# TRUTH COMES LIMPING

# TRUTH COMES LIMPING

## J. J. Connington

COACHWHIP PUBLICATIONS

Greenville, Ohio

# CONTENTS

# INTRODUCTION
## CURTIS EVANS

*Alfred Walter Stewart (1880-1947)*
*Alias J. J. Connington*

DURING THE GOLDEN AGE of the detective novel, in the 1920s and
1930s, "J. J. Connington" stood with fellow crime writers R. Aus-
tin Freeman, Cecil John Charles Street, and Freeman Wills Crofts
as the foremost practitioner in British mystery fiction of the
science of pure detection. I use the word "science" advisedly, for
the man behind J. J. Connington, Alfred Walter Stewart, was an
esteemed Scottish-born scientist who held the Chair of Chemistry
at Queens University, Belfast for twenty-five years, from 1919
until his retirement in 1944. A "small, unassuming, moustached
polymath," Stewart was "a strikingly effective lecturer with an
excellent sense of humor, fertile imagination, and fantastically retentive memory," qualities that also served him well in his fiction.
During roughly this period, the busy Professor Stewart found time
to author a remarkable apocalyptic science fiction tale, *Nordenholt's Million* (1923), a mainstream novel, *Almighty Gold* (1924),
a collection of essays, *Alias J. J. Connington* (1947), and, between
1926 and 1947, twenty-four mysteries (all but one true tales of
detection), many of them sterling examples of the Golden Age
puzzle-oriented detective novel at its considerable best. "For those
who ask first of all in a detective story for exact and mathematical
accuracy in the construction of the plot," avowed a contemporary

*London Daily Mail* reviewer, "there is no author to equal the distinguished scientist who writes under the name of J. J. Connington."[1]

Alfred Stewart's background as a man of science is reflected in his fiction, not only in the impressive puzzle plot mechanics he devised for his mysteries but in his choices of themes and depictions of characters. Along with Stanley Nordenholt of *Nordenholt's Million*, a novel about a plutocrat's pitiless efforts to preserve a ruthlessly remolded remnant of human life after a global environmental calamity, the most notable character that Stewart created is Chief Constable Sir Clinton Driffield, the detective in seventeen of the twenty-four Connington crime novels. Driffield is one of crime fiction's most highhanded investigators, occasionally taking into his hands the functions of judge and jury as well as chief of police. Absent from Stewart's fiction is the hail-fellow-well-met quality found in John Street's works or the religious ethos suffusing those of Freeman Wills Crofts, not to mention the effervescent novel of manners style of the British Golden Age Crime Queens Dorothy L. Sayers, Margery Allingham, and Ngaio Marsh. Instead we see an often disdainful cynicism about the human animal and a marked admiration for detached supermen with superior intellects. For this reason, reading a Connington novel can be a challenging experience for modern readers inculcated in gentler social beliefs. Yet Alfred Stewart produced a classic apocalyptic science fiction tale in *Nordenholt's Million* (justly dubbed "exciting and terrifying reading" by the *Spectator*), as well as superb detective novels boasting well-wrought puzzles, bracing characterization, and an occasional leavening of dry humor. Not long after Stewart's death in 1947, the Connington novels fell entirely out of print. The recent embrace of Stewart's fiction in recent publishing is a welcome

---

[1] For more on Street, Crofts and particularly Stewart, see Curtis Evans, *Masters of the "Humdrum" Mystery: Cecil John Charles Street, Freeman Wills Crofts, Alfred Walter Stewart and the British Detective Novel, 1920-1961* (Jefferson, NC: McFarland, 2012). On the academic career of Alfred Walter Stewart, see his entry in *Oxford Dictionary of National Biography* (London and New York: Oxford University Press, 2004), vol. 52, 627-628.

event indeed, correcting as it does over sixty years of underserved neglect of an accomplished genre writer.

Born in Glasgow on September 5, 1880, Alfred Stewart had significant exposure to religion in his earlier life. His father was William Stewart, longtime Professor of Divinity and Biblical Criticism at Glasgow University, and he married Lily Coats, a daughter of the Reverend Jervis Coats and member of one of Scotland's preeminent Baptist families. Religious sensibility is entirely absent from the Connington corpus, however. A confirmed secularist, Stewart once referred to one of his wife's brothers, the Reverend William Holms Coats (1881-1954), principal of the Scottish Baptist College, as his "mental and spiritual antithesis," bemusedly adding: "It's quite an education to see what one would look like if one were turned into one's mirror-image."

Stewart's J. J. Connington pseudonym was derived from a nineteenth-century Oxford Professor of Latin and translator of Horace, indicating that Stewart's literary interests lay not in pietistic writing but rather in the pre-Christian classics ("I prefer the *Odyssey* to *Paradise Lost*," the author once avowed). Possessing an inquisitive and expansive mind, Stewart was in fact an uncommonly well-read individual, freely ranging over a variety of literary genres. His deep immersion in French literature and supernatural horror fiction, for example, is documented in his lively correspondence with the noted horologist Rupert Thomas Gould.[2]

It thus is not surprising that in the 1920s the intellectually restless Stewart, having achieved a distinguished middle age as a highly regarded man of science, decided to apply his creative energy to a new endeavor, the writing of fiction. After several years he settled,

---

[2] The Gould-Stewart correspondence is discussed in considerable detail in *Masters of the "Humdrum" Mystery*. For more on the life of the fascinating Rupert Thomas Gould, see Jonathan Betts, *Time Restored: The Harrison Timekeepers and R. T. Gould, the Man Who Knew (Almost) Everything* (London and New York: Oxford University Press, 2006) and the British film *Longitude* (2000), which details Gould's restoration of the marine chronometers built by in the eighteenth-century by the clockmaker John Harrison.

like other gifted men and women of his generation, on the wildly popular mystery genre. Stewart was modest about his accomplishments in this particular field of light fiction, telling Rupert Gould later in life that "I write these things [what Stewart called tec yarns] because they amuse me in parts when I am putting them together and because they are the only writings of mine that the public will look at. Also, in a minor degree, because I like to think some people get pleasure out of them." No doubt Stewart's single most impressive literary accomplishment is *Nordenholt's Million*, yet in their time the two dozen J. J. Connington mysteries did indeed give readers in Great Britain, the United States, and other countries much diversionary reading pleasure. Today these works constitute an estimable addition to British crime fiction.

After his 'prentice pastiche mystery, *Death at Swaythling Court* (1926), a rural English country house tale set in the highly traditional village of Fernhurst Parva, Stewart published another, superior country house affair, *The Dangerfield Talisman* (1926), a novel about the baffling theft of a precious family heirloom, an ancient, jewel-encrusted armlet. This clever murderless tale, which likely is the one that the author told Rupert Gould he wrote in under six weeks, was praised in *The Bookman* as "continuously exciting and interesting" and in the *New York Times Book Review* as "ingeniously fitted together and, what is more, written with a deal of real literary charm." Despite its virtues, however, *The Dangerfield Talisman* is not fully characteristic of mature Connington detective fiction. The author needed a memorable series sleuth, more representative of his own forceful personality.

It was the next year, 1927, that saw "J. J. Connington" make his break to the front of the murdermongerer's pack with a third country house mystery, *Murder in the Maze*, wherein debuted as the author's great series detective the assertive and acerbic Sir Clinton Driffield, along with Sir Clinton's neighbor and "Watson," the more genial (if much less astute) Squire Wendover. In this much praised novel, Stewart's detective duo confronts some truly diabolical doings, including slayings by means of curare-tipped darts in the double-centered hedge maze at a country estate,

Whistlefield. No less a fan of the genre than T. S. Eliot praised *Murder in the Maze* for its construction ("we are provided early in the story with all the clues which guide the detective") and its liveliness ("The very idea of murder in a box hedge labyrinth does the author great credit, and he makes full use of its possibilities"). The delighted Eliot concluded that *Murder in the Maze* was "a really first-rate detective story." For his part, the critic H. C. Harwood declared in *The Outlook* that with the publication of *Murder in the Maze* Connington demanded and deserved "comparison with the masters." "Buy, borrow, or—anyhow get hold of it," he amusingly advised. Two decades later, in his 1946 critical essay "The Grandest Game in the World," the great locked room detective novelist John Dickson Carr echoed Eliot's assessment of the novel's virtuoso setting, writing: "These 1920s . . . thronged with sheer brains. What would be one of the best possible settings for violent death? J. J. Connington found the answer, with *Murder in the Maze.*" Certainly in retrospect *Murder in the Maze* stands as one of the finest English country house mysteries of the 1920s, cleverly yet fairly clued, imaginatively detailed and often grimly suspenseful. As the great American true crime writer Edmund Lester Pearson noted in his review of *Murder in the Maze* in *The Outlook*, this Connington novel had everything that one could desire in a detective story: "A shrubbery maze, a hot day, and somebody potting at you with an air gun loaded with darts covered with a deadly South-American arrow-poison—*there* is a situation to wheedle two dollars out of anybody's pocket."[3]

Staying with what had for him worked so well, Stewart the same year produced yet another country house mystery, *Tragedy at Ravensthorpe*, an ingenious tale of murders and thefts at the ancestral home of the Chacewaters, old family friends of Sir Clinton Driffield. There is much clever matter in *Ravensthorpe*. Especially fascinating is the authors inspired integration of faerie folklore into his plot. Stewart, who had a lifelong—though skeptical—interest

---

[3] Potential purchasers of *Murder in the Maze* should keep in mind that $2 in 1927 is worth over $26 today!

in paranormal phenomena, probably was inspired in this instance by the recent hubbub over the Cottingley Faeries photographs that in the early 1920s had famously duped, among other individuals, Arthur Conan Doyle.[4] As with *Murder in the Maze*, critics raved this new Connington mystery. In the *Spectator*, for example, a reviewer hailed *Tragedy at Ravensthorpe* in the strongest terms, declaring of the novel: "This is more than a good detective tale. Alike in plot, characterization, and literary style, it is a work of art."

In 1928 there appeared two additional Sir Clinton Driffield detective novels, *Mystery at Lynden Sands* and *The Case with Nine Solutions*. Once again there was great praise for the latest Conningtons. H. C. Harwood, a critic who, as we have seen, had so much admired *Murder in the Maze*, opined of *Mystery at Lynden Sands* that it "may just fail of being the detective story of the century," while in the United States author and book reviewer Frederic F. Van de Water expressed nearly as high an opinion of *The Case with Nine Solutions*. "This book is a thoroughbred of a distinguished lineage that runs back to 'The Gold Bug' of [Edgar Allan] Poe," he avowed. "It represents the highest type of detective fiction." In both of these Connington novels, Stewart moved away from his customary country house milieu, setting *Lynden Sands* at a fashionable beach resort and *Nine Solutions* at a scientific

---

[4] In a 1920 article in *The Strand Magazine* Arthur Conan Doyle endorsed as real prank photographs of purported fairies taken by two English girls in the garden of a house in the village of Cottingley. In the aftermath of the Great War Doyle had become a fervent believer in Spiritualism and other paranormal phenomena. Especially embarrassing to Doyle's admirers today, Doyle also published *The Coming of the Faeries* (1922), wherein he argued that these mystical creatures genuinely existed. "When the spirits came in, the common sense oozed out," Stewart once wrote bluntly to his friend Rupert Gould of the creator of Sherlock Holmes. Like Gould, however, Stewart had an intense interest in the subject of the Loch Ness Monster, believing that he, his wife and daughter had cited a large marine creature of some sort in Loch Ness in 1935. A year earlier Gould had authored *The Loch Ness Monster and Others*, and it was this book which led Stewart, after he made his "Nessie" sighting, to initiate correspondence with Gould.

research institute. *Nine Solutions* is of particular interest today, I think, for its relatively frank sexual subject matter and its modern urban setting among science professionals, which rather resembles the locales found in P. D. James' classic detective novels *A Mind to Murder* (1963) and *Shroud for a Nightingale* (1971).

By the end of the decade of the 1920s, the critical reputation of "J. J. Connington" had achieved enviable heights indeed. At this time Stewart became one of the charter members of the Detection Club, an assemblage of the finest writers of British detective fiction that included, among other distinguished individuals, Agatha Christie, Dorothy L. Sayers and G. K. Chesterton. Certainly Victor Gollancz, the British publisher of the J. J. Connington mysteries, did not stint praise for the author, informing readers that "J. J. Connington is now established as, in the opinion of many, the greatest living master of the story of pure detection. He is one of those who, discarding all the superfluities, has made of deductive fiction a genuine minor art, with its own laws and its own conventions."

Such warm praise for J. J. Connington makes it all the more surprising that at this juncture the esteemed author tinkered with his successful formula by dispensing with his original series detective. In the fifth Clinton Driffield detective novel, *Nemesis at Raynham Parva* (1929), Alfred Walter Stewart, rather like Arthur Conan Doyle before him, seemed with a dramatic dénouement to have devised his popular series detective's permanent exit from the fictional stage (read it and see for yourself). The next two Connington detective novels, *The Eye in the Museum* (1929) and *The Two Tickets Puzzle* (1930), have a different series detective, Superintendent Ross, a rather dull dog of a policeman. While both these mysteries are competently done—the railway material in *The Two Tickets Puzzle* is particularly effective and should have appeal today—the presence of Sir Clinton Driffield (no superfluity he!) is missed.

Probably Stewart detected that the public minded the absence of the brilliant and biting Sir Clinton, for the Chief Constable—accompanied, naturally, by his friend Squire Wendover—triumphantly returned in 1931 in *The Boathouse Riddle*, another well-constructed criminous country house affair. Later in the year came *The Sweepstake Murders*, which boasts the perennially popular tontine multiple murder plot, in this case a rapid succession of puzzling suspicious deaths afflicting the members of a sweepstake syndicate that has just won nearly 250,000 pounds.[5] Adding piquancy to this plot is the fact that Wendover is one of the imperiled syndicate members. Altogether the novel is, as the late Jacques Barzun and his colleague Wendell Hertig Taylor put it in *A Catalogue of Crime* (1971/1989), their magisterial survey of detective fiction, "one of Connington's best conceptions."

Stewart's productivity as a fiction writer slowed in the 1930s, so that, barring the year 1938, at most only one new Connington appeared annually (because of the onset of serious health maladies, Stewart was unable to publish any Connington novel in 1936). However, in 1932 Stewart produced one of the best Connington mysteries, *The Castleford Conundrum*. A classic country house detective novel, Castleford introduces to readers Stewart's most delightfully unpleasant set of greedy relations and one of his most deserving murderees, Winifred Castleford. Stewart also fashions a wonderfully rich puzzle plot, full of meaty material clues for the reader's delectation. *Castleford* presented critics with no conundrum over its quality. "In *The Castleford Conundrum* Mr. Connington goes to work like an accomplished chess-player. The moves in the games his detectives are called on to play are a delight to watch," raved the reviewer for the *Sunday Times*, adding that "the clues would have rejoiced Mr. Holmes' heart." For its part, the *Spectator* concurred in the *Sunday Times*' assessment of the novel's masterfully-constructed plot: "Few detective stories show such sound reasoning as that by which the Chief Constable brings the crime home to the culprit." Additionally, E. C. Bentley, much

---

[5] A tontine is a financial arrangement wherein shareowners in a common fund receive annuities that increase in value with the death of each participant, with the entire amount of the fund going to the last survivor. The impetus that the tontine provided to the deadly creative imaginations of Golden Age mystery writers should be sufficiently obvious.

admired himself as the author of the landmark detective novel *Trent's Last Case*, took time to praise Connington's purely literary virtues, noting: "Mr. Connington has never written better, or drawn characters more full of life."

With *Tom Tiddler's Island* in 1933 Stewart produced a different sort of Connington, a criminal gang mystery in the rather more breathless style of such hugely popular English thriller writers as Sapper, Sax Rohmer, John Buchan and Edgar Wallace (in violation of the strict detective fiction rules of Ronald Knox, there is even a secret passage in the novel). Detailing the startling discoveries made by a newlywed couple honeymooning on a remote Scottish island, *Tom Tiddler's Island* is an atmospheric and entertaining tale, though it is not as mentally stimulating for armchair sleuths as Stewart's true detective novels. The title, incidentally, refers to an ancient British children's game, "Tom Tiddler's Ground," in which one child tries to hold a height against other children.

After his fictional Scottish excursion into thrillerdom, Stewart returned the next year to his English country house roots with *The Ha-Ha Case* (1934), his last masterwork in this classic mystery setting. (For elucidation of non-British readers, a ha-ha is a sunken wall, placed so to delineate property boundaries while not obstructing views.) Although *The Ha-Ha Case* is not set in Scotland, Stewart drew inspiration for the novel from a notorious Scottish true crime, the 1893 Ardlamont murder case. From the facts of the Ardlamont affair Stewart drew several of the key characters in *The Ha-Ha Case*, as well as the circumstances of the novel's murder (a shooting "accident" while hunting), though he added complications that take the tale in a new direction.[6]

---

[6] At Ardlamont, a large country estate in Argyll, Cecil Hambrough died from a gunshot wound while hunting. Cecil's tutor, Alfred John Monson, and another man, both of whom were out hunting with Cecil, claimed that Cecil had accidentally shot himself; but Monson was arrested and tried for Cecil's murder. The verdict delivered was "not proven," but Monson was then—and is today—considered almost certainly to have been guilty of the murder. On the Ardlamont case, see William Roughead, *Classic Crimes* (1951; repr., New York: New York Review Books Classics, 2000), 378-464.

In newspaper reviews both Dorothy L. Sayers and "Francis Iles" (crime novelist Anthony Berkeley Cox) highly praised this latest mystery by "The Clever Mr. Connington," as he was now dubbed on book jackets by his new English publisher, Hodder and Stoughton. Sayers particularly noted the effective characterization in *The Ha-Ha Case*: "There is no need to say that Mr. Connington has given us a sound and interesting plot, very carefully and ingeniously worked out. In addition, there are the three portraits of the three brothers, cleverly and rather subtly characterised, of the [governess], and of Inspector Hinton, whose admirable qualities are counteracted by that besetting sin of the man who has made his own way: a jealousy of delegating responsibility." The reviewer for the *Times Literary Supplement* detected signs that the sardonic Sir Clinton Driffield had begun mellowing with age: "Those who have never really liked Sir Clinton's perhaps excessively soldierly manner will be surprised to find that he makes his discovery not only by the pure light of intelligence, but partly as a reward for amiability and tact, qualities in which the Inspector [Hinton] was strikingly deficient." This is true enough, although the classic Sir Clinton emerges a number of times in the novel, as in his subtly sarcastic recurrent backhanded praise of Inspector Hinton: "He writes a first class report."

Clinton Driffield returned the next year in the detective novel *In Whose Dim Shadow* (1935), a tale set in a recently erected English suburb, the denizens of which seem to have committed an impressive number of indiscretions, including sexual ones. The intriguing title of the British edition of the novel is drawn from a poem by the British historian Thomas Babington Macaulay: "Those trees in whose dim shadow/The ghastly priest doth reign/The priest who slew the slayer/And shall himself be slain." Stewart's puzzle plot in *In Whose Dim Shadow* is well-clued and compelling, the kicker of a closing paragraph is a classic of its kind and, additionally, the author paints some excellent character portraits. I fully concur in the *Sunday Times* assessment of the tale: "Quiet domestic murder, full of the neatest detective points. . . . These [characters] are not the detective's stock figures, but fully realised human beings."[7]

Uncharacteristically for Stewart, nearly twenty months elapsed between the publication of *In Whose Dim Shadow* and his next book, *A Minor Operation* (1937). The reason for the author's delay in production was the onset in 1935-36 of the afflictions of cataracts and heart disease (Stewart ultimately succumbed to heart disease in 1947). Despite the grave health complications that beset him at this time, Stewart in late 1936 was able to complete *A Minor Operation*, a first-rate Clinton Driffield story of murder and a most baffling disappearance. A *Times Literary Supplement* reviewer found that *A Minor Operation* treated the reader "to exactly the right mixture of mystification and clue" and that, in addition to its impressive construction, the novel boasted "character-drawing above the average" for a detective novel.

Alfred Stewart's final eight mysteries, which appeared between 1938 and 1947, the year of the author's death, are, on the whole, a somewhat weaker group of tales than the sixteen that appeared between 1926 and 1937, yet they are not without interest. In 1938 Stewart for the last time managed to publish two detective novels, *Truth Comes Limping* and *For Murder Will Speak*. The latter tale is much the superior of the two, having an interesting suburban setting and a bevy of female characters found to have motives when a contemptible philandering businessman meets with foul play. Sexual neurosis plays a major role in *For Murder Will Speak*, the

---

[7] For the genesis of the title, see Macaulay's "The Battle of the Lake Regillus," from his narrative poem collection *Lays of Ancient Rome*. In this poem Macaulay alludes to the ancient cult of Diana Nemorensis, which elevated its priests through trial by combat. Study of the practices of the Diana Nemorensis cult influenced Sir James George Frazer's cultural interpretation of religion in his most renowned work, *The Golden Bough: A Study in Magic and Religion*. As with *Tom Tiddler's Island* and *The Ha-Ha Case* the title *In Whose Dim Shadow* proved too esoteric for Connington's American publishers, Little, Brown and Co., who altered it to the more prosaic *The Tau Cross Mystery*.

ever-thorough Stewart obviously having made a study of the subject when writing the novel. The somewhat squeamish reviewer for *Scribner's Magazine* considered the subject matter of *For Murder Will Speak* "rather unsavory at times," yet this individual conceded that the novel nevertheless made "first-class reading for those who enjoy a good puzzle intricately worked out." "Judge Lynch" in the *Saturday Review* apparently had no such moral reservations about the latest Clinton Driffield murder case, avowing simply of the novel: "They don't come any better."

Over the next couple years Stewart again sent Sir Clinton Driffield temporarily packing, replacing him with a new series detective, a brash radio personality named Mark Brand, in *The Counsellor* (1939) and *The Four Defences* (1940). The better of these two novels is *The Four Defences*, which Stewart based on another notorious British true crime case, the Alfred Rouse blazing car murder. (Rouse is believed to have fabricated his death by murdering an unknown man, placing the dead man's body in his car and setting the car on fire, in the hope that the murdered man's body would be taken for his.) Though admittedly a thinly characterized academic exercise in ratiocination, Stewart's *Four Defences* surely is also one of the most complexly plotted Golden Age detective novels ever written and should delight devotees of classical detection. Taking the Rouse blazing car affair as his theme, Stewart composes from it a stunning set of diabolically ingenious criminal variations. "This is in the cold-blooded category which . . . excites a crossword puzzle kind of interest," the reviewer for the *Times Literary Supplement* acutely noted of the novel. "Nothing in the Rouse case would prepare you for these complications upon complications. . . . What they prove is that Mr. Connington has the power of penetrating into the puzzle-corner of the brain. He leaves it dazedly wondering whether in the records of actual crime there can be any dark deed to equal this in its planned convolutions."

Sir Clinton Driffield returned to action in the remaining four detective novels in the Connington oeuvre, *The Twenty-One Clues* (1941), *No Past Is Dead* (1942), *Jack-in-the-Box* (1944) and *Commonsense Is All You Need* (1947), all of which were written as

Stewart's heart disease steadily worsened and reflect to some extent his diminishing physical and mental energy. Although *The Twenty-One Clues* was inspired by the notorious Hall-Mills double murder case—probably the most publicized murder case in the United States in the 1920s—and the American critic Anthony Boucher commended *Jack-in-the-Box*, I believe the best of these later mysteries is *No Past Is Dead*, which Stewart partly based on a bizarre French true crime affair, the 1891 Achet-Lepine murder case.[8] Besides providing an interesting background for the tale, the ailing author managed some virtuoso plot twists, of the sort most associated today with that ingenious Golden Age Queen of Crime, Agatha Christie.

What Stewart with characteristic bluntness referred to as "my complete crack-up" forced his retirement from Queen's University in 1944. "I am afraid," Stewart wrote a friend, the chemist and forensic scientist F. Gerald Tryhorn, in August, 1946, eleven months before his death, "that I shall never be much use again. Very stupidly, I tried for a session to combine a full course of lecturing with angina pectoris; and ended up by establishing that the two are immiscible." He added that since retiring in 1944, he had been physically "limited to my house, since even a fifty-yard crawl brings on the usual cramps." Stewart completed his essay collection and a final novel before he died at his study desk in his Belfast home on July 1, 1947, at the age of sixty-six. When death came to the author he was busy at work, writing.

More than six decades after Alfred Walter Stewart's death, his "J. J. Connington" fiction again is available to a wider audience of classic mystery fans, rather than strictly limited to a select company of rare book collectors with deep pockets. This is fitting for an individual who was one of the finest writers of British genre fiction between the two world wars. "Heaven forfend that you should imagine I take myself for anything out of the common in

---

[8] Stewart analyzed the Achet-Lepine case in detail in "The Mystery of Chantelle," one of the best essays in his 1947 collection, *Alias J. J. Connington*.

the tec yarn stuff," Stewart once self-deprecatingly declared in a letter to Rupert Gould. Yet, as contemporary critics recognized, as a writer of detective and science fiction Stewart indeed was something out of the common. Now more modern readers can find this out for themselves. They have much good sleuthing in store.

# TRUTH COMES LIMPING

# CHAPTER I
## IN LEISURELY LANE

CONSTABLE JOSEPH DURLEY found little to complain about in his duties at Abbots Norton-on-the-Green. On the map, by virtue of its many syllables, it occupied more space than the neighbouring market town of Ambledown; but actually it was little larger than an overgrown village which had to content itself with a single picture-house. Only antiquaries and the Ordnance Survey ever troubled to give it its full title. The incoming motorist read "Abbots Norton" on the mustard-coloured plaque of the Automobile Association without dreaming that he was missing nearly half of the full description of this sleepy little place.

Constable Durley liked an easy life and, so far, he had found it in Abbots Norton. He preferred night duty; and in this law-abiding district, night duty meant mere routine patrolling interrupted only very rarely by the need for looking after straying cattle or the warning of some farmer who ignored the absence of a light on his vehicle. Poaching did occur; but its prevention was mainly a matter for the local gamekeepers, and Constable Durley was seldom called on by them for assistance.

He was a quiet, even-tempered man whose deliberate movements reflected the slowness of his mind. He had a good word for everybody and, possibly on that account, he was mildly popular with most of the Abbots Norton inhabitants, irrespective of class. He was especially beloved by children, and in the summer he whiled away the earlier hours of his patrol by surreptitiously whittling model boats for his little friends out of any odd pieces of wood which came his way. One could, if necessary, have tracked him down on his beat by the trail of wood slivers which fell from his pocketknife as he moved along.

He had reached the outskirts of Abbots Norton, beyond the last of the street lamps, when the sound of distant but approaching footfalls caught his ear. He halted, the better to listen, and now he picked up more than he had at first.

"Who's running at this hour o' night?" he speculated vaguely as the sounds drew nearer. "Two of them. Some kids' prank, maybe. I'll have a look at them."

He pulled out his electric flashlight and peered into the gloom ahead. The running footfalls drew nearer, and now, mingled with them, he heard gasps and an occasional ejaculation of "Oh! O-o-oh!" as if one of the runners was in an extremity of fear.

"That's a wench," Constable Durley inferred. "This is a rum go, surely."

He moved into the middle of the road and, as two dim figures emerged from the gloom, switched on his light. The beam revealed a young man and a girl bearing down on him, and he could see that the girl's face was distorted with panic.

"Halt, there!" he called sharply. "Now, then, what's all this about? Seen a ghost, or what?"

At the sight of his uniform, the two runners had slowed to a halt. Durley knew them well: one of the village lads, Bill Oulton, and his sweetheart, Tessie Marl. The girl was panting for breath and seemed on the verge of hysterics as she clung to Oulton's arm.

"There's a dead body up Leisurely Lane, that's what," Oulton jerked out in answer to the constable's questions. "Right in the middle of the path. Under the trees by the hoarding. We stumbled over it in the dark, we did. I lit a match to see what we'd tripped over. There it was. Blood all about it. Gave Tessie a turn, I can tell you! Ghastly!"

"Hold on a minute. Take my lamp," ordered Durley.

He pulled out his notebook and glanced at his wrist watch, motioning Oulton to hold the lamp so as to shine on the book.

"Time, 10:42 p.m.," he noted, jotting down the figures as he spoke. "Right! And what did you do then?"

"Tessie went right off the handle. And no wonder," Oulton explained. "It gave me a jar myself."

Durley, intent on noting down the statement, nodded curtly. "What then?" he demanded.

"Tessie took to her heels, shrieking for all she was worth. What else'd you expect? I went after her. Couldn't let her go off alone like that. For all I knew, murderer might be hanging about in the wood," Oulton declared, still rather breathlessly.

"Did you make sure the man was dead?" inquired the constable.

"He looked it. Jaw dropped and all. (It's all right now, Tessie, you needn't be afraid.) I didn't stop. Had to look after Tessie."

"Did you touch the body at all?" persisted Durley.

"Not much! What'd I want to touch him for? Besides, Tessie was off as soon as she set eyes on his face."

"Who is he? Anyone you know?" asked Durley.

"Not from Adam. Never saw him before. I'm sure of that."

"You've run all the way back?"

"You bet! As hard as Tessie could make it."

"Did you meet anybody or see anybody on your road down?"

"Not a living soul. Did you, Tessie?"

"No, oh, no," the girl confirmed, with a sob which caught her breath.

"'Twas dark, anyhow," Oulton pointed out. "And up there on the edge of the copse, it was darker still. Somebody may have been there. All I know is I didn't see anyone."

"Before it happened, you didn't hear anything?" persisted the constable. "No cries or anything of that sort?"

"Not a damn!" Oulton snapped. "Now look you here, Durley, my girl's about all in. I've got to get her home quick, after all this. If you want any more chat, you can come along with us. Bear up, Tessie, we're nearly there, now."

"Oh, I wish I was home; I wish I was home!" whimpered the overwrought girl. "I'll be sick in a minute, Bill. Take me home."

Oulton tucked her arm reassuringly into his own and began to help her along the road, without paying any further attention to the constable. Durley, making the best of it, shut off his flash lamp and fell into step with them as they made their way into the village. Once the houses were about them, Tessie seemed to recover a little from her panic, and Durley decided to make a suggestion.

"You'd better come along and see the inspector. He'll want to know all about it at once."

Oulton turned to the constable with an angry motion. "First thing I do's to take Tessie home to her mother. See? After that, I'll have time on my hands."

Durley saw there was no chance of turning him from this decision. And after all, he reflected, Oulton could give the inspector all the information necessary at the moment. If they wanted it confirmed by the girl, the morning would be time enough.

"All right," he acquiesced. "But you're not to hang about."

In a few minutes they reached the house of Tessie's parents and handed the girl over to the care of her mother, while Durley fidgeted impatiently, eager to make his report and get responsibility off his shoulders. He had not the slightest inclination to play Sherlock Holmes in an affair of this kind, even if it had been his duty to attempt that. "Pass it on to the man up above—and the quicker the better," was his unformulated rule of conduct whenever anything out of the common occurred.

Inspector Cumberland was actually attached to Ambledown, but his jurisdiction extended to include Abbots Norton and he preferred to live in the village rather than the town. A motorcycle allowed him to go to and fro with a minimum of delay, and the telephone linked him up in case of emergency. He was an excellent man for routine work, but a little lacking in finesse. That evening, as it chanced, he and three friends were playing bridge at his house, so Durley was able to get into touch with him without delay. He listened without comment, first to Durley and then to Oulton's story.

"Let's see," he said, reflectively, when he had, gathered all they had to tell him. "We'll need an ambulance to cart the body off. And someone to take a flashlight photo of the body before we shift it. And . . . All right! I'll get on the phone. Wait there."

He returned into his house and they heard him ringing up his headquarters in Ambledown, and giving instructions. Then he came back to the doorstep, on which he had left his visitors.

"I'll push off up there on my motorcycle," he explained. "You two can put your best foot foremost and follow me up. If the squad from Ambledown make up on you, stop them and get a lift." He turned to Oulton. "I'll have to see Miss Marl to-morrow. No need to worry her any more tonight. Let's see . . . No, that's all, I think. Beside the hoarding in Leisurely Lane, you say? Right. You'd better be pushing along."

With a gesture of dismissal, he went back into the house to break up his bridge party. Then, going to a shed, he brought out his motorcycle and set off. Abbots Norton was an early-to-bed village, and though it was only just after eleven o'clock, most of the houses were already in darkness.

"Not much chance of any other courting couples being up that way at this time of night," the inspector reflected as he left the last of the village lights. "Just as well, perhaps. But it cuts down the chance of picking up witnesses of any sort."

For a couple of miles, he kept along the road, meeting no one. Then, when he reached the end of Leisurely Lane, he stopped, dismounted, and propped his machine against the hedge. Further progress would be swifter on foot, for Leisurely Lane was little better than a field path leading up into the coverts of the Carfax estate, a rough, stony little byway quite unsuitable for even a motorcycle. The inspector pulled out his electric torch; then, thinking better of it, he returned it to his pocket. If, by any chance, the murderer happened to be still in the neighbourhood, there was no point in showing a light to warn him.

Leisurely Lane in daylight was passable enough; but in the dark it was a different matter, and the inspector stumbled once or twice over unevennesses in the track.

"Devil of a road for that girl to come down hell for leather," he reflected with a certain sympathy. "It's a miracle she didn't sprain her ankle in the dark."

Suddenly he halted and listened intently. Somebody was coming down the path towards him. The inspector strained his ears and was rewarded by the noise of a stumble, followed by an outbreak of profanity fervent enough to point to some bodily damage. Inspector Cumberland moved slightly off the track into the shadow of a tree, drew his torch from his pocket, and waited with his finger on the switch. The approaching steps came quite close and suddenly Cumberland threw his beam on the dim figure which he could see against the sky.

"Oh, it's you, is it?" he snapped, as he recognised the night wanderer. "Halt, there!"

His captive, cringing in the beam of the lamp, was anything but an attractive person. Cumberland had seen him about the village for a week or two: an untidy little man with small, cunning eyes set in an unhealthy white face. When the electric beam fell upon him, he gave a start so violent that it was almost a jump, and a coarse oath escaped his lips. Then he faced round on his interlocutor with an expression which mingled fear, rage, and—Cumberland imagined—disappointment.

The inspector was no believer in rules and regulations when they might hinder his work. He dropped his torch and sprang forward. One hand gripped his captive's collar, the other dived expertly into pocket after pocket in his prisoner's clothing. Then, apparently satisfied, Cumberland loosed his man, picked up his torch again, and threw its beam on something which he had extracted from one of the captive's jacket pockets.

"So that's your game?" he commented, as he recognised what he had secured. "I thought so, by the feel of them."

"May I die, guv'nor—" began his prisoner in a high, shrill protest. But Cumberland cut him short.

"Up with your hands till I run over you," he ordered brusquely.

"So help me, guv'nor, I'm carryin' nothin' in the way of a gun," the man protested. "Never had such a thing in me natural, never. You've been through me already."

"Then we can't prove you a liar, if we try," Cumberland pointed out. "Up over your head."

He had already satisfied himself that the man was unarmed, but now he went through his pockets meticulously by the light of the torch. All that rewarded him was a very dirty handkerchief, a pipe, a tobacco pouch, a box of matches, and some small change.

"Now don't you try to bolt," he warned, when he had finished, "for you won't stand an earthly if I have to start in and manhandle you. Answer my questions. What's your name?"

"Walton."

"First name?"

"Ben. Now look 'ere, guv'nor, you're wastin' your time, you are. There's somethin' serious I've got to tell you."

"I can guess it in one," retorted Cumberland. "'The Corpse in the Lane, or Who Did Him In?' We'll come to that in time, don't you fret yourself. Where do you live?"

"In Longstone Street, with the Moffatts. He's my brother-in-law."

The address did not seem to reassure the inspector. "Oh, with *him?* Well, it takes all sorts to make a world, they say. What are you doing up here at this time of night?"

Walton seemed to be recovering his nerve.

"Just 'avin' a stroll round," he said, impudently. "Takin' the fresh air, as it were."

"Looking for courting couples, maybe? The Peeping Tom game, eh? You look just the sort."

"Suit yourself," Walton retorted. "You seem to know more about it than what I do."

"No lip," ordered the inspector curtly, and Walton cringed at the tone of his voice. "Now about this dead man up above. Did you do him in?"

"So 'elp me Gord, 'e's nantee worster for me an' I'll kiss the Book on that," declared Walton fervently.

"Talk English for a change, if you can," ordered Cumberland. "Mean you did him no harm? Say so, then."

"I never laid so much as a finger on 'im," said Walton earnestly. "That's straight, guv'nor, dead straight. There 'e was, lyin' stiff, when I come down the lane. I fell over 'im—plunk!—I did! Gaw! *That* was a turn, give you *my* word. I came a purler, I did!"

"You never laid a finger on him, as you put it?"

"I never touched 'im. 'E gave me the shudders when I lit a scratcher an' took a glint at 'im. 'Orrid, 'e looked."

"Spare my feelings," interrupted Cumberland brutally. "Did you see all this with one match?"

Walton hesitated almost imperceptibly before replying. "I did. All I wanted, anyways."

"Ah! Then I'll borrow that match box of yours."

Walton reluctantly drew it from his pocket and handed it over to the inspector who stowed it away before continuing his examination.

"Let's see your hands," he demanded.

Walton held out two unclean paws backs upward. Cumberland inspected them closely with his lamp.

"Now the other sides."

Again a minute inspection failed to reveal anything and for a moment Cumberland seemed uncertain. Then he stepped forward and with a swift snatch extracted Walton's handkerchief from his pocket.

"If you never laid a finger on him, how did this blood get here?" he questioned, after a close inspection of the cloth.

"Me nose was bleedin' this afternoon," Walton countered with just a little too much readiness.

"But this happens to be quite fresh."

"Me nose bled again a bit after I come out this evenin'. I recollect wipin' it."

"Bled on your hands, didn't it? And you wiped them with this rag?" suggested the inspector, obviously wholly sceptical. "If you go on at this rate we'll be able to write a whole fairy tale, between what you remember and what you forget."

"Strike a light! but you are 'ard on a bloke, guv'nor. I may 'ave made a mistake in me 'urry. 'Oo wouldn't, after a shake-up like I've 'ad. It's on'y natural."

"More natural to you than telling the truth, I judge. Don't go making any more of these 'mistakes.' Understand? Did you meet anyone in the lane after you left the body?"

"Nary a one, mister."

The inspector seemed satisfied with this answer. He glanced at the horizon and saw the beams of two headlights approaching along the road below.

"And before that?" he demanded, turning back to Walton.

"'Fore I stumbled on the deader? No, I didn't meet nobody."

Something in his manner made the inspector go further. "Notice anything out of the common at all?"

"Well, now it comes back to me, I did hear a moll screamin' somewheres down the lane, this way."

"You didn't think of going to help?"

"I took it somebody was 'avin' a bit of a lark. W'y should I interfere with some fellow's sport? If I 'ad, I s'pose you'd 'ave called me a Peepin' Tom for me pains. No, I looks after me own business an' I wish other people 'ad the same sense."

"When did you hear this screaming?"

Walton scratched his head rather worriedly.

"A bit before I come on the stuffy. Five or ten minutes, mebbe. More like ten, or per'aps more than that. There wasn't a copper 'andy to ask the time off."

"That'll do. Anything else that's slipped your memory?"

Walton pondered for a moment or two as though making an effort to recollect further facts. Then he shook his head decidedly.

"No, Robin Hood," he said, with a touch of sullenness which Cumberland noted.

"No good? Sure? Well, you'll have time to think over it," he declared, as he caught the sound of his subordinates approaching up the lane.

Walton pricked up his ears at the last remark.

"You ain't holdin' me?" he demanded, evidently taken aback.

"Think again," said Cumberland. "Then you'll get used to the idea."

"But, Hell's bells? guv'nor, I've told you I never outed 'im."

The tone of his voice showed that his bravado had broken down completely.

"I'm not going to charge you for the present," Cumberland explained. "That means I can question you further when I want to.

But I'm going to detain you, just to have you handy when I feel inquisitive. That can be arranged, so don't raise a squall. And my advice to you is to brush up your Pelmanism and remember something more about how that blood got onto your hankie. That's one thing we'll want to be satisfied about. Think over it. It won't be time wasted."

And when his men came up, Cumberland handed Walton over to one of them without more ado.

# CHAPTER II
## RE MILES HUGGIN, DECEASED

OULTON AND CONSTABLE DURLEY had been overtaken and picked up by the police cars from Ambledown; and when Inspector Cumberland noticed them among the new arrivals he signaled to Oulton to join him.

"You know where the body is. Tell us when we're coming up to it," he ordered. "I don't want to fall over it the way you did."

For a few minutes the party trudged up the lane, flashing the beams of their electric torches hither and thither as they went, in the hope of detecting something of importance by the sides of the path. Nothing rewarded them. A nightjar churred in the copse; and once a hedgehog crossed the path in front of them, scurrying away from the lights into the shelter of the long grass. Except for these, the night life of the place was invisible and inaudible, evidently scared by the noise of the party's steps. They came to a black, tarred hoarding on their left, and then Oulton made a gesture of caution.

"It should be here or hereabouts," he said. "Just a bit further on. You'd better go cautious."

They rounded a turn in the path and in the light of the torches the inspector saw the body of a man lying on its back with the head almost touching the foot of the board fence. He stepped forward to examine it, motioning the others to keep back. Then he summoned Oulton to his side.

"Is it just as you left it?" he inquired.

Oulton looked down at the body. He had removed his cap and now he scratched his head as if a little in doubt.

33

"It is—and it isn't," he declared at last. "Seems to me as if it had been shifted. Nothing to speak of, though. I couldn't tell you just what's different. I only had a second or two to look at it before the match went out. I know; the arms aren't quite the way they were. They were like this, when I saw him"—he illustrated the position with his own arms—"and now they're a bit more spread out, like."

Cumberland remembered that Walton mentioned his tripping over the body. He made no comment on Oulton's description beyond a curt nod. Before making a closer examination of the corpse, he glanced about him to see the environment. On his left was the high tarred hoarding, carefully built so that it had no interstices through which in daylight the surrounding country could have been seen. At this point, the path made a double turning, so that the spot, even in the daytime, would be fairly free from observation. To the right rose a low bank covered with bushes and immediately beyond this lay a fairly extensive copse. Ahead, the right of way seemed to lead onward to some woodland.

The inspector glanced at the surface of the path and the earth of the bank. There had been little rain in the recent hot weather, and the soil was baked hard. Evidently it would be useless to look for footprints. He nodded again, as though satisfied on this point and then stepped forward, torch in hand, to examine the body itself.

"Lots of blood about," he said, rather unnecessarily, to the group which was now edging closer in curiosity. "Don't come too near till I've had a look round."

Taking care to avoid the sinister rills and pools, he knelt down by the body and began a methodical examination. "Here, sergeant," he said over his shoulder, "take this down as I dictate."

Sergeant Seabright, who had brought up the party in the police cars, obediently pulled out his notebook and stood, pencil ready, while one of his subordinates threw the light of his torch on the open page. Constable Durley had moved over to the inspector's side to give him the help of his lamp.

"His head's about six inches from the hoarding," the inspector announced, letting his tape measure snap back into its case. "Looks as if he'd been standing almost against it when he was knocked out, and just collapsed backward against it and then slid out over the path. But that's not much good, after people have been moving him. Leave it out. Respectably dressed, grey tweeds, well worn. You needn't put that down either. They'll note it all when he goes down to the mortuary."

He motioned to Durley to have the torch brought closer, and then made a careful inspection of the body's breast.

"I can see one wound, just over the heart as near as one can guess. It might have come from a small-caliber bullet. Looks like it, anyhow. We'll leave that to the surgeon. No signs of any violence that I can see, apart from that. Now for his pockets."

He slipped his fingers into them, one by one, dictating a list of his finds as he came across them.

"Left-hand jacket pocket: a leather tobacco pouch and a box of Swan vestas. . . . Left breast pocket: a silk handkerchief—artificial silk. . . . Right-hand breast pocket: a leather note case. Bring that light nearer till I see what's inside. . . . One-pound Bank of England notes. Wait till I count them. . . . Fifteen, sixteen, seventeen pounds. Put down £17 in Bank of England notes. It doesn't look like robbery on that basis. . . . Then in the stamp pocket of the case: seven three-halfpenny, two penny, and five halfpenny stamps. Not that they amount to much; still they'd better go in with the rest. . . . And in another pocket, eight visiting cards. This looks more like it. 'Mr. Miles Huggin, 47 Rookery Park, W.'—some number I can't read in this light."

He shuffled the cards, examining the inscriptions.

"They're all the same, so they must be his own. So he's a Londoner, else the name of the town would be there, most likely. That's going to make things easier for us."

He slipped the cards back into the note case and continued his search.

"Left-hand trouser pocket: three half-crowns, a florin, four shillings, and a sixpenny-bit. . . . Right-hand trouser pocket: sevenpence in coppers and a key ring with four keys on it."

Cautiously he slid his hand under the body.

"No hip pocket."

Then he turned his attention to the waistcoat pockets.

"Right-hand top vest pocket: empty. . . . Left-hand top vest pocket: a fountain pen and a pencil . . . Left-hand lower vest pocket: empty. . . . Ticket pocket in jacket: a railway ticket. Bring that light closer. Return half of a third-class ticket, dated to-day, valid between Abbots Norton and London. So I was right about his being a Londoner. . . . H'm! That's the lot."

He rose to his feet and stared down at the body, as though in hopes of recognising the dead man. But all he saw was a clean-shaven stranger who looked about forty, so far as could be surmised. Cumberland reflected for a moment or two and then became brisk again.

"He had matches and a pouch but no pipe. It should be somewhere about. Hunt for it."

It took little enough trouble in the finding. One of the party discovered it almost at once, in the grass at the foot of the hoarding, within a yard or so of the body. And not far from it lay a heavy walking stick.

Cumberland was quite satisfied in his own mind as to the cause of Huggin's death, but nevertheless he examined the stick with some care. It was, however, quite free from any trace of blood and he could find no adherent hairs or anything else which might have suggested its use as a lethal weapon. Round the shaft was a cheap silver band, but this carried no inscription to prove ownership.

The inspector put it aside and turned his attention to the pipe, a well-worn briar of a very common pattern. The bowl was three quarters full and, although most of the ash had been shaken out by the fall to the ground, enough remained to show that it had been smoked for a while before being extinguished by the concussion. Cumberland extracted some of the tobacco and compared it with that in Huggin's pouch. The two were identical, which satisfied him that the pipe was actually Huggin's. He put the pipe aside in its turn, but it had reminded him of something.

"Hunt about on the ground and see if you can find any spent matches," he directed.

His subordinates bestirred themselves, going hither and thither with their torches; and it was not long before the first find was made.

"Here's a Swan vesta, sir."

Cumberland took a piece of chalk from his pocket and made a cabalistic mark on the spot where the match had lain. Then he examined the match itself, which was burned down to about a quarter of its normal length.

"Try again," he ordered. "I want every spent match you can pick up."

A few seconds later, one of the constables discovered a paper match, and the same procedure was gone through. Again Cumberland examined the find, but this time he had something fresh. Apparently the match had failed to light when drawn across the prepared surface and had been thrown down unused. It was a blue-tipped match and one side of it bore the lettering: *McLaughlin's.* The inspector scrutinised it thoughtfully, testing the tip for any signs of softening. Then he went across and felt the surface of the ground for moisture, comparing it with the wayside grass which was already damp with dew.

"Go on," he directed. "There's more yet, if you hunt about."

Almost at once, his assistants discovered three match ends. They were burned down almost to the butts, but enough of them was left to show that their stems had been square and quite unlike the cylindrical Swan vestas. Cumberland took from his pocket the box of matches he had forced Walton to give up, and very little comparison made clear that the spent matches tallied with those left in Walton's box.

"Here's another Swan vesta, sir."

In this case the match had not been burned down so far as the first vesta had been, and the head still adhered to the stem. Cumberland tested it gingerly and satisfied himself that it was quite fresh.

At last two more spent matches were found. One corresponded to Walton's specimens and had been burned down fairly far. The other was a second paper match which had evidently ignited satisfactorily. It was only burned away a little, and on its side Cumberland read the lettering: "*De Luxe.*" Its head, also, seemed quite fresh and the paper was unaffected by dew. The inspector thoughtfully stowed away the spent matches in some envelopes which he took from his pocket, labeling each one according to the spot where it had been found.

"We can wait till daylight and see if any more turn up then," he decided. "This is something to go on with."

His assistants, who were growing rather tired of crawling about on their hands and knees, thankfully accepted the suggestion. They rose to their feet and waited for the next order. It did not, however, concern them directly. Cumberland turned to the official photographer.

"Can you take it by flashlight, or must you wait till daylight comes up? I'd rather get the body away now, if we can."

"I can manage the body all right, sir; but if you want the surroundings, I'd better come back in daylight and do the job properly."

"Well, get the body's position now, at any rate. You can come back to-morrow morning and make a panorama series. By the way, before you take the body, just put down some of your white disks on the spots where these matches were found. And a couple of labels to show where the pipe and stick were lying. Leave his cap where it is; it doesn't matter if his head hides it a bit."

"Very good, sir."

Leaving the photographer to set up his apparatus, Cumberland turned to an examination of the immediate environment. On one side of Leisurely Lane the tarred hoarding reared itself fourteen or fifteen feet into the air. It flanked one side of the lane for a hundred yards or more, a long smooth surface which—as Cumberland noted—gave not the slightest foothold to anyone who might attempt to climb it. The body lay almost at the mid-point of the hoarding and owing to the double bend in the lane, the spot was completely screened from the view of anyone approaching up the path, until he came almost up to it.

On the other side of the lane, bushes and undergrowth grew fairly thickly down to within a foot or two of the actual pathway. Cumberland moved up and down, scrutinising this side of the lane by the light of his torch; but nowhere could he detect any noticeable disturbance of the foliage, nor did he see any sign of heavy trampling down of the grass. Footprints it was useless to hunt for, with the ground baked hard in the recent hot weather.

He shut off his torch abruptly, as a bat, blundering into its glare, threatened to beat into his face. Cumberland hated bats—"verminous brutes," as he described them—and he had a horror of one alighting on him and possibly leaving some of its living cargo behind.

"Do you mind coming behind the camera, sir?" asked the photographer when his preparations had been completed.

The inspector obediently moved out of the field of the lens and in a moment the gloom of the evening was riven by the glare of magnesium light. Oulton, who had never seen a photographer's flashlight before, was amazed by the clearness with which even the grass blades stood out individually in that fierce illumination. In the foreground, the ugly form on the pathway appeared in ghastly relief, some freak in the lighting exaggerating the horrible disarray of a violent death.

"Gosh? It's as well Tessie didn't see it like *that!*" Oulton reflected to himself. "She only saw the face, and that was bad enough for her."

Then the flare died and swift darkness seemed to rush upon them out of the gloom of the copse, blotting out the vision and leaving them in a darker night. When Cumberland switched on his torch again its beam seemed a puny thing to Oulton's dazzled eyes.

While the photographer was shifting his apparatus to a fresh standpoint, Cumberland passed up the lane until he came to the end of the hoarding, then doubled the corner and began a careful scrutiny of the back of the fence. On this side it would have been easy enough to climb, since the supporting stays gave good footholds. But so far as the inspector could see, the tarring had been repeated quite recently and no marks could be found to suggest a climber. Cumberland had not expected any. He was merely being thorough in view of his report to his superiors. No one would think of climbing over a fence which could be circumambulated at the cost of walking fifty or sixty yards at most.

The successive flares which illuminated the top of the hoarding warned him that the photographer had got on with his work; so the inspector turned the lower end of the fence and came back up the lane again to the little group about the body.

"Finished?" he inquired, as the photographer began to dismantle his camera. "Right!"

He took his chalk from his pocket and, kneeling down, drew a heavy line round the outline of the body as it lay on the hard-beaten path.

"Now you can get him onto the stretcher and down to the road," he directed two of his subordinates. "Take him straight to the mortuary and warn Dr. Webber. I asked him to get started with his P.M. as soon as he could. Say I'll be down myself in half an hour or so. Oh, yes, and you'd better give Oulton here a lift into the village."

"An' w'at about me, guv'nor?" demanded an injured voice.

"You, Walton? The night's still young, my man. You won't mind sitting up until after your usual bedtime, just as a favour to me. I can't bear to part with you—at least not until I've seen you fixed up at the police station. Just stand round and look pretty until we want you."

He reflected for a moment, then added to the stretcher bearers:

"One of you can take my motorcycle back to Ambledown. Leave a car for me down below."

The body was shifted onto the stretcher, but before the party moved off with it, Cumberland had another idea.

"Look around and collect a lot of flat stones, if you can find them near by. We'd better cover up that place where he was lying. It might rain in the night. There's a touch of thunder in the air and I don't want these chalk marks rubbed out just yet. Lay that tarpaulin over the place and pin it down with the stones round the edges."

When this had been done to his satisfaction, he reckoned up his available forces.

"Let's see. Durley, you can stay here till you're relieved and see that no one comes round about here. Order anyone off and see that they go. Then you, and you," he nodded towards two of the other constables, "I want you to search round about here for anything you can find that looks interesting. Wait a moment!" He turned to the party detailed to remove the body. "You've got torches with you? Hand them over to those two; they'll need them in case their own batteries give out. That's all for the present."

He handed a torch to Oulton.

"You light up the road for these stretcher bearers. And remember that the Chief Constable will want to see you to-morrow morning, most likely. Perhaps he'll want to see Miss Marl as well. Goodnight."

The little group with the stretcher moved off and in a few seconds vanished round the corner of the lane. Cumberland watched them out of sight and then turned to his remaining subordinates.

"When you're hunting about, keep an eye open for a brace of dead pheasants. Or a couple of brace, maybe."

Walton incautiously broke out in an aggrieved protest.

"If you're meanin' as I was poachin', guv'nor, you can think again an' make a better job o' it. Pheasants is out o' season this month. You can't sell 'em, noways."

"No. But you and your friends can eat 'em," retorted Cumberland. "You may not have nabbed any, but you were trying to. I found the stuff in your pocket. You needn't try to get rid of the rest of it now," he added sharply, as he saw Walton's hand moving stealthily pocketward. "I've got enough to do for evidence."

Walton let his arm drop to his side again. Cumberland examined his features in the light of his torch and was slightly puzzled by what he read in them. Obviously there was not sufficient evidence to convict the man of poaching, and Walton must know he was on safe ground there. Yet he seemed apprehensive; and a man of his type does not show uneasiness plainly unless there is good cause for it.

"You come along with me," Cumberland ordered. "I'll find you a night's lodging and we'll say nothing about the expense. The Chief

Constable will want to see you in the morning, with the rest of them. Get a move on, now, and don't try any fancy tricks."

He took Walton by the arm and began to descend the path to where the police car was waiting.

# CHAPTER III
## CHRONICLES OF THE AMBLEDOWN HUNDREDS

WENDOVER GLANCED at his watch and found that it was past midnight. Then his eye turned to the chess table with its array of pieces and beyond it to the empty chair of his guest.

"Ungodly hour for people to start ringing up on the phone," he reflected, without paying any attention to Sir Clinton Driffield's curt replies to the person who had called him up.

Normally, Wendover would have been on the alert, for a telephone message at this time of night implied something out of the common; but a very busy day of physical exercise, followed by a dinner and wine worth lingering over, had lured him to relax completely that evening. Instead of playing chess, he and the Chief Constable had contented themselves with working over a game or two from a recent championship, and Sir Clinton had not found his host's critical comments quite up to the usual standard.

The Chief Constable put down the extension telephone and, without comment, came back to his chair. As he sat down, his knee came into contact with the table, and the jar upset several of the pieces. Had Wendover been more vigilant, he might have suspected that the mishap was not wholly accidental.

"It doesn't matter," said Sir Clinton, with a gesture of apology. "Neither of us seems much in the mood for studying gambits tonight, Squire. Let's change the subject. I drove through Abbots Norton this afternoon. That place doesn't seem to have altered much since I knew it first."

43

Wendover seemed to wake up at the change of topic. He took a mild pride in his native countryside; and he managed to keep himself remarkably well-informed about what went on in the Hundreds of Ambledown.

"It hasn't grown much, certainly," he agreed. "The Carfaxes are no particular friends of mine, but their policy fits in with my ideas up to a point, I'll admit. I don't like to see nice little villages growing up into something that's neither hamlet nor town, with all the faults of both."

"What have the Carfaxes got to do with it?" inquired Sir Clinton lazily, as he took a cigarette from the box on the table before him

"They own all the land on one side of the main road, there," Wendover explained, "and they've always set their faces against allowing any building extension on their ground. On the other side of the road, the lie of the land doesn't encourage building much; it would need fairly extensive draining before it could be used. So between these two factors, Abbots Norton remains pretty much where it was when I was a youngster. As a matter of fact, there's no great call for any extension. Industry—thank God!—has never put its foot into the place. It's a purely agricultural little village with no immigration to speak of. The population keeps almost steady, from census to census."

"So the Carfax policy meets your approval, and yet you don't like the Carfaxes, I gather. Why?"

Wendover waked up completely.

"Because they're damned bad landlords," he declared stiffly. "From father to son, it goes on just the same. There's a queer streak in that family, somewhere."

"Grasping?" queried Sir Clinton, striking a match for his cigarette.

He knew his friend's views well enough. Wendover hated industrialism. Anything which tended to accentuate the townward drift of the rural population was anathema to him. He held—and he had proved it often enough at the expense of his pocket—that the only true criterion of the landlord caste was the contentedness of the countryside. Anything which tended to uproot or even to unsettle the rural population was a bad thing; for if once you got a family on the move, it was sure, sooner or later, to drift cityward. One had to treat tenants decently, temper justice with understanding at times, suffer some financial loss if necessary, in order to keep them on the land.

"No," Wendover drawled doubtfully. "They're not grasping exactly. Not in the money-grubbing sense, at any rate. Take what I've just been saying, as a case in point. Young Carfax could make more in hard cash by doing a bit of building at Abbots Norton—cottages are rather hard to come by, thereabouts. But he won't look at the scheme. No, you couldn't say he was a money grubber of that sort."

Sir Clinton smiled at his host's obvious effort to be fair.

"And yet you don't like them. That's plain. Is it a case of 'I do not like thee, Dr. Fell'? Or have you any special grounds for this manifest aversion of yours?"

Wendover put down his cigar as though to emphasise his next words.

"They're damned bad landlords," he repeated, with just a shade of bitterness in his tone. "They're inconsiderate with their tenants, even with men who've been on their land for generation after generation. If rents aren't paid on the nail—out you go! And they pinch on repairs to what's a scandalous extent by my standards. It's not a mere matter of money, as you can see from what I've told you. It's simply that they haven't got a spark of sympathy with the people who live on their land. I don't wonder their tenants are the most dissatisfied lot in the whole neighbourhood. And that kind of thing's a bad influence all round, you know, Clinton. We may do our best to be decent to our own tenants, but still we all get tarred with some of the Carfax ill doings. It's not fair, I grant you; but it's only human nature after all. The decent landowners suffer for the bad ones, once this suspicion of unfairness begins to spread."

Sir Clinton smoked thoughtfully for a few seconds before replying.

"They sound rather like a survival of the less admirable side of feudalism," he commented. "The land's mine, and everything on it, to do as I like with, eh?"

"That's it, more or less in a nutshell," Wendover agreed. "I can't quite explain their position, even to myself. Land hunger, or the Divine Right of Carfax, or—or—or *something*."

"Very lucid, Squire. It's *something,* beyond a doubt. But I think I see what you mean."

Wendover grunted in disgust.

"Well, I'll give you one example," he said, after a pause. "When I was a youngster, there used to be a right of way across the Carfax ground—Leisurely Lane, they called it."

"Yes, let's hear about that," said Sir Clinton, with more interest than Wendover had expected.

"Well, it was a right of way and well recognised as such until a year or two ago. Then all of a sudden young Carfax—"

"What's his other name?" asked Sir Clinton.

"Druce," answered Wendover. "He suddenly put up fences on the border of his land at both ends and forbade any traffic over the path. There was a bit of a row, naturally. The place had been used mostly as a lovers' walk in the evenings. When the row got up, young Carfax took the high hand, and he made things no better by a lot of talk about morality and so forth. That roused bad feelings, naturally, and really it was hardly the line that the Carfax family could afford to take, considering their own history in recent times."

"Let's hear about that later, Squire. It sounds interesting. But finish about the right of way, first."

"Well, the villagers took the matter into their own hands and tore down young Carfax's fences for him. Then he brought an action for damages, and the whole affair was thrashed out in court. He hadn't a leg to stand on. Some society or other took a hand in the game, unless I'm mistaken. Anyhow, the right to walk over the path was legally established, and Carfax got nothing for his trouble but a little extra bad feeling on top of what he'd earned already."

"And that was the end of it?"

"Not quite. He was vindictive. The next thing was that a couple of village children were had up before the beak for damage to his property. They'd strayed off the right of way and picked some mushrooms in an adjoining field. He wasn't using the mushrooms.

All he wanted was to prevent anyone else getting any benefit from them."

"And the case was dismissed, of course?"

"Naturally. You can't prove actual damage to the soil in a case of that sort. So there he was, defeated again. Still, it didn't cure him. The next move was this. From one point in Leisurely Lane there used to be a magnificent view out over the countryside. People used to walk up Leisurely Lane to enjoy it. That was enough for young Carfax. It must have cost him a pretty penny, but he erected a huge tarred hoarding all along that side of the lane, so as to block the view completely. Pure spite. Nothing else. He can't keep people off the right of way, but he's done his best to prevent them getting any pleasure from the scenery."

Sir Clinton pulled at his cigarette as though pondering over this tale.

"A weird artist, evidently," was his conclusion. "The root of it seems to be pride of property carried to the limit and a shade beyond that. Is that it, Squire?"

"The way I look at it," declared Wendover gruffly, "is that he sticks to his rights but won't shoulder the corresponding duties. He's certainly very proud of being Carfax of Carfax Hall. And he doesn't care a damn for anyone else's opinion. I tried, once, to give him some fatherly advice—he's only about thirty, you know, and I'm old enough to put in a word without offence, I think. But he looks on me as a mere upstart because our family's only been at the Grange here for a couple of centuries. He did his best to send me off with a flea in my ear. He's not a tactful young man."

From an undercurrent in Wendover's tone, Sir Clinton surmised that the flea had been lodged so securely that it had not yet been ejected.

"He doesn't sound altogether attractive," he commented. "What's he like, physically?"

"He always reminds me of a bull in a bad temper," Wendover answered, so quickly that it was clear that his simile was no sudden discovery. "You know the way the beasts look at you. Well, he's like that. He's a big, red-faced fellow with a voice to match. If his father had lived, he'd have been kept in order, for Griswold Carfax was another of the same sort and would have stood no nonsense from the cub. But Griswold went West in the War, when the boy was only a youngster. You know what that meant in those days."

"A bit undisciplined, perhaps?"

"Completely," grunted Wendover.

"Hasty-tempered, too, from what you say."

"Well, they had him up once before the Bench for beating a groom with a hunting crop. You may remember the case."

Sir Clinton shook his head.

"I dare say it was reported to me, but I've forgotten all about it."

"You can guess how awkward it was for us to sit in judgment on a neighbour. But it had to be done, of course. We fined him five quid and costs—the most we could make it. And instead of being ashamed of himself, he was insolent to one of my colleagues afterwards."

"A nice young man, evidently. By the way, what was the father like? Killed in France, you said, didn't you?"

"To be exact, I didn't," Wendover corrected him. "He was blown to bits in one of the Zepp raids. You remember the one that smashed up Swan & Edgar's premises? That was it. Not an unsuitable place for him to die in, after all. He'd been up and down Piccadilly pretty frequently in his lifetime. It just happened that he went there once too often, that was all."

"You don't seem to have admired him either," remarked the Chief Constable with a smile which he did not trouble to conceal.

"I didn't," admitted Wendover abruptly. "Some men seem born to be a curse to women. Griswold was one of that breed, without a fine fiber in his whole make-up. It's queer how that type has a fatal attraction for just the sort of woman who's least fit to stand up to it. I suppose, in courting days, they get the idea they've tamed the beast. Something of the sort. They soon wake up from that dream once they're married."

"Go on, Squire, I see you're all worked up about it. Get your feelings off your chest. You'll sleep all the better for the relief," advised Sir Clinton ironically.

"Well, I shall, then," retorted his host, "and then we'll see if you like the sound of him. He was one of these big swarthy brutes, black-haired and dark-eyed, who start a sort of suspicion in one's mind that gypsy blood's got into the family at some stage or other. You've heard of a man going black with rage? Well, I've seen Griswold Carfax make that expression seem less of a hyperbole than one usually takes it for."

"Sounds a forcible sort of character, certainly," admitted Sir Clinton. "And his son evidently takes after him in that way. Go on, Squire. I shouldn't have interrupted you."

"You know all this stuff about the he-man, and the sheikh, and so forth," Wendover continued. "Well, Griswold Carfax was a he-man, and a sheikh, and a cave man, all rolled into one, long before our female novelists had popularised the types. A charming personality. He gave me a really concrete idea of what Neanderthal man must have been like. The one name always brings up the other in my mind, even nowadays.

"He started sowing wild oats before he was out of his teens. A couple of village scandals got hushed up, more or less. After that he settled down a bit. That's to say, he took a mistress and stuck to her for a while. What *was* her name? Judy—Judy— It's on the tip of my tongue— Oh, yes, Judy Finborough. That was it."

"Another village girl?"

"No, something round about the governess class of those days, I think. It was only a long time later that I saw her myself. She must have been in the early thirties by that time, but she still had more than the remains of good looks. She'd taken care of herself, physically, one could see. In fact, one got the impression that she was very well able to look after herself in every way. One of these hard, metallic people who can still be charming when they set about it. You know what I mean, Clinton. When a woman of that sort smiles, she looks all you could wish. It's only when she's off her guard that you see the hardness about the lips. And at seventeen or so, when Griswold got hold of her, she must have been a bit out of the common. She had good manners, too. Not 'quite the lady,' but still as near to that as makes no matter.

"However, looks, manners, and all the rest of it didn't make her a permanency. Not even the son she had. She managed to keep Griswold in hand for five years and then there came a burst-up between them. That was just after the Boer War, I think. It sticks in my mind because of that.

"Of course, we only heard about the affair at odd times. She lived in London while this business was going on, had a small flat up West, somewhere, I believe, and became rather notorious.

"Perhaps Griswold had got accustomed to some sort of regular life with her, or perhaps he felt he was getting on, now that he had got into the thirties, and that he'd better settle down. Anyhow, the next thing was the announcement of his engagement to another girl, Fenella Basnett. I don't know where he came across her, but she was quite a suitable match, so far as social position went. In other ways—well, I have my doubts. I had plenty of chances of seeing the two of them. In those days, people stuck more or less to their own countryside. There wasn't so much of this infernal modern restlessness; and one saw more of one's neighbours than one gets a chance to do nowadays. So, as I say, I'd fair opportunities of seeing the Carfax ménage pretty frequently in one way and another. Fenella, the very first time I set eyes on her, struck me as one of those romance-stricken damsels, if you know what I mean."

"It could be made clearer," Sir Clinton suggested, lazily. "When telepathy comes along, it'll save a lot of trouble, but in the meantime one has to depend on words and so forth. 'Romance-stricken'? Have another dip, Squire."

Wendover evidently had difficulty in finding words for what he wished to convey.

"Well, it's something like this," he began, doubtfully. "Most girls fall in love with a man and then manufacture a romance out of their feelings about him. He's not the least like the dream figure they make out of him; but at least there's something more or less real at the back of it. And, I suppose, when the dream stuff thins a bit, there's still enough left in the real man to make it worth while. But girls like Fenella Basnett don't go about it in that way. They manufacture the romance first of all and then go about looking for something that will fit into the center of it. And they don't look too closely at that 'something' when it comes along, if only it can be made to serve. It may be a poet, or a cave man, or a be-starred warrior, or an Arctic explorer. Anything will do, so long as it's out of the common. In Fenella's case, it happened to be Griswold Carfax with his 'romantic' and rather grimy past, and his obviously bad temper. Is that clear?"

"No, it isn't," said Sir Clinton, bluntly. "But I get a glimmering of your ideas. Let that serve. Go on."

"I'm no great hand at making psychological subtleties clear to crude minds," Wendover admitted with a wave of his hand. "If you can't follow me, you can't. She married him; that was in 1903. Marriage, on the Griswold Carfax standard, turned out to be not so romantic after all. Druce Carfax was born in 1904. Then another son, Franklin, turned up in 1905. He's dead. Next year came Julian. And then there was a still-born child in 1907, and that finished her, poor thing. A short life, and not a very gay one, after her marriage. For Carfax was damnably jealous. He was so with all his women."

Wendover paused in his narrative for a moment, as though his thoughts had gone a-wandering.

"She puzzled me, that girl," he confessed at last. "She was a slim, elfin sort of creature, you know, with a mass of chestnut hair and a tapering chin that made her face almost triangular. That sounds ugly, but she wasn't ugly. You'd have been struck by her looks at the first glance. And she'd a disturbing trick of smiling to herself at rare intervals. Not a vapid smile—far from it. The sort of covert smile she might have given if she saw a joke nobody else could see. I hate the look of *La Gioconda,* but Mona Lisa's smile has something in it that reminds me of Fenella's—too damned subtle to be quite comfortable to look at. What the joke was, I never could guess."

He paused again, seeming to search his memory for something more.

"Oh, yes, I remember it now. Griswold Carfax, you know, wasn't a man who troubled about people's feelings. I happened to be there to lunch when something had upset him: something about archery. He was mad on archery, curiously enough, and all the family were brought up on it. He tried to start a toxophilite society round about here, but naturally he was hardly the man for the job. But that's by the way. As I said, he'd been upset by something and had to take it out of somebody. He could hardly be rude to a guest—even he had to draw the line somewhere. So he spent his ill-temper on his wife, at the luncheon table, with the servants waiting behind us. Ugh! That was the sort of man he was.

"Naturally she simply sat tight and let him rage. She wasn't afraid of him. One could see that. She was perfectly cool through it all. No doubt, by that time, she'd got inured to his methods. I looked the other way, of course; but just by accident I caught a glimpse of her face, and there was that queer smile of hers, just as if she was enjoying some jest of her own. It came and went in a moment, but it was so unexpected that it's stuck in my memory. And the funny thing is that, in the ordinary way, she hadn't much sense of humour. These romantic people don't have it, as a rule, I've noticed."

Wendover mused for a moment or two before continuing, but Sir Clinton seemed quite content to let him take his own pace in his narrative.

"Fenella died in 1907, I think I told you. Griswold Carfax wasn't the man to mourn overlong, as you can guess. The next year he took another wife, a girl Ivy Ganton, a very ordinary sort of person. There was a son, Horace, in 1909; and then a daughter, Enid, in 1910. Easy enough to remember dates when they come like that. Then in 1911, Ivy had an accident when she was out riding. Her hack shied at a traction engine, reared and came down on top of her. So that finished her, poor girl. She wasn't thirty when she died, and her son Horace followed her in a year or so.

"Meanwhile the countryside had come to tolerate Griswold Carfax, as far as such a creature is tolerable at all. He'd lived a domesticated life for some eight years, you know, and that seemed to show that he'd decided to settle down. But when Ivy Ganton died, he blotted his copybook completely so far as the neighbours were concerned. He got in touch with that Finborough woman again, his old mistress, and he brought her and her son to Carfax Park as a permanency. Oh, no! He didn't marry her. He seems to have given up marriage as a bad job by that stage. He simply installed her and her boy without caring a twopenny damn for public opinion. Naturally it made things damned awkward. Nobody would call on them and they got no invitations. I don't suppose Griswold minded much, and I never heard what Judy Finborough thought of it. He used to take her to flower shows and that sort of thing. That's where I came across her. But nobody would look at them. It was a bit too blatant, altogether; and I believe he dragged her to these affairs just to make it as awkward as he could. He was that sort of fellow, you know. 'If you see a corn, tramp on it!' That kind of thing. Judy Finborough died early in the War. Somehow no woman seemed to thrive in Griswold's company.

"I never came across her son—Godfrey was his name—so I can't tell you anything about him. He stayed on at Carfax Hall after her death, brought up with the rest of that assorted family. But when Griswold was killed in the Zepp raid, his affairs fell into the hands of trustees, and they didn't see any reason for keeping the evidence of that scandal on the premises. They turned the boy loose. Gave him some capital to start him in life, I believe; or he may have got that under Griswold's will. Anyhow, they packed him off to London."

"What's happened to the rest of the family?" inquired the Chief Constable with just enough show of interest to keep the conversation alive.

"The present generation, you mean? Well, of course, there was a period of trusteeship until Druce came of age and took over the estate, about a dozen years ago. I've told you about him already. Then there's Julian. I don't think much of Julian. He's a born loafer and seems quite content to vegetate on a couple of hundred a year left him by an aunt or somebody of that sort. He lives at Carfax Hall on sufferance—free board and lodging at Druce's expense."

"What about the half-sister?" asked Sir Clinton.

"Enid? She must be about twenty-five or so, nowadays. I've come across her occasionally. Pretty girl with chestnut hair. She has a few hundred a year of her own since she came of age and she lives part of the time at Carfax Hall and the other part in London, I believe. Druce and she seem to rub along together, but I expect that's all there is in it. He's only a half-brother, you know, and I don't suppose she's absolutely enthralled with him."

"I take it that the old scandal's died away by this time?" interjected Sir Clinton.

"Oh, yes, long ago," Wendover confirmed. "Druce had a longish minority, and that helped people to forget about it. And, to be quite fair to the fellow, his eccentricities don't take the form that his father's did. He's rather strait-laced on that side, if anything. There's been no scandal of that sort about him. And, besides, times change. We don't visit the sins of the fathers on the children the way we used to do. There's no social bar up against the present generation, in this neighbourhood."

Sir Clinton glanced at his watch.

"Time's getting on, Squire. We'd better give the Carfax family a rest for the present."

Wendover rose from his chair and began to put away the chess pieces in the drawer of the table. Sir Clinton got up and crossed over to the hearthrug where he stood for a moment in silence. Then he put a question.

"Ever hear of a man Huggin, Squire? Miles Huggin?"

Wendover paused and looked round.

"Huggin?" he repeated. "No, I can't say I ever did, and if I'd heard a name like that I think I'd remember it. Who is he?"

"He isn't anybody, now. He was murdered this evening while we were talking chess."

"Hereabouts?" demanded Wendover, drawing an inference from his guest's last sentence.

"Just beside that hoarding in Carfax Park that you were telling me about. Inspector Cumberland rang up about it."

"Oh, so that was why you drew me out about the Carfaxes? You might have given me a hint."

"You'd have been so excited that I wouldn't have got an impartial story out of you," the Chief Constable retorted. "You always take sides in a murder case, Squire. It's apt to warp things. So I preferred to extract what I could while your mind was unbiased."

Wendover acknowledged the thrust good-humouredly.

"You certainly took me in," he admitted. "But what about the affair? Aren't you going to get a move on?"

"Cumberland will do all the buzzing about that's immediately necessary," Sir Clinton assured him. "Tomorrow morning will be time enough for me. You'd better come along with me after break-fast. Your local knowledge will be invaluable when it comes to over-hearing footprints, measuring clues, and what not. After all, it's most unusual for a man to be murdered in a strange place by a total stranger. Though it might happen, of course. But in the mean-time, I propose to go to bed, without bothering to build up any theories to-night. I'd advise you to do the same. That's why I'm giving you no further news at present."

# CHAPTER IV
## PHEASANTS AND BANK NOTES

"JUST ROUND THIS CORNER," Wendover explained, as the car ran along the byroad. "There it is. Stop!"

Sir Clinton pulled up opposite a rough gap in the wayside hedge. On the highway side stood a notice board bearing the recently-painted inscription:

PUBLIC RIGHT OF WAY TO MALLARD CHASE

whilst a companion board, obviously of earlier date, was planted almost in the gap itself and announced in faded lettering:

TRESPASSERS PROSECUTED.

The Chief Constable solemnly inspected them in turn.

"Conflict of evidence here, at the very start," he said sardonically. "This is the thing you told me about, Squire. An obvious case of ingrowing landlordism of an acute type, probably inherited from a long line of noted land stealers in the days of the enclosures. Ah! There's the inspector's motorcycle stowed behind the hedge. He's up the lane, probably. We'll go through here and follow the path."

They stepped through the gap in the hedge and began to ascend the path which wound upwards towards some wooded ground.

"I expected a crowd of interested inhabitants," Wendover commented, glancing round. "A murder always draws the morbid-minded ones like a magnet."

"That's why you're here, eh?" retorted the Chief Constable pleasantly. "I always do admire candour, Squire. But as to your congeners, Cumberland has probably sent them off with fleas in their ears. We can't have a horde of rubber-necks trampling over everything until after we've seen all there's to be seen. When we've finished our job, they can swarm up here if they like; but meanwhile, I'm against intrusion. It may not be exactly legal, but it's common sense."

"Cumberland rang you up this morning, didn't he?" demanded Wendover. "Has he made any progress with the case?"

"About as much progress as a glacier would make in the same time," Sir Clinton answered. "And that's quite good going in a case of this sort, Squire. It's less than twelve hours since the murder, and Cumberland hasn't had much chance of getting witnesses together yet. You can't rout people out of their beds at midnight on the off chance that they may have seen something useful. Cumberland has done as much as can be expected."

The Chief Constable always stood up for his subordinates, as Wendover knew from long experience.

The path was one which had obviously been made by the feet of passers-by and it was just wide enough to allow two people to walk abreast on its rather rough surface. At first it led through meadowland; but then, round the shoulder of a slope, it curved and as they walked on briskly the end of a tarred hoarding came into view.

"This is that eyesore I told you about," Wendover explained, pointing to it.

"It must be visible from his own windows," Sir Clinton ruminated. "Rather a case of cutting off one's nose to spite one's face, by the look of things. The house is just about half a mile away, isn't it? I noticed it as we came up the path. In that direction."

He indicated a point beyond the hoarding along the edge of which they were now passing.

"Yes, that's it. A big place in the Palladian style."

At this moment they caught sight of Inspector Cumberland, rounding a turn in the path as he came to meet them. He saluted as he came up to them.

"Haven't kept you waiting?" Sir Clinton hailed him.

"Only a minute or two, sir."

He turned and walked behind them, the path not being broad enough for the three to go abreast.

"I've got one or two fresh points, sir," he explained with a certain satisfaction.

"Let's take things in their order, if you don't mind," Sir Clinton suggested. "First of all, has Dr. Webber made his examination of the man's body?"

"He's not finished all he wants to do, sir. But he's made some preliminary examination. The wound corresponds roughly to what a .45 bullet would make, he thinks. There was no powder blackening or singeing of the cloth of the waistcoat. And apparently the shot must have gone clean through the body. He can't find any trace of the bullet, and of course there's the exit wound in the back. I mean the shot didn't just break the skin at the back and stick there. It must have gone through and come out. I've got my men hunting for it on the ground, now. But they haven't spotted it, so far."

"There was no pistol or revolver near the body?"

"No, sir, nothing of the sort, so far as we've found. So it's not suicide."

"That hardly settles it," Wendover pointed out. "He might have shot himself and then somebody else might have picked up the weapon and carried it off."

Cumberland had it on the tip of his tongue to say, "Pigs might fly," as sufficient criticism of this suggestion; but he stopped himself in time and substituted, "That is so, sir," with so much scepticism in his tone that he might almost as well have used his first choice.

"Mr. Wendover believes in looking at all sides of a question," Sir Clinton said, seriously. "It's not a bad plan. And, by the way, Inspector, just give Mr. Wendover an account of your doings up to the time you phoned me last night. He knows nothing about the case, and it'll help to refresh my memory as well, before we begin to look round."

Cumberland gave his chief a glance of suspicion. Was this a dodge of Sir Clinton's to test whether he would make a slip? But the expression on the Chief Constable's face evidently reassured

him, and with Wendover's obvious eagerness as an encouragement
he plunged into a bald summary of the events which had occurred
since he took up the case. But when he had finished, Wendover's
reaction to the tale was not exactly what he had expected. The
Squire had something of the pictorial imagination in him. He could
visualise a scene for himself, if he were given some details to build
upon. And he had a kindly feeling for any girl.

"Phew! What a transformation scene for those two!" he said
sympathetically. "This nice lonely lane. The young fellow and his
girl in the after-dusk with only some stars out overhead; a cock-
chafer or two flying about, and perhaps a bat flickering over their
heads. All still, except a nightjar in the wood, maybe. A kiss or
two; young blood all keyed up with emotion. . . . And then, in the
flare of a match, that blood—and other things! Then panic, and a
flight down that path, stumbling over the rough ground, and the
girl, no doubt, expecting to feel a murderer's hand on her shoulder at every step. She must have gone through it, poor girl!"

"They didn't stop running, except to catch their breath, until
they got to the village," Cumberland amplified, in the tone of one
whose business it is to record facts and leave emotion out of the
question. "Nearly burst their bellows, I gather, by the time they
met the constable."

"Well, that's the tale," Sir Clinton said, turning to Wendover.
"It puts you abreast of the case. Now we'll see what's to be seen
hereabouts."

The spot where the body had lain was still marked by the stones
which had been heaped upon it the night before. Cumberland made
a movement as though to remove them and disclose the surface of
the ground; but Sir Clinton checked him.

"Don't bother. I'll see the photographs," he said, as he stepped
past the little cairn and began to scrutinise the surface of the tarred
hoarding. For a few moments he let his eyes range over it, as though
expecting to pick up some easily discernible object. Then he seemed
puzzled and began a much more thorough examination, foot by
foot, of the planks. Wendover guessed that he was looking for the
mark left by the bullet after it had traversed Huggin's body.

"Can't you find it?" he demanded, moving over to assist.

"See for yourself," Sir Clinton advised, drawing back a little to allow Wendover and Cumberland to search.

They examined the planking meticulously, and Cumberland carried his exploration to a dozen yards or more on either side of the place where the body had lain. At last he gave it up and turned to the Chief Constable.

"I don't see any trace of an impact, sir," he reported. "And yet . . ."

A thought struck him and he turned to his subordinates who had been searching the ground for the bullet.

"Find it?" he demanded.

"No, sir," one constable reported, answering for his companion also. "There's no sign of it hereabouts that we can see. It may be amongst the grass and maybe we missed it. But we had a rare good hunt."

"I see it!" ejaculated Wendover.

Then, at the expressions on the faces of the constables, he made himself rather clearer:

"I mean, I see what's happened. You've been assuming that he was shot here, on this spot. But what is there to prove that? He might quite well have been shot somewhere else. The body could have been dragged along and dumped here after he was dead. That would account for there being no mark behind him on the fence, although the bullet went clean through him."

Cumberland listened to this hypothesis with obvious interest but also with growing scepticism.

"That's neat enough, sir," he admitted, "and it gets us out of this hole. But it lands us in a worse one, to my mind. If he'd been dragged here, there'd be a regular break in the bushes hereabouts. There's no sign of that, as far as I can see."

"He may have been shot further along the path," Wendover pointed out. "Then there'd be no need to trail him through the bushes at all."

Cumberland was still unconvinced.

"There'd be some sign of dragging," he objected. "A body's a heavy thing and leaves marks. I looked into that when I came up this morning. There isn't a sign of anything of the sort, either up or down the path."

"He may have been carried," suggested Wendover, fighting hard for his idea.

"Then there'd be a blood trail all the way—no matter how you look at it, dragging or carrying—and what's more, the man who carried him would have got blood all over his clothes from the wounds."

"You said that you found evidence of blood on this fellow—what's his name?—Walters."

"Walton, sir. No, that cock won't fight, I'm afraid. Walton had some blood traces, but nothing like what he'd have had if he'd been carrying that body about. I went over his clothes after I got him locked up. There was nothing soiled to any extent bar his handkerchief."

"Then how do you account for this?"

"I don't account for it, sir. Not at present. Later on, we'll see better, perhaps."

During this mild passage of arms, Sir Clinton had evidently been thinking along a line different from that taken by Wendover. He now turned to the two constables who were standing by.

"You've been searching round about here? And you haven't seen any trace of a pistol or revolver?"

"No, sir," admitted the senior constable. "We've done our best, hunted everywhere that looked likely. Every square foot of ground near by's been gone over carefully. There's no sign of it, sir."

"Didn't come across an empty cartridge case, did you?" asked Sir Clinton.

"No, sir. We'd orders to keep our eyes open for anything of the sort, but we didn't find it."

"The shot might have come from a revolver," Wendover pointed out. "It's only automatics that eject after each shot."

"Then it wasn't an automatic that did the trick, sir," Cumberland declared. "These men are very careful searchers. I can vouch for that. They're not likely to have missed a thing like a brass cartridge case. It isn't so very small—a .45 one."

Sir Clinton gave a nod, as though agreeing with this.

"We'll need a complete large-scale plan showing all the trees, bushes, and so on, if it ever comes to a trial. Better put your best man on to it. One never knows what will be required. And unless it's done now, it might not be accurate enough. Mr. Carfax may take it into his head to clear up the undergrowth or make some other changes. It's his land; and his ideas of improving it aren't like other people's."

He pointed rather contemptuously at the unsightly expanse of the hoarding in illustration.

"Very good, sir," said Cumberland. "I'll see to it."

Sir Clinton turned to another matter.

"How about these matches you found? Have any more turned up?"

Cumberland threw a glance of inquiry at his constables, whereupon the junior one began to feel in his pocket. He pulled out a notebook and from between its pages he took a spent match, a square-stemmed one which the inspector recognised as another from Walton's box.

"I found this under a tuft of grass over there, sir," the constable explained, holding it out to Sir Clinton. "I've marked the place where I picked it up."

"Very good. I like to see people careful in their work," said Sir Clinton, encouragingly. "It's fairly well burned down," he pointed out—rather unnecessarily, since he held it up for inspection. "Now about this match business, Inspector. Would you mind explaining to Mr. Wendover just what you found, including this one. By the way, you'd better add it to your collection."

The inspector stowed away this fresh exhibit and then turned to Wendover.

"We've found two Swan vestas, corresponding to a Swan vesta box that was in Huggin's pocket, sir," he explained. Then there were five cheap square-stemmed matches. They corresponded to the ones in a box I took from Walton. And finally, there were two paper matches, one that hadn't struck right, and the other just lit and thrown away before it had got well alight."

"Go on," suggested the Chief Constable. "Let's hear how you account for all this fireworks display."

"I don't know if Mr. Wendover heard that we found a pipe as well," began Cumberland. "Huggin's pipe, it must have been, since he'd a pouch in his pocket and the pipe was lying over there"—he pointed to the spot—"just where it might have got knocked out of his hand when he came down."

He smiled with mild triumph as he added:

"And that seems to show he was killed here, doesn't it, sir?"

"You have me there, I admit," Wendover conceded with an answering smile. "But I hadn't heard about this pipe, you know, when I made my suggestion."

"You didn't wait for the whole evidence, sir," Cumberland pointed out. "You see there's something to be said for holding judgment in suspense, like I'm doing."

"Don't rub it in," said Wendover, placably. "I admit I ran a bit ahead of the facts. Please go on."

"The way I look at it is this," Cumberland explained. "The two Swan vestas were Huggin's, and he lit his pipe with them. The fact that they're fairly far burned down is enough to show that. His pipe must have gone out on him, I expect, which accounts for the second match after he'd got it going with the first one. If you pass that as sound, sir, then he must have been here for some minutes, between the times he lit the two vestas. That fits in with the amount of unsmoked tobacco in the pipe bowl, too, assuming he started by filling his pipe when he arrived here."

"Wait a bit," interrupted Wendover. "Sorry to interrupt you, but I believe in admitting when I'm wrong. You've convinced me you're right, Inspector. He must have been killed here, on that evidence, taken all together."

"I wish everyone was as fair-minded as you, sir," said Cumberland, obviously restoring Wendover to favour again. "Now we've got those five burnt matches with the square stems. Walton used them. They tally with the ones left in the box I took from him. He smokes gaspers and he hadn't a pipe on him when we got him to the station."

"He couldn't have smoked five cigarettes in the time that Huggin took to smoke a quarter of a pipeful of tobacco," Wendover threw in.

"Nor would the matches be three quarters burned down if he'd used them for cigarette lighting," Sir Clinton added. "Up to a point, his tale's evidently correct. But he didn't take a mere fleeting glimpse at Huggin's body. He spent five matches over it, so he must have examined it pretty thoroughly. Judging from your description of Walton, Inspector, I infer that he went through Huggin's pockets. And that he lit at least four matches to examine his catches as he came across them."

"You're absolutely right there, sir," confirmed Cumberland. "I've got evidence to prove it. But we'll come to that later on. We've still got a couple of matches unaccounted for—the two paper ones. Neither Huggin nor Walton had any paper matches on them, and there's no sign of the carton stub anywhere about. So neither of them had these two matches left on a stub and used them up before starting on the other kind. The stub would be about somewhere, if that had happened, for they'd have thrown it down after taking the last match out of it. So there must have been a third man here."

"And he must have smoked one cigarette," Wendover put in. "One paper match was a dud; it didn't light. The other one is barely burned, which points to a cigarette and not a pipe. You didn't find any cigarette stub about?"

Cumberland gave a nod of denial after consulting his subordinates with a glance.

"Then the interview must have been a short one, so far as this third man was concerned, otherwise he'd have finished his cigarette and thrown the stub away."

"Unless he put himself in your place and took the trouble to carry his stubs away with him," Sir Clinton pointed out. "He may have been a chain smoker who used only one match for a series of cigarettes. I don't say he was. Still, it's a possibility and we're apparently considering every possibility."

His tone suggested that he had no great belief in the hypothesis.

"I've got my own ideas about what happened," the inspector resumed, "but I'd rather leave them aside for the moment. There's more evidence. I'll give you it later, sir. What I'm trying to do just now is to clear up the points connected with this place, so that you're on the spot if you want to look into anything a bit further."

"Sound view," Sir Clinton agreed. "Well, produce your evidence."

Cumberland made a gesture, and one of the constables brought out something which had been laid down behind a bush. As he turned back, Wendover saw that he had two dead pheasants in his hand.

"Just show us where you found them," directed the inspector.

The constable led the party up the lane to beyond the end of the hoarding, then, leaving the path, he walked into the copse and finally pointed to a spot amongst the undergrowth.

"In there, I found them, sir," he reported to the Chief Constable. "They was well poked in, out of sight; but he'd disturbed the twigs a bit, doing it, and I spotted things wasn't just natural."

"You've got sharp eyes," commented Sir Clinton.

Wendover had been examining the brace of pheasants with a frown on his face.

"These have been poached, of course," he said, crossly. "It's the close season yet. They weren't shot. Caught in a springe, by the look of them, and not earlier than yesterday, I should think."

"That was Walton's doing, sir," explained the inspector, though he did not trouble to give any proof of his statement.

"Oh, it was, was it?" grunted Wendover.

All his feelings as a preserver of game were rasped by the thought of a poacher, and it was clear that Walton's reputation had now sunk to zero in his eyes.

"But wait a bit!" he continued. "The pheasants must have gone to roost long before all this match striking began. How do you account for that?"

"That's an easy one, sir," the inspector explained. "My notion is that Walton came up here yesterday afternoon and did his poaching. He got this brace of birds. He may have got more. But it was broad daylight, then, and he couldn't get the game away. So he hid them, and came back in the dusk to pick them up. That was what brought him up here in the evening."

"Where are the nearest pheasants?" asked Sir Clinton.

"About a mile or so up the lane, and then off to the left," the inspector said, pointing approximately in the direction which he had indicated.

"So he wouldn't bring them down the lane in broad daylight and hide them here immediately after his poaching," inferred the Chief Constable. "He probably hid them somewhere further up, at first, and then in the evening he picked them up and brought them down. Then he hid them again where the constable found them— most likely because he heard someone coming up the lane and didn't want to be spotted with the game in his hands. Well, we'll go into that when we question him. Anything more, Inspector?"

Wendover could see by Cumberland's face that he had now reached the culmination of his tale. Obviously, too, it had required no little restraint on his part to reserve this titbit for the last. He put his hand in his pocket, drew out an envelope, and handed it to the Chief Constable with a gesture which was almost a flourish.

"There's this, sir. I told you my men here didn't miss much."

Sir Clinton kept the envelope in his hand and turned to the constables.

"Where did you find this?" he inquired.

"Just over here, sir." The junior constable led the way to a rabbit hole a few steps beyond the bank which edged the path. "Down there, sir. Shoved in, a full arm's length. It cost me a bit of wriggling to get it out, once I'd felt it was there. It wasn't in the envelope you have, sir. All in a roll, sir, and maybe I didn't get the whole lot. But we can dig down, sir, and make sure. Only I didn't want to disturb anything till you'd seen it, sir."

"Very good indeed," said the Chief Constable, heartily. "You must have been pretty busy if you examined all the rabbit holes hereabouts."

As he spoke, he slipped his fingers into the envelope gingerly and drew out the corners of some one-pound Bank of England notes.

"You haven't been handling these, I suppose?" he inquired of Cumberland.

"Not more than I could help, sir. I just slipped them into the envelope as they were."

"Not that it matters," said Sir Clinton. "These things pass through too many hands to make it worth while to look for finger-prints. Still, we'd better not examine them closely till we get to a less exposed spot."

He shook the notes back into their place in the envelope and returned it to the inspector. As he did so, Wendover caught a glimpse of Cumberland's face and saw that he had still to produce his last sensation.

"There's one thing I *did* notice, sir. A big splotch of blood on one of the notes."

# CHAPTER V:
## "GOD SEND YOU BACK TO ME"

"Now," suggested Sir Clinton to Cumberland as they settled themselves round a table in one of the rooms of the police station at Ambledown, "I think this will be the best plan. Give us any further points you've got since last night, first of all. Then we'll interview young Oulton. That won't take long; and we needn't bother the girl—what's her name? Marl, isn't it?—at present. You can see her yourself and get her to confirm Oulton's story. But that can wait. And when we've got all that clear, we'll tackle friend Walton. I can foresee a bad five minutes for him."

"Very good, sir," agreed Cumberland. "Would you like me to begin with Huggin's movements last night, so far as I've been able to trace them?"

Sir Clinton nodded; and the inspector, pulling out his notebook to refresh his memory, began his account.

"He had the return half of a London ticket in his pocket when I searched the body, a third-class ticket it was. So the first thing was to make inquiries at the station, sir. When I got hold of the porter who took the tickets last night and showed him the photograph of the body, he was pretty sure he'd seen the man. So I sent him along to the mortuary—he didn't much like the job!—and made a certainty of it. Huggin arrived here last night on the train that gets in at 7:11 p.m."

"One moment," interrupted Wendover. "Let's extract all we can from this before we go on."

Sir Clinton shrugged his shoulders impatiently.

"You remind me of the story about the Scotsman when a fly fell into his whiskey. He lifted it out and wrung it dry before he threw it away. Get on with your wringing, then."

"My point," Wendover explained, with a slightly ruffled air, "was simply this. He didn't come by car. That might mean one of two things."

"That he hadn't a car to come in?" interjected Sir Clinton.

"That's one possibility," Wendover proceeded. "The other is that he didn't want to leave any trace of his visit. Someone might have noticed the number of a car if he had used one."

"Something in that, sir, perhaps," conceded the inspector.

"Further," pursued Wendover, evidently gaining confidence again, "there's the fact that he traveled third class. That doesn't look like affluence and it suggests that he hasn't got a car."

"We can check that up through the registration lists if it's necessary," Sir Clinton said. "But by the time we get that length, we'll probably know all we want about him. Go on, Inspector."

"Well, sir, he had no luggage with him. He simply stepped out of the train with his walking stick in his hand and passed through the ticket barrier with the rest of the passengers. He went along the High Street and turned into a public house there: The Barleycorn. I expect you've noticed it."

"What sort of place is it?" inquired the Chief Constable.

"It's quite a decent little pothouse, sir. Lots of the village lads make it a center in the evenings. They can give you a scratch meal there, or even put you up, if it comes to a pinch, though it's not exactly a pocket Ritz. It's clean, and well-conducted; but it's not a real hotel, like the Green Lion just outside the station. Huggin passed it on his way to The Barleycorn. When he got to The Barleycorn, he ordered something to eat. I got a list of what he had, if you want to hear it, sir."

"No, thanks," said Sir Clinton. "Give it to Dr. Webber in case he wants to check up the digestion period or anything of that kind."

"Very good, sir."

Wendover could not refrain from putting in his oar.

"This evidence confirms what I said before," he pointed out. "If Huggin hadn't been hard up, he'd have gone to the Green Lion for his meal."

The inspector smiled covertly at this inference, but made no comment

"People don't always go to the most expensive restaurants when they've enough money to do so," objected Sir Clinton. "Huggin may have gone to The Barleycorn in search of tripe and onions, which he wouldn't get at the Green Lion. Some people have morbid tastes and will go any length to gratify them. What next, Inspector?"

"He had no luggage with him, sir, and he made no inquiry about sleeping accommodation at The Barleycorn. That points to his having meant to get back to London again by a later train, I think."

"There is a later train?"

"There's one at 10:40 p.m., sir. Now, if you reckon out the time he would take to walk up to where we found him and back again to the station, it's pretty clear that he was allowing himself just time and no more to put his business through, whatever it was."

"Yes, go on," urged Sir Clinton.

"He ate his meal at The Barleycorn, sir, paid the bill, and left there about half past eight. No one seems to have paid any attention to him after he left The Barleycorn."

"He didn't ask for directions from anyone?"

"Not that I've been able to find out, sir."

"It would be none too easy for a total stranger to find his way to Leisurely Lane," mused Wendover. "He must have made some inquiry, surely."

"One could do it with the help of an Ordnance map," Sir Clinton pointed out. "And besides, he may have been here before, for all we know. Just let me interrupt your narrative for a moment, Inspector. There's been a dearth of nature study in it, so far; and I think it's time we had something of the sort. On the evening of Huggin's death, the sun set at 8:17 p.m., summer time. The moon, I may say, set at 7:59 p.m., so it doesn't come into the picture. I got these details out of Whitaker's Almanac. Now this man Huggin left The Barleycorn about 8:30 p.m. and walked up to the spot where he was found dead, so it's likely he didn't arrive at the killing place before, say, 9:15 p.m."

"It's at least two and a half miles from the village. He'd take forty minutes to walk it, at three miles an hour," rectified Wendover. "Say he got to the hoarding at 9:20 p.m."

"Say what you like. It really doesn't matter a damn," agreed Sir Clinton politely. "The real point is that he got up there in the dusk, just about lighting-up time, when there was still light enough to see fairly clearly at short distances. If he meant to catch the 10:40 train back to London, he'd have to leave the hoarding again by 9:50 at the latest. That doesn't allow much time for an interview, if he went up there to meet someone by appointment."

"Obviously he had an appointment," Wendover declared.

"Somebody had an appointment with him, anyhow," said Sir Clinton, with a touch of grimness.

"Who?" demanded Wendover.

"A bony old gentleman called Death," said the Chief Constable. "'To all mankind upon this earth, he cometh soon or late,' as we learned in our school days. But I expect he took Huggin unawares. And now, Inspector, let's have a look at these bank notes. They seem to fit into the tale hereabouts, so we may as well see what we can make of them."

Cumberland produced the envelope from his pocket and with care he drew out the notes from it and placed them on the table.

"I'd better count them, sir," he suggested, suiting the action to the word. "As you see, there are some ten-bob ones amongst them and nothing higher than a quid . . . seventy-five, seventy-six, seventy-seven pound notes; and a dozen ten-bob ones. . . . That makes eighty-three pounds in all. A tidy little sum," he concluded, half enviously, as he finished his task.

"Just go through them again and pick out any that are marked with bloodstains," said Sir Clinton.

The inspector obeyed, throwing aside a note here and there, until four had been selected. Two had large ominous brown stains on them, and two were more lightly blotched. Sir Clinton examined them thoughtfully for some moments, then he turned to the inspector.

"Have you looked at that note case you found on Huggin's body? I mean, have you examined it again in daylight?"

The inspector shook his head.

"No, sir. I just had a glance at it when I took it out of his pocket up there, by the light of a flash lamp. Since then, I've been about run off my feet collecting information about Huggin's movements and so on. I've had no time to re-examine it."

"It's here, isn't it? Suppose we have a look at it now."

Cumberland got up and left the room, returning in a moment or two with the suede leather note case in his hand, which he passed to Sir Clinton. The Chief Constable opened it and examined the note pocket meticulously.

"Our friend Walton isn't easily rattled, evidently," he commented, laying the case on the table.

Wendover picked it up and scrutinised it in his turn. It still contained the seventeen Bank of England one-pound notes which the inspector had found in it when he first discovered it. They seemed free from any trace of blood. But on the inside of the pocket which contained them, the soft leather bore faint ominous stains which might well have escaped a hasty examination. Wendover passed the case to Cumberland who, enlightened by Wendover's actions, found the marks at once.

"H'm!" he admitted, stiffly, "I missed this, sir."

"Considering that you were working with a flash lamp, I don't wonder at it," Sir Clinton replied. "It takes daylight to show up that kind of thing plainly. The point is, what are we to make of it, now we've got it?"

"What do you make of it, sir?" inquired the inspector, cautiously.

"Only a guess," Sir Clinton said. "But it may be right. Look at it in this way. Walton said he stumbled over Huggin's body and came down on the ground. Suppose he landed with his hands outspread— one usually does—and one of them flapped, palm down, into a patch of blood. He probably didn't notice what had happened, in the shock of the fall. I mean he wouldn't bother about his hand being moist. Then he lighted a match and saw what he'd stumbled over.

Suppose that he went through the dead man's pockets. He doesn't seem to be the sort of person to be troubled by scruples, you know. He goes into the breast pocket with his 'clean' hand and brings out the note case. Remember, he's holding a match in the other hand, so he hasn't both hands free. The match goes out, which frees his other hand; and he uses that to extract the notes *en bloc* from the case. Naturally, in doing that, the top and bottom notes get heavily marked by the blood on the inner side of his hand; and when he strikes a fresh match, he notices that. But he forgets that quite likely some blood may have worked onto the back of his hand and marked the case lightly as he was drawing out the notes. One can't think of everything, in a situation like that, you know. Then it occurs to him that it might be safer not to take all the notes. Better to leave a few behind, so as not to suggest robbery. So he slips some clean notes out of the middle of the bundle, slides them back into the case again, and strips off the top and bottom ones—once they're in—to make sure he's left no stains on the remainder. That gives you two heavily marked notes—the top and bottom notes in the original pile—and two lighter-marked ones representing the top and bottom ones of the smaller packet before he put it back into the case. And it gives you the marks on the leather of the case also. It may not be right, but it's the nearest guess I can make at present."

"And then he went off and hid the bigger packet in the rabbit hole, sir?"

"Well, before that, I think, he cleaned his hands with his handkerchief. You remember you spotted he'd done that, Inspector. He'd want to get rid of the blood as quick as he could. And that would account for the extra matches he struck. He probably used them up in making sure that he'd got his paws clean."

"That seems to fit, sir," the inspector agreed.

"Pure hypothesis," said the Chief Constable. "Still, we may be able to trip him up with it when we come to question him. But we haven't done with these notes yet. Two points still."

He glanced at Wendover as though inviting a suggestion, but got no response.

"Well," he continued, "how does this fit in with the idea that Huggin was so very hard up? Here he was, with plenty of money in his note case. I don't go about myself with sixty or seventy quid in my pocket normally. I prefer to keep it in the bank, unless I happen to be paying bills or something of that sort. How do you square that with a third-class ticket and a scratch meal at a pub? And that brings up the second point."

"What's that, sir?" demanded the inspector, without troubling to speculate or to give Wendover time to do so.

"Just count up," suggested the Chief Constable. "You found eighty-three pounds in that pile of notes, didn't you? And last night you found seventeen pound notes left in the case? What's the total? One hundred pounds. *A round sum.* That seems suggestive, doesn't it? Couple it with Mr. Wendover's idea that Huggin was hard up when he arrived in Abbots Norton last night."

"You mean somebody gave him £100 between the time he left The Barleycorn and the time Walton found his body, sir?"

"It's on the cards, isn't it? That's as far as it's safe to go at present. But if we could find out where these notes came from, it might be a help. It's a pity there wasn't a fiver or two amongst them. One-pound notes are almost impossible to trace back. We may as well have a look at them, however."

He drew the pile of notes towards him and began to examine them one by one, scanning both the back and the front of each note as he came to it. Suddenly he paused in his operations and with a smile of amusement spread out one note for the inspection of his companions. Across the back of it, written in indelible-pencil script, were the words:

GOD SEND YOU BACK TO ME.

Wendover and the inspector leaned across to examine it.

"Somebody with a queer sense of humour," Wendover commented. "He's hardly likely to see his prayer granted, I fear."

"I don't care whether he does or not," said the practical inspector. "It's a noticeable note. That's what you mean, sir, isn't it? Some bank clerks must have had a snigger over it and they'll remember something about it. A fair godsend."

"If the writing had been on the face of the note, it would have been noticed more easily. Bank clerks count notes face upward, usually. However, it's always something," Sir Clinton observed. "You'd better begin by trying the local banks, Inspector. See if anyone remembers it. If you fail there, it'll be a troublesome business; for it might have come from anywhere."

"I'll have a try, sir, locally. Perhaps we'll have a stroke of luck. And now, would you like to have Oulton in? I don't want to keep him hanging about longer than's necessary. It takes him off his day's work, this."

"Very well. Bring him in."

The inspector retired and in a moment or two ushered in his witness. Oulton seemed slightly taken aback to find that he had three people to encounter. He made a movement, half between a nod and a bow, and then stood twisting his cap in his hands as if perturbed by his position. But Wendover noticed that when he was addressed, he looked the speaker straight in the eyes; and as time went on he lost his initial nervousness and grew more at ease.

"Nothing to worry about, my man," said the Chief Constable. "All we want from you is your story; and if you make it full enough, we shan't have to trouble Miss Marl at all, probably. The inspector will take down what you say, and you can read it over after we've done, and sign it. Just tell us what happened last night. Start from, say, the time you met Miss Marl."

Oulton turned out to be a fairly good witness. He told his tale concisely, yet with sufficient detail to obviate the need for more than an occasional question. He and Tessie Marl had been engaged for some months. He had met her in the village after supper—shortly before eight o'clock, so far as he could remember. They had arranged, a day earlier, to go for a walk if the night was fine; otherwise they meant to go to the pictures. It was a fine night. They strolled out of the village for some distance. Then they had sat down for a while—he could not say exactly how long. After that, they had gone on—sauntering, not in a hurry—to Leisurely Lane. They met no one in the lane itself. He couldn't say when they got to the entrance to the lane; he hadn't looked at his watch. They had sat down again on a bank by the wayside. No one passed them while they were there, in either direction. Then they had moved on again in the dusk. And so, finally, they had stumbled on the body; the girl had taken fright; and they had run back towards the village, without meeting anyone until they came upon Constable Durley.

"That's quite clear," the Chief Constable said, when Oulton had finished his narrative. "Now just a couple of questions. Did you, after you got into Leisurely Lane, hear any sound that struck you as out of the common?"

Oulton reflected for a moment or two before replying.

"No, sir. Nothing that I can remember."

"No sound of a shot? Or cries for help? Anything of that sort?"

"No, sir, nothing. If we'd heard anything like that, finding the body wouldn't have been such a knock-out as it was. We'd have been expecting something, wouldn't we?"

"Possibly," the Chief Constable admitted. "Now another point. You lit a match to see the body. Did you throw down the stub there?"

Oulton took half a minute to consider this before answering.

"I wouldn't take my oath on this, sir," he said frankly. "But I *think* I kept the match stick in my hand and threw it away while I was chasing after Tessie. I believe that's what happened. But I couldn't swear to it. A bit flustered, I was then, and I can't remember just what I did do."

"Well, that's all we need," said the Chief Constable. "Thanks for your trouble. You might listen while the inspector reads over what he's written down, and then you can sign it, if it's all right."

The formality was soon over. Oulton, breathing heavily, scrawled his name at the foot of the last sheet and initialed the others. Then he was allowed to go, evidently relieved to find that the ordeal had not been so bad as he had feared. When he had left the room, Sir Clinton turned to the inspector.

"What sort of character has this girl, Tessie Marl?"

"Oh, she's a decent girl, sir. Never a word against her. Young Oulton's the first she's taken up with, and they're dead nuts on each other—I should say, sir, that they're very much attached to one another. I expect they'll be getting married as soon as they've got enough to make ends meet on and can get a cottage to live in."

"That clears one possibility out of the way, perhaps," the Chief Constable decided. "And now, Inspector, I think we'll try our hands on Mr. Walton. I'm afraid he won't be quite so satisfactory."

# CHAPTER VI
## THE POACHER

WALTON PROVED TO BE a slovenly little man with large, outstanding ears and bad teeth. Wendover glanced at him with hardly concealed distaste as he entered the room in charge of the inspector.

"An obvious slum rat," he thought, "the fine flower of this industrial civilisation. Here, in the country, he looks as much out of place as a rusty meat tin in a well-kept flower bed. Oulton is a gentleman, compared with this miserable creature."

Walton's manner was a mixture of familiarity and cringing. He nodded cavalierly to Wendover at which the Squire flushed with suppressed anger—and then began to sidle up to the Chief Constable. Apparently he was one of those people who cannot address a listener in comfort except when they have come within touching distance.

"Stand back there," ordered Cumberland roughly, restraining Walton with a hand on his shoulder.

"I didn't mean no 'arm, guv'nor," protested Walton, evidently sorry for his own sake that he had made an initial bad impression.

"Well, stand where you're put and answer straight off when you're asked a question," Cumberland advised.

He went back to his own chair, picked up his pen, and pulled a fresh sheet of paper towards him. The movement drew Walton's eyes to the table, and Wendover saw him start slightly as his glance fell on the pile of bank notes which lay at the Chief Constable's elbow.

"What's your name?" demanded the inspector, with his pen poised to note down the reply.

"Ben Walton."

"Where are you staying in the village?"

"At 16 Longstone Road. I'm livin' with me brother-in-law, name o' Moffatt. I told you so last night."

The inspector noted down the address and then put a further question.

"Where do you live? You're only a visitor here."

"At 12 Badger's Rents, in Brandford, mostly."

"Married?"

"Not me, guv'nor! Cheaper to buy milk than to keep a cow, as they say."

"How do you come to be here?" Cumberland asked.

Walton was not the kind of man who can tell a straight story. He had, first of all, to collect his wits and get his tale into order; and this, apparently, involved scratching his head: a purely mechanical process designed to give himself time to pull himself together.

"This is the way of it, guv'nor," he began at last. "Back in the spring, I got a sort of cough w'at didn't seem like as if it was doin' me much good. Fair 'ackin' it was, o' nights. Kept me awake somethin' cruel. So I tried 'em at the 'ospital over it, expectin' to get a bottle o' some dope or other outen 'em for it. But they didn't give me nothin'. They fussed a lot, instead, an' 'ad me back twice; an' they asked me a lot o' questions about where I dossed an' so forth. An' when they 'eard as I lodged in Badger's Rents, they shook their 'eads over it an' talked about gettin' me into some kip-house or other, a thing they called a Sannytorium. I wasn't much took with the notion. I'm a man as likes 'is liberty, by natur'; an' confinement goes agin the grain with me. So I turned *that* down, pronto, I can tell yer. That set 'em aback a bit, I could see. They told me I'd got T.B.—what you'd call chewberkewlosis—an' then, instead o' 'tendin' to my case, they started layin' off a lot o' talk about the risk o' me infectin' other blokes if I stayed on in Badger's Rents. By their way of it, I was full o' bugs. An' that's a lie!"

"They meant you were loaded up with germs," explained the inspector, testily. "It's doctors' slang for bacilli."

"*You* say so," said Walton, obviously unconvinced. "It's not a thing anybody's got a right to say about me, that's all. An' you can kiss the Book on that! I'm a partickler man, as it 'appens, in that sort o' way."

"Get on with your tale," ordered the inspector. "We'll go into your personal habits by and by, if it's necessary."

Apparently Walton read a threat into this last remark, for he hurriedly continued his story.

"They give me a lot o' chat about fresh air, an' open windows, an' such like, sleepin' out under the sky an' so forth, till it fair give me the creeps to listen to 'em. It reminded me o' George Robey doin' his Pre'istoric Man turn on the 'Alls, more than anythin' else. Me, sleepin' out in the open air, with a cough fit to split me ribs! I ask yer, as man to man, is there any common sense in chat like that?

"An' this talk about infectin' the neighbours give me a scare, too, for that sort o' thing always gives 'em a pull. They can yank you off to 'ospital, w'ether you like it or not, if yer infectious with scarlet fever or typhoid. So it seemed best to humour 'em a bit, lest worse befall. Then, thinks I to meself, w'at about Emma? She's a sister o' mine. I 'adn't seen 'er for donkey's years. All I used to get from 'er was a pitcher post card on me birthdays, sayin' as 'ow she 'oped I was as well as this left 'er, in the pink. But she lives down 'ere in the tooral-looral district, right in the midst o' the fresh air. She's married to a bloke Moffatt. So I puts it to the sawbones, an' they seemed to take not unkindly to the notion of me goin' down to w'ere the milk comes from. An' so, after thinkin' it over a bit, I faked 'er a screeve, an' down 'ere I comes on the rattler, leavin' Badger's Rents in mournin', no doubt. I 'aven't written to ask."

"So you're staying with your sister. What does her husband do for a living?" asked Sir Clinton.

Walton considered for a few moments before answering. Possibly he had been weighing the question of loyalty; but if so, he decided not to let it interfere.

"W'at I do myself, more or less," he explained, without shame. "'E's got more wits than most, like me; an' 'e lives on 'em. Mugs an' easy money, you find 'em in the country just as well as in the Big Smoke, if you knows w'ere to look for 'em."

"What does your brother-in-law do with these wits of his?" asked the Chief Constable. "You needn't wrap it up."

"Well, 'e does a bit o' bettin'. An' sometimes 'e gets mixed up in 'orse deals. They tell me 'e's a rare 'and at fakin' up a screw an' makin' it look better nor new. 'E's a vet by trade, if 'e's anythin'. One way an' another, 'e turns enough honest pennies to live on."

"He does a bit of poaching, too, in a quiet way," interjected the inspector. "I've had him through my hands for that."

"Well, mebbe 'e does, or mebbe 'e doesn't," said Walton cautiously. "There's a lot o' ill-meanin' people in this world as is always ready to look on the worst side o' things. An' a lot more who'll swear away a poor man's character without turnin' a 'air over it. So I've found, by 'ard experience, meself."

He glanced perkily at the Chief Constable, as though expecting him to share in the joke.

"Well, that accounts for your being in this neighbourhood," said Cumberland, blotting his latest sheet of writing and laying it aside. "We'll be able to check your story, by and by. Which of the Brandford hospitals did you attend?"

"The Victoria," Walton replied, so glibly that it was plain he was telling the truth in that matter.

"Very good. Now we come to your doings of yesterday evening. Go on with the tale. And don't miss out anything."

Walton glanced at the blood-stained notes on the table, fidgeted uneasily, stared up at the ceiling as though calling in the aid of higher Powers, and then spoke in sulky tone.

"First of all, I wants to know w'ere I stands in this 'ere affair. If you're chargin' me with anythin', say so. Then I can talk or keep my trap shut, just as suits me best. You 'aven't cautioned me, I'll point out."

Cumberland nodded as though he had expected something of the sort.

"Been through it before?" he said, with very little interrogation in his tone. "I thought as much. Well, it saves bother, since you know the ropes. I'm not bringing any charge against you just yet in the matter of that murder. Not yet. But unless you make a clean breast of things now, I'll have to think about it. There's a lot that wants explaining. So you'd better get started."

Walton turned his little, cunning eyes on the Chief Constable.

"You're the boss, 'ere," he said ingratiatingly. "We all makes our little slips, 'uman natur' bein' w'at it is. You must ha' seen a deal o' trouble in yer day—other people's trouble, I mean. You 'ave a sympathetic 'eart, sir, I'm sure."

"I've got a salary to earn, too, if that's of interest to you," Sir Clinton pointed out. "I'll give you one hint. Poaching's a much less serious crime than murder. Just ponder on that, if you feel inclined to tamper with the truth. Go on with your story."

Walton evidently saw that he might get himself into a tight corner if he tried to be too clever. These notes on the table were plain proof that the police knew a good deal more than he had bargained for, before he entered that room. He considered for a moment or two whether he could keep his brother-in-law's name out of it, but family ties proved weaker than his desire to save himself at any cost.

"I'll tell yer as straight's I can," he began with an effort to appear wholly honest. "I 'ad to pay my way some'ow, w'ile I was livin' down 'ere. I've always been 'andy with me fingers, from boy to man, an' it don't take a watchmaker to learn 'ow to fix a snare for rabbits an' w'at not. My brother-in-law, 'e taught me all about it. After that, we 'unted in couples, so to say. It doubles the profits an' 'alves the risks, specially in places w'ere they keeps only one keeper, like Carfax does. Him an' me, we used to work different warrens, an' the keeper couldn't be in two places at onc't."

"Much more of this?" demanded Cumberland, ostentatiously consulting his wrist watch.

"I'm comin' to it, I'm comin' to it," protested Walton in an aggrieved tone. "You don't give me 'alf a chanst, breakin' in that way, every minute. I've got to make things clear, 'aven't I?"

But despite the inspector's urgency, he paused and scratched his head as though in perplexity. Then he seemed to recall the words of the Chief Constable and took a decision.

"Now, yesterday afternoon, long before this 'ere 'Uggin got done in, I was up in Carfax's place, settin' snares for some pheasants."

"Pheasant shooting hasn't begun yet," interrupted Wendover, all his feelings as a game preserver aflame against this self-confessed poacher. "What could you do with pheasants at this season?"

"Eat 'em, o' course," returned Walton, contemptuously. "We weren't thinkin' o' sellin' 'em to the Fishmonger's 'All, if that's w'at's worryin' yer. Any'ow, that's by the way. As I was goin' ter say, I picked up a couple—a brace, they call it, 'ereabouts—an' the next bother was 'ow to get them damn birds back 'ome. You can't stuff a couple o' pheasants up yer round-the-'ouses an' then walk down the village street like that, even if you did get off the ground without the keeper spottin' yer. So I 'id 'em, careful, an' then I slung me 'ook."

"Where did you hide them?" demanded Sir Clinton.

"Not far from w'ere I picked 'em up. I got 'em in that bit o' wood—spinney, they call it, 'ereabouts—Apsley Spinney's the name. You get to it up this 'ere Leisurely Lane an' then cut across a field or two."

He broke off, dipped his hand into his pocket, and pulled out several Valencia raisins which he stuffed mechanically into his mouth, apparently before he realised what he was doing.

"Good feedin', these," he declared, with a rueful grin which displayed the badness of his teeth. "Specially when you're lookin' to catch pheasants. Open 'em up, stick a grain o' Indian corn inside, an' a pheasant's as keen on 'em as an alderman on turtle soup. Lay a trail of 'em to your snare, and there you are! Moffatt, 'e taught me that. You can't beat 'im. But 'e 'as a dawg to 'elp. I've got to make out on me own."

His eye caught a restless movement which Wendover made, and he hurried on with his narrative.

"W'en it got dusk, last night, I went back up there again. That Leisurely Lane through Carfax's ground, it's a right o' way, an' no one can make any fuss s'long's you stick to it. So I stuck to it so far's it served, an' then I lay down a bit, waitin' for dark to come on, so's I could get them birds."

"What time was it then?"

"Search me!" suggested Walton ironically. "'Ow should I know? I left 'ome about 'alf past seven an' 'ad one for the worms at The Barleycorn before startin' off."

"You didn't see this man Huggin at The Barleycorn?" interjected Wendover.

"'E wasn't in the taproom that I can call to mind," Walton declared, after a pause to rummage his memory.

"Huggin was in the private parlour, getting his meal, sir," Cumberland pointed out. "He didn't go into the taproom, so far as I know."

"Oh, quite so," said Wendover, rather vexed at having missed this point. "I ought to have thought of that, of course."

"Did you meet anyone in Leisurely Lane?" the inspector demanded, turning to Walton.

"Not face to face on the path, if that's w'at you're after," was the reply. "But, now I come to think, I did see a big fellow movin' across the fields towards that 'oardin' as I was comin' up to it."

"Ah!" exclaimed the inspector, eagerly. "Did you recognise him? Would you know him again if you saw him?"

Walton shook his head decidedly.

"Not me!" he replied. "It was gettin' dark by then. All I really saw was somethin' movin' in the dusk. Once he come up against the sky for a jiffy an' that's what makes me think 'e was on the big side. It's just an idea, like. But recognise 'im! You might about as well ask me to pick out a black cat in the dark and swear to it."

"We shan't trouble you to do that," Cumberland assured him ironically. "Now go on. You were lying down—hidden, I suppose—somewhere up the lane beyond the hoarding. What happened next?"

"I was waitin' till it got dark enough to go after them birds. By an' by it was dark enough, an' I legged it over to w'ere I'd hid 'em an' got me 'ooks on 'em, easy as kiss yer 'and. I got back to near the path again an' sat down to wait a bit. No use goin' down into the village till most people was gone to bed. They're an early lot in these parts. So down I squats and waits."

"What time was that?" asked the inspector.

"'Ow the 'ell do I know?" retorted Walton in genuine exasperation. "The way you busies go on, one'd think everybody in the ruddy world 'ad nothin' to do but look at 'is watch from mornin' to night. It's all very well for them as has soft jobs in the police to go notin' down the time every three secs. People as 'as their livin' to make is differently posted. Just make a note o' that an' it'll be useful to you w'en you draw yer pension an' come out into the real world. Strike me blind! *I* dunno w'at time it was and if you don't like that, you can lump it."

"Stick to your tale," advised the inspector, crossly.

"Oh, all right, *all* right! Well, as I was sayin', it got darker, an' I was just thinkin' about gettin' a move on, when all of a suddent I 'ears a moll screechin' fit to bust, down the lane a bit. Give me a fair start, it did, comin' that unexpected like after all that stillness. I'm not one for interferin' with the neighbours' sport, so I sat still for a bit, listenin' and tryin' to make out w'at it was all about."

"You didn't think of going to her help?" inquired Wendover acidly.

"Not me! I'm all for people mindin' their own business, an' I sets 'em a good example. I thought mebbe it was some bloke 'avin' a lark with a moll, and she'd cut up rough. No affair o' mine that I could see. If you get mixed up in things o' that sort, you're called a Peepin' Tom for yer pains"—he stared malevolently at the inspector—"an' most likely you get a bat on the 'ead as a gentle 'int that ye're not wanted at the moment."

"Wait a bit," interrupted Sir Clinton. "While you were sitting there, did you hear any unusual sound *before* the girl screamed?"

Walton seemed to rack his memory unsuccessfully.

"No," he answered, "I can't call to mind as I 'eard anythin' you'd call unusual. A bird squeakin', mebbe, amongst the trees. But that ain't anythin' to call for comment, I take it."

"You'd have pricked up your ears if you'd heard a shot?"

"You bet I would! But 'earin' no such thing, I left my ears alone."

"Go on, then."

"Well, as I listened, the moll's yells seemed to get further away, as if she was runnin' down the lane towards the road. It was no call o' mine to go after 'er. 'Sides, I was on business an' I 'adn't no call to play the shivvaleer. Not much! An' just then it crossed my mind that this moll—'oo-ever she was—'ad got me into the soup with 'er damned caterwaulin'. If the keeper 'eard it, 'e'd be down that way in two shakes o' a lamb's tail, as they say round about 'ere. No chanst then o' gettin' them birds away on the quiet, after all that racket. 'Ard lines, wasn't it, guv'nor, after me takin' all that trouble? But there it was. Not a hope in 'ell of gettin' the stuff off the ground that night. Fair perishin' luck, I call it."

"Very sad," said Sir Clinton unsympathetically. "So?"

"I 'ate to be beat," continued Walton. "But there it was. So I cut me losses. An' as there wasn't no further point in lyin' up any longer in the dew an' gettin' me clobber soaked, I just 'ides them birds in a quiet 'ole near by w'ere I was. Then I got back on to the path an' doddled off towards 'ome, cursin' me luck an' that moll till I could think o' nothin' else to say."

"Her cries had died out by that time, I suppose?"

"They 'ad, as you say. By that time, it was dark, an' that path's no Regent Street to walk on, give yer moi word! I got to the bit that's fenced along one side—w'ere that 'oardin' is—an' by that time I was steppin' out, not wishin' to be run into by the keeper, if 'e 'appened along. All of a suddent, I tripped over somethin', an' down I came, a reg'lar purler. Tore the knee of me round-the-'ouses, I found out afterwards. But I didn't think o' that point just then, for w'en I put out me 'and I felt a boot. It didn't move, so thinks I: ''E's 'ad 'is load. 'E must 'ave 'ad 'is nose in the suds pretty deep to be as blotto as all this.' Then it crossed me mind that 'ere was w'at 'ad scared the moll. 'E must 'ave given 'er the jumps if she fell over 'im like I did. Like enough, I thinks, that's w'at made 'er go off the deep end the way she did. I gets on me knees an' pulls out me box o' lights, an' you can guess the rest. It was this 'ere fellow"—he turned to the inspector—"'Uggin you said 'is name was, didn't yer? It was this 'ere 'Uggin, as dead a bit o' meat as ever there was."

"Sensation!" interjected Sir Clinton. "Don't describe your feelings, for they don't matter. Tell us what you did, and be sure it's the truth."

Walton glanced furtively at the blood-stained notes on the table, as though calculating how much the police might know.

"You're not out of the wood yet, by any means," added the Chief Constable menacingly, as he saw the undecided expression on Walton's features.

This seemed to tip the scale in the mind of the witness. Apparently he decided that the safest policy was to speak out.

"I 'ad a good look at 'im by the light o' the scratcher," he went on, "an' 'e was a stuffy for sure. So thinks I: 'No 'arm in fannin' 'im, seein' there's no one about.' It's an idee as would 'ave crossed anyone's mind, in the circs. So I lit another scratcher—I must ha' struck three or four altogether—an' I went through 'is sky. W'en I got at 'is dummy, it took me breath away. It was fair stuffed with oncers. Dozens of 'em. I didn't know there was as much geld in the whole world as there was in that wad.

"I stood with that packet in me 'and, thinkin'. There was this pore bloke—I didn't even know 'is name then—gone to 'is long 'ome, as the Good Book says, an' no more needin' money than w'at a cock angel needs boot polish. It would do 'im no 'arm if I swiped the lot. I stood there with them notes in me 'ooks—a bloody foretune to be 'ad for the takin'. I was tempted, sir, an' I fell."

"Just what one might expect," said Sir Clinton, in a matter-of-fact tone. "You can cry over it, by and by. Cut out the pathos and get on with your story. Don't miss anything out."

Walton gazed at him reproachfully.

"The troubles o' the poor are not your troubles, sir, an' it's easy to see you've never 'ad real temptation put in front o' you like I 'ad." Then, catching the look in the Chief Constable's eye, he continued hastily, "I was just goin' to pouch the lot, w'en, thinks I to meself, 'It might look rummy if the whole lot was pinched. Better leave one or two in the dummy.' So I skins off a pile. An' w'ile I was doin' that by the light o' another scratcher, I sees blood all over me 'and. I must 'ave fallen in it w'en I come that crash. So I cleaned me paw with me wipe an' slipped some clean notes back into the dummy an' the dummy back into his sky again. It fair broke my 'eart, to let them oncers go. Finnios is 'ard to change, but anyone'll take a oncer from yer an' no questions asked. Then I went off the path a bit an' stuffed the balance of 'em down a rabbit 'ole for safety. 'Ow you got yer claws on 'em, beats me."

"What happened after that?" asked Cumberland.

"Well, w'at d'you expect I'd do? Kiss 'im good-bye? All I wanted was to get out, an' quick, too. 'E wasn't pretty, with all that blood about. I've known better company. So I lighted out down the lane after the moll, an' not strollin' neither, I give yer moi word! An' the next thing I knew I was bein' 'eld up by you."

"And through all these adventures of yours you met no one from the time you left the village until you ran into the inspector?" Sir Clinton demanded.

"Not a soul."

"Have you ever had a firearm in your possession?"

"Never, so 'elp me!"

"You never borrowed Moffatt's gun, did you?"

"I couldn't 'ave 'it an 'aystack with it. W'at use would it 'ave been to me, I ask yer?"

"You never met this man Huggin before?"

"I didn't know 'im from Adam, except by his tailor."

"Well, read over what the inspector has written down and if it's correct, sign it."

"Can you read?" inquired the inspector as he handed over the manuscript.

"I can so," declared Walton. "I was as well eddicated as w'at you was, only mebbe I've forgotten more. See's yer dockyment an' I'll give it the once-over."

Cumberland handed him the sheets, and Walton, with some obvious difficulty and much heavy breathing, struggled through it.

"It's your 'and o' write as makes it difficult," he complained. "But you seem to 'ave got it down more or less straight, I'll say that. I'll put my monaker to it."

He did so, laboriously, with the pen which Cumberland passed to him. Then he straightened himself up with the sigh of a man who has completed a heavy task.

"An' now, I s'pose, I can shift me barrow?"

"After we've had time to check things up a bit," Cumberland answered, exchanging a glance with the Chief Constable.

"Is it all right about them pheasants?" persisted Walton anxiously.

"We'll think the matter over," was all the comfort that Sir Clinton gave him as Cumberland led him out of the room.

When the inspector returned, he had a sheet of paper in his hand which he put down on the table.

"That's a nasty little beast," Wendover commented. "But his tale sounds as if it might be true. Still, I can't quite swallow it when he says he never heard a shot fired."

"Oulton said the same thing," the inspector pointed out.

"Yes, but Oulton came on the scene much later, remember."

"Mr. Wendover's quite right," Sir Clinton confirmed. "If Walton's tale holds water, he met no one and was passed by no one until he ran up against you, Inspector. Therefore, he must have been ahead of Huggin, or he'd have come across him at the hoarding if Huggin actually had an appointment at that spot. So he must have been in the neighbourhood throughout the interview—if there was an interview at all. Which way was the wind blowing, when you went up, Inspector?"

"Not a breath of wind that evening, sir."

"Well, a shot sounds a long way off on a still night. You'd better test that point. You have an automatic, I think?" he said, turning to Wendover. "Lend it to the inspector and he can find out whether the report can be heard at Apsley Spinney when a shot's fired at the hoarding."

"Druce Carfax won't be pleased to have you startling his pheasants," said Wendover, with a smile. "However, you can have my pistol whenever you need it, Inspector."

"And, of course, your men who take part in the experiment will have to be able to swear to the results," Sir Clinton pointed out, turning to Cumberland.

"I'll see to that, sir."

"The most suggestive bit of Walton's evidence was what he said about seeing a big man coming down towards the hoarding as he went up the lane himself," Wendover said, ruminatively. "That man, if he existed, didn't go up the lane after he got onto it, or he'd have passed Walton while Walton was lying beside the path waiting for the night to get darker. And he didn't pass Oulton, either, on the lower stretch."

"Why not?" objected the inspector. "Oulton and his girl didn't come straight up to Leisurely Lane. They sat down for a while before they got into it at all. This man if he *was* there at all, may have got into the lane at the hoarding and turned off down to the road, passing Huggin on the way, and been off along the road in the opposite direction to the one Oulton and his girl were coming."

"That's true," Wendover conceded, after thinking it over.

"Well, we're not getting much forward on this line," Sir Clinton declared. "Have you had any answer from Scotland Yard yet?"

"It's just come in over the phone, sir," Cumberland explained, picking up the sheet of paper before him. "This is what the sergeant took down a few minutes ago. Shall I read it?"

"Yes, do," Sir Clinton asked.

"'Re your inquiry' . . . and so forth," Cumberland read. "Miles Huggin, of 47 Rookery Park, W., made a living by writing books and articles for the press. His landlady, Mrs. R. Hassop, gives him a good character: quiet, well-conducted, but behind with his rent at times though he always paid up in the end. He shared her rooms with another man, George Fairbank, but had hardly any visitors. He had tea in his rooms yesterday afternoon, then went out, saying he would not return for dinner. This morning she found his bed had not been slept in. She asked Fairbank about Huggin at breakfast-time, but Fairbank had been to the theater the night before and knew nothing about Huggin's absence. He can throw no light on the matter. The usual precautions have been taken. They ask us to give them further information. That's the gist of it, evidently, sir."

Sir Clinton reflected for a moment.

"I gave you last year's *Who's Who,* didn't I?"

"Yes, sir. It's here, if you want it," said Cumberland, rising and taking the portly volume from a shelf. "It's been useful to us in getting people's names right at times."

The Chief Constable opened the book and turned over the pages.

"Hudson . . . Huggard . . . Huggins . . ." He turned back a page. "No, nothing between Huggard and Huggins. He's not here."

"Then he's evidently not a best seller, whatever he is," commented Wendover.

"That exactly what I was thinking myself," said Sir Clinton, dryly. "Care for a trip to town, to-morrow, say? I shall have to go up and your company would be cheering. I'll stand you a lunch at my club, if you'd like to meet a literary young friend of mine, not unamusing."

"Well—I can manage it," Wendover conceded, after a momentary hesitation. "But what about—"

"This affair? Well, Huggin lived in London, didn't he? I'm going to combine business with pleasure, for once."

"Oh, if it has to do with the murder, of course I'll come," Wendover agreed at once. "But have you the faintest idea of what you're looking for?"

"A needle in a bottle of hay, probably."

"So long as it isn't a mare's nest," Wendover retorted.

He recognised that the Chief Constable was not in a communicative mood just then, but he could not resist an attempt to draw him.

"Have you *any* notion who's at the back of this business?" he demanded.

"Yes, I think so," replied the Chief Constable unexpectedly. "But it's no certainty."

"Then who is it? It's not Oulton. Is it Walton?"

"My impression is that it's Mr. A."

"Mr. A?" repeated Wendover, irritated by this evasion. "I suppose you mean Mr. X—an unknown quantity. I know as much as that myself, without being overclever."

"No, I said Mr. A," returned Sir Clinton, with a quizzical look in his eye. "As a matter of fact, he's an old friend of yours. I shouldn't wonder if you came across him even before you met me."

"Hereabouts?" demanded Wendover in a puzzled tone.

"Yes, hereabouts."

"Do you mean Car—" exclaimed Wendover.

But Sir Clinton interrupted him before he could complete the name.

"Remember the law against slander," he warned.

"Oh, nobody here's going to repeat what's said," Wendover protested, with a glance at the inspector. "Who is it?"

"Mr. A," repeated Sir Clinton with a teasing smile. "An old friend of yours. Now, it's no use fishing. I've said more than I ought to do, for I may be wrong after all. But if I'm right, I'll remind you of it."

# CHAPTER VII:
# GRUB STREET

SIR CLINTON WAS A MEMBER of two clubs, and Wendover noted that it was to the quieter and lesser-known one that they drove from the station. In the entrance hall, the Chief Constable paused to make an inquiry at the desk; and while he was so engaged a young alert-looking man ran up the steps from the door.

"Oh, you're here already, are you?" he said, with a nod to Sir Clinton. "I got your wire. Just a moment. I'll join you at your table. Trot along."

Sir Clinton was saved the trouble of a reply, for already a swing-door had closed behind the newcomer, who was evidently a person incapable of punctilio. The Chief Constable finished his instructions to the desk keeper and led Wendover towards the luncheon room.

"I seem to know that fellow's face," Wendover mused aloud as he accompanied his host upstairs, "but I don't remember meeting him before."

"You've probably seen his photograph somewhere. He's Robert Denzil—Bob to his friends. He writes crime yarns in the shilling magazines and elsewhere. Sometimes I vet his stuff for him before it goes into print, so I've no hesitation in making him useful if I can. But that may wait till after lunch. Here he comes."

Denzil, after a passing glance at the carver's table, came up and was introduced to Wendover. The Squire, though well-read, was shy of modern writers and for a few moments he feared lest he should be expected to discuss his fellow guest's shop. Denzil soon relieved him of his apprehensions. He was one of those people who have the knack of "getting on terms" with strangers almost immediately by sheer naturalness and a happy personality.

"Well, made your choice?" inquired Sir Clinton.

"The alguazil's paying for this lunch," Denzil reflected aloud, "so expense is no drawback—to me. For once I can live as well as my characters always do. I've often longed to be in that position. Here goes, then! I didn't see any plovers' eggs in that display over there. But we can ask for them. My characters always take plovers' eggs," he added confidentially to Wendover.

"In season and out of season," interjected Sir Clinton. "I often wondered how they managed it, Bob."

"Don't plovers nest all the year round? Well, my readers know no better, so it doesn't matter. Don't write to the papers about it. Ignorance is bliss. As a matter of fact," he added, again taking Wendover into his confidence, "I never tasted a plover's egg in my life. But that doesn't hinder me from writing about them. After all, I've never committed a murder either, and yet I've described 'em often enough. The artist's imagination can stretch to anything, if you give it a chance. And that reminds me," he continued, turning to Sir Clinton, "my characters always drink the best that's going. Has this club any Imperial Tokay in its cellars, alguazil?"

Sir Clinton shook his head.

"Ah, then it'll be whiskey and split for me. Some of the pre-War stuff. So much for the nectar. As to the ambrosia, anything will suit me, so long as it doesn't taste of onions or garlic. I leave it to your generosity and good taste. I know you always fix up a good meal. In fact, I'm going to jot down the menu on my shirt cuff. It'll come in handy, next time my characters lunch at the club."

"I understand now why the old literary hacks congregated in Grub Street. The name must have drawn them like a magnet," said the Chief Constable.

He consulted Wendover and then gave his orders to the waiter. During lunch, he exerted himself to put his guests on the best of terms with each other; and when it was over, he led them to a corner of the smoking-room which seemed to promise some privacy.

"Now I want to dig some information out of you, Bob," he explained, as he rang for coffee. "You don't live in New Grub Street nowadays, but it isn't so long since you shifted out of it. As an author, you'll understand I'm speaking metaphorically. Did you ever come across a man called Huggin—Miles Huggin? I've an idea that he was a hack writer of sorts."

"I've met him," said Denzil promptly, "and that's no plover's egg story. But I didn't much take to him. One meets all sorts, in Grub Street."

"Tell us what you know about him. The cold truth, please. Nothing you say will be used against him officially."

Denzil glanced at his host with a shade of suspicion.

"So you're up in town on business, are you, Dogberry? And you want me to be a nose, nark, or snout for you, as the case may be? After creeping into my confidence with all this information about plovers' eggs."

"He's dead, as it happens, so nothing you can say will hurt him."

"Dead, is he?" demanded Denzil. "He looked as well as usual when I saw him a week or two back. What did he die of?"

"Well, our surgeon diagnosed a dose of lead pills, if I may borrow the vocabulary of your characters."

"Shot?" exclaimed Denzil in unaffected surprise.

"Unless it was an overdose of iron tonic—that's your characters' euphemism for stabbing, isn't it? He's dead, anyhow."

"Murdered?"

Denzil's tone showed that he could hardly believe what he heard.

"It looks like it," Sir Clinton said, testily. "I'll send you a copy of our local paper when the inquest comes on; I haven't time to give you the whole story just now. We're trying to find out all we can about him. You seem to have knocked up against him, as I hoped. What sort of man was he?"

Denzil had been temporarily sobered by the Chief Constable's statements.

"What sort of man was he?" he repeated slowly. "I wasn't a friend of his, you know. I came across him casually, from time to time. But the first time you met him, you saw he was a disappointed man. You know how it shows at the mouth corners, quite unmistakably. You see, he was round about forty; he'd been writing for close on twenty years, and he'd never made a real success. You can turn into a best seller after forty, of course. But not if you write Huggin's kind of stuff. No matter how long he lived, he'd never have risen to be more than a hack. It wasn't in him, poor devil."

"Know anything about his career?" demanded the Chief Constable.

"Some odds and ends. They talk a lot, in New Grub Street, and one can't help picking up things here and there. He published his first novel when he was twenty-five. I expect he was like the rest of us, then. Golden days . . . pen running without effort . . . when you finish a sheet you can read it over and say to yourself: 'That's good! That's damned fine stuff!' We've all been through it, or we wouldn't be blackening paper still, as we do. Next morning, of course the stuff didn't seem quite so brilliant."

Sir Clinton nodded without speaking.

"He told me all about it, once, after his fifth glass of whiskey," Denzil continued. "He wrote some other novels. The best of them, they say, was *That For Which Virtue*. It was well reviewed when it came out, and he thought he'd made a hit. But the public bought only eight hundred copies of the thing in two years, and his publishers remaindered the rest of the edition. That took the heart out of him, I suppose."

"Poor devil!" interjected Wendover.

"I'm evidently making him out to be a pathetic character," said Denzil with a smile. "But if you'd met him in the flesh, I don't know that you'd feel so soft-hearted. He wasn't a likable creature, somehow. Anyhow, by the time I got to know him, all the fine frenzy had passed away. From the way he talked, it was plain that he sat down to his typewriter like a tired journeyman going to work on a task that had lost its relish. 'How many words have I turned out to-day?' interested him more than any experiments in phrase or refinements of style. He knew he was a failure. He'd shot his bolt and missed the target. He'd ceased to trouble about Fame and all that. He was the only man I met who quoted Johnson regularly. You know the phrase: 'Nobody but a fool ever wrote, except to make money.' That was Huggin's favourite quotation. And the worst of it was, from his point of view, that he didn't make much. He was always damnably hard up and quite ready to sponge on anyone."

Wendover's mind swung back to the inventory of Huggin's effects. Deduct that round hundred pounds, that mysterious windfall, and what was left? Three half-crowns, a florin, four shillings, a sixpenny-bit, and sevenpence in coppers—fourteen and sevenpence in all. Not even a ten-bob note, except the ones in the "round sum."

"How did he manage to make a living?" Sir Clinton asked.

Denzil made a careless gesture.

"Hackwork, of one sort and another, I believe. He edited an anthology of verse, *The Silver Casket,* for Sebbon & Co. the schoolbook publishers. It was meant for girls of fifteen. I don't suppose he got much for that. Sebbon & Co. pay cash down for their work, so although the thing had a big sale, Huggin would have no interest in the figures."

"Anything else?"

Denzil pondered for a moment.

"Oh, yes, he acted a secretary to two literary men, I remember. You know the sort of thing, Dogberry."

"My duties never took me down New Grub Street," Sir Clinton reminded him. "You're our Virgil for that Inferno."

"Well, you can take it from me, Dante, that there are about as many kinds of secretaries as there are types of literary men. One of Huggin's bosses was a very busy fellow with more ideas than he could work out single-handed. His method was to ring for a secretary, give him a plot in outline, and let him write it up. Then it was published under the author's name. And sold by the thousand on the strength of the name. I've heard people wondering at Mr. X's wonderful versatility in the matter of style. The solution didn't cost me a moment's thought."

"You mean that Huggin was what they call a 'ghost'?" interjected Wendover. "Damn it, that was hardly honest."

"Oh, rot!" said Denzil, lightly. "I don't suppose you enjoyed Dumas's works any the less because they were written by someone else. 'A rose by any other name would smell as sweet.' Some attribute that to Shakespeare, but it was Bacon as like as not."

"It's selling goods under a false label," grumbled Wendover.

"What does that matter, so long as the public likes the goods?" retorted Denzil. "But to proceed. Huggin's other author was by way of being a learned one. All present and correct, except the learning. So Huggin's job was to go to the British Museum Library and excavate the erudition which went into his boss's historical romances. You know what I mean? Looking up to make sure that Charles II really did say 'Oddsfish!' in lighter moments. Finding out what a bassinet was, when it wasn't a child's cradle. That sort of thing. You know how it lends verisimilitude to the most unconvincing narrative. It's teamwork applied to the typewriter, or mass production in the fiction factory. Quite in the modern vein."

"What else did Huggin do for a livelihood?" demanded Sir Clinton, who evidently had no desire to be drawn into moral problems of this sort.

"Oh, hackwork journalism of one sort and another, I believe. The kind of thing that wears a good man out but does a hack no great harm. He did some book reviewing, too, for obscure journals."

At this moment the smoking-room door opened to admit a page boy carrying a telegram on a salver. He advanced into the room, intoning lugubriously: "Sir Clinton Driffield—Sir Clinton Driffield—Sir Clinton—"

The Chief Constable snapped his fingers. The page boy, apparently human enough to feel relief at having run down his quarry, came over and presented the envelope. Sir Clinton opened it, studied the wire intently for a moment or two, and then indicated that there was no answer. When the boy had left the room, he tossed the form onto the table in front of his friends.

"Care to try your teeth on it?" he asked, with a smile. "It's simple enough."

Wendover spread open the form so that both he and Denzil could inspect it. They leaned over and read:

HNRDNL DNSRBL DOEADY OABNTD AFXABF
RMREZZ UDEICU IGCIBE NTPIBL CLAKOC
RADYEO EUDRZZ CUMBERLAND

"Simple, you say?" mused Wendover. "Then, by the general look of the thing and the relative numbers of vowels and consonants, I'd say it was a rearrangement cipher and the Z's are dummies. Is that right, so far?"

"So far, it is," said Sir Clinton gravely. "But 'so far' isn't far."

He glanced at Denzil, who shook his head.

"I'm all right at making up puzzles," he confessed. "But I couldn't solve even one of my own if you gave me a year to do it in. You can leave me out of this guessing competition."

"What about you, Squire? We haven't all day to spare, you know."

Wendover reluctantly gave it up.

"It's from one of my inspectors, in charge of Huggin's case," Sir Clinton explained to Denzil. "Sometimes it's handy to be able to communicate with them in cipher without the trouble of dragging a codebook about with one, so we use the 'rail-fence cipher' which was used by the Union forces in the American Civil War."

"Oh, that's it, is it?" exclaimed Wendover, suddenly enlightened. "I'll have it out in a jiffy. And the Z's *are* dummies. I was pretty sure of that."

He took an envelope from his pocket and wrote for a few seconds.

"This is it, isn't it?" he asked, looking up from his writing. "'*Hundred, including scribbled note, paid by local bank to D. Carfax, day before murder.*'"

Then his glee in his solution was submerged in a certain anxiety produced by the tenor of the message.

"I say! I don't quite like that! It looks pretty bad, Clinton. It does indeed!"

Denzil, knowing nothing of the course of events, could not see the cause of Wendover's perturbation. Tactfully, he kept to the cipher question.

"Your interpretation means no more to me than the original did," he pointed out. "Still, I'd like to know how you got it."

Wendover recovered himself immediately.

"It's simple enough," he explained. "Suppose you want to send this message: 'Get the hay mown in the Long Meadow.' You write the first letter in the top line, the second in the lower line, the third in the top line, and so on, alternately. Like this:

G t h h y o n n h l n m a o
e t e a m w i t e o g e d w

Then you write the top line in groups of six letters—that's to make it easy for the telegraph officials—and when you've finished the top line you run the second line on after it. If the top line doesn't contain a multiple of six letters, you add on Z's to fill the missing space and to make it easier for your correspondent to see where to start, without the bother of counting the letters. That gives you this for 'Get the hay,' and so forth:

GTHHYO NNHLNM AOZZZZ
ETEAMW ITEOGE DWZZZZ

To read the thing, you just write the second half—from ETEAMW onwards—in zigzag fashion under the first half as I put it in making the cipher. And then you can read it straight off."

"Easy as winking—if you know how," admitted Denzil, with a grin. "The bother is, I never know how. That game needs a special brand of mind."

Sir Clinton picked up the telegram and stowed it away in his pocket.

"Anything more about Huggin?" he demanded, turning to Denzil. "Anything you know about him may be useful, whether it seems important to you or not. What's he been doing, lately, do you know?"

Denzil searched his memory for a few seconds before answering.

"As it happens, I do know one thing he's been busy with for the last few weeks at any rate. I ran into him once as he was coming

out of Somerset House. To make conversation, I asked him casually what took him there. Then it came out that he's been in to
hunt up some records about Eustace Atherfold—his will, or his
death certificate, or something of that sort. Huggin was in great
form that day, I remember. Up in the flies, almost. It seems he'd
got the job of writing Atherfold's life—"

"Eustace Atherfold, that best-seller novelist?" interrupted
Wendover. "I didn't care for his books. I only read a couple of them
but they weren't my sort. A rank bad influence, Atherfold. . . . He
wasn't a friend of yours, was he?" he added, rather afraid lest he
had been discourteous.

"A friend of mine? No," replied Denzil, turning down the corners of his mouth as though in distaste. "I'm all for good healthy
fiction with the corpse in plain sight and the loving pair clinched
in the last chapter. I write for the bored businessman and I try to
bring a little joy into his leisure. After all, it's something to be able
to brace up these Atlases for their tasks. Atherfold was off my beat.
I met him, of course. One meets nearly everybody sooner or later.
I've even eaten his salt—and some better-tasting things as well—
at his dinner table. But he wasn't my sort, really."

"I congratulate you," said Wendover heartily.

"We proceed?" Denzil went on. "Re Huggin deceased. As I told
you, Huggin seemed very cock-a-hoop at having got this job. It took
the prospect of hard cash to make Huggin enthusiastic. So I had a
fair notion of what he was after, even before he told me he was
going to be 'quite frank' as a biographer of the late Eustace. 'Quite
frank'! I kept a straight face and asked him if he was thinking of
printing it in Paris or issuing it for private circulation only. But
his line was plain enough. He'd got the chance of a lifetime, writing up the career of a celebrated dirty dog. It was a sure best seller,
even if it wasn't *quite* frank."

"I remember something about this fellow Atherfold now,"
Wendover put in. "Wasn't he mixed up in that nasty business, the
Lordsmead divorce case?"

"And half a dozen others, in his lighter moments. A 'quite frank'
life of him would be a real 'human document' in the Zola sense.
Huggin kept me standing there for a while, telling me about his

luck. It seems Atherfold's sister had given him carte blanche. She must be a rum artist! She'd handed over all Atherfold's letters and even a diary in umpteen volumes—'locked volumes,' as Huggin described them with a leer that made St. Mary-le-Strand rock on its foundations. In fact, he'd come into a perfect Golconda of esoteric information about the *faits et gestes* of the late lamented."

"Then he had a prospect of getting a fair amount of cash as soon as the thing was published?" Sir Clinton asked.

"Undoubtedly. He was so full of it that he blurted out the terms. Often, you know, these things are paid for by a sum down and the literary executor cops the royalties. But Huggin was to get a royalty of so much a copy, which, in this case, meant a lot more. Naturally, being Huggin, he proposed to make it salable at any cost short of colliding with the Obscene Publications Act."

"But meanwhile he was hard up," Sir Clinton mused. "By the way, Bob, you say you came across this man Atherfold. Let's hear your own impression of him."

"Atherfold? A nasty little fellow like a faun with a squeaky voice. I don't see myself what those women found to admire in him. But you can't get over facts. Perhaps it was his money they liked. He had plenty. Never grudged himself anything he fancied. You ought to have seen his study. The literary man's dream and the connoisseur's nightmare, rolled into one. Chairs that seemed to suck you into them when you sat down. Three dictaphones on stands, ready to roll anywhere you wanted them at the touch of a finger. The very last touch in desks. Shelves on shelves of rare editions, all uniformly bound in leather. That stamped him. Fancy tearing the original covers off rare editions just because he wanted uniformity! And lacquer. And Whistler etchings on the walls, with Japanese prints. You know that Hokusai print, the worst of the lot? Well, he had that hung over his mantelpiece as large as life. You'd only to look at that study to see the man had neither taste nor decency. No one with a spark of feeling could have crammed so many discordant styles into one room."

"Three dictaphones seems a lot," commented Sir Clinton. "He must have kept his secretary busy, if he had one."

"Secretaries? He had a regular procession of them. They were always good-looking girls and they lived on the premises—till he got tired of them. But I doubt if they did much typing while it lasted. No decent girl would have stayed a minute on the premises after one look above the fireplace."

"Suppose, for a change, you tell us something about the man himself," Sir Clinton suggested. "All you've done is to describe his furniture."

"I don't pretend to draw character," Denzil retorted. "They tell me it's not needed in detective stories. The impression I got of him was that he'd no morals. I don't think it was a case of his having gone to the bad. He'd been born like that. He'd stick at nothing to get what he wanted—usually it was a woman, I gathered. If he had any guiding star it was hedonism. It sticks out everywhere in his books."

"If the two I read were fair samples, I can believe you," Wendover confirmed.

"Oh, it wasn't a pose," Denzil continued. "His private talk ran on the same lines. He once mentioned to me in passing, that he'd never kept faith with any woman since he was seventeen. Some men would have said that as a bit of brag. He didn't. It was quite natural to him and he thought nothing of it. Women were there for his amusement, if he fancied them; and that was all about it. When they ceased to amuse him, he didn't waste any time thinking about their worries."

"Get back to Huggin," said Sir Clinton. "Were you ever at his rooms?"

"Lord, no!" Denzil declared flatly. "He was no pal of mine. I wouldn't have crossed the street to speak to him. He lived somewhere in the suburbs, I heard."

"That's all you remember about him?"

Denzil nodded affirmatively.

"You've dragged me into this, alguazil," he pointed out, after a pause. "I didn't ask to read your crime serial, you know. But since I've started your dime novel, I've a craving to hear the beginning of it and to see the next instalment, whatever it is. Am I to be left out in the cold?"

"I see your drift," Sir Clinton assured him solemnly. "'Situation wanted by rather dull-witted gentleman, age thirty, with literary tastes. No cryptograms or ciphers. Apply Watson, Box No. So-and-so.' Speaking as between friends, Bob, and entirely in the public interest, I don't see what use you'd be. This isn't a city job. I'm going back to Talgarth to-night. I'm not even at home, so I can't offer to put you up. Besides, it may be long enough before we get on the track of anything that would interest you—like hidden treasure, masked monks, shrieks in the night, secret societies, and so forth. In fact, I don't believe we'll come across one of them. It would be deadly dull for you."

"I'll chance that," Denzil pleaded.

Wendover had an impulse to ask the author to stay at the Grange, but on second thoughts he refrained, since it was clear that the Chief Constable was not eager for Denzil's company while he was busy with this case.

"It wouldn't amuse you," Sir Clinton declared. "You wouldn't find it half so exciting as the bit in your last story where the supposed corpse rises in its coffin and throws a tame octopus into the villain's face. How the devil you think of these things is beyond me. It must be either lunacy or genius; and somehow, Bob, you never struck me as a genius."

"He's very hard to please," said Denzil in an audible aside to Wendover. "Personally, I thought that tame octopus rather a good touch. Give one a jar, wouldn't it? to get a devilfish slung into one's face unexpected like? I shouldn't care about it myself."

He stopped short and an impish grin crept over his face. "After all, it's a free country," he remarked irrelevantly. "Is there a good pub at Talgarth?"

"It doesn't keep Imperial Tokay in its cellars or plovers' eggs on its table," Wendover explained. "Hardly up to the standard of your characters, I fear."

"I'm not proud, so long as the beer's drinkable."

"It's not a tied house," Wendover answered. "But you needn't expect lifts, or private suites. And the bar's not the quietest place you could think of, until after closing time. They get rather excited at times, I believe."

"I can imagine it. The fat stock prices on the wireless always make me want to leap out of my chair and do some great deed. And of course they must come more directly home in a farming district. You tempt me, Mephistopheles, I'll think over it. After all, it's a public duty to help the police."

"Help?" said Sir Clinton witheringly. "Then you'd better bring your tame octopus along to throw at the criminal when you've spotted him. I don't want you, Bob, and that's putting it politely."

"Well, I'll think over it and decide what's in the interests of the public, of which I am an important member. Thanks for your warm encouragement."

# CHAPTER VIII
## MELCHIZEDEK

ROOKERY PARK was a long, depressing street flanked on either side by high terraces of grimy brick, with sooty little twenty-foot gardens separating them from the roadway. Here and there, in a heavily-curtained window, stood a card bearing the word: APARTMENTS. Though it had possibly seen better days, Rookery Park was one of those thoroughfares which seem inevitably fated to end up as a phalanstery of boarding houses and lodgings, a place where no one knows the name of his next-door neighbour and in which the floating population changes from year to year. Although one end of it abutted on a roaring High Street along which an almost continuous stream of buses sped to and from the further suburbs, Rookery Park itself was a backwater. Lodging-house cats formed its chief visible population through most of the day. Once a week, a dilapidated man briskly pushing a barrow passed down it, chanting in a high, exhausted voice, "Rag-bone! Rag-bottle-er-bone!" but his visits seemed a mere formality, so far as actual trade was concerned. Humanity in quantity was seen in Rookery Park only when its inhabitants, armed with jugs for beer, sallied forth to the nearest public house at hours governed by the local licensing regulations.

The taxi drew up before number forty-seven and Sir Clinton, after paying the fare, mounted the flight of worn-down stone steps which led to the front door. Wendover followed him and arrived just as the door was opened by a short, stout woman, evidently the landlady.

"Are you another of 'em?" she demanded, with the air of one who has already suffered more than is good for her temper.

"I've called to see Inspector Summerfield. I believe he's here just now."

The landlady stood squarely in the doorway, blocking the entrance.

"Are you from the Press? He says not to let you in, if you are. I've been run off my feet, answering the bell to reporters that won't take no for an answer. Impident fellows, too, some of 'em."

Sir Clinton produced his card, and after examining it she became a shade less hostile.

"Well, you can come in," she said, grudgingly. "But if this is a try-on, I hope the police'll do something to you. In there," she explained, pointing to the door of a room at the back of the house.

Sir Clinton knocked and then pushed open the door without further formality. A man in a dark lounge suit was seated before a desk, going through some papers. He looked up as they entered and ran a pair of very steady eyes over them. At the window stood a uniformed constable.

"My name's Driffield," Sir Clinton explained. "Inspector Summerfield, isn't it? This is a friend of mine, Mr. Wendover."

The inspector rose swiftly from his chair and made a gesture of acknowledgment.

"I'm just going through his papers, sir, to see if there's anything in them. Nothing that's any use, so far as I've gone. I started with his bedroom, upstairs, but there's nothing in it except his clothes and a few odds and ends."

"Did you find the addresses of any relations amongst his papers?"

"No, sir. But that's not surprising, after all. Most people tear up their letters when they've read them. I do, myself."

"Any letters for him by to-day's post?"

"Only a couple of circulars, sir."

"We don't seem to be getting much forrarder, on that basis. Is there any business correspondence? He must have kept that, at least."

"There's one file, sir, full of stuff dealing with books and so on. Nothing that you'd call personal."

"At any rate it's some link with the outer world. May I see it, please?"

The inspector opened a drawer in the desk, took out a folder, and passed it to the Chief Constable who spread it on the desk and began to turn over the leaves, reading scraps aloud as he went on.

". . . 'We enclose their usual statement, showing the sales of your book. . . . We regret to note that, at that date, there was a balance standing against the book.' I suppose that means that the royalty on the sales didn't cover the advance payment. . . . That's from Rodsley & Co., the literary agents. . . . Here it is again, the same tale. Denzil wasn't far wrong about his success, evidently. . . . And yet again. . . . Let's come up to date." He turned to the final documents on the file. "'I have pleasure in sending you enclosed a copy of the formal agreement dated 23rd February, 1936, between yourself and Messrs. Spratthall & Co.' . . . It's about that Life of Atherfold that Denzil told us about," he explained, with a glance at Wendover. "The rest of the stuff deals with small items, evidently newspaper articles and that kind of thing," he added after he had run through the remaining pages. "He can't have been a very lucrative client for Rodsley & Co."

He closed the file, took out a pocketbook, and jotted down the address and telephone number of the literary agents.

"They're not likely to know much about him, personally, but it's always a chance. Is his passbook there, Inspector? And his chequebook?"

"They're here, sir," said Summerfield, diving into another drawer and producing them. "There's nothing interesting in them that I could see, except that authorship doesn't seem as paying a game as I supposed. That reminds me, sir, there's a lot of type-script in this desk. I just glanced at it. It's unfinished—a biography of Eustace Atherfold, I gathered from what I saw. It beats me why anyone wanted to write a life of *him*."

"Read his books, have you?" asked Sir Clinton, with a twinkle in his eye.

"No, sir. My wife got one of them out of the library once, I remember. It wasn't much in her style. She doesn't care for hot stuff. No, my interest in Atherfold was purely professional. We always expected to have him on our hands, sooner or later, from what we picked up here and there. And most likely he'd have come to grief before long if he hadn't got knocked out in that taxi smash-up. A rank bad lot, he was."

Sir Clinton nodded and began to examine Huggin's bank passbook, making comments for Wendover's benefit as he proceeded.

"There's a steady dribble of small cheques paid in at irregular intervals. . . . These would be from his literary agent, most likely. . . . Here's something bigger than usual. 'By cash, £65,' on 5th May. . . . Then a run of items like £4-14-6 . . . £2-16-8 . . . £6-13-5 . . . Oh, I see. I'd forgotten the agent's ten per cent. commission. These really represent payments of five guineas, three guineas, and so on, less the commission. That accounts for the odd pence in the cheques. As you say, Inspector, his brand of literature doesn't seem to have brought in much. . . . Now let's try the chequebook counterfoils. . . . Mrs. Hassop, three guineas, on the 15th August. . . . Mrs. Hassop, three guineas, at the end of the week before that." He turned back to the passbook. "Yes, that runs right back. Payment for these rooms, obviously. It doesn't seem dear for a bedroom, a sitting-room, and board."

"He shares this sitting-room with another man, sir. That accounts for it."

"Oh, yes, I remember. Fairbank's his name, isn't it? Have you seen him?"

"No, sir. But I arranged that he was to come back here about this time and see you. I thought that would suit you better."

"What's his line of business, do you know?"

"He's a stockbroker's runner, sir, whatever that may be."

"Oh, is he? I'm not well up on the point, but I think you'll find it means that he works to get clients for a broker and has a share in the commission for his trouble. But let's get on with these counterfoils. . . . Here's another regularly recurring item, four pounds once a month. Pocket money, perhaps. He certainly doesn't sound a new Croesus. . . . And then sundry cheques to various people. They look like accounts to tailors and firms of that sort, to judge from the figures."

Sir Clinton made a movement as though to push the books across the desk to the inspector, but hesitated at the last moment.

"Let's see what his present bank balance amounts to," he suggested, taking out a pencil.

He consulted the passbook for the balance of the last audit, rapidly added up the figures entered on the chequebook counterfoils, made the subtraction and then whistled softly.

"Well, he was certainly running things pretty fine," he said. "His current balance is £1-17-4. And he had three guineas to pay for his rooms at the end of the week. I wasn't so far out when I talked about Grub Street, evidently. But probably he was counting on that windfall of £100."

"What windfall of £100, sir?" asked Summerfield, evidently perturbed lest he had missed some point in his search.

"He had £100-14-7 in his pocket when he was murdered," Sir Clinton explained. "Judging by what these books show, it's likely enough that fourteen and seven-pence was what he left London with that night. The round hundred was a windfall from somewhere unknown. It's the simplest explanation. Not that it explains much, really," he added, with a smile.

Wendover did not smile in reply. The obvious explanation had grown clearer to him since he first heard of that hundred pounds; and that obvious explanation, if correct, would mean a washing of dirty linen in the Hundreds of Ambledown which was by no means to his taste. And would it stop at a mere washing of dirty linen? With a dead man thrown into the problem and the police on the track? And that infernal "God Send You Back To Me" bank note already identified?

Then a fresh aspect of the matter occurred to him and for a time banished his forebodings. But on further examination this slight comfort seemed hardly so good as it had looked at first sight. In any case, he decided, this was not a matter to discuss before the inspector. He could wait till he had the Chief Constable alone.

Sir Clinton glanced round the room and lighted upon an old-fashioned bookcase with glass-fronted shelves and cupboards below the shelving.

"Have you gone over the contents of that?" he asked.

"Yes, sir. We picked the lock and had a look inside. There's nothing in our line there. These volumes you see the backs of on the shelves are manuscript stuff. Each volume has a lock on it, but I could see it was manuscript by opening out the leaves a bit. There's a gold lettering on the back: *Diary of E. Atherfold.* I expect Huggin had it to write up that Life he was busy with. And these cupboards down below are simply stuffed with old letters, Atherfold's correspondence apparently. I expect he borrowed them for the same purpose. If we could have laid our hands on that diary while he was still alive, it might have meant something to us. But he's dead now, so there's nothing doing."

"You'd better take good care of it," Sir Clinton pointed out. "It belongs to Atherfold's literary executors, whoever they may be. Huggin had no property in it, so far as one knows. It'll have to go back to the executors intact along with the letters. See that none of it goes astray. Perhaps it would be safest to take it away with you; it would be awkward if anyone tampered with it while it's more or less in our charge."

"Something in that, sir," agreed the inspector, though it was evident that he thought Sir Clinton a shade fussy in the matter. "I'll take the whole lot away in a taxi and see it's put in safety."

"I think I'll have a few words with the landlady. Her name's Hassop, isn't it?" the Chief Constable asked. "Is she married or a widow, or what?"

"She's married. The husband's employed at the Tube station up the road. There's one daughter, about nineteen, in the dressmaking line. They're quite respectable people, sir."

Sir Clinton rang the bell and in a few minutes Mrs. Hassop appeared.

"Sit down, Mrs. Hassop," said the Chief Constable. "I just want to ask a question or two. How long has Mr. Huggin had these rooms?"

"Five years, sir."

"Then you've had no complaint to make about him, obviously?"

"No, sir, he was a quiet gentleman, fairly regular in his ways and easy to get on with. He gave no trouble."

"Had he many visitors?"

"Hardly ever, sir. Now and again he had a gentleman to dinner, which was extra, but not often."

"What arrangements were there between him and this other man— What's his name?— Oh, yes, Fairbank."

"They had bedrooms upstairs, sir. They shared this sitting-room between them; and they had their meals in the room below this. Their bills were quite separate."

"Were they great friends?"

The landlady evidently hesitated over a definition so Sir Clinton tried to help her out.

"Did they go about much together and that sort of thing?"

"No, they didn't, so far as I know. I can't say what they did outside the house, of course, but inside it they didn't see very much of each other. Mr. Fairbank, he used to leave the house immediately after breakfast every day except Sunday and not come back until dinnertime. After dinner, as like as not, he'd go out again for the evening. Mr. Huggin, he was a writer and he did most of his writing in the mornings and afternoons. We could hear his typewriter going. He didn't use it in the evenings unless Mr. Fairbank was out. I expect the noise of it annoyed Mr. Fairbank if he happened to be in. I've heard him making remarks about it."

"What did they do on Sundays. Spend the day together?"

"No, sir. Mr. Huggin had his breakfast in bed and didn't come down till late in the morning. Mr. Fairbank read the Sunday papers and went for a walk till lunchtime. Then he usually went out and didn't come back till it was time for dinner. Often he was out in the evening as well."

"You've had no difficulties about money with either of them?"

"Oh, no, sir. Mr. Fairbank always paid my bill the minute I presented it. Sometimes Mr. Huggin let it run on for a week or two, but he always paid in the end. He used to grumble at times about money coming in irregularly, sir, and having to wait for newspapers and magazines to pay up."

"Did he ever talk to you about his affairs?"

"No, sir," said Mrs. Hassop rather indignantly. "I don't gossip with my gentlemen, ever. And besides, Mr. Huggin was a very quiet gentleman, not the talkative sort."

"And Mr. Fairbank?"

"I don't gossip with my gentlemen. I make them as comfortable as I can, and that's all there is to it, so far as I care."

"Any other residents?"

"I've a Mr. Highlever. He's a shopwalker at Tring's in the High Street. He has a bedroom and eats his meals downstairs. He has them at a different time from Mr. Fairbank and Mr. Huggin. He hardly knew them—just a matter of 'Good morning' if they met on the stair."

"You saw Mr. Huggin for the last time on Monday? What did he do, that day?"

"He got up and had his breakfast as usual, sir. He told me at breakfast-time that he wouldn't be in for dinner that night. After breakfast, he came up here. I brought him a cup of tea at eleven o'clock, and he had the table here all covered with a lot of old letters and stuff that he usually kept in that cupboard under the bookshelves. That's his own bookcase. He bought it at an auction sale last March. He was making notes out of these old letters, I think, when I brought him his tea. He had his lunch at half past one and then he did some more work with the papers, I think, for when I brought him his afternoon tea at half past four he was putting all the old papers and stuff back into the bookcase. He went out about five o'clock, and that was the last I saw of him. Sometimes he goes out for dinner and doesn't come home till late, so I didn't know he hadn't come home until next morning when I found his bed hadn't been slept in."

Wendover had little difficulty in perceiving that Mrs. Hassop had told this story many times before to other listeners; but he gave her a good mark as a witness since she had fined down her tale to the essentials and omitted irrelevant details.

"What about Mr. Fairbank and Mr. Highlever?" demanded Sir Clinton.

"Mr. Fairbank went out after breakfast as usual on Monday, sir. He didn't come home to dinner. He went to the theater, I think, for I saw the programme lying on his dressing table next morning. He came home after midnight, as he often does. I heard the front door when he came in, for I'm a light sleeper. Mr. Highlever put on his dress clothes that evening and went out to a social or a dance that Tring's were giving their staff. He came home after midnight, too. It was a Cinderella, he told me in the morning, and he'd had a very pleasant time."

"Did Mr. Huggin keep a car?" Sir Clinton inquired, with a quizzical glance in Wendover's direction.

"Oh, no, sir. Mr. Fairbank has a car. He garages it in a shed belonging to a friend of mine not far away from here. Mr. Highlever used always to be talking about buying a car, but he's just got engaged and I don't think he'll want one now. He borrows someone else's when he needs one for an afternoon."

Evidently, Wendover reflected, Mr. Highlever was a communicative man, able to force personal information upon even gossip-hating landladies.

"Have you a telephone, Mrs. Hassop?" inquired the Chief Constable.

"Well, sir, we have and we haven't, in a manner of speaking. Mr. Fairbank had one put in and his name's in the book. But he lets us use it any time we want and he trusts us to make a note of our calls and pay him for them once a week. You could use it, sir, if you pay me for the call."

"I may have to, later on, thanks. Now that's all I have to ask you at present, I think, Mrs. Hassop. Just one question. Do you know the addresses of any of these visitors Mr. Huggin had from time to time?"

"No, sir," the landlady replied, shaking her head decidedly. "I don't even remember their names. They didn't come regularly, you see. Most of them came only once and I paid no attention to them beyond seeing they had a good dinner."

Mrs. Hassop withdrew, rather reluctantly Wendover thought, and Sir Clinton turned to the inspector, who had resumed his search through the documents in the desk.

"Anything further of interest?" he inquired.

The inspector shook his head.

"Nothing that I can see, sir," he said gloomily. "This Huggin seems to have been like that old Melchizedek you hear about in church—without father or mother and without descent. One runs across people like that at times, in the way of business, and they're the biggest nuisance of the lot, if they get sunk. No relatives, no intimate friends, no documents. There's no way of laying one's hand on information about them, if one wants it in a hurry. If everyone in the country were ticketed and cross references given, it would save people like me a lot of trouble at times."

"And give employment to a lot of extra officials," said Wendover with a smile. "Isn't the income tax big enough for you yet?"

"I don't suppose it bothers me as much as it does you, sir," retorted the inspector, giving smile for smile.

The sound of a latchkey in the front door interrupted this exchange.

"That'll be Fairbank, sir, I expect. I'll bring him in," said Summerfield, getting up and going out of the room.

They heard a short talk in the hall, and then the inspector ushered in a dark, good-looking man. Wendover, who liked to see a fine physique, eyed him up and down with satisfaction, for he was nearly six feet in height, well-built, and still under forty by his looks. Evidently he took pains to keep himself in first-rate condition, and Wendover was led to wonder whether he played badminton. If he did, that might account for some, at least, of his evenings away from his rooms.

The newcomer seemed a shade surprised to find two people waiting for him, but he betrayed it no more than was courteous. He glanced from one to the other, waiting for a lead, which the inspector gave him at once by introducing him to Sir Clinton.

"Sad thing, this," he said to the Chief Constable when he had identified him "Poor Huggin! It beats me to guess who could have had a grudge against him. If I can do anything to help, I'll be glad to lend a hand. Just ask what you want to know."

Wendover could judge people by their manner, so far as social standing went; and in Fairbank he recognised "one of his own sort."

"Come down a bit in the world financially," he surmised, "but he knows how to behave properly. And his tailor's got a good cutter."

Sir Clinton apparently thought much the same. He dropped his "official" manner when he spoke.

"A nuisance that we have to trouble you, Mr. Fairbank," he said, "but your friend's affairs aren't too clear to us. Perhaps you can help. You've lived with him in these rooms for a number of years, haven't you?"

"When you say 'friend,' you're putting it too high," Fairbank corrected pleasantly. "It suited both of us to share these rooms. We didn't see much of each other, not enough to get on our nerves. But I left his affairs alone and he didn't pry into mine. He wasn't in my set and his friends weren't my sort."

"So your association was purely one of financial convenience? These were better rooms than he could have afforded if he hadn't joined company with you?"

"That was it. And once you get used to a place, you stay on."

Wendover noted the underlying suggestion that Fairbank could go elsewhere if he chose.

"Can you tell us anything about his personality?" asked Sir Clinton.

"You mean what sort of a man he was?" Fairbank said in a cogitative tone. "Soured, I should say. Missed fire in life, I think, and wasn't big enough to get over it. That kind of thing. Always hard up, too, poor chap. He used to touch me at times when he ran short. Always paid up in the end, though, I'll say that for him."

Again Wendover caught the tacit suggestion that Fairbank had been the more prosperous of the two.

"Anything else you can think of?" prompted Sir Clinton.

"Virtues and vices, you mean? He stuck at his work though he didn't make much out of it. The dogged type, you know, that doesn't let go easily. He never lied to me. But then he'd no need to. I never saw him drunk or even near it. As to women—well, what does any-one know about any of us in that field? He hadn't much use for them, if one went by his talk. But I can't say much about that."

He made a slight gesture as though to suggest that he knew very little about his late housemate. On reflection, Wendover could see that this state of affairs was not improbable. They had not been more than acquaintances brought together purely by financial con-venience at first, and obviously they had so little in common that association had led to no intimacy between them. Huggin's death left no blank in Fairbank's life, and evidently there was no need to pretend regrets which he did not feel. It was much better than shed-ding a lot of crocodile tears.

"When did you see Huggin last?" Sir Clinton asked casually.

"At breakfast on Monday morning."

"He didn't say anything about his plans for the day?"

"He never did. We didn't talk much at breakfast as a rule. He was always sulky at breakfasttime. Some people are like that. So we used to read our newspapers and say nothing to each other be-yond 'Pass the toast' or things like that. I saw nothing out of the way in his manner, if that's what you want."

"You didn't come home for dinner that night, I believe?"

Fairbank shook his head.

"No, I went to the Crescent second house to see Thelma Campion's turn. Have you seen her in this new thing? One of her best. You shouldn't miss it."

"I'm afraid I shan't have time on this visit," Sir Clinton said with a touch of regret. "She has a wonderfully magnetic personal-ity, hasn't she? You've seen her?" he asked, turning to Wendover.

"Oh, yes. She manages to grip you as soon as she comes on to the stage," Wendover agreed. "It's a great gift, that."

"You didn't notice, when you came in, that Huggin hadn't got back?" asked the Chief Constable, turning again to Fairbank.

"Not I. He was out at night occasionally and I thought nothing of it. I came in here and had a whiskey and soda. Then I went straight to bed. His bedroom door was shut, I remember. But that meant nothing one way or the other."

"No, of course not. Now, Mr. Fairbank, I want you to think carefully. Can you remember anything—anything whatever—that could throw light on this affair? Don't mind how unimportant it seems to you. Let's have it."

Fairbank frowned in obvious concentration for some seconds, then apparently he gave it up.

"Not a thing," he said at last, with the reluctance of a man who dislikes to admit failure. "Seems silly, doesn't it? But I can't think of anything that fits. I didn't know his set, but I can't think why anyone would want to do him in. He'd no cash to speak of, I'm sure of that. And I doubt if it was a woman, from what I did know of Huggin. No, it beats me. Unless—he couldn't have been taken for someone else, by chance? Short of that, I can't make even a guess at it."

Sir Clinton tried a fresh line.

"Think again," he suggested. "Relations? Habits? Correspondence? Health? Literary work? Does none of these call up anything?"

Once more Fairbank pondered without success.

"No, I give it up," he admitted. "I never heard of any relations of his. He didn't show me his letters. And you've been through them yourself," he added, with a glance at the desk. "His health was sound enough, so far as I know. Mrs. Hassop could tell you more about his habits than I can. They give me no clue. Literary work, ditto."

He paused momentarily and then changed his tone.

"That reminds me of one point. He was writing a life of Eustace Atherfold. I got him the job. At least, I put him on the track of it. Atherfold was a client of mine. He knew my . . . I mean, we had common acquaintances before he was my client. When he died, I put it to Huggin that he might get the job of writing the man's life, if he got in first with his offer. He snapped at the chance and got it."

Fairbank made a gesture towards the bookcase with its serried ranks of volumes.

"All this stuff here was handed over to him for that work. What about it? Shall I get it sent back to Atherfold's executors? It might get lost, if it's not looked after. And I suppose it's valuable, in a way. I looked into it when Huggin was working on it. Some of it's hot stuff. Not the kind of thing to leave about."

"We'll look after it," Sir Clinton assured him. "That reminds me, do you know if Huggin left a will? It's not amongst his papers?"

He turned for confirmation to the inspector, who nodded.

"No, it isn't here, if he made one. Do you know the name of his solicitor, by any chance?"

Fairbank shook his head.

"I doubt if he had one. And I don't suppose he made a will of any sort. Why should he? He'd no money. He was broke, half the time. And his personal property, apart from manuscripts, would have gone into a suitcase. You can advertise, if you think it worth while, but I bet you draw nothing by that."

"Did you never hear him mention his relations?"

"Never. I doubt if he had any left. I don't know, of course. That's just my own view."

Sir Clinton deliberated for a moment or two before speaking again.

"We'll need somebody to identify him for the coroner's jury," he pointed out. "You could do it for us, couldn't you?"

Fairbank made no concealment of his distaste for this proposal.

"I'm not keen," he said dryly. "I'm a busy man and it would cost me a day to get away to this place—where is it?—Newton Abbas?"

"Abbots Norton," Sir Clinton supplied, as Fairbank sought for the name.

"Abbots Norton, is it? I knew it was one of these old-fashioned ones. No, unless you're stuck, I'd rather cry off that job. Can't you get Mrs. Hassop or her husband to do it for you? They knew him by sight as well as I did and it would be a day in the country for them. Besides giving them heaps to talk about when they got back."

Sir Clinton did not press the matter.

"I see your point," he admitted. "We'll not trouble you. But I wish you could have thrown more light on Huggin's affairs for us. If you think of anything, later on, you'll let us know, please?"

"Of course," Fairbank agreed. "And now, I take it, you'll want to get on with your work. As I can't help, I needn't hinder. If anything occurs to me later, I'll let you know at once."

"Thanks. By the way, you own the telephone here, I'm told. May I make a call or two?"

"Of course," Fairbank assured him readily. "Anything I can do to help, you know."

And with that he took his leave. They heard his steps going up the stairs towards his bedroom, and then Sir Clinton turned to the inspector.

"Would you mind seeing if you can lay hands on that music-hall programme the landlady spoke about? Just check it, when you get it. He brought it in on Monday night, Mrs. Hassop said."

"Certainly, sir, if it's to be had, I'll get it. It'll be the current one, of course." He glanced at the Chief Constable as he spoke. "You're not suspecting Fairbank, are you?"

"I wish I had reasonable grounds for suspecting somebody definite," said Sir Clinton with a pretense of despair. "No, it's merely that I like to see no loose ends in a case; and this time it happens that it will cost no trouble to check Fairbank's visit to the Crescent. If you can give me good ground for suspicion, you won't find me hanging back, Inspector. But unfortunately we simply have nothing against anyone, so far. Now let's see. Oh, yes, pass me that folder of Huggin's literary correspondence, please. I want to look up his agents' number. It's on the letter paper."

When he had secured it, he went off to the telephone and was out of the room for some minutes.

"I wonder if you'd mind parceling up that unfinished MS. you found—the Atherfold Life. I've promised to hand it over to Rodsley's. There's no objection to doing that. You'd better ring and see if Mrs. Hassop can give you some wrapping paper and twine."

While he waited for the parcel to be made up, Sir Clinton glanced at his watch. Then he turned to Wendover.

"You'd better amuse yourself till six o'clock. I've a couple of calls to make and one of them's on a lady who might be scared if two of us descended on her en masse. Sorry to leave you at a loose end, but there it is. Duty calls, in more senses than one. Meet me at my club—the one we lunched at—at six o'clock. And, by the by," he turned to the inspector. "Here's a phone number which will get me between six and half past, if you've anything to report. I can leave you in charge here, but I expect you'll find nothing worth much. You'll remove these diaries and letters? Thanks. Then that seems to be all I can do here."

He bade the inspector farewell and left the house, followed by Wendover.

"It's the High Street and a taxi for me," he explained "No use offering you a lift, Squire. We're not going in the same direction unless you'd like to take a stroll in the Strand. It's lucky that Huggin hadn't got far with his masterwork. I do hate carrying large parcels."

# CHAPTER IX
## MISS GERTRUDE ATHERFOLD

HAVING TIME ON HIS HANDS, Wendover filled it in as best he could by doing some desultory and unnecessary shopping; and it was not until close on six o'clock that he returned to the club to await the reappearance of the Chief Constable. He was not kept long in suspense, for Sir Clinton came in within a few minutes of his own arrival.

"Anything fresh?" demanded Wendover, laying down the paper which he had been reading to pass the time.

Sir Clinton shook his head, though not despondently.

"Nothing much to the point, so far as Huggin is concerned," he said, taking a chair beside Wendover. "Still, it's always interesting to know how the next man lives, or the next woman for that matter. At least I've discovered how Eustace Atherfold's sister came to authorise the publication of his biography."

"I can't imagine how any woman would sponsor a thing of that sort," grumbled Wendover. "We've a pretty good idea now what kind of stuff it was going to be. Denzil made that fairly plain, didn't he? She must be a rum artist, as he put it. I suppose she's one of these mannish females who couldn't catch a husband while the going was good, and who pride themselves on not being shockable by anything short of an earthquake."

"What an imagination you have, Squire," observed the Chief Constable. "You're lost as a country gentleman. Take my tip and go into Denzil's line. With a little practice you'd beat his tame octopus hollow. No, curiously enough, she's not in the least like your character sketch. In fact I found her rather likable, even by my rather finicky standard. But she doesn't come into the tale at first."

He took out his cigarette case and leaned over to extract a match from the supply on the nearest table.

"After I left you, I drove first of all to Rodsley's office. I'd rung them up from Rookery Park and prepared them for the bad news that the Life of Atherfold had got stuck on the way. They hadn't heard about Huggin's death, of course. They received the unfinished MS. with moderate joy—very moderate, since I don't suppose it's much use to them as it stands. Then we got to business."

He paused to light his cigarette.

"Like everyone else, they seemed to know next to nothing about Huggin's private affairs. He was just a client to them, naturally, and I gathered that they didn't care much for him owing to his continual grumbling because they didn't find him more contracts. Their point of view, I gather, was that they'd find him contracts if he'd write salable stuff; which seems more or less common sense to me. And with this biography of Atherfold, both sides seemed satisfied. I asked how the matter cropped up at first, and it seems that Huggin proposed it almost as soon as Atherfold died."

"That fits in with what Fairbank told us about his drawing Huggin's attention to the chance of snaffling the job," Wendover pointed out.

"It does. But the thing was a bit complicated by the late Eustace employing a lawyer who had no acquaintance with literary affairs. Eustace, quite obviously, meant to leave his sister nothing of any cash value. All his money was left to various females of whom the less said the better. And even the copyrights in his published novels went to the same people. I don't suppose he had the slightest wish to be kind to these dames in particular. It's more likely that he meant to keep his sister out of everything that he could. All he left her was 'any family papers.' There were two sets of executors: one lot for the ordinary property, and Rodsley's, whom he appointed as executors in anything connected with literary affairs. So you see the only things that came to Miss Atherfold were old letters and, possibly, his locked diary, which might be reckoned as either unpublished literary stuff or as 'family papers.'"

"He must have been rather a beast to leave his sister hard up like that," commented Wendover.

"They hadn't much in common," Sir Clinton said. "But to get on. Apparently the diary was inspected; and from what Rodsley's told me it was not in the class of 'publishable documents' by a long chalk. So the two sets of executors had no difficulty in deciding that it was 'family papers' and they handed it over to Miss Atherfold along with the old letters. Then came Huggin, with his proposal. And obviously that diary and the letters acquired a commercial value in the light of it. Rodsley's handled the business as was natural in the circumstances. And, except for another point, that was about all I could get from Rodsley's."

"Not very much," said Wendover, critically.

"No. It seemed next door to impossible to find out anything useful about the late Huggin. I'd got to the stage of clutching at any straw, so I asked Rodsley's to ring up Miss Atherfold and let her know I was coming to see her. I made the excuse that we had her brother's diary and these letters and we wanted to know what to do with them. I didn't expect to pick up anything from her. Still, she had met Huggin and he might have dropped something that would help us. Luckily, she was at home this afternoon."

"So you went round straight away?"

Sir Clinton nodded.

"You heard Denzil's account of the late Atherfold's abode, Squire. Reeked of money, didn't it? Well, none of that money had come in his sister's direction. When I was shown into her flat, the first glance round made that clear. Old-fashioned furniture, well-worn carpet, dingy wall paper, cheap little wireless set. But everything as spotless as care could make it. You remember what 'shabby-genteel' meant when we were youngsters?"

"Trying to keep up appearances on next to nothing," paraphrased Wendover. "That's a disheartening business. Evidently she and her brother didn't hit it off very well or he'd have done something for her. He could afford it."

"Oh, quite easily," Sir Clinton confirmed. "But one or two things in that shabby little room suggested why these two didn't hit it off, as you put it. On the mantelpiece was a card, a notice of some church function or other. There was an occasional table with a Bible and a prayer book on it, I noticed. And the only portrait in the place was one of a plump man in a clerical collar. I hope you see how well these fit in with your imaginary portrait of a mannish dame of the unshockable brand, Squire."

"Church mouse, you mean?" inquired Wendover, not troubling to answer the gibe.

"Church mouse is right. She came into the room before I pursued my investigations further. She's just what one might expect from her surroundings, rather faded, with eyes of an uncertain blue, but a very nice mouth and what our mothers would have called a 'sweet' expression on her face."

"I know the sort," said Wendover soberly. "The kind that gets all the thankless jobs to do and never sees how it's being put upon. We don't get so many of them nowadays. It's no wonder they didn't pull well together. Eustace Atherfold didn't trouble church much, I bet. Mohammedanism was more in his line."

"Even that would have cramped him," Sir Clinton surmised.

Wendover nodded rather absent-mindedly in reply.

"But how could a woman like that agree to let Huggin write her brother's life?" he mused. "It doesn't fit, Clinton. If you've given me the right impression of her, it's the last thing she'd want."

"So I thought myself. Then it came out, quite accidentally. She wanted the money. . . . Oh, no, not for herself, Squire. It seems the poor creature has given herself one luxury in that starved life of hers—her subscriptions to foreign missions. She's a fanatic on the conversion of the Heathen—you can see she always thinks about them with a capital H. When this suggestion of a Life of her brother was put before her, all she saw in it at first was some hundreds of pounds in royalties which she could spend in the mission field. That dazzled her—the chance of giving pounds where she'd only been able to spend shillings—and she agreed straight off in general terms. I'm giving you the gist of what I got from her. It took a little fishing to elicit it all, though she was quite frank, really.

"It seems she's too innocent to realise exactly the kind of life her brother had been leading. They hardly ever met, and he never let her come to his house. But she guessed vaguely that it would never square with the standards of her Vicar. And she'd never read Eustace's books. The Vicar advised her to leave them alone, and she had a fair idea that they were deleterious productions. And here you come up against her moral problem, Squire. On the one hand, can you touch pitch—or the proceeds of the sale of pitch—and keep your hands and your conscience clean? On the other, have you the right to reject money which can be turned to a good purpose, the conversion of the Heathen—with a capital H? It was too much for the poor old lady. She couldn't see her way through it.

"It's really pathetic, Squire. She has a certain naïve artfulness, if you know what I mean, and she constructed a hypothetical case which she laid before the Vicar. To her surprise, and much to her relief, he came out quite strongly in his verdict. 'If I were in a position to use Satan's money to forward a good cause,' he told her, 'then I would, without a moment's hesitation, take his money and turn it to hallowed uses.' Or words to that effect. He was most impressive, it seems, and she came away from that interview with her mind at ease. I expect the Vicar knew pretty well what was really in her mind when he gave that advice."

"I shouldn't quarrel with it myself," Wendover admitted, "though I suppose some people would call it a bit Jesuitical."

"Well, she swallowed it," Sir Clinton went on. "And after that, her obvious plan was to rake in as much of Satan's money as she could. And so, naturally enough, she jumped at the suggestion of this biography of her brother. The proceeds would be so much more money for the conversion of the Heathen. And then, when she'd committed herself, she began to reflect a bit. That Lordsmead divorce case! What would the church people say to that being raked up again? And would the Vicar approve of her name being flaunted on a book which mentioned *that,* even in a good cause?

"Then came Huggin to interview her. She didn't like him. I could see that, well enough. And it was plain to me that he simply diddled her, without the slightest scruple. One could see that running through her whole account, though she was too innocent to twig it herself. He spotted her weak point and played on it. Rodsley's original suggestion had been that he and she should collaborate and that both names should appear on the title-page. But before Huggin had finished, he'd persuaded her—easily enough, I suspect—to make an agreement which gave him a completely free hand and the major part of the spoils as well. If she'd had even a glimmering of how he meant to write that book, she'd have refused point-blank. But he didn't talk to her as he talked to Denzil, of course. It was to be a critical biography, that was all. And he was to get all the available documents from her, including the diary. Huggin took care that she had no say whatever in the text of what he proposed to write. She wasn't even to see the proofs or have any right of censorship."

"She'd never opened the diary, I take it?"

"Of course not! Nor the correspondence, either. She just passed them over to Huggin without the slightest examination. And now here's the point I got from Rodsley's. Huggin wanted the publishers to pay him an advance before he started work. They didn't see it. They wouldn't go beyond the usual cash advance on the day of publication. So Huggin had to make the best of that."

"You've spent an afternoon in confirming what we knew already: that Huggin was hard up," Wendover pointed out rather unsympathetically. "I've been worrying over something more important."

"Yes?" said Sir Clinton, knocking the ash from his cigarette into the ash tray beside him. "I take it that you're perturbed about some possible repercussions of this Huggin case in your own locality. I don't say you're wrong there, Squire. From all we've heard, the late Huggin was hard up and quite unscrupulous, so it's more than likely there was something dirty behind his sudden demise. But let's have your reconstruction of the affair. There's just time for it before we go for our train."

"Then in one word: Blackmail," said Wendover. "It stares you in the face."

"It does," the Chief Constable agreed. "And I may say that I've been staring back at it for quite a while. Almost from the very start in fact. It hasn't escaped my notice, Squire, though you might think it had. But I'd like to hear just what you make of it yourself. So go ahead."

"Very well, then," Wendover began. "Huggin's bank balance was £1-17-4, and when he left Abbots Norton he had fourteen and sevenpence in his pockets: total £2-11-11. He owed his landlady three guineas for his board and lodging that week, which leaves him worth just eleven and a penny less than nothing. And he wasn't likely to touch anything from that Life of Atherfold for the best part of a year at least."

"He could still carry on a sort of half-time job at writing for the papers," Sir Clinton objected. "He didn't need to spend all day and every day at the biography."

"He just made ends meet when he worked full time at journalism and such things," Wendover pointed out. "If he did less, he'd starve. So in any case, he had to look forward, probably, to a year of steady running into debt. Would his landlady have stuck that? I doubt it."

"Say well over £100," Sir Clinton estimated. "Yes, you seem to have the right end of the stick up to this point. What next?"

"He turned up in Abbots Norton with fourteen and sevenpence, plus whatever he paid for his meal at The Barleycorn. A couple of hours later, he's found dead with an extra hundred quid in his pocket. That hundred pounds was all in one pound and ten shilling notes, you remember. Now, nobody carries £100 in small notes in the ordinary way. It makes too big a packet. Fives are more likely, or notes of even bigger value."

"But one-pound notes are practically untraceable," interjected the Chief Constable. "I see your point."

"Therefore," Wendover continued, "he must have got that £100 from someone in return for something."

"And the someone is your neighbour Druce Carfax, apparently, since Cumberland has traced the 'God Send You Back to Me' note to him. And so the local aristocracy are going to get shown up, in the person of Druce Carfax. Hence your perturbation, Squire. You don't like the idea. Neither do I, but there it is, and I have my salary to earn. People shouldn't do these things if they don't like the consequences."

"Perhaps he gave the note to someone else—the man who handed it on to Huggin," suggested Wendover feebly.

"Possibly. But don't forget that Walton saw 'a big fellow' in the dusk, making towards the hoarding as he himself was coming up the lane. Your friend Carfax is 'a big fellow,' isn't he?"

"You might call him so," admitted Wendover.

"Then if Druce Carfax uses McLaughlin's De Luxe paper matches, it will be fairly clear that he met Huggin at the hoarding."

"I suppose so," Wendover conceded reluctantly.

"You need cheering up, evidently," said the Chief Constable in a lighter tone. "Suppose we look at another side of the matter for a change. Take the defence which could be put up. First of all, meeting Huggin isn't in itself a crime."

"Of course not," Wendover agreed, looking rather puzzled at Sir Clinton's change of front.

"And paying money to Huggin isn't a criminal act?"

"No, I don't suppose it's criminal to be blackmailed."

"How do you know it was blackmail, Squire? What's your proof?"

Wendover pondered for some moments, his face gradually brightening as he did so.

"There isn't any *proof*, I admit," he confessed finally. "But it looks damned fishy, doesn't it?"

"A smart lawyer would make short work' of that in court," said Sir Clinton. "First, he'd want to know what proof we have that Druce Carfax was ever blackmailed. There isn't any. Then, no doubt, he'd cook up some other explanation for the transfer of that money. I could suggest a dozen myself, if I were put to it. So that line would count for very little. I don't say it isn't true. It may be, for all I know yet. But it can't be established in the witness box."

"But it could be used to prejudice a jury against Carfax, all the same," objected Wendover.

"That's the jury's affair, not mine," replied the Chief Constable. "But there's a more troublesome point in the background."

"What's that?"

"No one we've come across yet can testify to the firing of the shot that killed Huggin. Oulton didn't hear it. Walton didn't hear it. The keeper would have been on the spot as quick as he could get there, if he'd heard it; for he'd have mistaken it for poachers shooting. And yet the keeper never appeared. What do you make of that, Squire?"

"The pistol must have had a silencer on it, obviously."

"Which means, if you use that argument, that you've got to establish Carfax's possession of a pistol *and* a silencer. I grant you he may have a pistol. Plenty of people seem to have them as antiburglar equipment and for other reasons. But a silencer is rather different. How would you go about buying a silencer yourself, Squire, if you wanted one?"

"I suppose I'd go to a gunsmith's and order one," said Wendover rather reluctantly as he saw where he was being led.

"So as to leave a nice little trail? An excellent idea. Silencers are not articles in common demand, Squire. Any gunsmith would prick up his ears if you asked for one; and he'd have some little difficulty in supplying you with one, I suspect."

"You haven't tried to follow up that line yet," Wendover asserted. "So your 'nice little trail' hasn't been much use to you."

"Oh, yes, we have," replied the Chief Constable swiftly. "Purely as a matter of form, we've started inquiries. But I doubt if we'll hear anything."

"Well, then, a handy man can make a silencer of sorts without going near a gunsmith," Wendover pointed out as an alternative to his first suggestion.

"It's been done, as we know," admitted Sir Clinton. "But it would take a handy man to make the thing. Is your friend Carfax a skilled metal worker?"

"Not that I know of," confessed Wendover. "I never heard of his being anything of the sort."

"So there's not much support for the home-made silencer notion. Then, again, Squire, there's an alternative suspect who could be dragged across the trail by a smart lawyer."

"Walton, you mean?"

"Walton would be an awkward witness for the Crown. Remember that he's admitted robbing the body and he's the only link connecting Huggin with the actual round sum of £100. All we found on Huggin's body was £17-14-7. Suppose a smart barrister got hold of Walton in the witness box, wouldn't it be fairly easy for him to give the jury the impression that Walton was really the man responsible for the whole affair? In that case, provided that Carfax could cook up some fairly plausible tale about why he paid the money over to Huggin, he would be fairly safe."

"I'm not so sure about that," declared Wendover in a tone of doubt mingled with growing relief.

"Very well, I'll reconstruct the crime for you, without prejudice of course."

"Meaning that you don't believe in your solution?"

"I'm putting myself in the position of a barrister who has to get Carfax off, that's all. He begins by admitting a meeting between Carfax and Huggin quite frankly. And he produces some good solid-looking reason why Carfax should pay Huggin £100, on that occasion. He also produces an equally plausible reason why Carfax went to Leisurely Lane to meet Huggin, instead of having Huggin calling on him at his house. That's a point which seems to have escaped you, Squire. Our barrister then suggests that there was present at that meeting, though in hiding and unknown to the two others, a third party. Call him Mr. A. Mr. A. sees the transfer of a fat wad of notes from Carfax to Huggin and sees Huggin pocket it. Remember that screen of bushes and undergrowth at the side of the lane opposite the hoarding? It would give perfect cover."

"But why should anyone be in hiding there?" demanded Wendover.

"Well, he might be a poacher bringing a brace of pheasants down the lane. Hearing steps approaching, he'd naturally efface himself. Or he might be a Peeping Tom or something of that sort. It's not hard to find a tale to fit the case."

"Go on," said Wendover, with increasing relief as he saw the trend of suspicion leaving his fellow landowner.

"There's nothing much left to suggest. Carfax parts from Huggin and goes off home. Mr. A. then does Huggin in, for the sake of the cash. After that, he conceals some of his plunder and when he has done so, Cumberland arrives on the scene. And there you are."

"It has a kind of plausibility," admitted Wendover, "but do you think it would stand testing?"

"A smart barrister wouldn't risk it coming to a test. He'd introduce it into his speech purely as an hypothesis to account for some of the evidence. All he would want from it would be something to shake the jury. 'Can you risk condemning a man to death when this possibility exists?' Juries aren't bloody-minded ogres, you know, Squire. Give them a grain of doubt, and they shy at a conviction. And quite right, too. Judicial mistakes do occur. Men have been hanged for the murder of people who turned up all alive and kicking when it was too late to help the prisoners. A smart barrister would be careful to recall these cases."

"I suppose you're right there," Wendover confessed. "I can't say I yearn to serve on a jury in a murder case myself, unless it was an absolutely lock-fast affair."

"And now there's another point which a smart barrister would fasten upon for the defence," Sir Clinton continued. "Take that alternative hypothesis I gave you. It provides a perfectly sound motive for murder, assuming that Mr. A. is a person to whom £100 is a lot of money. You wouldn't think it a fair price for the risk of a murder, but murder's been done in the past at very cheap rates, as you well know. There was Dickman, who shot a man in a railway carriage on the chance of making about £300 off it. Milsom and Fowler got about £100. Burke and Hare murdered several people for the sake of the tenner they got per corpse from the anatomists. All that Muller secured was a watch valued at £3-10-0. Lefroy murdered the first prosperous-looking man he came across in the train; and he made such a bad choice that he got only a few shillings for his trouble. As these things go, £100 seems quite good payment. It must seem quite a tidy sum to Walton, for instance."

"That's admitted," Wendover confirmed. "I remember one case where all the murderer got was a gun-metal watch."

"Now take the Carfax defence from this point of view," Sir Clinton continued. "Where's the motive? We haven't come across any at all, so far. That's the irritating thing about the whole affair. In spite of a couple of days' work, Huggin's not much more than a name to us, so far as real information about him goes. How did he come in touch with Carfax at all? I don't know, and I don't suppose Carfax is likely to give us much useful information on the subject now that Huggin's mouth is effectively shut. You look wise and say, 'Blackmail.' But blackmail doesn't cover the ground, or anything like it. It merely brings in fresh bits that won't fit into the jigsaw."

"I don't see that," objected Wendover. "It gives you a motive, and that's what you're crying for, isn't it?"

"Very well, then, Squire. Let's assume that Huggin was blackmailing Carfax. First of all, we can't guess—I can't, at any rate—what the basis of the blackmail was. Second, if Carfax paid over that hundred pounds in notes to Huggin and then did Huggin in, why in the name of all that's sensible didn't he go through Huggin's pockets and remove the notes? Why leave them there to form the basis of all this scaffolding we're setting up now? They were the only things that could prove a direct connection between Carfax and Huggin. Anyone above the intellectual level of a cretin would have grabbed them from Huggin's pocket before clearing out. Better still, he need never have made the actual payment at all, if he meant to kill Huggin. There was no point in paying the man and then murdering him."

"Unless it was done to put Huggin completely off his guard," suggested Wendover. "That's always a possibility."

"In that case, why not have removed the notes from the body? And if the notes were to be left on the body, why did Carfax go to his bank and draw these notes *en bloc,* as he seems to have done? According to Cumberland's wire, he simply presented a £100 cheque and took the money in pound notes and ten-shilling ones. That in itself, as a preliminary to a murder, is little less than insane, if the notes were to be left on the body."

"Perhaps he was disturbed before he could get them out of Huggin's pocket."

"The evidence is all against that. Who was there to disturb him?"

Wendover considered this point carefully before answering.

"Well, here's a possibility. I don't say it's more than that. But suppose Carfax was blackmailed twice over: once by Huggin and then, after the murder, by Walton *who'd seen the murder done?* Assume that Walton, coming down with his pheasants, heard the voices of two men on the path ahead of him. He'd slip off the lane and hide. Suppose he actually saw the murder done and then came out and made an offer to keep his mouth shut in return for the money. Wouldn't Carfax pay? Of course he would."

"And wouldn't Walton have taken the round £100, in that case? Of course he would. He wouldn't have left anything on the body and neither would Carfax. No, that brilliant idea won't work, Squire. Not from what we know of Walton's character. I don't say he wouldn't be capable of blackmail—he's just the sort for it—but he'd have pouched the round sum. And Carfax would have seen to it that he did, too, if he'd the glimmerings of intelligence. It won't fit."

"It was too complicated, anyhow," confessed Wendover frankly. "I see that, once the first flush of creation's over. But to get back to the roots of things, are you sure that blackmail comes into it at all?"

"Morally certain of it," said the Chief Constable. "You remember I went over Huggin's bank passbook? All the entries we came across on the paying-in side were cheques—bar one. 'By cash, £65' appeared on 5th May of this year. Now where would a man like Huggin, making his income by writing, get £65 in cash to pay into his bank? All his intake would be in the form of cheques from his agent, in the natural course of things. That £65 couldn't come from the literary side. And from what one heard of Huggin's general condition, he hadn't a single asset that he could have sold for £65 cash. It's no certainty, but it seems most likely that this £65 was the unspent balance of another £100 cash contribution from Carfax, so that the £100 Huggin received the other night was the second payment within four months or so. Now if that was hush money, it was on a pretty fair scale, for you can bet that a successful blackmailer wouldn't stop after four months. He'd have come again, a month or two later. And if Carfax was prepared to pay £200, with the probability of having to go on paying—"

"There must have been something pretty black that he was hiding," completed Wendover in a gloomy tone. "I see your point."

"Something of the sort," confirmed Sir Clinton. "But it's beyond me to put a name to it. How could Huggin, living the life he did, have come in contact with Carfax at all? And, to judge from what you've told me of Carfax, he doesn't seem quite the man to be carried off his feet easily. If your character sketch was right, Squire, I'd have expected him to thrash a blackmailer within an inch of his life and then tell him to do his worst. He'd have been fairly safe if he'd taken that line. He could have split to us, without risking much, for you know we can always keep a victim's name out of the papers nowadays. And Huggin would have gone to gaol for a cert. if we'd got our hands into the business."

"That explains one thing, perhaps," said Wendover hastily. "I never thought of it before. Why did they meet at that hoarding and not in Carfax's house? Because Huggin was afraid of a trap, with some of your subordinates behind a screen taking down what was said. Out there, it was fairly safe. He could have a look round before Carfax arrived and make sure that no one was lurking about in earshot. And he could walk up and down the lane while he talked to Carfax and so make it hard for any eavesdropper to get the whole of the talk consecutively. Funny I never thought of that before."

"There's a good deal in that," admitted the Chief Constable. "If blackmail comes into it, you seem to have hit the mark there, Squire, beyond a doubt. And if Carfax did Huggin in, it was Huggin who played into his hands by that arrangement."

"Another thing," Wendover continued. "If Carfax did murder Huggin, it must have been done on the spur of the moment. Otherwise he would have been more careful in the matter of these notes. He could easily have drawn some tens and twenties and changed them in paying accounts and buying odds and ends in London, say, getting pound notes as change and so leaving no trace. He'd have been sure to think of that, if the thing had been pre-planned. The notes on the body fit nothing but a crime carried out on a sudden impulse."

"It certainly looks like it," Sir Clinton admitted, "but then most murderers are fools. So you can't argue that because a man makes an obvious slip, therefore he isn't a murderer. But I don't mind admitting that your portrait of Carfax gave me the impression of a headstrong fellow who might very well act impulsively and do a stupid thing on the spur of the moment. You didn't lay great stress on his intelligence, so far as my recollection goes."

"What's your next move to be?" inquired Wendover.

"We shall have to go into this business of the £100 drawn from the bank; and the only person who can tell us about that—I mean what happened to it eventually—is Carfax, obviously. But you were asking what my next move is to be. As it's near train time, I think it had better be to the station. Come along."

# CHAPTER X
## DRUCE CARFAX'S STATEMENT

"I'M A SHADE DOUBTFUL about the best line to take this morning," Sir Clinton explained to Wendover after breakfast at the Grange. "Druce Carfax will have to be interviewed, obviously. Now if I send the inspector to do it, that'll look official in the extreme."

"It will," agreed Wendover, dryly. "Cumberland will go with his notebook and an air of 'whatever you say will be taken down and used in evidence; please sign these notes on the dotted line.' And knowing Carfax as I do, I expect your inspector will get very little except a good view of the outside of the front door as he leaves the premises. No, Clinton, you'll have to think of something better than that."

"Well, I bow to your local knowledge," said the Chief Constable. "Suppose I go and see Carfax myself. That injects a certain amount of courtesy into the officialism. The big bug of the police approaching the big bug of the countryside on more or less equal terms, eh? Still, it would look damnably formal, wouldn't it? And the less official we are on the surface, the more likely we are to get on happily with Master Carfax, unless you've misled me, Squire."

"I see your trend," admitted Wendover still more dryly. "You're going to propose me as your chaperon. Or, rather, I'm to act as your anaesthetist while you extract a truth or two from Carfax. You want a sort of semiofficial, semi-social function in the hope that he'll be off his guard a bit? Amen, so be it. I go as your social sponsor, introduce you to him, and supply the tact at the awkward places?"

"That was my idea," confessed Sir Clinton. "It seems the only method that's likely to yield any results at all."

Wendover was secretly delighted with the project, since it would give him further chances of seeing the case develop under his own eyes.

"Then suppose I ring him up now?" he suggested. "You don't want to speak to Cumberland again, do you? I heard you talking over the wire to him before breakfast. If we wait any longer, Carfax may be out, you know."

"Go ahead, then," Sir Clinton agreed. "And give him the impression, if you can, that I'm calling on him purely as a matter of form. Say it's to ask him about maps of his estate which we might use for evidence in court or some stuff of that kind. No, you'd better find some other excuse, for he might refer us to the Ordnance map and ring off. Let's see . . . Oh, tell him I want to consult him about Walton's poaching. That ought to fetch him."

"Sound idea," Wendover approved. "I'll take that line." In a few minutes he came back with the invitation he had angled for rather skillfully.

"Carfax is at home," he announced, "and I'm to trundle you round now. Ready?"

It did not take long to reach the gates of Carfax Park. As they drove up the avenue, Sir Clinton studied the lie of the land. The nearer park was rolling country and presented nothing to catch the eye except a couple of red flags which apparently marked holes on a small private links. The roof of a wooden hut, possibly a golf shelter, appeared above a green slope which concealed the rest of the structure. And beyond it, in the distance, half a mile or more away, the ugly hoarding on Leisurely Lane made a blot on the landscape.

They were shown into a morning-room where Druce Carfax awaited them. At first sight, Sir Clinton was struck by the aptness of Wendover's simile of a bull in a bad temper. Druce Carfax had something of bovine mass and clumsiness in his appearance, and in his rather protruding eyes were signs of that quick-kindling irritability which marks the savage type of bull. He wasted no time in courtesy, barely acknowledging Wendover's introductory phrase.

"Want to see me about this poaching?" he demanded. "Damnable, isn't it? Snaring pheasants in the close season. Be none left when the shooting begins, at this rate. If I could lay my hands on one of these swine, I'd give him a lesson he wouldn't forget."

The tint of his red face deepened as he spoke, and it was clear that he was lashing himself into a passion over his grievances. Sir Clinton intervened rapidly.

"Mr. Wendover agrees with you, I'm sure," he said. "It's a thing we want to put down. How many keepers have you?"

"One," said Druce Carfax crossly. "How many do you expect me to keep, on a place this size?"

"We might be able to lend you a constable, or perhaps a couple, when there's any likelihood of trouble. Of course, you'd need to let us know beforehand. Your keeper must have some notion of when they'd be most useful. On some nights, I take it, you're fairly safe from disturbances."

"Fat lot of good that would be," Druce Carfax commented, in an ungracious tone. "D'you think I want a lot of flat-footed policemen stamping all over my place, disturbing every pheasant on the place? Why, yesterday I caught them in the middle of a regular corroboree down Leisurely Lane. Letting off toy pistols, so please you, on my ground. Frightening every bird in the neighbourhood. I soon kicked them out."

"I'm sorry you've been troubled," Sir Clinton hastened to apologise. "It shan't occur again."

"I should hope not! I'd as soon have poachers about as see your bobbies prowling round the place. They're quieter, for one thing. I suppose it's this Huggin affair they're excited about?"

"Yes," said the Chief Constable. "That's a nasty business. I had to go up to town yesterday in connection with it, to look through Huggin's papers."

Wendover, with his eyes on Druce Carfax's face, saw a sudden change in its expression. The pugnacity died out and a calculating look replaced it, as though Sir Clinton's remark had given Druce a problem which must be thought out swiftly. He nodded, pondered for some moments, and when he spoke again it was in a far less aggressive tone.

"Find anything useful?" he inquired with an unsuccessful effort to pretend indifference.

"Oh, one or two things," answered Sir Clinton, cryptically. "I think you could help us with a couple of pointers. He came down here to meet you, didn't he?"

Wendover could almost see the furious calculation going on in Druce Carfax's brain. The police had been through Huggin's papers, had they? What had they found there? And if they had found anything how much had they guessed from it? How far would it be safe to bluff and where would it pay to be frank? These were evidently some of the questions which were racing through Druce Carfax's mind while he hesitated before speaking again.

"Yes," he admitted reluctantly, "he came down here to see me, as you say."

"On business of some sort?"

"Yes—on business, of course."

And here Wendover realised, with some relief, that Druce Carfax had a story to tell. Once he started, there was no further hesitation.

"This is the way it was," he went on. "We're a pretty old family in this neighbourhood. Wendover here can tell you that. And we've always had some family pride. After all, there's something in being able to say who your seventh ancestor was and to know that he held the same ground as you do. I dare say John Smith has as long a family tree as I have. But it's not the same kind of tree. You see what I mean?"

"I see what you mean," Sir Clinton admitted with an irony so faint that it escaped Carfax completely.

"Well, naturally," Druce Carfax continued, "one would like to see some permanent record made. As time goes on, it's likely some things slip out of memory. More difficult to track down the facts. Something of the sort was in my father's mind, but he let it slide. Was always going to get it started, but never screwed himself up to make a move, you know. So when it came to my turn, I thought I'd

better not put off any more time. I'd leave something behind me
that would let my successors know who they were and where they
came from."

"A family history?"

"Just so. But a thing of that sort needs an expert to do it. I'm
no hand with a pen, never was. I've sense enough to know I'd make
no fist at the thing. Besides, my time's valuable. Cheaper to hire
one of these writing fellows and tell him what I wanted done. So I
got hold of Huggin. He agreed to do the business for me."

Druce Carfax paused and looked sharply at the Chief Constable's face as though he expected to read something in its expression at this point. Then he continued in a more assured tone.

"I got him down here to talk the matter over. I'd some ideas of
my own, about how it should be written. Since I was paying the
piper, naturally I wanted the thing done according to my ideas."

"Naturally," confirmed Sir Clinton.

"Huggin agreed, of course. So that was that. We didn't settle
details at the time. He was busy with some other stuff he'd con-
tracted to write. I was in no hurry."

"And you arranged all this when you met him in Leisurely Lane
on Monday night?" asked the Chief Constable.

Wendover saw a gleam of acute suspicion in Druce Carfax's eyes
as the question was put.

"No, no. All that was fixed up earlier," he explained after a full five
seconds' pause. "On Monday night I just mentioned one or two points
that had occurred to me lately. That took only a minute or two."

"You didn't think of writing to him about them, instead of bringing him down here specially?"

"I'm no hand with a pen," said Druce Carfax sullenly. "Hate
writing, even business letters. Besides, why shouldn't he come
down here? He was my dog, wasn't he? I was paying him for his
trouble. Why should I run after him?"

"That's true," Sir Clinton admitted. "So you made an appointment with him. Why didn't you tell him to come here?"

"To the house?" asked Carfax. "Well, you've seen Huggin.
Needy-looking fellow. Not quite out at the elbows, but a bit shiny

at the corners. My sister had a friend to dinner that night. Naturally I didn't want Huggin hanging about the premises. Not the sort you'd care to have your friends running into. Wendover will understand what I mean," he added, as though Sir Clinton could not be expected to appreciate the finer feelings of the landed gentry.

"So you met him in Leisurely Lane. Did you notice anyone else in the neighbourhood at the time?"

Druce Carfax gave this question even more than his usual consideration. At last he shook his head doubtfully.

"I can't remember anyone," he admitted finally. "Wasn't paying much attention to that, you know. Busy thinking what I was going to say to Huggin when I met him. Besides, it was dusk, then. Not much chance of noticing anyone unless one was on the lookout. There may have been other people about, for all I can say. I didn't notice anyone, that's all."

"That's what our other witnesses said," Sir Clinton said, as though lending support to Carfax's statement. "It's a nuisance. No one seems to have seen anybody, and yet there were four people on the ground in addition to Huggin. By the way, when did you leave Huggin?"

Druce Carfax shook his head again.

"Now you're asking," he replied. "About ten o'clock, I'd say. But that's no better than a guess. It was round about then, though."

He seemed to have recovered from his momentary discomfiture and he gave his estimate with apparent confidence.

"One of our witnesses complained that he didn't run about with his eye on his watch all day long," Sir Clinton volunteered, with a smile. "I quite understand your difficulty. Round about ten o'clock, then. By the way, do you mind if I smoke a cigarette? I'm ashamed to say that I'm rather a slave to the habit."

Druce Carfax pulled out his case, but Sir Clinton already had his own in his hand. Then, with a look of annoyance, he felt in his pocket unavailingly.

"I'm afraid I'll have to trouble you for a match," he said apologetically.

Wendover's hand went to his own pocket but came away empty as an idea crossed his mind. Carfax produced a carton of paper matches and the Chief Constable lit his cigarette and passed the stub back to his host. He retained the used match in his hand for a moment, and when Wendover looked again, it had vanished. But as the carton passed from hand to hand, the Squire had seen the lettering on the outside: "McLaughlin's De Luxe." So the paper matches beside Huggin's body came from Druce Carfax's supply and there was no reason to look for an extra man outside the list already known.

"Apart from this literary business, did you know anything about Huggin personally?" Sir Clinton pursued. "We've had difficulty in finding out much, so far. Anything might help. How did you get in touch with him at the start?"

Druce Carfax did not reply for several seconds. When he did so, it was with a puzzled air, which Wendover surmised to be pretence.

"Funny I can't remember who it was that recommended him to me. Might have been Lauriston. . . . No, it wasn't he. . . . Somebody gave me his name, I know. . . . Parfitt, perhaps. . . . No, not Parfitt. . . . I'm damned if I can remember exactly who it was. . . . But someone told me he was a likely fellow for the job, I know. It'll come back to me by and by, probably."

"Well, never mind that. Can you tell us anything about him that might be useful?"

Druce Carfax made a hopeless gesture.

"I barely came across the fellow," he explained, candidly enough. "I wasn't interested in his joys and sorrows. He was hard up. But anyone could see that by looking at him."

"In the matter of this book," Sir Clinton went on. "Did you make a definite agreement with him? In writing, I mean."

"Not I," Carfax replied. "Why should I?"

"Well, if you made no agreement, the copyright in it would be his and you'd have no control over it. Seeing that it was to be a history of your family, that might have caused difficulties."

"I hadn't thought of that," Carfax admitted. "I know precious little about books."

"When did you arrange to meet him on Monday night?"

"Oh, about 9:30 or thereabouts."

"By the way, how did you make the arrangement?"

This question evidently took Druce Carfax completely aback. Wendover could see that he had no answer ready and was unable to invent one on the spur of the moment. After a second or two, he took refuge in a display of anger which was only partly feigned.

"What the hell's that to you?" he demanded. "D'you think I've nothing better to do than answer all sorts of prying questions about my private affairs?"

Sir Clinton looked at the red, angry face in front of him with the cool scrutiny of a fencer waiting for an opponent's mistake.

"There are no private affairs when it comes to a murder case," he pointed out incisively, "especially for people who may come under suspicion."

This last phrase seemed to stagger Druce Carfax.

"Do you mean me?" he demanded, with a sudden fail in his truculence. "Why, damn it, man, you must be mad. The notion's absurd! Why should I—"

Then, in mid-sentence, he pulled up as though he had seen something which had not occurred to him before.

"I'll just point out how you stand, Mr. Carfax," the Chief Constable explained in a chilly tone. "You met Huggin by appointment at 9:30 on Monday night. He was found murdered shortly after ten o'clock. I don't say you murdered him. But in the circumstances, you can see for yourself how advisable it is for you to give us all the information you can. If you aren't frank well, we shall have to draw conclusions which might not suit you. Now, I've asked you a plain question, and I don't see why you shouldn't answer it. How did you make this appointment with Huggin?"

With a manifest effort, Druce Carfax pulled himself together. The red of his complexion had grown mottled, as though the blood had ebbed from the surface while still flowing in the tracery of capillaries.

"Oh, if you think it's important, I don't mind telling you," he replied huskily. "He rang me up—I mean, I rang him up and made the appointment."

"Have you a London directory here?"

"No," Carfax admitted, after a momentary pause. "I rang up London and they looked up his number for me."

"The local office will have a record of that trunk call, of course," Sir Clinton commented, as though he attached little importance to the point.

Druce Carfax seemed to have trouble with his saliva. He gulped twice before he could get out his next sentence. "I suppose they will."

"We shall have to check that, of course, merely as a matter of form," explained the Chief Constable. "Now, another point. You had come to a verbal agreement with Huggin about this family history. Did you pay him a retaining fee?"

Carfax was evidently fighting for time to consider this question.

"A retaining fee? What d'you mean, exactly?" he asked.

"I'll put it plainer. Did you pay Huggin any money when you met him on Monday night? Now be careful what you say."

The last sentence came out so sharply that Carfax started. He had apparently meant to lie, but thought better of it at the last moment.

"Yes, I paid him something in advance," he admitted finally. "A hundred pounds. He said he was hard up."

Sir Clinton's face lost its hardness and became almost genial. He raised his eyebrows slightly as if surprised at this method of doing business.

"And you'd no hard-and-fast agreement?" he queried. "Very generous on your part. A good many people would be eager to do business with you, Mr. Carfax, if they heard about that. You won't see your money again. Huggin's assets don't amount to much, we found. I hope that was the only payment you made to him. Was it?"

Again the last phrase had a minatory twang, and Druce Carfax winced as he heard it.

"I'd paid him £100 before that," he admitted sullenly.

"Phew! £200 in advance? And you'd made no written contract with him and he hasn't written a line of this family history yet! I'm afraid you'll have to write off that £200 as a bad debt. By the way, when did you make this other payment?"

"About the end of March or the beginning of April," Carfax confessed. "I could tell you the exact date by the counterfoil in my chequebook."

"You paid him by cheque?"

"No, in cash," Carfax corrected. "He asked for it in cash. Don't know why."

Sir Clinton considered for a moment before putting his next question.

"So you met him in March or April. Was that your first meeting with him?"

"Yes."

"Down here? In this house?"

"Yes. He came down to talk over the affair with me then."

"How much did he ask for doing the work?"

"Four—no, five hundred pounds."

"Was there any talk about an arrangement with a publisher? Had you fixed on one?"

"No, he didn't raise that. And I never thought about it. I know nothing about books."

"By the way, you got a receipt each time, of course?"

Carfax shook his head.

"You're singularly confident," commented Sir Clinton rather contemptuously. "Now, another point. Have you any revolvers or pistols on the premises?"

Carfax shook his head decidedly.

"Not that I know of," he said with a frankness which contrasted with his earlier tone.

"So I supposed," Sir Clinton said. "I asked that merely as a matter of form. Now, let's get back to the affairs of Monday night. How did you go when you went to meet Huggin?"

"Across the fields, direct," Carfax answered promptly, with a gesture to indicate the line he had taken.

"And you saw no one?"

"Nobody that I noticed, until I met the man."

"You discussed this affair of the family history with him, you say. How long did that take?"

"Oh, only a few minutes," Carfax replied, with a certain eagerness.

"And yet you brought him all the way down from town for that?"

"It seemed worth while," Carfax declared rather hesitatingly.

"Were you smoking when you met him?"

Carfax reflected for a moment or two.

"I lit a cigarette while I was talking to him. He was smoking a pipe, I think."

"When you left him, what road did you take?"

"I came straight back here, over the fields, the way I'd gone to meet him."

"Did you hear anything unusual on your way back?"

Carfax shook his head quite decidedly.

"Nothing at all unusual. I didn't hear the shot, if that's what you mean."

"You didn't hear a girl screaming?"

"No, nothing of that kind."

Sir Clinton rose to his feet, and Wendover could see a flood of relief come into Carfax's expression at this sign that the interview had reached its end. It passed as swiftly as it came, however, when Sir Clinton gave a final warning:

"Jog your memory a little, Mr. Carfax. I think you'll find more in it than you've told us. Just think over that."

All the original bluster had gone out of Carfax and Wendover saw that he looked both perplexed and apprehensive as he led them to the door. At one point he hesitated, as though he wished to say something; but immediately some counterforce stifled the impulse to frankness and he moved on again. Wendover could see that the Chief Constable had frightened him and yet, apparently, something frightened him still more and kept his mouth shut.

It was plain that he feared Sir Clinton knew more than he had admitted and that there might be something damaging still in reserve. His misgivings had been evident when he learned that the police had gone through Huggin's papers. What had he feared they would find amongst them? By this time, Wendover had not the slightest doubt about Huggin being a blackmailer; and it seemed manifest that Druce Carfax was in terror lest an examination of Huggin's effects had brought to light the basis of the blackmail. It must have been something serious if it had cost £200 in three months to keep it hushed up. Besides, as Wendover knew, initial payments of blackmail were mere flea bites compared with the demands which came later, once the victim was well entrapped. It would probably be thousands, instead of hundreds, by and by.

When they reached the front door, Wendover noticed an empty Wolseley standing on the gravel sweep beside his own car. It barely caught his attention. He was more interested in getting away, now, so that he might learn what the Chief Constable thought of these latest developments in the Huggin case.

"Well, what did you make of him?" he demanded, as they drove down the avenue.

"He's a poor liar," was Sir Clinton's estimate. "But whether that's due to want of practice or lack of brains, I can't say. Both, perhaps. I wish he hadn't been so free with his fairy tales. He's given us a lot of points to check. And that will have to be done, worse luck, even though we know the answers already."

"I can guess some of them, but give me the list."

"First of all, we'll need to find out if Huggin actually did come down here in March or April. Then we'll need to see if Carfax drew a £100 cheque about that date and took cash for it to pay Huggin his first £100. Then we'll have to check that tale about his trunk call to Huggin, though it's plain enough that his story was a lie."

"Noticed he fumbled a bit there," Wendover agreed. "First he said Huggin rang him up. Then he corrected himself and said he rang up Huggin."

"Where he bungled was in saying he got Huggin's number from the London exchange. Huggin had no telephone. It was in the house at Rookery Park under Fairbank's name, and the exchange couldn't have known that if Carfax asked for Huggin's number."

"But Huggin might have given Carfax the number," Wendover objected.

"Then Carfax wouldn't need to ask the exchange to look it up," retorted the Chief Constable. "No, Squire, Carfax blurted out the truth in the first instance when he said that Huggin rang him up to make that appointment on Monday."

He reflected for a moment and then turned to Wendover with a question.

"Did you swallow Carfax's tale about his family history?"

"You never know what antic idea a man may get into his head," Wendover replied cautiously. "But a family history of the Carfaxes would beat chloral as a soporific. Why, Clinton, they've lived on that estate for generations and not one of them, so far as I know, has ever managed to make their name known outside a radius of fifty miles from Carfax Park. They've existed, that's all. A family history of them would read like the generations of the sons of Noah in the book of Genesis: 'And Eber lived four and thirty years, and begat Peleg . . . and Peleg lived thirty years and begat Reu' . . . and so on. Not one of these Carfaxes so much as got into Parliament, in spite of their chances. Family pride can do a lot, but it can't make bricks without straw. There's nothing to write about."

"I had a suspicion of that," Sir Clinton concurred. "You've given me a good deal of the county's history at one time or another, and I never heard you mention the Carfaxes till this case came on. But here's a rum point. Carfax's transactions with Huggin were both cash ones. No cheques taken. On that showing, why did Huggin give his name to Carfax at all? If it was a black-mailing business, he'd have been better to sail under false colours or else remain anonymous. And yet Carfax knew something about him. He knew he was a literary hack, at any rate, or he wouldn't have had this family-history tale all ready for us. Curious, isn't it?"

"I suppose Huggin must have been a fool," declared Wendover. "It's a common enough characteristic."

"No," said the Chief Constable doubtfully. "I'm not so sure that Huggin was as big a fool as all that. He seems to have run his show fairly well, for an amateur, if you ask me. It's not so easy to go in for blackmail nowadays and get away with it. The Court and the Press are quite ready to suppress the prosecutor's name, so he doesn't suffer, in the ordinary way. Whatever it was that Huggin got hold of, it must have been something out of the common, something that meant more to Carfax than the normal basis of blackmail. Something that he *daren't* allow to come out. And that being so, it's no good thinking of worming it out of him directly."

# CHAPTER XI
## TATTLE AT THE BARLEYCORN

"YOU HAVEN'T SHAKEN OFF your young friend with the tame octopus yet," Wendover announced with a smile as he replaced the telephone receiver. "He's come down to see things for himself, he says. Apparently you're one of the things; for he rang up to say he'd be here in a minute or two, and he asked specially if you were on the premises. He's put up at the Talgarth Arms, it seems."

"I wish he'd stay there," growled the Chief Constable inhospitably. "He seems to think murder's amusing. Written so much fancy stuff about it that his perspective's all askew, I suppose. I'm not in the mood for this funny-dog business at the moment."

"Huggin's affair seems to be hanging fire," reflected Wendover aloud, with a certain lack of tact. "You don't seem to be making much progress."

"You can't put a jigsaw together properly when half the pieces are missing," retorted Sir Clinton restively. "This Huggin business seems to be all blank ends. A fine field for speculation with no facts to speak of. It's irritating."

"Somebody must be more worried than you are," Wendover pointed out cheerfully.

"The murderer, you mean? One can't even be sure of that. Some murderers have no moral feelings."

"Sounds like a paradox, that," said Wendover. "I shan't think it out at the moment."

In a few minutes, Denzil was ushered in, evidently in the best of spirits.

151

"And what have you been doing with yourself, Bob?" inquired Sir Clinton after they had greeted the newcomer.

"Me? Let's see. Well, one can't beat Caesar for conciseness. *Veni, vidi, vici.*"

"Construe and paraphrase. Perhaps it'll make sense, then," the Chief Constable suggested.

"Oh, certainly. (I'll have a cigarette, thanks.) *Veni,* I came down in my car. *Vidi,* I had a look round. *Vici,* I won all hearts. Amplification of foregoing. I've been elected one of the lads of the village. Special medal with crossed tobacco pipes and pot of beer on the reverse. I've heard the whole truth—and a bit more—about Huggin's demise. I've tapped gossip at the fountainhead at the local pubs. And I've wormed my way into the confidence of the Carfax family—or the best-looking member of it, anyhow. Not bad going for a mere matter of twenty-four hours. In fact, despite your long start, I'm level with you already, alguazil. You don't know who the murderer is; neither do I: so we're neck and neck. When the moment comes, I shall tread on the gas and rush home, an easy winner."

"More than ten capital I's in that short piece," commented Sir Clinton. "Are there any other characters in the story?"

"Heaps. I know you're dying to hear all about it. Wouldn't be human if you weren't. I won't keep you in suspense. I arrived last night at the Talgarth Arms. Decent little pub. I dined there. No good for my characters, though. No ortolans on toast or peacocks' tongues. Plain mutton. Trimalchio would have found it dull. In view of my plans for the evening, I didn't draw on the cellar; but I found they stocked some cigars at one-and-ninepence the half dozen."

"Did they call them cigars?" demanded Wendover ironically.

"No. They're quite honest. The barmaid called them 'smokes.' I can't speak of them from personal experience; but they were highly appreciated by the people I gave them to. They smoked 'em down to the band and were quite sorry to take it off when they came to it. It looked rather classy."

"And what happened after all this high living and plain thinking was over?" inquired the Chief Constable.

"I'd got my bearings from the waiter," Denzil explained. "A warm-hearted fellow, simply dripping with information. Told me all about both of you, but I spare your blushes. By his aid, I located the center of things; and after dallying with the cheese, I betook myself to The Barleycorn Inn in Abbots Norton."

"Care to have a voice lozenge?" asked Sir Clinton. "We seem to be leaving you to do all the talking."

"Don't trouble. I can go on for quite a while yet. To resume. To a man of my gifts, it was child's play to become the popular hero. I lost money at Darts until they thought they'd discovered a new Rand. That was where the cigars came in handy. Then I picked up a game of billiards with a retainer from Carfax Hall. I'm not clear yet whether he was a valet, a butler, or a chauffeur. A bit of all three, perhaps. He knew the roll of the Barleycorn table to a dot, anyhow. A perfect education to see him make a losing hazard with the ball running into the pocket along a curve like a blown kite string. A new game to me. Fascinating. And while he performed these wonders, he gave me all the gossip of Carfax Hall. Most entertaining."

"You must have felt quite at home," suggested Sir Clinton.

"They took me to their bosoms as long as I seemed to have a stiver left," said Denzil. "Then I chummed up with the oldest inhabitant who could still swallow beer. A pleasant old man with a tongue like a serpent's tooth. If he didn't know anything to the discredit of the local gentry, he was ready to draw on his imagination without stint. A most obliging old chap, really. And, as a beer-lapper, positively in a class by himself, so long as I paid."

"That would be Caleb Yerbury," interjected Wendover, with a wry grimace.

"We took such a liking to each other at first sight that we dispensed with introductions," Denzil explained. "But no doubt you're right. Anyhow, before we were turned out of that pub. I had the popular verdict sized up to an eyelash. 'Who did him in?' 'Druce Carfax, my Lord.' And loud applause from the gallery. They don't seem fond of Druce. In fact, if the jury's drawn from that push, there isn't a barrister in the Kingdom who could get him off. I hate to hurt your feelings, alguazil, but public feeling's much against you for not nipping off and arresting Druce as soon as the body was found. It was the least they expected, as rate-payers."

"I shan't lose sleep over it," Sir Clinton assured him unnecessarily. "Pray proceed with your most entertaining monologue."

"Delighted," Denzil assured him. "All that's by the way, preliminary to my thoughts and discoveries." He turned to Wendover. "I hope I'm treading on no corns. Are the Carfaxes bosom pals of yours?"

"I don't even drink with them in The Barleycorn," Wendover explained. "You can say what you please. And I shan't repeat it."

"Splendid! These Carfaxes occupied quite a stretch in your friend Caleb's reminiscences. He began with the late one, Gris—Gris—"

"Griswold?"

"That's the lad. Griswold Carfax. He seems to have been hot stuff in a quiet neighbourhood. Perhaps Caleb laid it on too thick, but I gather that Griswold raised two village scandals before he was twenty. One of the girls was Caleb's niece. Which perhaps accounts for his excessive interest in the Carfax family. Likewise his venom."

"I believe that's true enough," confirmed Wendover.

"Then there was a mistress, I gather. A woman Finborough. This is where I get the personal touch. I met her son this morning. . . . You seem surprised?"

"I didn't know he was back here again."

"He is. But he'll keep. At present I'm checking Gaffer Caleb with your kind help. Griswold gave his mistress the push and got married. Four children by his first wife. 'Fair wore 'er out wi' childbearin', pore thing; she 'adn't the 'ealth to stay that pace.' So Caleb assured me. Then he married again and had a son and a daughter—more about that daughter in the next thrilling instalment—before the second wife died also. And then, after earning social ostracism by taking back his ex-mistress, ''e got blowed up by one o' them Zepps in the War, an' a good thing too,' if I'm to believe

Mr. Yerbury. Well, a family of nine is good going, even if three of them came on the wrong side of the blanket. And, by Caleb's account, this fellow Griswold was as jealous of his wives as a whole syndicate of Pashas rolled into one. There was some yarn about his blacking somebody's eye at a flower show because the poor chap was polite to the first Mrs. Griswold."

"That's correct," Wendover corroborated. "He was always in trouble with that sort of thing."

"Caleb doesn't embroider as much as I thought," admitted Denzil. "But these mass-production families don't seem good articles for wearing purposes. One of the first lot was still-born and another died in infancy. That correct? And only the daughter survived in the second lot. That leaves Druce Carfax, his brother, and his half-sister still alive. Now we come to Druce, the present head of the clan. Unpopular fellow, I gather?"

"He's a damned bad landlord," interjected Wendover in explanation. "And spiteful, too."

"So Caleb assured me, at some length. Evictions, rights of way, trespassers will be prosecuted, general fussiness, and so forth. I spare you the details. Mr. Yerbury tells me that Druce has the devil's own family pride. Though what he finds to be proud of in the last generation is beyond me, entirely. Caleb says he's not a scandalous liver. And if Caleb draws blank in scandal, Druce Carfax must be a *chevalier sans reproche* in very sooth, I imagine. Rather strait-laced on that side, if anything."

"Oh, he's quite all right so far as *that* goes," Wendover confirmed.

"His brother's rather a poor creature, according to Mr. Yerbury. 'Anyone could steal the boots off him and he'd thank them for takin' the trouble to do it,' was my informant's judgment."

"He's got just enough to exist on and he never did a stroke of work in his life," said Wendover. "Out of courtesy they put him in the village cricket eleven—last man in. It's his only distinction."

"'About as much character as a hodmandod,' according to my esteemed informant. What is a hodmandod, anyway?"

"A snail," explained Wendover. "Caleb Yerbury wasn't far out there. Julian Carfax has about as much backbone as a slug. A born loafer, I must say, if ever there was one."

Denzil leaned over and helped himself to another cigarette.

"I just wanted to get things straight," he continued. "You have the advantage of me in past history. But now we come to the Stop Press Column and the latest tips from the stable. Attend, and learn from me. I got some of this from my friend the valet-chauffeur while he was robbing me on the Bump-the-Bumps, with a patronising air which I found insufferable. It appears that this week, Mr. Godfrey Finborough, Druce's half-brother on the wrong side of the blanket, has been infesting Carfax Hall. He and his half-sister get on well together. As thick as thieves, in fact."

"They were brought up together after Griswold took his old mistress back to the Hall."

"Indeed? Well, they're quite chummy, as I saw with these very eyes. But Druce Carfax differs. Perhaps he dislikes to see the blot on the scutcheon wandering about the premises and reminding folk of the bad old days. Anyhow, relations began as chilly and then got heated. In fact, there seems to have been hell's own racket between the two noble kinsmen. My Special Correspondent at the Front—I mean the keyhole—informed me that he heard Godfrey refer to his brother as 'a damned cuckoo.'"

"I've heard worse things said in anger," interjected Sir Clinton critically. "If that was the level of the conversation, they can hardly have been more than slightly vexed with each other, surely."

"Well, it may have been the tone rather than the actual words. Probably it was, for my valet-chauffeur shark spoke highly of his employer's general bad temper. Seemed to think he'd earned the Order of the Black Dog, with Monkey up, and three Tantrums on the ribbon. But let's brush these details aside. This exchange of compliments occurred yesterday, after dinner; and this morning Godfrey got his walking-ticket. Or so I suppose. He took his hook, at any rate. I have inside information, exclusive, on that point. But of that, anon."

"Pushed your valet friend off the keyhole and took his place, did you?" inquired the Chief Constable. "Well, it takes all sorts to make a world, they say."

"No. I wasn't even tempted to do it, alguazil. In fact, I wasn't invited into the house at all."

"Ah, that explains why you didn't. But if I may interrupt your reminiscences, Bob, I'll point out that you were supposed to be investigating the matter of Huggin's death. At the present rate of progress, you'll get the solution on Judgment Day, when it'll be common property."

"*Vox populi, vox dei*," replied Denzil. "The popular verdict is that Druce Carfax did him in, and I've nothing against it. They say in the village that he was 'the big fellow' Walton saw before the murder."

"And the motive?" demanded Wendover.

"No motive. Done in a fit of ill-temper because Huggin crossed him in something. Supporting evidence: a tale about some groom that Druce thrashed within an inch of his life for some trifle or other."

"That would be no more than manslaughter," the Chief Constable pointed out. "And that's not a hanging offence, so your gore-thirsty friends at The Barleycorn would be disappointed. They'll have to put up a better case than that, if they want their own way. Doesn't Huggin come into it more effectively than as the mere raw material for a murder?"

Denzil considered for a moment or two before answering.

"Well, no names, no pack drill," he said cautiously. "I'm not going to tell you who fished up this bright thought. But somebody did say blackmail."

"Oh, so they've got that length, have they?" said Sir Clinton, with no great surprise in his tone. "And did they say anything further on these lines?"

"They did," admitted Denzil, rather reluctantly. "I don't think I'd repeat this as mere tittle-tattle. Not quite the game. So I'm passing it on semiofficially. The police ought to know what sort of chat's going round. Give somebody a word of warning, perhaps, before there's harm done. Catch my meaning?"

"Too much cottonwool round it, I'm afraid," said Sir Clinton. "Unwrap it a bit."

"Well, this is it," said Denzil, seriously. "They say it was Enid Carfax who slipped on the moral stairs and that Druce was paying hush money on her account for the sake of the family name."

"Egad!" exclaimed Wendover. "I never thought of that possibility. . . . It's just on the cards from what I've heard about her at times. I don't much like this, if it's got so far that a casual stranger can pick it up in that village."

"This is official now, Bob," said the Chief Constable, turning a steady eye on Denzil. "Not for publication, of course; but you must put your cards on the table. What, exactly, did you pick up on this line?"

"A bit here and a bit there," Denzil answered soberly. "I can't give you the individual bits. But putting 'em together, they amount to this. Enid Carfax. . . . By the way, what age is she, do you know?"

Wendover remembered without much difficulty. "About twenty-five."

"So I gauged," Denzil said with a nod. "She came into three or four hundred a year, didn't she, when she came of age?"

"I seem to remember something of the sort," Wendover agreed. "Under an aunt's will, I think it was."

"Yes, that's sound enough, so far," Denzil continued. "That made her independent of Druce and his ideas. She could go where she liked and do what she liked, within limits. She got into a bad set in London just after that. A proper lot of young wasters, I gather. Some cash, fewer brains, and no morals. One of them was a married man, who took a fancy to her. He's separated from his wife. Got a free hand. His wife won't divorce him, no matter what happens. She's a Roman Catholic, I believe. This gang, including Enid Carfax and the man, used to wander about at week-ends to hotels which don't much mind what you do, so long as your money's genuine."

"How did our village sleuths get hold of all this?" demanded Sir Clinton. "It sounds rather outside their ambit, doesn't it?"

"Enid took her maid with her, the first time or two," explained Denzil. "I fancy that's how the tale got round. After that, she left the maid at home when she went off week-ending. So probably the rest of the story owes a bit to local imagination, stimulated by the absence of the maid from these little affairs. It doesn't take much to make your villagers talk, I've learnt."

"No, it doesn't," confessed Wendover sourly. "I don't like that kind of thing; but it's easy enough to see how a young girl might get herself into a fix amongst a gang of that sort. And so they think Huggin was blackmailing her? It's possible, though he'd hardly be staying at hotels of that sort, one would think. Still, once you go on the racket, you never know who you'll run up against."

Denzil, having got his tale off his mind, returned to his normal style.

"I think that covers the ground. Unless you'd like my personal impressions of Miss Carfax? Ah! Your eyes light up! The human touch, eh? With that encouragement, I proceed. Having nothing on hand this morning, I took my car over to Abbots Norton. The victor revisiting the field of battle. No, I didn't count the dead men. Caleb takes his out of a mug. Then I found I'd run out of cigarettes. Not much hope of finding a special brand in a place like that. However, I entered the likeliest shop I could see. An amazing place, really, after the highly-specialised emporia of Bond Street. A nice old lady kept it; and so far as I could see at a glance she sold marking ink, playing cards, sweets, newspapers, fly flaps, ham frills, picture postcards, dolls, tea, sugar, and paraffin oil. I didn't see the paraffin oil. It suggested itself, somehow. And she sold tobacco. She actually had the very cigarettes I wanted. Observing my obvious joy, she kindly told me she stocked them specially for one customer: Miss Carfax of the Hall. She always smoked that brand, it seems. A link between us, evidently."

"Is this an anecdote or a serial?" interrupted Sir Clinton.

"I'd just paid my money," continued Denzil, ignoring him, "when a car drew up at the door. First thing I saw was two neat ankles, then a pair of those legs that look best in short skirts. There aren't so many of that sort about, so I grew interested. Faces are often disappointing. Hers wasn't. I always describe each of my heroines as 'the most beautiful girl in England.' I'll save trouble here by leaving it at that. She was quite my style in looks. Nothing of the shrinking violet about her, though. She gave me an inquiring glance as she came in. Not brassy, but pleasantly interested, I'd call it."

"I know exactly what you mean," Sir Clinton broke in. "I've seen that expression on the faces of people examining 'The Great What-Is-It?' in Barnum's show in the old days. Let me collaborate in this story. She was Miss Carfax and you picked her up. Now go on."

"If you mean that I lifted my cap and said: 'Ahem! Haven't we met before, somewhere, Miss . . . ,' you're in error, alguazil. She's not quite like that. Still, reflecting on Tennyson's advice to grasp the skirts of happy chance, I decided to try a grab. Association with the police makes for unscrupulousness. Hence the existence of the criminal classes. As soon as I heard the nice old lady greet her as Miss Carfax, I withdrew. Passing her car, I unostentatiously gave the petrol cap a half turn. Luckily it was one of those spring ones which come adrift with a single twist. The rest was child's play. I followed up when she drove off. In about twenty yards her petrol cap fell off on the road. I picked it up, overtook her outside the village, introduced myself as the *deus ex machina*, restored the cap, and before you could say Abracadabra or Chrononhoton-thologos, we were as friendly as could be. She's by no means backward, and my well-known charm of manner did the rest."

"You don't lack impudence, evidently," was Wendover's comment.

"I wanted to get a footing at Carfax Hall," said Denzil. "As a mere matter of public duty it seemed necessary. Well, it ended in my going up to the Hall with her to walk over the private nine-hole course there. I'm playing a couple of rounds with her to-morrow."

"Oh, so it was your Hornet I saw standing at the door yesterday morning, was it?" asked the Chief Constable.

"Round about eleven o'clock? Yes, it was. But to proceed. We strolled over the course, talking of this and that. By and by, just off the fairway, I saw some archery targets, beside a little wooden hut. One doesn't often see that sort of thing nowadays. So we fell into talk about toxophily and toxophilites. She's very keen on it. In fact, she got a bow or two and some arrows out of the hut to give me a lesson. I did very well. I hit the wide, wide world, which is about the biggest game one could bring down. But she's a marvel, really. I wonder more girls don't take up archery. Shows off the figure better than any other sport I know. She reminded me of Diana and Atalanta, and all that lot. Arrows in the gold nearly every time. My best was a magpie, and even that was an accident."

"Curb your enthusiasm," suggested the Chief Constable. "I can read the Badminton archery book for myself in my spare time. It's on the shelves here."

"Well, I was deep in the mysteries of parrot beaks, four-and-ninepenny arrows, nocking, loosing, bracing, flirting—I don't mean what you mean, alguazil—tips, and the use of deer's fat, when unfortunately we were interrupted. A large athletic-looking person hove in sight. He put me off my stroke, for usually I look slightly down on people and I had to look up at him. Six foot high and, despite my natural prejudice, good-looking. To cut matters short, she introduced him as Mr. Finborough; and Caleb's local directory enabled me to place him at once as her half-brother, the one with the bar sinister across him. Though they were polite, it was plain that I was now *de trop*. They had something to talk about which wasn't my affair. In fact, Finborough said he'd come out to say good-bye to her. So I evanished, gracefully. When I looked back, they were evidently much engrossed with each other. Not even a parting wave from Diana. And so home to cold roast beef and pickles at the Talgarth Arms."

Wendover rang the bell, and a maid brought whiskey and soda. Denzil received it gratefully.

"You think of everything. My throat *is* a bit dry after all that narrative. About three thousand words, I reckon it at. For the same trouble, I could have dictated a short story and made untold gold, alguazil, so you owe me something."

"Psychology was never a strong point in your yarns," Sir Clinton pointed out. "You started by offering your impressions of Miss

Carfax, didn't you? Apart from the fact that she had neat legs and reminded you of Diana, I haven't gathered much in that field. Weren't you interested in anything except her physique?"

"You have me there. Perhaps I dwelt too much on externals. Let's see. I'd say she's remarkably well able to look after herself—when she wants to. Pretty cool, except when excited, I mean. Still, she looks as if she could show a good turn of temper if she were crossed. Might flash up and explode to some purpose if she got peeved. In fact, though she's just my style in looks and for fair-weather sailing, I don't know that I'd want to hitch up with her permanently. Too much chance of squalls in the offing, I fear."

"Did she give you the impression of having anything to worry her just now?"

"No, I can't say she did. Very cheery, I thought. Still, now you mention it, she did fall silent once or twice and threw the burden of the talk on me. I remember that now."

"If all you've told us is true," Wendover pointed out, "these family squabbles would account for that, perhaps."

"Now, another point, Bob," Sir Clinton broke in. "When you came on these archery targets, did she seem to want to talk about them much or did you lead her on?"

Denzil reflected for some moments before answering.

"Difficult to remember exactly how talk goes," he confessed ruefully. "I expect I began it, but she didn't seem averse, so far as I remember. It was she who suggested taking the stuff out and letting me make an ass of myself."

"And the bows, arrows, parrot beaks, bracers, and so forth were left on the ground when you departed?"

"Yes, naturally. I had to tear myself away from the family farewelling. I left Finborough to help her to clear the ground."

"Still another point. Did you notice if the hut is kept locked?"

Again Denzil reflected for a moment.

"No, it's just on the latch. At least, she didn't use any key to get into it. Why should she, when it's on private ground?"

"True. I just wondered. And now, Bob, suppose you drink up your stirrup cup and clear out. Wendover and I are early birds, and I'd hate to see you overstaying your welcome."

"Always somebody moving me on to-day," grumbled Denzil. "First Finborough and then you, alguazil. Well, anything to oblige the neighbours."

He rose from his chair and, as Wendover made no effort to restrain him, went away.

"Early birds!" said Wendover ironically, when he had gone. "You seem to live that Truth may die, Clinton. You know we don't turn in for a good while yet."

"I usually go to bed about one or two a.m.," Sir Clinton pointed out. "That's early in the morning, isn't it? Anyhow, I've had about as much of Bob Denzil as I can stand, this evening. He's all right in small doses; but this began to look like a 'long pull.' And now, Squire, since we are alone at last, have you guessed who Mr. A is, yet?"

"Mr. A?" echoed Wendover. "Oh, I remember now. You said the murderer was Mr. A."

"He has other names as well, but you should have got him taped down by this time, surely. Well, I'll help you with the context:

*B was a Butcher, who had a big dog.*
*C was a Captain all covered with lace . . ."*

"*D was a Drunkard who had a red face,*" Wendover completed the verse. "Now I see what you meant, confound you! '*A was an Archer who shot at a frog.*' Is that it?"

"I told you he was an old friend of yours. You must have met him in the nursery. In this case, I think he shot at a toad, if there's any truth in the superstition that toads are venomous. It's an insult to any honest frog to liken him to the late Huggin."

"It was your talk about Mr. A and all the rest of it that tangled me up," complained Wendover.

"Well, it was plain enough, wasn't it? Nobody heard the noise of a report when he was shot; and a silencer was unlikely. The wound was of the same caliber as a .45 but no bullet was discoverable. Doesn't that tally perfectly with an archer using an arrow of the same diameter as a .45 bullet and pulling out the arrow after Huggin was dead? There's no difficulty in that, for the target-practice arrow has no barb to cause trouble."

"But the thing went clean through him," objected Wendover. "Even a bullet would hardly do that, except at close quarters."

"What a pity people put books on their shelves without reading them," regretted Sir Clinton. "You bought the whole of the Badminton series as a pious duty, I suppose, to have the complete set. But you only read the ones that interested you."

He stepped over to a bookcase and took down a volume.

"Here you are," he said, turning the pages till he reached the passage he was seeking. "*Range and Penetration of the Long Bow.* This is by C. J. Longman, and gives the results of some experiments he made himself. He used a self-yew bow with a sixty-five-pound pull and a five-shilling arrow. That, I may say, Squire, is not one that he bought for five bob, but an arrow with a weight equal to that of five silver shillings. With this outfit, at seven yards he shot at a panel of seasoned timber, one inch thick. The arrow broke clean through, so that the pile—that's the metal tip, Squire—stood out on the further side."

"That's good going," admitted Wendover. "I'd hardly have expected quite so much penetrating power."

"It surprised me a bit, too, when I looked it up. Here's another instance. Longman used field-gun-trial penetration pads for it, each pad made up of forty-five sheets of the toughest and stoutest brown paper tightly bound together with wire clips. When he used a 14-bore gun with medium game shot on this at seven yards range, two of the shot broke all forty-five sheets, seven broke thirty-nine sheets, and twelve broke thirty-seven sheets. The rest of the shot apparently got stopped somewhere between the thirty-sixth and the thirty-seventh. Now when he turned to the bow and used an eight-and-sixpenny arrow at the same range, his arrow penetrated two whole pads and fourteen sheets of a third pad. In other words, at equal ranges the shotgun had less than half the penetrating power of the bow."

"Surprising!" said Wendover. "Did he try with a bullet instead of small shot?"

"He did, using a lead spherical bullet weighing an ounce and one eighth and loading his cartridge with 2½ drachms of black powder. At ten yards range, that bullet penetrated five complete pads, the bullet being found in the fifth pad. At seven yards range, you remember, his arrow went through two complete pads and one third of the way through the third. So although the bullet won, there wasn't so much difference as you'd expect. Of course, a sixty-five-pound bow is a bit out of the common. A fifty-pound bow is good enough for most people, apparently."

"H'm! After that, one begins to realise better what the French thought about the English archers at Crécy and Poictiers."

Sir Clinton replaced the volume on its shelf and, coming forward, poured himself out some whiskey and soda.

"Well," he said, putting down his glass again, "'A was an Archer' seems to fit the case neatly enough. One saw that fairly early in the business. But what were A's other names, Squire? That's the rub. And why did he shoot at the frog?"

"Don't ask me," answered Wendover, gloomily. "It must have been one of the Carfax Hall lot. They're the only archery cranks hereabouts."

A sudden suspicion crossed his mind, apparently.

"Why did you ask Denzil these questions about the girl and the hut and the rest of it?" he demanded.

"Curiosity, Squire. Sift out the answers for yourself and see what you make of them."

# CHAPTER XII
## THE DEATHS IN APSLEY SPINNEY

"ANYTHING IN THE PAPERS, this morning?" inquired Sir Clinton as he took his seat at the breakfast table.

"Nothing world-shaking, thank goodness," said Wendover contentedly. "It's the kind of news I'm glad to see, in these days. One gets overmuch of the other sort. There's a short account of the inquest on Huggin in the local rag. You can send a marked copy to Denzil. You promised him that, didn't you?"

"Bob can buy it himself, if he wants to. I washed my hands of him when he came butting in here on his own. They brought in the usual verdict, I suppose?"

"Murder by some person unknown," confirmed Wendover. "Nothing fresh came out. But, by the way, there is a bit of news I was sorry to see. Thelma Campion's dead."

"I'm sorry," said the Chief Constable sincerely. "It must have been a very short illness, surely."

"She took ill suddenly last Monday. They got her into a nursing home and operated at once. Everything seemed all right, but she had a bad relapse later on and died yesterday evening. It's a pity. She gave one the feeling that she must be a good sort off the stage, and not every actress manages to leave that impression."

Sir Clinton nodded agreement and was about to say something when a maid entered the room carrying the extension telephone which she plugged into its socket.

"Inspector Cumberland has rung up, sir," she intimated to the Chief Constable. "I told him you were at breakfast, but he said it couldn't wait."

Sir Clinton picked up the receiver with no very genial expression. "Yes, he's speaking. . . ."

There was a long pause during which Cumberland delivered his message. Wendover waited anxiously for the Chief Constable's comments, since the look on his face showed that the news was important.

"Apsley Spinney, towards the eastern end, you said? You have somebody on duty to keep people off, of course? Then there's no special hurry for a minute or two. . . . By the way, where's the nearest point that a car can reach? . . . Thanks."

Sir Clinton put down the instrument and turned to his host.

"More trouble, Squire. And higher up in society this time. Your friend Carfax is done for, now, and his gamekeeper as well. It looks like a poaching affray, for they were done in at Apsley Spinney where Walton got that brace of pheasants. We may as well make what breakfast we can, for there's no saying when we'll see lunch. You needn't trouble to put on a mourning air. He was no friend of yours."

"No," admitted Wendover. "Still—"

He took the Chief Constable's hint, however, and poured out a second cup of coffee for himself.

"Cumberland says that if we take a car up to Piney Ridge Farm it's as near as we can get. Then over some fields past Ferny Hollow. Know the way from that?"

"Oh, yes. It's easy enough. But what exactly's happened?"

"I've no details worth repeating," Sir Clinton said curtly. "We'll hear all about it when we see Cumberland."

During the drive up to Piney Ridge Farm and the walk across to Apsley Spinney, Sir Clinton discouraged any conversation, and Wendover was left to rack his brain over this fresh act in the local tragedy. Was this latest affair directly related to Huggin's death, he wondered, or had Druce Carfax and his gamekeeper been murdered in some chance poaching affray which had no connection whatever with the Huggin case? The fact that the keeper had shared his employer's fate certainly strengthened the latter view. What possible connecting link could there be between him and a stranger like Huggin? It seemed fantastic to suppose such a thing.

Then a fresh hypothesis crossed his mind and threw all his previous speculations back into the melting pot. Suppose these three killings had been the work of a homicidal maniac. That would cover the ground completely. Given an aimless slayer, seeking merely to glut his lust for blood, then the victims would be elected by the mere chance of their passing their murderer at a given moment. Instead of Huggin, it might have been Walton, or Oulton and his girl, or Carfax himself as he left the rendezvous. And if this irresponsible and capricious killer chose to roam over the Carfax lands at night, the keeper was as likely a victim as any. Or Carfax himself, if he had been abroad in the dusk for some purpose or other.

And then Wendover recollected the questions which Sir Clinton had put to Denzil. That hut by the archery targets contained an outfit of bows and arrows, accessible to anyone, since it was left unlocked.

Wendover found this new hypothesis taking a firmer hold on his mind than he liked. If by any chance it were true, then all this search for a motive, all these tedious investigations of Huggin's past history, all these attempts to elucidate the relations between Huggin and Druce Carfax had been no better than pure time wasting. And, *a fortiori,* any endeavour to link together the Huggin case and the twin murders of the previous night would be foredoomed to failure, since no connection could exist between them except in the gruesome brain of a demented assassin.

The appearance of Cumberland on the fringe of the spinney interrupted Wendover's speculations. The inspector led them among the trees until they reached a tiny clearing; and as they emerged into it the first things which caught Wendover's eye were two bodies lying on the grass, about ten feet apart. One of them he recognized as Carfax's; the other, which had a gun at its side, must be that of the gamekeeper. In the background was a little group made up of a police sergeant, two constables, a couple of rustics, and a nervous-looking young man whom Wendover recognised as Druce Carfax's brother Julian. Wendover did not go forward to examine the bodies more closely, but waited until the Chief Constable had finished his inspection.

Meanwhile, he joined the little group. As he came up to them, Julian Carfax gave a half-hearted sign of recognition and pulled a cigarette case from his pocket as though to offer it to Wendover. Then, suddenly thinking better of that, he fumbled with it for a moment or two as though undecided what to do with it, and then returned it to his pocket. It was plain that he was much agitated by the tragedy which had occurred so unexpectedly. Wendover tried to put him at his ease by a few sympathetic commonplaces suitable to the occasion, and succeeded in extracting some information eventually.

"How did it happen?"

"This? Oh, I don't know. Dreadful, isn't it? Some poaching affair, I should think. I always expected there'd be trouble in that way, sooner or later. Druce, poor chap, was always so ready to take violent measures, you know, and I don't think violence pays, do you? It's apt to breed counter-violence, isn't it? And then one gets this happening, doesn't one? After all, what does it matter if one loses a brace of pheasants now and again? They're not worth risking trouble over, really."

"I suppose that's one way of looking at it," said Wendover, non-committally. "Still, I shouldn't have thought our local poachers would carry things to this point. They might go the length of fisticuffs occasionally, if they were caught at their work. But hardly murder, from what one knows of them."

"You think so? Quite likely you're right. Of course, there's no denying that poor Druce made himself unpopular hereabouts. Lots of people didn't like him, hated him in fact, didn't they?"

Sir Clinton finished his examination and came over to the group, when Wendover introduced him to Julian Carfax.

"Would you mind telling me what you know about this?" the Chief Constable asked, when this formality was over.

"I?" said Julian, in a tone which suggested that he was almost surprised at being asked for information. "Well, really, you know, I don't know anything about it. I haven't a notion how it can have happened, not the very faintest. It's a mystery, altogether."

"How did you first learn about this?" Sir Clinton pursued patiently.

"About this? You mean about his being dead? Maverton told me."

"And who is Maverton?"

"Maverton? He's our man and Druce used him for a valet. He came and waked me up this morning and told me one of the gardeners brought the news, that one over there, Gossage. He comes through the spinney here on his way to the Hall, and he found the two of them lying here."

"When did you see your brother last?"

"When did I see him? Let's think I saw him at dinner, and after that he went up and changed his clothes and I saw him again before he went out. He'd changed into the clothes you see him in now."

"Is that usual with him?"

"Oh, no, I don't think so. No, I think I know why he changed. He'd had a letter."

"It happens to most of us at times," said the Chief Constable with exemplary forbearance. "What sort of letter?"

"What sort of letter? Oh, it was an anonymous letter. At least it was signed 'A WELLWISHER.' But that's hardly a signature, is it? One would call a letter signed like that an anonymous letter, wouldn't one?"

"Possibly. Did you see this letter?"

"Did I? Yes, he showed me it, you know. It was just a line or two warning him about poachers, I remember."

"Ah! It annoyed him, perhaps?"

"Annoyed him? Well, yes, it did, you know. He was always very bitter against poachers, very bitter. Perhaps too bitter, I sometimes thought. After all, a brace of pheasants is neither here nor there when one thinks it over. You know the old saying about pheasant rearing, don't you? 'Up goes a guinea; bang goes a penny; and down comes half-a-crown.' Of course prices have changed a bit since those days, you know. Cartridges cost twopence now, and I don't know what a pheasant sells for nowadays. But the principle's the same, isn't it? The things cost far more to rear than they're worth when you've shot them."

Sir Clinton evidently felt that extracting information from Julian was as uneconomical a process as rearing pheasants. He turned to Cumberland.

"What have you made of it?" he asked.

"Well, sir, you've seen the bodies. One's Mr. Carfax's, the other one is John Phelp, the gamekeeper. He lived with a widowed sister at the lodge on the Ambledown road. She keeps the gate. I've seen her this morning, and this is her story. Yesterday afternoon, Mr. Carfax came down to the lodge in a towering rage. She didn't hear what he said to her brother, but from his tone it was plain enough he was angry about something. She saw a paper in Mr. Carfax's hand, and he tapped it while she was looking at them. They were in the avenue outside the cottage. As it happened, she was coming out to see a friend in the village and spend the evening with her at the pictures afterwards, so she left the lodge while her brother and Mr. Carfax were still talking. She got back about eleven, and found her brother had gone out. He'd had his evening meal and fed the cat before he left the cottage, and altogether he seems to have followed his ordinary routine. He took his gun with him. That's it there. I know it quite well. Sometimes he used to lend it to me for a bit of rabbiting. That's all she can tell us, so far as last night goes. This morning, Phelp didn't come to breakfast as usual, and she began to feel worried; but the first she heard of this murder was from us, after Gossage had given the alarm at the Hall."

"That's the gardener over there, isn't it?" asked Sir Clinton. "I'll have a word with him now."

But Gossage could throw little light on the tragedy. He had come through the spinney about a quarter to eight and had seen the two bodies. He had not disturbed them in any way, merely satisfied himself that both men were dead and that he could be of no help to them. Then he had gone straight to the Hall and given the alarm.

"Did anyone hear shots fired in the night?" inquired the Chief Constable.

"A good many imagine they did," complained the inspector sardonically. "A perfect fusillade, some of them would have you believe, sir. But actually I've got only two reliable witnesses and they agree on two shots with some minutes between them, about a quarter to ten or so. In the ordinary way, we'd have had people up Leisurely Lane; but since Huggin's murder, the villagers avoid that place at night. It was the valet Maverton and Miss Carfax's maid that heard the shooting. They were out for a stroll in the dusk, on the golf course, and they seem to have heard the reports. They put them down to poachers. The valet didn't look on it as part of his business to do the gamekeeper's job; so beyond having a bit of a laugh over it, they paid no attention."

"That's roughly about the same time as Huggin was killed— between half past nine and ten?" mused Sir Clinton. "It's a bit early for poachers to be abroad. But it's about as late in the evening as one could see to shoot at any reasonable range. Too dark, in fact, for anything but fairly close-range shooting."

"Moffatt and that hanger-on of his, Walton, may have been out last night," said the inspector. "The only person to give them an alibi is Moffatt's wife; and I wouldn't bet much on her evidence."

The Chief Constable made no comment on this.

"What did you find when you examined the bodies?" he inquired.

"Well, sir, as you see, they're both lying face up and the wounds are in front in each case. Suppose they'd been standing facing each other and let drive at each other with guns, you'd get much the same result as what's here. But there's only one gun here. It was lying beside the keeper, just where you see it now; and it's got two discharged cartridges in the breech. That fits with the two shots that Maverton and the girl heard."

"What's the exact distance between the bodies, measured from feet to feet?"

"Eleven feet two inches, sir."

"Did you measure the dispersion of the shot in each case?"

"Yes, sir. In each case the main bulk of the shot made a big continuous wound in the flesh; but the outlying pellets could be covered with a five-inch circle in Mr. Carfax's case and by a one-and-a-half-inch circle in the case of the keeper."

"You've used this gun, you say? What is it—choke or cylinder?"

"It's a half-choke, sir. I remember Phelp telling me that."

Sir Clinton ransacked his memory for a moment or two, then he turned to Wendover.

"You can check me roughly, I think," he said. "From a half-choke you get a five-inch circle of spread somewhere about a five-yard range, don't you?"

Wendover at one time had made an examination of this problem and he agreed to Sir Clinton's estimate with a nod.

"And a dispersion of one and a half inches means that the gun must have been fired quite close up, within a couple of yards at most?"

"Somewhere about that," Wendover confirmed.

"What about the card wad which lies on top of the shot in the cartridge?" asked Sir Clinton, turning to the inspector. "Did you find these on the ground anywhere?"

"I found one, sir, about halfway between the two bodies." He consulted his notebook hurriedly. "It was about six feet three inches from the keeper's feet and a bit to the side of the line joining the bodies."

"You didn't find the other corresponding wad? It must have lodged in the wound in Phelp's case. If so—we'll find out definitely from the P.M. results—then Phelp must have been shot from quite close, a couple of yards at most. That fits in with the slight traces of burning on the cloth round the wound. But you can't trust burning as an accurate criterion. Powders differ so much from each other. But see that the police surgeon is warned to look carefully for the wad in the wound. It's sometimes missed."

"Very good, sir."

"Mr. Carfax had no gun with him?"

"No, sir. He was carrying a hunting crop. We found it in the grass where it dropped from his hand when he was shot."

"What do you think about it all?" demanded Sir Clinton.

"Well, sir, one look at the wounds excludes a number of possible suggestions. Neither of those men could use a gun after they'd been shot themselves."

"That seems likely, on the face of it," Sir Clinton agreed.

"So Phelp didn't shoot Mr. Carfax and then get shot by Mr. Carfax, or *vice versa.*"

"I don't contest that in the slightest."

"Then there's the chance that Phelp shot Mr. Carfax first and committed suicide afterwards. But you say the shot that killed Phelp came from a couple of yards away, roughly, and that excludes suicide entirely. So we can rule that out. And that implies, doesn't it, sir? that there must have been a third man present."

"It looks like it, doesn't it?" admitted Sir Clinton. "And if your premises are correct, then we know something about the third man, straight away."

"I don't quite see that, sir," said Cumberland doubtfully, after a moment or two's consideration.

"Well, if you're sure that only two shots were fired, and there are two exploded cartridges in the breech of Phelp's gun, and if Phelp was as powerful a man as he looks, I think we'd be safe in making one assumption about the third man. Just think it over, Inspector. I don't want to rob you of the pleasure of the inference."

He paused for a moment as though to give Cumberland the chance of a reply; then, as none came, he issued some routine instructions about the removal of the bodies after they had been photographed *in situ*. This done, he turned to Julian Carfax, who was standing near, apparently completely detached from the proceedings.

"I must see some of the people at Carfax Hall," he explained. "This man Maverton, and the lady's maid he was with last night. And Miss Carfax, if she's on the premises. And I want to see that anonymous letter, if it can be found. I've got a car over yonder"—he made a gesture towards Piney Ridge Farm—"so the easiest way will be for you to come back with us to the Hall. There's nothing more for us to do here. Inspector Cumberland will see to everything."

Julian Carfax seemed to awaken suddenly from his introspection.

"Yes, yes," he agreed, "of course, if you think so. I think that would be the best thing to do, wouldn't it? Quicker than walking back to the Hall, of course, and you couldn't leave your car up here and come back for it afterwards, for that would be an extra walk. Yes, we'd better do that, as you say."

He moved off with Sir Clinton. Wendover, glad to leave the little glade of the tragedy, followed them among the trees.

# CHAPTER XIII
## RIFTS IN THE LUTE

"In the first place, Mr. Carfax, I'd like to see your sister's maid for a few minutes. What's her name?"

"Tobin," answered Julian. "I'll send her to you."

"And while I'm talking to her, would you look about and see if you can find that letter which your brother got yesterday, the one warning him about poachers? I wish to see it."

"I'll hunt for it," Julian promised. "It may be in the pocket of the suit he was wearing yesterday afternoon."

Wendover glanced after him as he retreated to the door. It was surprising to see how little real emotion he had shown under the stress of his brother's tragic death. Possibly he had been stunned by the suddenness of the calamity, but somehow that was hardly the impression given by his manner. He seemed rather to be following his normal trivial trend of thought, wholly undeflected by the catastrophe which had befallen the family.

"I suppose it's introversion," Wendover concluded with a shrug. "He's got so wrapped up in his own little interior world that he's lost all perspective in the real events going on around him. He can put this whole affair aside without an effort, simply because it doesn't touch him where he lives. No wonder he never made anything of his life. He's no better than a dope fiend."

His reflections were interrupted by the entrance of Tobin, the lady's maid; and he glanced up to examine her. Well-trained, he judged at the first glance. She knew how to stand, and what to do with her hands; and she showed no signs of nervousness. Good-looking, too, in a hard sort of way, but he didn't like the set of her mouth. She hadn't exactly a vinegary expression, but she might develop into a shrew in time. In fact, Wendover concluded, she was just the sort to give her mistress the courtesy she was paid for while taking a real delight in sneering at her behind her back.

"You're Miss Carfax's maid?" Sir Clinton began. "I'm told you were out after dinner last night, on the golf links?"

"I was, sir."

"You were with the valet, I believe?"

"I was, sir."

"You heard some shots? Where were you at the time?"

"Just about the fifth green, sir. There's a plan of the course in the hall, if you'd care for me to show you exactly where we were."

"Don't trouble. I looked at it as I came in. Near the fifth green, you say?"

"We were in the golf shelter between it and the fourth green, sir."

"You heard some shots? What time was that?"

"I couldn't say exactly, sir. It would be towards ten o'clock, I think."

"How many shots did you hear?"

"Two, sir."

"Only two?"

"Only two, sir."

"How long was there between them, can you tell me?"

"It was some minutes, sir."

"Five, or ten?"

"About five, I think, sir."

"What did you say to each other when you heard them? I suppose you took some notice?"

"We thought it was some poachers in the spinney, sir."

Sir Clinton seemed satisfied with this. He turned to a fresh subject and began to question Tobin about the rumours which Denzil had picked up in the village.

"Miss Carfax had a flat in town, hadn't she?"

"She has it still, sir, but it's shut up just now."

"You were with her there, I believe. She had friends in London, hadn't she? What sort of people were they?"

"They weren't what I'd been used to in previous situations, sir," Tobin answered in a tone loaded with insinuation.

"That doesn't tell me much," Sir Clinton pointed out suavely.

"They were always drinking at odd hours, sir. Very noisy, too. And they were too free altogether, specially when they went away for week-ends, from what I saw myself. When some of the maids took morning tea to the ladies, they found the rooms empty, they told me, as often as not."

"Did you ever find Miss Carfax's room empty when you took tea to her in the morning?"

"No," admitted Tobin reluctantly. "But Miss Carfax isn't a fool, like some of them."

"Tell me some more about these people."

"Well, sir, they generally went week-ending in couples, if you see what I mean. And Miss Carfax went with Mr. Bulstrode. They were keen on each other. He's a married man. A maid sees more than she gets credit for. I've seen them kissing each other in the flat, often."

"Kisses don't count for much, nowadays," commented Sir Clinton carelessly. "You're perhaps giving them too much weight. How often did Miss Carfax take you with her to these hotel week-ends?"

"Just once, sir. After that she left me at the flat."

"And you imagined things?"

"Well, sir, one can't help thinking—"

"I don't want to know what you thought," Sir Clinton pointed out incisively. "I want to know what you saw."

Tobin apparently racked her memory for something discreditable, but failed to find it.

"I can't think of anything like what you mean, sir," she admitted at last, "but I can put two and two together."

"Are you good at arithmetic?" asked Sir Clinton with interest.

"Fairly, sir," declared Tobin, rather taken aback by this literal interpretation.

"Are you sure you haven't added two and two and made five, or even six, out of them? If you haven't, some people in the village have managed it. Did you tell any of them what you thought?"

Tobin was plainly taken aback by this question.

"Not any of the villagers, sir. I may have dropped a hint to some of the staff here; and Mr. Druce Carfax knew about it."

"How do you know that?"

"Because he asked me questions about it all. And he had a talk with Miss Carfax about the kind of company she was keeping. She was angry about that and gave me notice."

Wendover had little difficulty in guessing the cause of Tobin's obvious spite. She was plainly embittered by her dismissal from what must have been a fairly easy post.

"When did this happen?" continued Sir Clinton.

"Last Saturday, sir."

"When did Mr. Finborough come down here?"

"On Wednesday, sir. The day before yesterday. He came in time for dinner."

"Did Mr. Finborough visit Miss Carfax's flat often?"

"Fairly often, sir. Once a week or so."

"He saw the company you complain about, then? Perhaps he formed a different opinion of them."

Tobin reflected for a moment over this and then said spitefully:

"He could hardly be particular, considering who he is."

Sir Clinton ignored this reference to Finborough's parentage.

"He seemed quite friendly with these people?"

"Well, he was making money off them," Tobin declared, with no less spite. "He was rooking them at cards and getting them to put money into shares and things. He wasn't likely to quarrel with his bread and butter."

Sir Clinton considered for a moment or two, then apparently decided not to ask any further questions.

"If I were you," he cautioned the maid seriously, "I'd be careful after this. What you've said to me is official; but if you go talking in that strain outside, as you've been doing, you'll get yourself into trouble. Don't try to make mountains out of molehills. And if there's any fresh talk in the village, we'll know where it comes from, you understand? You can go now. Send Maverton to me at once."

When the door closed behind the lady's maid, Wendover turned to Sir Clinton with a wry face.

"That's a nasty creature," he commented. "There's nothing behind all that stuff, except spite and a foul imagination. You can wash it out, Clinton."

"Oh, I don't think the time was entirely wasted," said the Chief Constable. "I'm beginning to get interested in these family affairs. But if she'd liked her mistress, I doubt if we'd have heard so much about the doings in that circle. I suppose there's jealousy of some sort at the back of it all. It sounded like it. Probably Miss Carfax is better looking or something like that. We'll be able to judge when we see her."

"Are you going to worry her with all that?" demanded Wendover, discontentedly.

Before Sir Clinton had time to answer, Maverton the valet presented himself. He was a man of about thirty-five, with an underhung jaw and little twinkling eyes which seemed ever on the lookout for a possible advantage.

"Your name's Maverton?" asked Sir Clinton, in a tone a shade more "official" than he had used with the lady's maid. "You were on the golf links last night, I'm told; and you heard a couple of reports? Where were you at the moment?"

"In the golf shelter halfway between the fourth and fifth greens, sir, up towards Apsley Spinney."

"What time was it when you heard the shots?"

"About a quarter to ten, sir, or near about then."

"You heard only two shots? Were they shotgun reports?"

"I should say they were, sir. I certainly took them for that at the time."

"How long was it between the two shots?"

"Five or six minutes, I'd say, sir; but I didn't look at my watch."

Wendover wondered whether the valet and the lady's maid had pooled their recollections, since they both seemed to have the story pat.

"You thought that poachers were at work, didn't you? Natural enough conclusion; but had you any special reason for drawing it?"

"Mr. Carfax put that into my head, sir, in the afternoon. He was always very bitter against poachers and I gathered that he'd had some sort of warning about their making a raid last night. Someone had sent him a warning letter about it. I heard him say something about that to Mr. Julian Carfax in the afternoon, and very angry he was."

"You didn't think of going up into Apsley Spinney yourself when you heard the firing?"

"Certainly not, sir. Apart from everything else, I had strict orders from Mr. Carfax never to go near any of the spinneys if I went for an after-dinner stroll. We were all warned to keep to the golf links or the park lands. Mr. Carfax was very strict about our going anywhere near his pheasants."

"You heard nothing but the two shots? No cries?"

"Just the two shots, sir. And I saw nobody. It was too dark, for one thing."

"Very well," Sir Clinton said, as though he expected nothing further. "Now another point. I believe there have been some slight disagreements among the members of the family lately. Can you throw any light on that subject?"

Maverton hesitated perceptibly at this question.

"I'm not quite sure . . ." he began, dubiously.

"You needn't treat the police worse than you do your acquaintances at The Barleycorn," said Sir Clinton bluntly. "You've chattered pretty freely there, Maverton, and it can be made hot for you if it suits us. So let's have no shuffling, if you please."

Maverton threw a quick glance at the Chief Constable's face and, apparently finding on it an expression which helped him to make up his mind, he decided to abandon subterfuges.

"Miss Carfax and her brother had a bit of a row on Saturday," he divulged, with a certain zest in his tone. "After it, they didn't seem on good terms from what I saw when I was waiting the table. I do that as well as valet Mr. Carfax, sir. It was plain enough to me. Then on Wednesday, Mr. Finborough turned up. He's a—"

"I know all about who Mr. Finborough is," interrupted Sir Clinton. "Go on."

Evidently Maverton felt that he had been robbed of the chance of communicating a spicy bit of news.

"Well, sir, he came down on Wednesday," he explained rather sulkily, "and I don't think Mr. Carfax was over-pleased to see him. He let Mr. Finborough come about the place at times, but they didn't get on well together. Anyone could see that, though they were polite enough on the surface usually. But this time, there was a regular row, probably over Miss Carfax's affairs I should think."

"How did you manage to pick up all this assorted news?" demanded the Chief Constable. "You seem remarkably well informed."

"I'm not so stupid, sir, that I can't see you're being ironical. You're suggesting I had my ear to keyholes. Quite unnecessary, sir, I can assure you, when Mr. Carfax lost his temper. He had a voice like a bull, sir; and when he was in one of his bullying moods, he shouted fit to bring the house down. One could hear him through any door, without having to bother about the keyhole."

"And you were lucky enough to be at hand to catch his remarks on these various occasions?" asked the Chief Constable sardonically. "How very fortunate. Well, give us the results. What happened between him and Miss Carfax on Saturday?"

"I didn't hear what Miss Carfax had to say, sir. She doesn't raise her voice, even when she's angry. But Mr. Carfax went on for long enough about the sort of life she was leading at her flat in London and the kind of company she kept there. Very angry, he was, about it all. He used very coarse language, part of the time, as he always did when he got into one of his tempers, sir. He was always a nasty one to cross, sir, for he'd bite as soon as bark. I often wonder I've stuck this place as long as I've done."

Sir Clinton showed no desire for further insight into Miss Carfax's biography.

"What makes you think the strain between them persisted over the week-end?"

"I could see it plain enough at table, sir. Usually, they talked a bit at meals, general conversation. After that row on Saturday, they sat down and never took the least notice of each other. They did talk, but it was to Mr. Julian only, not to one another. And that made it fairly clear something was up, sir, for Mr. Julian's no hand at real dinner-table talk. Usually he sits and dreams over his plate and says 'Yes' or 'No' when anyone speaks to him. Or else he gets started and tells some long story full of detail and with no point in it when he comes to the end of it. So when they wouldn't talk to each other and insisted on talking to him, the man hardly got a mouthful, and Mr. Carfax was getting redder and redder in the face and crosser and crosser with him as time went on. Miss Carfax didn't show it; but I expect she felt the same, for talking to Mr. Julian is no treat to anyone."

"Then on Wednesday Mr. Finborough appeared? What is he like, in appearance?"

Maverton considered for a moment or two.

"He's dark, sir, and tall—round about six feet, I'd say. And he's got white teeth and smiles a lot. He'll be thirty-five or thirty-six, I'd say, but he carries himself as if he was younger, for he's in good condition."

"Is there a photograph of him in the house?" asked Sir Clinton.

Maverton shook his head.

"I haven't seen any," he declared. "Not in any of the public rooms. And neither Mr. Carfax nor Mr. Julian was very fond of him. Miss Carfax might have one in her room, perhaps. I never saw one."

"Very well. When did Mr. Finborough arrive here on Wednesday?"

"Before dinner, sir. He came down in his car."

"They all had dinner together? You seem to study your employers' behaviour at table, Maverton. What struck you on that occasion?"

Maverton paused for a few seconds before answering, as though to muster his memories.

"Well, sir, as far as I can recall it, Miss Carfax and Mr. Finborough talked a good deal to each other and left Mr. Carfax out of it mostly. He tried to get even by talking to Mr. Julian, but he didn't make much of that, as one might expect. It wasn't quite as uncomfortable as when Mr. Finborough wasn't there; but it wasn't just a friendly happy-family atmosphere. A sort of strain over things without much to show for it, if you see what I mean, sir."

"What happened after lunch?"

"Miss Carfax got up at once and went away out of the room. Mr. Finborough waited till Mr. Carfax got up and then he said: 'I want a talk with you, Druce,' or something like that. He and Mr. Carfax went into the lounge. Mr. Julian stayed behind at the table, with a cigarette. They talked low in the lounge to start with. Then Mr. Carfax lost his temper and began to bellow like a bull of Bashan, like he always did when his temper went; and Mr. Finborough raised his voice a bit to keep level. I couldn't help hearing a phrase or two. Mr. Carfax said something like 'do anything for money.' Mr. Finborough said something sneering about 'give your family pride a knock.' Then Mr. Carfax called him a 'come-by-chance,' and I thought they'd be sure to get to blows over that. But Mr. Finborough kept cool, like he usually does. He said something that sounded like 'I'd keep off that, if I were you, you damned cuckoo.' Then Mr. Carfax gave him a lot of abuse, getting angrier and angrier, it seemed. And then I heard Mr. Finborough say, 'We're both in the same boat. I can't put the screw on you, and you can't touch me without it all coming out. Awkward, isn't it?' He was quite cool about it, whatever it was. And, by the by, I heard them both mention 'Enid'—that's Miss Carfax—about the start of the talk, when they began to get angry. Finally, Mr. Carfax ordered Mr. Finborough to get out of the house. Mr. Finborough just laughed at that and said something I didn't quite catch, about not taking orders from him. I don't know what Mr. Carfax said to that, but Mr. Finborough didn't leave the house till next morning. At dinner, they each behaved as if the other wasn't there. Mr. Finborough and Miss Carfax talked to each other as if they were alone at table. Mr. Julian sat there as if he was noticing nothing, and probably he wasn't. Mr. Carfax sat at the head of the table and glared at the three of them time about, as if he could hardly hold himself in, but he didn't say anything through the whole dinner."

"And after dinner he changed his clothes and went out, didn't he?" Sir Clinton asked, as Maverton seemed to have finished his tale.

"I didn't know that at the time, sir. He went upstairs and changed without saying anything to me. I went out myself, after dinner, as I told you; and it was only when I came to look to his room that I found he'd changed and left his dinner jacket and things about."

Sir Clinton nodded, as though this satisfied him on the point. Then, with a critical glance at the valet's face, he put a fresh question:

"What's all this gossip about Miss Carfax?"

Maverton seemed obviously uncomfortable at the raising of this subject.

"I don't know anything about it, sir," he protested, uneasily.

"Then why did you put it afloat?" demanded the Chief Constable with a black look.

"Me, sir? I didn't."

"You needn't trouble to lie about that. I know what you've been saying."

Maverton shrank a little under the Chief Constable's eye. He changed his line of defence without the slightest regard for consistency.

"It's common talk, sir. I've said no more than other people."

"That's no defence, if Miss Carfax chooses to haul you up for it. Keep off that subject in future, Maverton. And look up the law about slander at the nearest free library in your spare time, just in case you feel inclined to let your tongue wag in future. Pass that hint round to your friends, too, if you want to do them a good turn. There will be trouble, if that sort of chatter doesn't stop."

"Very good, sir," acquiesced Maverton in a tone which showed that he had got a fright. "I never meant any harm. I just passed on what I heard myself."

"Well, bear my advice in mind. That's all I want from you at present. Go and ask Miss Carfax if she'll be good enough to spare me a few minutes."

## CHAPTER XIV
## A NOTE OF WARNING

WHEN MAVERTON HAD LEFT the room, Sir Clinton turned to Wendover.

"That should stop their mouths," he declared with a certain satisfaction. "Nothing like using a gossip monger to stop gossip. He can spread the tale quicker than anyone else."

"The Carfaxes haven't been lucky in their servants," grumbled Wendover. "Not much of the old family retainer about these two, is there? But probably no decent servant would consent to stay in the house of a man like Druce Carfax. . . . I really shouldn't say that, with the fellow lying dead; but it's just the truth."

He paused, rather shamefacedly, since he felt that he had overstepped the bounds of his code. Then, to cover this up, he put a question.

"Can you make head or tail of all this business about a family quarrel?"

"Oh, like Miss Tobin, I can put two and two together," said the Chief Constable with a smile. "But the result's a bit unusual, like her total. When I put two and two together in this case, I make it just two and no more."

"Very amusing," said Wendover, testily. "You're evidently pleased with yourself about something, though I don't see why you should be. Denzil was right when he said you and he were neck and neck in this affair because neither of you knew anything about it."

Sir Clinton's smile deepened into what looked like an impish grin.

"For that, Squire, I shall keep my ideas to myself. Bob and I— and you also, Squire—have all had the same information about this

186

particular point. The difference between us is the old one between Eyes and No Eyes. It's a matter of letters, by the way. So now all you've got to do is to make the same guess as I'm making, and you'll be level with me and, I expect, one move ahead of Bob Denzil."

"Letters?" echoed Wendover. "Oh, you mean this warning note that Druce Carfax got yesterday? I haven't seen it. How do you expect me to infer anything—"

The opening of the door cut him short and he rose to his feet as Enid Carfax came into the room. As she looked from one to the other of her visitors, Wendover had to admit the aptness of Denzil's description: "An inquiring glance, not brassy, but pleasantly interested." In the matter of her ankles, also, Denzil seemed to have hit the mark; and her face, under its chestnut hair, was quite pretty enough to justify the enthusiasm he had shown about it.

Sir Clinton did not wait for the Squire to introduce him. "You know Mr. Wendover, of course," he said to the girl. "My name is Driffield. . . ."

"Oh, yes," answered the girl composedly. "You're the Head Constable, aren't you?"

"The *Chief* Constable," Wendover corrected, stung by the suggestion that he made intimate friends so low down in the police force as a Head Constable.

"I apologise," said Enid Carfax, with a suspicion of mockery in her smile. "Apparently I've put my foot in it at the start. The *Chief* Constable, not the *Head* Constable, of course. I'd better call you Sir Clinton—I do know that—and steer clear of slips of the tongue. Won't you sit down?"

She seated herself and again glanced from one to the other as though waiting for them to explain the reason for their presence. Wendover, examining her covertly, felt a certain slight fall in the sympathy which he had been ready to extend. This girl had lost a brother—well, a half-brother—in the tragedy in Apsley Spinney; but so far as he could see, there were no signs of tears about her. Then he remembered that make-up could obliterate such things. Still, she seemed wonderfully cool. But then, he reflected, some people took a pride in not showing a wound to strangers. What he took for hardness might possibly be merely pride and self-restraint.

Sir Clinton did not plunge straight into business as Wendover feared that he might. He began by saying a few words of sympathy with the Carfaxes in their loss; and Wendover had to admit to himself that the Chief Constable steered most adroitly among the reefs of that subject. Enid Carfax seemed to appreciate his careful reticence, and she thanked him gracefully enough, though without any excess of warmth. Then once more she sat silent, leaving it to Sir Clinton to make the next move.

"I'm sure you'll understand, Miss Carfax," the Chief Constable began, "that I wouldn't trouble you at present if it could be avoided. But if we are to lay our hands on the person who caused your brother's death, we shall need all the information available. You'll believe me when I say that in some things I may have to ask I'm not fishing out of vulgar curiosity; and I'm sure you won't regard the questions as offensive, even if they touch you closely. We must have all the information we can get, for we can't tell whether a fact is important or not until we can fit it in along with the others."

Enid Carfax lifted her head and examined the Chief Constable's face for a moment. Wendover, noting the shrewdness of that glance, was again reminded of Denzil's verdicts: "Pretty cool, except when excited. Still, she looks as if she could show a good turn of temper it she got peeved." Evidently, at the moment, Enid Carfax was "pretty cool," to judge by her manner.

"Yes, I quite see that," she agreed.

"I've been told that your brother received a letter warning him that a raid was going to be made on his pheasants last night," Sir Clinton explained. "Did he say anything about that to you?"

"Not to me," Enid Carfax replied.

It was clear to Wendover that Enid Carfax would make an excellent showing in the witness box. She answered the questions put to her but volunteered nothing. Unfortunately, the characteristics which tell in the witness box are not those which are most useful to a detective making a fishing inquiry. Wendover felt that this lack of fluency was deliberate. She might not have anything to conceal, but she certainly did not intend to encourage the Chief Constable to widen his field of investigation into her own affairs.

"I think I understand," Sir Clinton pursued. "That afternoon, you and your brother were not on very good terms. That was it, wasn't it?"

Enid Carfax glanced at him sharply for a moment as he made this suggestion. She evidently realised that the servants had been talking.

"That is so," she admitted.

"May I ask what the disagreement was about?" persisted Sir Clinton.

"It was a purely private affair," Enid Carfax declared, in a tone which was clearly intended to stop further inquiry.

Sir Clinton refused to be staved off so easily.

"I'll put my cards on the table, Miss Carfax," he said with a pleasant smile. "We have some information which leads us to think that blackmail was one of the factors in this intricate affair."

"Blackmail?" the girl ejaculated in a tone which seemed to leave no doubt that the suggestion came as a complete surprise to her. "Who was being blackmailed?"

"Well, I'll put it to you formally, Miss Carfax. Were *you* being blackmailed by anyone?"

"I?" exclaimed the girl, and this time Wendover felt sure that her astonishment was quite unfeigned. "I can't imagine how you got that idea. As you put a formal question, I'll give you a formal reply. I was certainly *not* being blackmailed by anyone." Then she seemed to recover from her surprise and to grow indignant. "Who dared to suggest anything of that sort? I know there's been some ill-natured gossip going round, about my affairs; but this is over the limit."

"Another formal question, Miss Carfax," Sir Clinton went on, ignoring her anger. "I have to put these things to you because I want a definite denial of them, you see? Do you think it possible that some ill-disposed person may have gone to your brother with some tale about you and may have induced your brother to pay money to hush the matter up?"

Miss Carfax reflected for a moment, as though this question had suggested a train of thought to her. When she did speak, it was not in direct reply to the Chief Constable's question.

"I think I see it," she said frankly. "I have a friend, a Mr. Bulstrode, a married man. We go about together a good deal, and I know there's been a lot of ill-natured chatter about us: how we stay for week-ends at hotels, and that kind of thing. There's nothing in it. We're just good friends. Some rumours of this did get round to my brother, who was rather a strait-laced man. He didn't understand modern ways of living, and he took offence at the affair. We had a talk about it last Saturday, and I think we both lost our tempers. He talked a good deal about the honour of our family. He was always very strong on that, I should tell you. Of course I was angry that he should swallow this kind of gossip and refuse to take my word about the matter. As it happens, my half-brother, Mr. Finborough, knew a good deal about the circumstances; so I wrote to him, asking him to come down. He lives in London and was often at my flat there so he knew most of my friends and had every opportunity of seeing what my relations with Mr. Bulstrode actually were. So I asked him to come down and tell my brother Druce that the whole thing was a mare's nest. But it never struck me that anyone might be using that business as a basis of blackmail or that my brother Druce would ever dream of paying hush money on that account. The thing's too absurd."

"Still, you can't definitely say that it didn't happen?" Sir Clinton inquired.

"No, naturally I can't say that," Miss Carfax admitted in a less assured tone. "Now that I think over it, there is just a possibility that my brother Druce might have been induced to do it, with his notions about family honour and high standards in social affairs. Still, really, I think you might put it aside as unlikely."

Sir Clinton did not persist along that line of inquiry.

"I understand that your brothers—half-brothers, I believe they are—had a very marked disagreement when Mr. Finborough came down on Wednesday? There was a heated discussion, wasn't there?"

"So Mr. Finborough told me," Enid Carfax admitted. "I wasn't present at it."

Sir Clinton seemed quite satisfied with this.

"I'm sorry to have worried you so much, Miss Carfax," he apologised. "But you can understand that in a serious case like this, we have to go into many things which may turn out to have no bearing on the matter, once we've investigated them. That's my excuse for troubling you at such a time. I'm sure you'll forgive me. Oh, by the way, I think I've come across Mr. Finborough somewhere. Have you a photograph of him? I'd just like to make sure."

"I'll send my maid to you with it, if you wish," Enid Carfax promised as she rose to her feet.

"That's very good of you. And now, I mustn't trouble you any longer. Thanks for giving us the facts," Sir Clinton said, as he moved over to open the door. "I'd like to see Mr. Julian Carfax, if he's not busy."

"I'll send him to you," Enid Carfax agreed, with a friendly smile as she took farewell of them and passed out of the room.

"Well, that seems clear enough," Wendover remarked when she had gone. "I don't hold with modern manners much, but one has to take them as they come. And obviously that lady's maid has been making a mountain out of a molehill. The girl's quite straight, if I'm any judge."

"If you're any judge, certainly, Squire. But since you confess that you're out of touch with the modern generation, I'm chary of taking your opinion as Gospel. Pretty girl, isn't she?" he added slyly.

"Too pretty to be wasting herself on a married man," retorted Wendover, stoutly. "She ought to be looking round for someone more suitable."

"Thinking of applying yourself?"

Wendover laughed at the suggestion.

"No," he said. "Your young friend Bob Denzil seems to me to have hit it off when he opined that she'd be 'all right for fair-weather sailing.' She looks as if she might occasionally take a strong line and hold to it, if she chose. She may be a handful for whoever gets her in the end."

Sir Clinton was about to make a retort when the door opened hesitatingly and Julian Carfax came into the room, blinking at his two visitors as he advanced towards them. He had an envelope in his hand, which he held out to the Chief Constable.

"That's the letter you asked for," he explained. "At least, I think it is the one. It seems to be."

Sir Clinton paused before taking it from its envelope.

"Many people been handling this?" he asked.

"I should think so. In fact, it's very likely," Julian answered with as much decision as he seemed capable of showing. "A good many. You see, Druce was so angry when he got it that he showed it to nearly everyone in the place and I expect their finger marks will be on it, if that's what you're thinking about. He had it himself and he handed it to me, and he told me he showed it to the keeper, poor chap, and I think Godfrey may have seen it as well, and most likely he let other people have a look at it, too, though I can't remember anyone else at the moment. He left it on his desk; so probably some of the servants may have taken a glance at it out of curiosity since he'd been making such a fuss about it."

"Not much hope for our finger-print expert, then," said Sir Clinton, as he drew the paper from the envelope.

When he had read the note, he passed it to Wendover.

20th August, 1936

It will please you to hear that some of the village lads are going to have a try for a pheasant or two to-night in Apsley Spinney.

They say that poaching on your ground is as easy as taking toffee from a baby, and I'm not sure they're wrong about that.

I don't like you any better than most people do, but I like to see fair play so I send you this warning just in case you'd care to stir yourself to protect your birds.

Good luck and a pleasant evening to you.

A WELLWISHER.

"It's typed on a sheet torn off one of these cheap writing pads they sell in the chain stores, by the look of it," Wendover pointed out. "You can see the roughness at the top of the sheet, where it's been torn off the pad. The watermark's CIVIC BOND. Not much of a clue to the typist. What about the envelope?"

"Chain-store stuff too, one would think," Sir Clinton replied.

He examined the typed address and then the postmark, first with the naked eye and then through a Coddington lens which he took from his pocket.

"These stamps get worse and worse," he grumbled. "I wish the Postmaster-General would look into that side of his business. In the old days, one could see at a glance where and when a letter was posted. Now, it's a case of original research, with about a fifty per cent. chance of failure. One can just make out that this envelope was posted in Abbots Norton; and with a bit of imagination one could venture on 20th August. The time looks like 11 a.m., but it might be 10. The last figure's almost invisible through lack of ink. Luckily that doesn't matter much. We can check it at the post office. When did it reach Mr. Carfax?" he asked, turning to Julian.

"By the one o'clock post, I think," Julian replied carefully. "At least, it's what we call the one o'clock post. Sometimes it comes before one o'clock; sometimes it comes a little later, if the postman has a heavy round that day; and I've known it to come in as early as half past twelve. I can't say exactly when Druce got this letter. You see, he may have been out when the postman arrived. . . ."

"Quite so," Sir Clinton cut abruptly into the stream of minute explanation. "We can find out from the postman himself when he delivered it. Now I want to ask you a further question or two, Mr. Carfax. Your brother wasn't married, so far as you know?"

"No, I never heard of his being married," Julian admitted. "He may have been, of course. One hears stories about secret marriages sometimes, I know. But Druce had such an idea of our family, you know, that I can't see him going in for anything of that sort. No, I don't think it's at all likely. Though of course you never can tell, can you?"

"The man who invented that phrase should have a monument," Sir Clinton declared. "Now, another question. Your brother inherited the estate on your father's death. Could he do what he liked with it? Or was there any provision in your father's will that governed such a case as this?"

Julian rubbed the back of his head as though in some perplexity. Then, after staring up at the cornice as though seeking information, he replied with his usual caution.

"I'm not altogether sure of my ground in these legal affairs, you know; they're too intricate for me, with all these phrases like 'declaring always and specially providing' and 'to the contrary notwithstanding' and 'hereinbefore mentioned.' You'll have to go to our lawyers if you want the thing explained officially, for although I've got a general notion of how things stand, I really can't guarantee to give you it all offhand like this, you know. But I've some recollection, which I think's probably fairly near the mark though I won't stake my oath on it, you understand, that if Druce died without issue, the estate was to come to me next and then if I died without having a family, it was to go to my sister Enid. But that's just my recollection of what our lawyers told me when I came of age and got some capital my father left me. The lawyers explained the will to me then. I know Druce came first and I came next. But our lawyers know all about it; and you'd better try them, really, if you want to be sure about it all."

"Who are your lawyers?" asked the Chief Constable, taking out his pocketbook.

"Fentiman and Forester. We always called them F. and F., because the names are so long. Their office is in Ambledown."

Sir Clinton jotted down the name of the firm and replaced his notebook in his pocket.

"Now, another question," he said, turning to Julian. "Did you always get on well with your brother Druce?"

"Did I always get on well with my brother Druce?" echoed Julian as though trying to gain time for thought. "Oh, yes; at least, that is, on the whole, I mean. We had a spat, now and again, for he was sometimes difficult to deal with if he got his back up over anything and he was apt to be a bit quick-tempered, you know. But on the whole I should say we got on quite well, for I'm fairly easy-going myself and I hate to have trouble. It's easier to give in, even if the other man happens to be in the wrong, I always think. What's the use of squabbling over something or other which isn't really of much importance anyway? Yes, I should say that he and I got on quite well, all things considered."

"I understand that there's been some friction lately between your brother Druce and the rest of your family?"

"Well, yes," admitted Julian with the faintest reluctance. "It was really no affair of mine, you understand? I took neither side but just kept clear of it so far as I could, for there didn't seem to be any need for me to shove my oar into a business which didn't concern me directly. Some people are always rushing in to take sides in family squabbles, but I always think that the more you keep out of these things the easier it is to get on with people. One never knows who's in the right, really, in things of that kind."

"Have you any idea what it was all about?" demanded Sir Clinton.

"I didn't take much interest," Julian explained frankly. "It wasn't anything that touched me, you see. Druce and my sister got across one another about some fellow Bulstrode, I think I've never met him, don't know anything about him, really; so naturally I didn't mix myself up in the squabble at all but just let them wear themselves out over it. I find that far the best way to save trouble, for the more people you get mixed up in affairs of that sort, the more difficult it is to smooth things down in the end. At least, that's what I find myself."

"Then Mr. Godfrey Finborough got mixed up in it, didn't he?"

"Yes, he came down here on Wednesday night. Now that just proves what I was saying, doesn't it? What need was there for him to come butting in at all? It only meant that he got across Druce, for they never did get on well with each other, somehow. If he'd stayed in London, the whole thing would have been over when Druce and my sister had talked themselves out; but he just brisked up the blaze again by interfering. It made things very uncomfortable for me, for I hate to live in an atmosphere of that kind."

"There was an acute disagreement between your brother and Mr. Finborough, I understand?"

"Oh, yes, if you like to put it that way. I mean, they quite lost their tempers and Druce, I believe, ordered Godfrey off the premises finally. But then, you know, he never did like having Godfrey about the place. Some people seem to dislike having old scandals raked up, though what it matters nowadays I never could see. Everybody knows about it, you know, so it's no use trying to pretend they don't, though Druce seemed to think if you shut your own eyes everybody else does the same. But I don't see much use in that, really. Everybody knows that our father was an old rip and that Godfrey was his son, so what's the good of pretending? I quite admit that Judy Finborough was a bit notorious in the West End at one time—a sort of reprint of Skittles, you know—and Druce hated to see her about the place when my father brought her and Godfrey back here when I was a boy. And when they stayed here, Godfrey and Druce didn't get on together. They were always scrapping and giving trouble. In a way it was a good thing when our trustees packed Godfrey off to London after my father died. There was really no peace in the house, with those two on the premises. But that's all over and it's no good raking it up now, I think."

Sir Clinton seemed to weary of the Carfax family troubles.

"What did you do with yourself after dinner last night?" he asked.

"What did I do with myself?" repeated Julian, evidently put out by this sudden change of subject. "I'm not quite sure, but let's see. I generally take a little nap after dinner, just for a quarter of an hour or so, for I find that refreshes me and I wake up again much brighter. I suppose I had my usual nap last night. Yes, I had. I went into the billiard-room and lay down on the settee, now I come to think of it. Then, when I woke up, what did I do? Let's think. Oh, yes, I remember I felt a bit stuffy and I thought a stroll would do me good, get some fresh air and that kind of thing. So I went out and strolled about a bit and smoked a cigar and thought about one thing and another. And then I came in again and read the evening paper for a while, and then it was about time to go to bed, so I went upstairs."

"Did you see your brother Druce after dinner?"

"Did I? Oh, yes, I did, now I come to think of it. I met him in the hall just as I was going out. He'd changed his clothes and he had a hunting crop in his hand, I remember, the one they found up in Apsley Spinney, beside him. I didn't say anything to him then; I could see he was in a bad temper and it was always best to leave him alone when he was in a rage, so I said nothing and he said nothing to me, but just went out. I had an idea he was off after these poachers, you know. It wasn't any business of mine."

"Where did you go for your stroll?" inquired the Chief Constable. "Not towards Apsley Spinney, I suppose?"

"Oh, no. I just walked down the avenue a bit and then came back to the house again."

"Did you see Miss Carfax when you got in again?"

"No, I didn't," Julian explained. "To tell you the truth, I was a bit tired of all this arguing and quarreling and squabbling that was going on and I preferred to keep out of the way until it had died down a bit. It seemed the easiest thing to do; so I didn't look about for either Druce or my sister when I came in. I just went up to my room."

"What time was that?"

"I really don't know," Julian declared. "It might have been after ten or thereabouts, but really I can't tell you exactly, or anywhere nearer that, for I didn't look at my watch after dinner so far as I can remember. After all, one doesn't look at one's watch much in the evening anyway, for one knows pretty well without looking at it whether it's time to go to bed, so I can't give you even a rough idea of the time, really."

"Did you meet anyone during your stroll?"

"I? No, not that I can remember. I wouldn't expect to see anyone on the avenue at that time of night, you know, for if there had been a visitor he'd have come earlier in the evening, most likely, for we're fairly early birds here and most people know it. They don't drop in, late in the evening, unless they ring up to say they're coming. At least, that's true so far as Druce and myself were concerned. My sister's friends sometimes dropped in later on in the evening, for she sits up later than Druce and I do, usually."

"That seems to be all I have to ask you just now," Sir Clinton said, to Julian's evident relief. "Your sister said she'd send her maid with something for me to look at."

"Just ring the bell, then, will you?" suggested Julian. "You're nearest it. And if you don't want me any longer, I'll be trotting along. All this business has been very worrying, as I've no doubt you can imagine for yourselves, and it takes it out of one, somehow. Emotional strain's always exhausting, I think, even if one doesn't show it. In fact, perhaps it's most exhausting when one doesn't show it, now I come to think of it. I hope I haven't made an ass of myself in that way—showing my feelings, I mean, and making people uncomfortable."

"You've borne up wonderfully," Wendover assured him with an irony which seemed quite lost on Julian.

"Well, if you want to get any more information about things, just ring up F. and F., will you?" Julian suggested as he began to close the door behind him. "They'll be able to tell you just what's what, I expect, better than I can, for really it's so long since I bothered my head about the estate that I can't pretend to remember details nowadays. But F. and F. will be able to give you all the information, I'm sure."

And thus, lingeringly, he took his departure.

Sir Clinton rang the bell and in a few moments Tobin came in with a photograph frame which she handed to the Chief Constable. He glanced at it, but waited until she left the room before making any comment. Then he handed the portrait to Wendover.

"I thought so," he explained.

"It's that fellow Fairbank that we saw at Huggin's lodgings," ejaculated Wendover at the first glance.

"Yes, I told you I'd put two and two together and made two of it."

"You said something about letters," said Wendover, "What's this got to do with letters?"

"Well, I took the initials of George Fairbank and Godfrey Finborough—G.F. and G.F.—and I put them together and made only one G.F. out of them: George Fairbank *alias* Godfrey Finborough.

Of course the odds and ends of description of Finborough that we got from Bob Denzil put me on the track, plus the fact that there was some connection between Huggin and Carfax Hall."

"But why does Finborough call himself Fairbank in London?" asked Wendover. "Why doesn't he use his own name?"

"As our friend Julian would say: 'I don't know, really.' But considering that he was packed off to London a good many years ago, I can imagine that at that period his mother's name was still pretty well remembered in the West End as Julian informed us—and perhaps Godfrey thought it advisable to avoid it. It's an uncommon name, and I expect he didn't want to have people referring to him as 'a son of Judy Finborough, you know, the notorious one.' That seems a possible explanation."

"But why keep the same initials?"

"Because, Squire, in the lowlier strata of society in those days, people put their initials on their linen. It would save comment—and the cost of a complete new outfit—to keep the initials the same in the new name. If you live in lodgings, your linen goes through your landlady's hands, and she might get a bit suspicious if you turned out to have the wrong initials on your shirts. That's my explanation of it; and if you want a better one, then you can look for it yourself."

"Might be something in what you say," Wendover admitted, though rather grudgingly. "Then you think that Fairbank-Finborough is the link connecting Huggin with Abbots Norton?"

"I'm not certain of it," Sir Clinton admitted, "for I don't see what's at the bottom of the Huggin murder even yet. No, it's something that Fairbank said in our interview that sticks in my throat a bit, and yet it might be explained easily enough. But turn to something more definite, Squire. What did you make of that warning letter about the poachers? Anything strike you as curious?"

"Of course one thing stares you in the face," Wendover pointed out. "It's the close season for pheasants, so what good would poachers do themselves by taking birds they couldn't sell?"

"They might eat them, as our friend Walton explained to us."

"Then a brace or so would be all they'd want. They wouldn't come up here to make a *battue,* would they?"

"In that case, I'd have thought that snares would be more in their line than night forays; but I bow to your superior *expertise,* Squire. You may be right. As a matter of fact, I wasn't thinking of that side of the thing at all."

"What struck you, then?" inquired Wendover. "Let's see the letter again, please."

The Chief Constable opened it out on a table and Wendover conned it over carefully.

"The spelling's all right," he said. "It doesn't come from an uneducated man."

"Uneducated men haven't access to typewriters in the ordinary way," Sir Clinton pointed out. "No, it isn't that, however."

"I don't see it, then."

"If you look at the spacing between the lines, you'll find that there's enough and no more to take in an interlinear correction," Sir Clinton explained. "Now in the ordinary business communication, you find the spacing closer than that, because if the professional typist makes an error—which a good one seldom does—she erases it and writes in the correction in the blank space left by the erasure. So she doesn't need this wider spacing such as you have here. Of course, you can adjust the spacing by moving a lever. But would it occur to anyone to do that, if they started to write on a machine, unless there was some special reason for making the change? It's possible, of course, but really I don't think it's quite the sort of thing one would expect to find done, if you understand what I mean, as Julian would tell you in his concise way. Especially when one can find a simpler explanation by assuming that the type spacing wasn't altered. I'm so convinced of my own sagacity in this matter, Squire, that I'm going to put Cumberland and Bob Denzil on the job. It's in Bob's line, to some extent, and he'll be company for the inspector while they're working at it. Besides, it'll get him out of Abbots Norton at the moment, and that's always something gained. I'm nervous about that young man's doings. He's a bit too enterprising, in some ways."

"He won't get his round at golf now, at any rate," Wendover surmised, not altogether unkindly "That's hard lines on him. But what are you driving at in this typescript business, Clinton?"

"No, no, Squire. Do your own thinking. I've given you the data. *'I said it very loud and clear; I went and shouted in his ear.'* What more do you want?"

"Posing as Humpty Dumpty, are you?" asked Wendover ironically. "Well, you know what happened to him in the end. And there's more likeness than I thought, at first sight. Humpty Dumpty had a way of talking so that no one could make out what he was driving at. 'Impenetrability!' Wasn't that one of his remarks?"

"Yes, I remember," Sir Clinton admitted. "That meant 'that we've had enough of that subject and it would be just as well if you'd mention what you meant to do next, as I suppose you don't mean to stop here all the rest of your life.' I agree with you. Let's go now."

# CHAPTER XV
## THE VICISSITUDES OF A TYPEWRITER

"MATE IN FOUR MOVES," said Sir Clinton.

Wendover studied the board for a moment or two before giving a nod of resignation.

"I ought to have seen what you were after, when you sacrificed your knight," he confessed. "Can't think how I came to overlook it."

He began to set the board for the next game, but the Chief Constable glanced at his watch.

"Not worth while starting another," he said, with a restraining gesture. "Cumberland rang up just before they left London; and Bob Denzil will cover the distance under three hours, roughly, at the rate he usually drives. They may be dropping in on us any minute now. We may as well wait."

Wendover glanced at his own watch and began to stow the chessmen away in the drawer of the chess table.

"So you actually did send Denzil to town with Cumberland?" he inquired.

Sir Clinton nodded.

"Yes," he explained, half seriously. "First of all, I wanted to get that young man safely off the premises at the moment. Things seem complex enough without having him bustling about the place. Gifted amateurs are all right in books, Squire, but I've no use for ungifted amateurs in real life, especially when they talk as much as Bob Denzil does."

"Something in that," Wendover admitted. "It's just on the cards he might hit on something important and give it away in his enthusiasm. Especially as he seems to have wormed his way into the Carfax circle by his cheek. Safer to send him to town, certainly."

He reflected for a moment or two, and then put a question.

"What do you think of Julian Carfax, Clinton?"

"Not much," said the Chief Constable concisely.

"A bit of an egotist?"

"Something in that line. Egocentric might fit better."

"He comes into the property, now that Druce has gone," Wendover mused. "I wonder what he'll make of it."

"As a landlord? No worse than his brother, from all you said."

"He'll let things go to rack and ruin through sheer laziness," grumbled Wendover.

"Cheer up!" suggested the Chief Constable sardonically. "Perhaps he'll die suddenly. One never can tell. Then, I suppose, Bob's young friend will come in for the property. . . . Talk of the devil! There's the car."

In a few moments, Denzil and Cumberland were ushered into the room.

"*Eh Bien! Nous voilà encore une fois,* as the French don't say," Denzil began, after greeting his host. "The return of the conquerors, eh? after a most interesting day's sleuthing. You'll find it all in my next book *Tracked by the Typewriter*, Sunburst Press, Ltd. Seven and sixpence, net. At all bookstalls. Order it, if they are sold out, as they probably will be. Thanks, whiskey and soda for me."

"I hear the safety valve fizzling, Bob," said Sir Clinton wearily. "If we don't let you get your wind out, I suppose you'll burst. Not that that would be any great loss, I suppose; but it might make a mess of the room. So you *can* tell your tale, such as it is; and I'll get the facts from the inspector, later on."

"I'm not used to this fine old Spanish courtesy, alguazil," protested Denzil with a gesture of deprecation. "You leave me, positively, with no option but to proceed with my tale, regardless of age or sex. Where was I? Oh, yes, at the beginning, I think. It was a bright sunny morning, and so forth, when I, accompanied by my able but official coadjutor, stepped into my almost-Rolls car and set off for London, the Home of Big Ben. Cumberland, very properly, wished to get the blessing of New Scotland Yard on our enterprise, so we went there first. I'd never been inside before. Disappointing, I found it. The corridors look like any other corridors. I can't speak for anything else from personal experience. I suggested to a passing catchpole that I might drop into the Black Museum to while away the time; but he told me it was not available at the moment. Gone to the wash, or something."

"They found it gave simple souls like yourself the idea that crime was easy," Sir Clinton explained. "So they closed it to avoid such misunderstandings."

"The catchpole did say something of the sort," Denzil admitted. "And he gave me quite a nasty look, too, the way they do when they ask for your driving licence. Cumberland can tell you. He hove in sight just then, or I might be doing three days hard for loitering with intent or leaving car unattended.

"The next port of call was just as dull, though different. Cumberland, here present, desired to visit the Crescent Theater of Varieties. Tact hindered me from asking what took him there. Young blood—up in London for the day. We all know how much it means. We've been young ourselves, Cumberland. But I must say you stayed inside a devil of a time: three cigarettes at least. And as no performance was going on then, you can't have been merely watching a turn from the wings."

Cumberland seemed to regard Denzil as a chartered libertine. He threw an understanding grin at Wendover. Then, becoming official, he fished two papers from his pocket and handed them to the Chief Constable. From the pictures on the front, Wendover recognised them as copies of the Crescent programme which he had often seen.

"These are the two, sir," the inspector explained as he passed them over. "I've endorsed them: one from Scotland Yard, the other from the Crescent office. I've checked them. They're identical. And here's the inset issued with the second one."

He handed over a slip of white paper. Sir Clinton glanced at it, nodded as if satisfied, and laid the three papers on the table beside him.

"Go on with this biography of yours," he said, turning to Denzil, and excluding any cross-questioning on his byplay with the inspector.

"A little lesson in geography now, to give you the local colour?" Denzil suggested, taking in good part his exclusion from official confidence. "Like Caesar's Gaul, London is divided into three parts: the bit you know; the bit you think you know something about; and the bit you know you know nothing about. The third part is the biggest; and if you venture into it without the price of a taxi in your fob, you're lost for good. It was this third part that Cumberland dragged me into, in search of Number Forty-seven, Rookery Park. We found it, eventually; and I can't speak too highly of my tenacity in the quest. The further we went into these wilds, the less chance there seemed of our ever having lunch that day, unless we took rooms for the week in one of the innumerable lodging houses. We found a promising 'pull-up for car men'; but man cannot live by beer alone, though it wasn't bad beer, really. Cumberland took porter, I believe."

Cumberland seemed about to interrupt, but Denzil waved him aside.

"It may have been stout, I admit," he said graciously. "But don't let's argue over nonessentials. The point is that Ganymede—I mean the bartender, of course—helped to put us on the right road and we reached Rookery Park. Number forty-seven was a depressing place with a Manx cat sitting on the doorstep."

"We've seen that house," interjected the Chief Constable. "Don't waste your descriptive talents on us, Bob, but get on with the tale."

"A lady, no longer young, answered the bell, and turned quite puce in the face at the sight of such distinguished visitors. 'Are you more of them?' she inquired when she could choke down her emotion. Cumberland produced his official card and we led her inside to administer the Third Degree.

"'Where is the typewriter of Huggin?' Cumberland asked her in the style of the First French Primer. And at that her colour deepened. I don't know what comes next to puce in the spectrum, but that was how she looked. 'Guilty, my Lord!' written all over her. I made a note of it for future reference. Cumberland, stout fellow, gave her no time to recover her wits, if she had any. And so the sad tale came out.

"The late Huggin, it seems, had departed this life without paying his bill to her. A trifling sum to one of my characters, but important to her. It seems she had lamented it to one of her lodgers and he had advised her to dispose of some of the late Huggin's portable property to square the account, suggesting this typewriter as being about the mark in the way of price. This might seem a bit high-handed to us, but Cumberland tells me that a death in the house is not infrequently the signal for the lower classes to loot all that they can in the hope that minor articles won't be missed; so perhaps her reaction to the suggestion was not unnatural. I don't know how it stands in law, in this particular case."

"Never mind the law," said the Chief Constable. "Get on with the tale."

"I shall continue my narrative," said Denzil, "when these unseemly interruptions cease. Quite done? Thank you. I proceed. Our hostess, it appears—her name's Hassop, by the way—had thereupon transported the typewriter of the late Huggin to a second-hand emporium round the corner, in the High Street; and, being an honest old thing apparently, had parted with it for the sum which exactly squared her with the deceased. She was, I gather, rather put out a day or two later when, passing the shop, she observed the typewriter in the window with a ticket pricing it considerably higher than the sum she'd obtained for it. The margin of profit struck her as being overlarge, it seems. But that's by the way. We secured the address of this marine store or whatever it was, and bade her farewell, after Cumberland had informed her that perhaps she'd hear more about the matter. I gather she expressed the strongest desire *not* to hear more about it. A most incurious woman, really."

Denzil interrupted his tale to drink from the glass beside him, but Wendover surmised that the interruption was meant for dramatic effect.

"This is where the interest quickens," he announced, putting down his tumbler. "We called upon this dealer in debilitated goods and, with the aid of Cumberland's official card and my intuitive powers, we extracted from him a strange story. Yes, he had acquired a typewriter from Mrs. Hassop for three guineas. Yes, he had placed it in his shop window, ticketed £4-10-0. No, he had not placed it in the forefront of the battle; he just showed it in at the side quite inconspicuously. It stayed there for one day. Then there arrived in his shop a man in the uniform of the Corps of Commissionaires who pointed to the typewriter in the window, paid cash down for it, had it wrapped up, and removed himself and the typewriter with no further ado.

"So the next port of call was obviously the Strand, where the Corps of Commissionaires received us with all politeness. Cumberland's card did the rest. They hunted up their records. From these it appeared that they had received a letter asking them to send a Commissionaire to the second-hand emporium previously mentioned in my story. He was to buy the typewriter, as described, and £5-10-0 in notes was enclosed in the letter to cover cost and expenses. The balance, if any, was to be sent to an address given in the letter."

Cumberland produced a fresh sheet of paper which he passed over to the Chief Constable. Sir Clinton glanced at it, then scrutinised it more carefully, and finally put it down on the table with the others, without comment.

"When the commissionaire obtained the typewriter," Denzil continued, "the instructions were that he was to deposit it in the Left Luggage Office at Euston Station. The receipt for it was to be enclosed in the letter along with the balance of cash and posted to—"

He turned to the inspector.

"John Saltram, 93 Annfield Terrace, Minard Road, Blackheath, S.E. 3," Cumberland read from his notebook.

"This had been done by the Corps of Commissionaires with their usual efficiency. And there, so far as they were concerned, the matter ended. Now," continued Denzil, "up to that point, as you have seen, this valuable piece of sleuthing had gone just as in the books. Clues had been spread before us in neat succession and we had plodded along without the slightest difficulty. In fact, I don't mind telling you, I began to acquire the idea that Scotland Yard and all the rest of them were a bit overrated. It seemed so easy that anything above a moron could have done it. But now came a snag, hitch, stumbling block, oppilation, or embarrassment. Blackheath is off my beat. So far as I am concerned, it lies in London, Division III. I communicated this to Cumberland, and his Napoleonic mind at once evolved a solution of the difficulty. He asked for a Post Office Directory, which the Corps of Commissionaires most kindly supplied before you could say Aldiborontiphoscophornio or recite one stanza of 'Mary Had a Little Lamb.' And, believe it or not, there's no such address in Blackheath, S.E. 3. Sensation!"

"But then the letter would come back to the Corps of Commissionaires through the Dead Letter Office," objected Wendover. "Why hasn't it turned up?"

"It takes weeks for a letter to come back to the sender via the Dead Letter Office," Sir Clinton pointed out. "Probably they're trying all the Annfield Terraces in the country at present, on the off-chance of the address being wrong in some detail or other. That letter won't turn up for weeks yet. And, in the normal way, the Corps could do nothing with it, when it did come back to them, since the only address they had was a false one. And the typewriter was apparently buried in the Left Luggage Office, where it would stay for months until it was sold off as unclaimed property. A neat scheme, I must admit."

"But," interrupted Denzil, "as Poet Burns remarks:

> The best laid schemes o' mice and men
> Gang aft a-gley.

Especially when two competent sleuths like Cumberland and myself take a hand. We dashed to Euston Station Left Luggage Office. Cumberland produced his official talisman. After interviewing numerous officials, we bore off the long-sought typewriter. Cumberland pretended it was stolen property, which it may or may not be. I'm hazy on the point. But Cumberland, stout fellow, never blenched as he made the claim, so for the sake of his morals I hope it was correct."

Sir Clinton glanced at the inspector, who nodded: "It's outside in the car, sir. Shall I bring it in?"

"Let Mr. Denzil finish first, I think. Then we shall be able to get to business without interruption."

"You encourage me to continue?" asked Denzil. "We next had a long-deferred lunch. And that reminds me, who pays for all this petrol and other items which I have furnished to-day? I hate to seem grasping, but—"

"Send your bill to us and our accountant will disallow what he thinks fit. Considering the amusement you've had, Bob, and the amount of advertisement you've given yourself since you began, I think if you handed us five bob we might call it square."

"No wonder the Lord Chief Justice writes books about The New Bureaucracy!" complained Denzil. "But let that pass for the moment. Refreshed by food and drink, Cumberland decided to call on Messrs. Rodsley, the literary agents, from whom he collected some paper or other."

Again the inspector felt in his pocket and produced a paper which he handed across to Sir Clinton, and again the Chief Constable, after a glance, placed it with the others.

"Finished?" he inquired of Denzil.

"Well, we came back here, just in case you haven't grasped that fact yet."

"And are you not going to tell us the interesting part of the story, Bob?" asked the Chief Constable suavely. "I mean, the point of it all. You seem to have left that out, somehow. Now suppose you restrain yourself and give the inspector a turn. He'll tell us the important things."

He turned to Cumberland, inviting him to speak.

"Well, sir," the inspector began. "First of all, I'd like to say how very useful Mr. Denzil has been. He's taken a lot of trouble, driving me round, and saved me a lot of time. I'm very grateful to him for what he's done."

Wendover glanced at Denzil and repressed a smile at the expression on the face of the author when he heard this tribute from which all acknowledgment of brains was omitted.

"May I have these papers, sir?" the inspector continued. "Thank you. Here's the programme of the Crescent Theater that I got from New Scotland Yard. That's the one Inspector Summerfield got at Rookery Park the day you were there. Fairbank brought it in with him from the theater. Now here's the second copy, which I got at the Crescent office. Just the same as the other."

He handed them across to Wendover to examine, rather with the air of a conjurer beginning a trick. Then he turned back to Sir Clinton and addressed him.

"You were quite right in your guess, sir. The same programme's handed out at both the six-fifteen and the nine o'clock performances so Fairbank's copy is worthless as a proof that he was at the Crescent second performance on the night of the murder. Actually, at the second performance that night the programme had a cyclostyled inset to say that Thelma Campion had been taken ill at the first performance and couldn't appear in the second one. If Fairbank had had that, then he'd have had a lock-fast alibi or near it. As it is, he may have dropped the inset while he was reading his programme, so we can't say one thing or another. But it's perfectly possible that he dropped into the 6:15 performance for a few minutes, bought a programme, and cleared out again immediately. That finishes that subject."

"You didn't think of seeing Fairbank and asking him if he had the inset?"

"No, sir, I didn't," admitted the inspector.

"Never mind, then. Go on with your report."

"We went next to Rookery Park, as Mr. Denzil told you, sir. I questioned Mrs. Hassop about the typewriter. It was Fairbank who suggested the sale of it to cover Huggin's debt, so she said. I just asked her, in passing, as it were, so as not to let her think it was important."

"Find out when she sold it?"

"On the morning of the twentieth, sir. That's the morning of the day Carfax was murdered. I checked that by asking the second-hand dealer when it had been brought in."

"Very good. Then you went to the Headquarters of the Corps of Commissionaires and got the letter ordering them to send a man to buy the typewriter and take it to Euston. We'll take that letter along with the specimen letter that Rodsley's gave you, one of Huggin's old letters to them. Got them? Thanks."

He spread the two letters side by side on the table and compared them carefully for a minute or two. Then with a movement of his finger he swung them round so that Wendover and Denzil could follow what he said.

"You see the spacing between the lines is the same in both?" he pointed out in the first place. "Being a literary person, Bob, you'll probably appreciate why a literary man uses that spacing. It's to allow for the corrections these literary people make when they've found themselves unable to say what they want to say, straight off," he explained to the inspector. "With this spacing, they can put a correction between the lines of the MS."

"Quite so, sir. I understand."

"Further," Sir Clinton pointed out, "the margin is of the same breadth in both cases. And again, if you look closely, you'll find that the letter 't' in both documents is just a shade too much to the right. It's out of alignment, laterally, as they say. Whereas the letter 'p' is out of alignment vertically. It prints too high in every case where it appears. I dare say we could find other points of similarity if we looked for them. These are ones which struck me almost at a glance."

"They're both written on the same machine—Huggin's typewriter," Wendover agreed, after examining the documents. "But then—"

He hesitated for a moment and Denzil took the opportunity of breaking in.

"There's one difference that's escaped your eagle eye, alguazil. The letter 'e' in Huggin's own letter is quite sharp, but the loop of the 'e' is blurred wherever it appears in the letter to the Corps of Commissionaires."

"What a filthy state your own machine must be in," commented Sir Clinton. "Do you never run a brush over your type to clean the dirt out of the corners?"

"Oh, I see," said Denzil, unabashed. "It just happens that Huggin hadn't cleaned his machine for a while before he departed this life, eh? But it was cleaned shortly before he wrote this letter to his agents, some months back. That's quite all right, now I come to think of it. I often let my own type get clogged up a bit before I brush it."

Sir Clinton drew out his pocketbook and extracted from it a fresh document which he added to the pile on the table.

"This is the letter of warning, signed 'A WELL-WISHER,' and sent to Druce Carfax on the morning of Thursday. Have a look at it, all of you. Again you'll notice that the spacing is the same as in the other two letters. Also, the 't' is a shade too much to the right and the 'p' is just a fraction above the line in both cases. Furthermore, the loop of the 'e' is blurred by clogging in both the 'WELL-WISHER' letter and the directions to the Corps of Commissionaires. And, finally, if you look at these last two epistles you'll find that the paper is the same. It's come off a cheap writing pad in both cases. Compare the watermarks, for instance. They're both 'CIVIC BOND,' in a special brand of lettering. But obviously Huggin didn't write either of them. He had gone to his long home before they were typed. And, as an extra piece of evidence, although the margins are the same in all three, the paragraphs in Huggin's own letter start with an indention of five spaces, whereas the paragraphs in the Commissionaires' orders and the WELLWISHER' letter are indented ten spaces from the margin. Which is further proof that these last two documents came from the same hand."

"But, damn it, alguazil, the letter to the Corps of Commissionaires was sent to them after old Mrs. Hassop had sold the typewriter to that second-hand dealer! That's so, isn't it, Cumberland?"

"That's so, sir," confirmed Cumberland. "I saw the entry about it in the books of the Corps myself."

"Did you take a good look at the man who kept the second-hand shop, Bob?" inquired Sir Clinton genially. "A good detective has the knack of observing trifles, you know, even when they don't seem to have any direct bearing."

"Oh, I could identify him again, all right," declared Denzil confidently. "Snuffy little fellow with a slight lisp."

"A bit summary, as a description, especially as the snuffiness could be removed if necessary and the lisp might have been assumed. Notice the colour of his eyes?"

"Some light colour, blue or grey or something."

"Bulgy, or deep-set, did you observe?"

"About ordinary, I'd say."

"His ears, now. Were they large or small? Did they lie close to his head or flap out like an African elephant's? Had they large or small lobes? Were the tops rounded or pointed? What slant had the antitragus? Come along, Bob, answer smartly when you're asked important questions. You'll get muddled if you take too much time to consider."

"I don't remember trifles of that sort," said Denzil, rather crossly.

"Well, take it from me they're worth remembering, Bob, if you set up as a tec. These details, and some others, are permanent in a man, short of plastic surgery. They can't be disguised. Put that in your next thriller."

"Let's get back to business," suggested Wendover, anxious to play peacemaker. "What it amounts to is this. Mrs. Hassop sold that typewriter on Thursday. The secondhand dealer— What was his name, by the by?"

"Dewberry, sir," said Cumberland.

"Thanks. Well, then, this typewriter passed into Dewberry's hands on Thursday. And yet, on Thursday morning, a letter written on that typewriter, was posted in Abbots Norton about 11 a.m. Further, Dewberry put the typewriter in his window, where Mrs. Hassop saw it. Next day, Friday, the Corps of Commissionaires got a letter from 'John Saltram,' *written on that very typewriter and correctly dated*, ordering them to buy the machine and deposit it in Euston Left Luggage Office. And the sum enclosed was fairly correctly gauged to cover cost and expenses. You didn't see the actual envelope that letter came in, did you?" he asked, turning to Cumberland.

"No, sir. I asked about it, but they'd thrown it into the waste-paper basket when they filed the letter itself."

"Still, there's no doubt about the facts," said Wendover. "It's the dates that puzzles me. And it would have been easy enough to omit the date from both the 'WELL-WISHER' letter and the one to the Corps of Commissionaires. You didn't think of making some inquiries about this fellow Dewberry? When he set up in business, and so forth?"

"Not at the time, sir. But that's a matter of routine if it has to be done. The London people can find out for us quick enough."

Sir Clinton seemed tired of this subject.

"Nothing like making absolutely certain of things," he agreed, "so suppose we make sure of the typewriter itself. Will you bring it in, Inspector, please?"

Cumberland went out to the car and came back with the type-writer which he placed on a table which Wendover cleared for the purpose. Sir Clinton sought out some sheets of paper, clipped them into the machine, and typed out a copy of the "WELLWISHER" note. When he had finished, he showed them the result.

"Not much doubt, is there? There's that clogged 'e' showing up, as well as the other peculiarities. You'd better take charge of this typewriter, Inspector. Pack it up and seal it, so that no one can tamper with it. It looks as if we may need it."

"Very good, sir."

"By the way, you didn't see the commissionaire who actually took it to Euston Left Luggage Office?"

"No, sir. I inquired about him, but it seems he's gone on holiday just now, so I couldn't get hold of him."

"We can always lay our hands on him if we need him for the witness box. We've got all he could tell us already, I expect."

Denzil had been fidgeting slightly during this last episode, and Wendover got the impression that he was feeling rather out of the picture. He now broke in, speaking with a certain air of triumph.

"I may not have the plodding intelligence which makes notes of eyes, ears, toenails, and so forth, alguazil; but still when it comes to the really important points, you have to come to me."

Sir Clinton turned round to look at him.

"Well, then, assume that we have come to you, Bob. Where are the important points?"

And he pretended to fix a monocle in his eye.

"I went round to The Barleycorn again last night," said Denzil.

"Well, what of it? That hardly comes under the head of Society News."

"I had a chat with my old friend Gaffer Yerbury. His epiglottis is still working well. So is his tongue. I kept both of them in action. Not without effect. And I learned something worth hearing."

"Well, let's hear it, then, instead of beating about the bush."

"Ah, you're interested, alguazil? That's nice. Then I shan't keep you on tenterhooks, whatever they may be. I shall come straight to the point."

"Do," said the Chief Constable, politely.

Denzil made a gesture of waving him aside.

"You may remember, possibly, that in his young days the late Griswold Carfax sowed a wild oat or two in the local cabbage patch? Well, I'm informed on the best authority—Gaffer Yerbury—that one of these wild oats has now grown to maturity under the name of Moffatt. Now, Moffatt, I may recall to you, took to wife the sister of one Walton. And Moffatt and Walton have the name of poachers in this countryside. And, if you will cast your mind back, you will recollect that Walton is, or was, detained on suspicion in connection with the Huggin murder. Not being a wild oat myself, I can't speak with authority as to its feelings towards the tame variety of the same parentage. But my imagination suggests that they might not be too friendly. Especially when the wild oat poaches the preserves of the tame oat and so rasps the feelings of the game preserver."

"Interesting, if true," commented the Chief Constable. "But I take it you have some ideas on the subject? Elucidate them for us, pray."

"You're intrigued? I take that as a compliment. Then how's this for a possibility. Moffatt and Walton plan to raid Apsley Spinney one night. A third party—I leave his identity to your intelligence—gets wind of the scheme. Knowing there's bad blood between Moffatt and Carfax, this *tertium quid* blows the gaff to Carfax, hoping for trouble. The rest works out according to plan or even better, perhaps. Carfax and his demirelation come to blows in the spinney and Carfax and the keeper are left on the ground, in both senses. Which turns the *tertium quid* into a *tertium gaudens,* no doubt."

"Neater than I expected from you, Bob, I must admit," said Sir Clinton. "But just one question. Where does the Huggin murder fit in with this scheme of yours?"

"Didn't you suspect Walton of that? Do you know whether Walton could tell Carfax from Huggin by sight, before the murder? Huggin may have been mistaken for Carfax and eliminated under a rather unfortunate misapprehension."

"Your imaginative powers are evidently good for a short burst, but they soon flag, I suspect, Bob. Your first try was quite good, but this second one is simply rotten, if I may say so without offence."

"Quite. Quite," said Denzil, blandly. "But, between you and me and the bedpost, has Moffatt got an alibi for the Apsley Spinney affair?"

He turned to Cumberland, who shrugged his shoulders rather sulkily.

"Not one that I'd give tuppence for," he admitted.

"There you are!" said Denzil. "Now you work along these lines and you'll find something. I don't want the credit. Take it all, as you no doubt will do without hesitation. I'm content with the satisfaction of having shown the way."

"'This Way to the Mare's Nest,' eh?" interjected Sir Clinton. "No, Bob, I think you can safely use that as a basis of one of your thrillers. Nature won't plagiarise from you. If you could have fitted the

Huggin business into your scheme with any sort of probability, I'd have looked at it. Not otherwise."

Denzil seemed in no way cast down.

"Very well, then," he declared, "I shall work along these lines myself. And that reminds me. Society Jottings: Mr. Godfrey Finborough has returned to Carfax Hall. So Mr. Yerbury assured me, between gulps. 'Now that that there Druce is out o' the way, this 'ere Godfrey's come 'ome to roost,' as my esteemed informant put it. He also quoted Scripture about the eagles and the carcass, or words to that effect. Quite a well-read fellow, it seems."

Sir Clinton seemed to have little interest in Caleb Yerbury's characteristics. He turned to the inspector.

"Anything further to report?"

"I've got the results of the P.M. on the two bodies, sir."

"I got it myself to-day, thanks. They found that card wad in the keeper's wound, so that shot must have been fired at fairly close quarters, obviously. Oh, by the way, Inspector, don't forget to take this typewriter with you and put it in some safe place."

Then, seeing the inspector eyeing the heavy machine rather ruefully, Sir Clinton turned to Denzil.

"You'll give the inspector a lift, won't you? It's no distance to Abbots Norton, and you're going part of the way anyhow."

Denzil agreed pleasantly enough, though it was plain that he realised that he was being disposed of. When the two had gone, the Chief Constable turned to Wendover.

"Do you see a glimmer of a motive behind this case, Squire? I don't, I'm free to admit. And short of a motive, the thing's a washout."

"Blackmail," suggested Wendover. "It stinks of it, to put it vulgarly."

"Oh, blackmail, certainly," agreed Sir Clinton with a gesture of impatience. "But you can't go into Court and say: 'Gentlemen of the jury, the incentive here has been blackmail,' without telling them who was blackmailed, and why, and by whom. The whole affair, so far, has been like building a house and beginning above the ground floor. There are no foundations. I wish I knew what's behind the business."

# CHAPTER XVI
## THE INSET IN THE PROGRAMME

As WENDOVER STOOD with the Chief Constable on the broad steps of Carfax Hall, waiting for the door to be opened, he had the feeling that at long last the Huggin-Carfax mystery was on the verge of solution.

Pondering over it on the previous night, he had been driven to the conclusion that Godfrey Finborough was the machinator of the whole sinister business. Tools he might well have had, to do the actual bloodshed. There was this poacher Moffatt, with his scurvy brother-in-law, Walton. And Moffatt had his own grudge against the Carfax family, making him a handier instrument for the work. But there was no traceable connection between Moffatt and Huggin which would serve to account for the first homicide, if Moffatt had been the chief agent in the whole affair.

If one looked for a man in the key position, Finborough filled all requirements. He shared rooms with Huggin and possibly was in Huggin's secrets—whatever they might be—whilst on the other side, he had a foot in the Carfax camp. His alibi for the time of the Huggin murder had broken down; for without the inset about Thelma Campion's illness, the Crescent programme by itself was useless as a proof of his presence in the music hall during the second performance on the fatal night. Then there was the quarrel between Druce and Godfrey which Maverton had overheard, with Finborough's taunt: "I can't put the screw on you, and you can't touch me without it all coming out." That hinted only too plainly at strife ending in a deadlock between them. And that deadlock probably ended with Druce's murder, leaving Finborough as the winner.

Little wonder, then, that with these ideas in his mind, Wendover had accepted the Chief Constable's rather casual invitation to go with him to this interview, despite the obvious awkwardness of his presence on the scene. Surely, he thought, the next half hour would bring enlightenment.

"I wish to see Mr. Finborough," explained Sir Clinton, when the maid opened the door to them.

She showed them into the room which they had seen before; and in a few moments Godfrey Finborough came to join them. Wendover scanned him swiftly as he entered, not unprepared for some signs of nervousness; but Godfrey Finborough showed nothing of the sort. He had the same frank, unembarrassed air which had struck Wendover so favourably at the previous interview in London.

"I'm not quite sure how you'd prefer to be addressed," Sir Clinton pointed out. "You were George Fairbank, last time I saw you, you remember; now, I believe, you're Godfrey Finborough."

Finborough's smile showed that he had taken no offence at this opening.

"Sounds peculiar, doesn't it?" he admitted. "But really it's quite simple. When I was a youngster I was sent to London by my father's trustees. They started me in life with a certain amount of capital, and for reasons which seemed good to them, they insisted on my changing my name by deed poll. It wasn't my suggestion, but I had nothing against it; so I agreed to change my name to George Fairbank, and you'll find the deed registered at the proper office at the Courts of justice. That was nearly twenty years ago, and I suppose that since then I've been George Fairbank for all legal purposes. But in this neighbourhood the old name sticks, and everyone calls me Finborough. I don't object. Why should I? I suppose it looks, to a stranger, as if I were using an alias; but there's nothing in it, as you can imagine. If there's any blame in the matter, you'll need to put it on the shoulders of my father's trustees; and I'm sure they acted for what they believed to be the best in the matter."

Finborough's concluding gesture made it perfectly clear that he attached no importance whatever to the name question. And from his account it was plain that he himself had no responsibility for his dual nomenclature. Wendover gave him a good mark for his reticence in suppressing the real reason for the change of name. No use washing dirty linen in public when it could be avoided.

"That's quite satisfactory," Sir Clinton declared. "As a matter of fact, we weren't wholly in ignorance; but it's best to have these things confirmed definitely by the person most likely to know just how they stand. So I asked you as a matter of form."

"I quite understand," said Finborough, pleasantly. "I expect you have to ask a lot of questions which really bring out nothing that's fresh to you. But it's as well to have everything shipshape. Anything I can do, you've only to ask it."

"That brings me to another field," the Chief Constable explained. "As you can guess, we have to check up the movements of a lot of people who turn out in the end to have had nothing to do with the case. It's a pure matter of routine and unfortunately most of it is a mere waste of time. Still, for form's sake, we have to do it."

"I quite understand," Finborough repeated with a smile. "You mean you want me to account for my own movements in the last week or so? I've no objection. Luckily, I keep a diary of business engagements, so I think I can supply you with a fairly detailed account of my time. Where do you want me to start?"

"Let's take the night of Huggin's murder," Sir Clinton suggested. "I remember you told us at our last meeting that you'd been to the Crescent that evening?"

"Yes, I dropped into the second house. It started at nine o'clock."

"Buy a programme?"

"Yes, I did buy one. But if you were to ask me to produce it, I'm afraid you draw blank. I didn't keep it."

"Do you remember anything out of the common in that programme?"

Finborough seemed to reflect for a moment or two before answering. Then he smiled as though he had seen the Chief Constable's point.

"Oh, I can guess what you're driving at," he said. "That's very neat, by Jove! You mean the inset about Thelma Campion's illness? It was enclosed in the ordinary programme, of course, at that performance. Now let's think. . . . Yes, I believe . . . Well, we can soon see if it's there."

He crossed the room and rang the bell. When the maid appeared, he ordered her to send Maverton to him. In a minute or two the valet presented himself.

"Go up to my room and bring down the jacket of the dark lounge suit you'll find at the right-hand side of the wardrobe," directed Finborough. "I think that's the one I was wearing that evening," he explained, turning to Sir Clinton. "I've a hazy recollection of stuffing that inset into my pocket after I'd glanced at it. I hate to strew papers about and I believe I put it into my pocket, meaning to pitch it away into a waste-paper cage when I got outside. I can't remember doing that. But, frankly, my memory's very vague indeed about it, and I'm not guaranteeing results. However, we'll see when Maverton brings the jacket."

In a few minutes, Maverton came back with the garment, and Finborough, with a gesture, ordered him to hand it direct to the Chief Constable.

"Always best to see things with your own eyes; it's the best way, and saves a lot of talking. So would you mind going through the pockets yourself, to see if that paper's there? It ought to be in the right-hand one, I think. . . . Yes, that's all, Maverton."

The valet withdrew, obviously with reluctance. Wendover had a strong suspicion that he would linger outside the door, hoping to pick up some of the further conversation. Sir Clinton waited until Maverton had left the room, then, putting his hand into the indicated pocket, he produced a sheet of paper which had been folded and refolded on itself until it was only a couple of inches square.

"Yes, that seems to be it," Finborough explained. "I don't know why, but I've got a knack of folding up any small bit of paper that comes into my hands. I do it mechanically, without thinking about it. Often when an inspector comes along in a bus and wants to see my ticket, I find I've been folding it and unfolding it unconsciously until it's cracked at the seams and the poor fellow's hard put to it to recognize the thing when he examines it."

Sir Clinton unfolded the slip and glanced at the cyclostyled wording on it.

"Yes, this is it," he said. "It's lucky you stowed it away unconsciously and didn't come upon it till now. If you had put your hand on it, most likely you'd have thrown it away. Well, that's that. Now, you mentioned a diary, didn't you? If you can lay hands on it now, I'd like to get done with these formalities."

"I have it here," Finborough explained, putting his hand into his pocket and taking out an engagement book. "There's nothing private in it. Have a look through it yourself and pick out what you need. Or keep it, if you want to. I can easily start a fresh one."

"Thanks," said Sir Clinton. "That will save time now. Mind if I glance over the entries for the last week, just in case any questions suggest themselves?"

"Not a bit. I'm only too glad to give any information I can."

Sir Clinton took him at his word, turned over the pages of the little volume, read an entry here and there, and then closed the diary.

"There's nothing here worth troubling you about," he said. "I'm only concerned with these murders, and your private engagements are quite beside the point. I see you made a note of your visit here on Wednesday, but I knew about that already. Miss Carfax asked you to come down, I think?"

"Yes, I got a letter from her on Monday morning. The matter didn't seem urgent, and I had some business engagements in town which kept me there until Wednesday afternoon. I came down here in time for dinner. That was after I'd seen you in town—under my alias," he added, with a smile.

"I gather that there had been some friction in the family and that you were brought down to pour oil on the water, if possible?"

"I don't know that I made much of a success of it," Finborough confessed rather ruefully.

"So I inferred. You and Mr. Druce Carfax seem to have had a sharp disagreement, I'm told. Perhaps your sister has told you that she gave me some information about it all."

Finborough nodded.

"Yes, she gave me the whole story of your interviewing her. I may as well tell you that I wasn't overpleased at being dragged into that affair. Druce Carfax and I never managed to hit it off, and I think it was a mistake to bring me on the scene. But Miss Carfax asked me to come down and tell her brother about some things; and I couldn't let her down."

"Now here's a point I want cleared up, because although I've done my best to put an end to local gossip about the Carfax affairs, there's always the chance of tittle-tattle still going on. In that squabble with your brother both of you raised your voices a bit, and part of your talk was overheard. You called him 'a silly cuckoo,' didn't you?"

Finborough laughed a little when Sir Clinton brought out the phrase.

"Well, you see," he explained, "I wasn't exactly pleased to find how he'd been behaving to Miss Carfax. He'd got hold of some ill-natured gossip and made a mountain out of it. Played the silly ass, in fact. Naturally I told him what I thought about it. I don't re-member calling him a silly cuckoo, but likely enough I did. It's a very mild description. I'm surprised I didn't say worse."

Wendover sympathised with Finborough's feelings. In the mat-ter of his sister's reputation, Druce Carfax had behaved like a fool and a boor; and Wendover was not ill-pleased to find that Finborough had stood up for her and told him the truth about him-self. Then, suddenly he remembered that Druce was dead, and he felt rather ashamed of thinking so hardly of him.

"There was another phrase," Sir Clinton went on. "Something about your both being in the same boat, so that neither could put the screw on the other. I needn't point out the meaning that ill-disposed people might put on that, in the circumstances."

"I see. You want it explained?" Finborough seemed to hesitate for a moment, and then continued. "It's not exactly my own affair. Miss Carfax comes into it and perhaps I ought to ask if she has any objection. . . . Oh, well, I'm sure she won't mind if I tell you. You can get her to check what I say. Or send for her now, if you like."

"If it's an awkward subject, better leave her out of it for the present," Sir Clinton suggested. "Give us the gist of it."

Finborough betrayed his approval of this by a gesture. He was obviously relieved that Enid Carfax was not to be dragged into the interview.

"I don't mind. It wasn't actually illegal, you know, though I admit it came near sharp practice, so naturally I don't want it spread abroad. I'm a stockbroker's runner, as you probably know. Naturally, in that line, one's in the way of hearing things. I heard of a scheme set afoot by some sharks to fleece the small investors. A bit of share manipulation on a minor scale. Knowing their trick— I'd learned about it on the quiet—I could play the same game independently and take my share of the profits without appearing on the surface. But I needed capital. So I mentioned the thing to Miss Carfax—without saying it was a ramp, of course—and asked her to back me with as much cash as she could spare. We were to divide the profits on a fifty-fifty basis. She sent me a good deal more dibs than I expected; and the thing went through just as I hoped. But when it came to squaring up, I found that she'd mentioned it to Druce Carfax, and most of the money had come from him. Naturally I was angry. I don't say that all I'd done was the sort of thing one would like to have turning up in a law court. One sometimes gets one's inside information in queer ways. But most certainly I hadn't run risks for the sake of putting cash into Druce Carfax's pocket. So I paid Miss Carfax her share, on what she herself had put in; but all that Druce got was his capital back again with a note of thanks and no profits. Naturally he was furious. And in that squabble on Wednesday he threw it in my teeth. I took the trouble to point out to him that if there was a screw loose in the business, he'd made himself an accessory by furnishing capital for the scheme, so he couldn't afford to say anything without letting people know that he was both a rogue and a fool. You see the point of the phrase, now?"

"Miss Carfax didn't know it was a ramp, you say?"

"Oh, no," Finborough declared bluntly. "She knows nothing about financial affairs. But when she mentioned it to Druce, he saw through it, all right. But that didn't keep him from coming in, though no one had invited him. He practically forced his cash on Miss Carfax, I believe, from what she told me; and he asked her not to tell me that he was interested. She let it out, though, in sheer innocence."

"Miss Carfax could confirm this, you say?"

"Certainly. In fact, I'll send for her now, if you wish. And you can examine my books if you want to, and see the records. There's nothing in them beyond the dealings on 'Change, of course. I don't propose to give myself away. But you can check up the share transactions with her statement and you'll find they tally all right."

"I don't think we need trouble Miss Carfax," said Sir Clinton in a colourless tone. "Now that finishes my questions except for one. Have you any inkling of a motive in Huggin's murder and the murders of your brother and the keeper?"

Finborough shook his head definitely.

"Not a glimmer," he declared. "It beats me completely. And how Huggin came to be murdered down here is more than I can conceive. I didn't so much as know that he had any connection with Abbots Norton."

"I've said already that there's been a good deal of chatter in the neighbourhood," Sir Clinton pursued. "In some of it, blackmail's been mentioned as a possibility."

Again Finborough laughed unconstrainedly.

"Blackmail? Good Lord! What next? Who's supposed to have been blackmailed?"

"Druce Carfax."

"Rot!" said Finborough bluntly. "I didn't love him much and I'm not in the mood to deliver a panegyric on him; but I'll say this: he was absolutely straight so far as sex affairs went. No, they're barking up the wrong tree there. In fact, there isn't so much as a tree for them to bark up."

"Rumour goes that he was being blackmailed on account of Miss Carfax."

Finborough flushed with obvious anger, and again Wendover found himself in sympathy.

"Who the devil's been saying that?" Finborough demanded with scarcely suppressed rage in his tone. "Give me his name, will you? and I'll fix him so that he won't dare to put stuff like that about. I'll—"

"I shouldn't, if I were you," interrupted Sir Clinton. "Want the thing broadcasted? A favour to Miss Carfax, that would be. I've taken steps to put a stop to it myself. Let it go at that."

Finborough's anger had been so genuine that it was unnecessary to push the matter further. Quite obviously he had been touched to the quick by the slur thrown on Enid Carfax; and, equally clear, he wholly disbelieved that the scandal had any basis.

"There's something in what you say," he admitted. "But I'd like to get my hands on the fellow. I knew Druce had picked up some scandal, since that was what brought me down here on Wednesday. But I thought he'd nosed it out himself. It never crossed my mind that it was being talked about all over the place. Well, if I come across anyone spreading that tale, I'll find *some other grounds* for half killing him. Thanks for the hint."

"I'd rather you took my other hint," said Sir Clinton seriously. "Frankly, I don't think it's likely to be a popular topic hereabouts in future. Better let it alone and not run the risk of stirring it up again. That's only fair to Miss Carfax."

"I'll think over it," said Finborough, with a touch of sullenness in his tone.

Sir Clinton rose, as if to go; then something seemed to occur to him.

"This is a pure formality," he said, and his tone confirmed it. "You've no interest, direct or indirect, in the Carfax estate. That is so, isn't it?"

"Not a glimmer," Finborough confirmed. "I've seen my father's will at one time. I was given a few hundreds when I came of age; and that was in full quittance of any claim, moral or otherwise. You can reckon me as wholly disinterested, so far as the Carfax estate goes. Druce came first, and now it's gone to Julian. If he leaves no heirs, then Miss Carfax comes into possession. After her, some relations might come in, but they're so far off that I don't even remember their name. You can count me out, completely."

"That was what I thought," Sir Clinton said. "Well, I don't think I need trouble you any longer."

"You'd like to see Miss Carfax, perhaps?" suggested Finborough.

Sir Clinton shook his head.

"No, thanks. I've seen her before, and I don't need her to check your evidence. It's quite convincing without her support."

Finborough accompanied them to the door and waited until their car moved off. Wendover sat in silence for a while thinking over the interview. Sir Clinton at last broke into his reflections.

"Well, Squire? You must feel rather upside-down in the theory department. I know you went there with the idea that Finborough was the villain of the piece. And now you've got to start looking for a fresh scent."

"I suppose so," confessed Wendover, "but I don't see how it's to be picked up. Everything seemed to point towards Finborough."

"Barring the plain fact that there's no motive in sight in his case."

"There's no motive in sight anywhere," grumbled Wendover. "I must say, though, I rather liked the way he stood up for his sister. They're evidently very fond of each other. That's to his credit. But I didn't much like that tale about the share swindle. I suppose he was hinting that he'd done a bit of bribery to get that inside information he bragged about."

"Something like it," agreed Sir Clinton, indifferently. "Well, go on with your suspect hunt, Squire, and I'll do the same. As soon as you catch one, let me know. Every little helps."

When they reached Talgarth Grange, Sir Clinton went to his room for a moment and when he came down again he handed to Wendover a long blue envelope.

"I like to be forearmed, you know," he said, as Wendover took it from him. "This is a copy of Griswold Carfax's will, Squire. If you glance through it, you'll see that I was quite accurate when I described my last question to Finborough as a mere formality. I knew that he hasn't the slightest claim on that estate. In fact, he's explicitly excluded, as you'll see when you've looked over that document."

Wendover drew the papers from the envelope, sat down, and began to read through the will. Sir Clinton went across to a desk and began to write. But in a moment or two he turned round to his host.

"Sorry to interrupt you, Squire. You've got a London Directory, haven't you?"

Wendover looked up from the sheet he was reading. "It's in the library, on the bookcase between the windows. Ring the bell, if you want it."

"I'll get it for myself," the Chief Constable decided, getting up and leaving the room.

Wendover continued to study Griswold Carfax's will until he came to an unusual clause which he read twice over, to see if he could find a loophole in it.

> I hereby explicitly exclude in all circumstances from any participation whatsoever in any benefit under this will any descendant of mine who was born out of lawful wedlock.

"Well, that seems definite enough," reflected Wendover. "There was no need for a provision of that kind, so far as my knowledge goes. Moffatt and Finborough were out of the picture in any case unless Griswold had gone out of his way to provide for them specially. They've no legal claim. But Griswold evidently meant to make sure that no mistakes were made. The life rent of the estate went to Druce; and if he had had any heirs they would have come in after him. Failing heirs of his body, Julian was to get it. And, again failing heirs, Enid comes in if Julian peters out. It's as plain as a pikestaff, as a will."

Sir Clinton came back and sat down at the desk to consult the Post Office Directory which he had brought back with him. Wendover allowed him to finish his letter, which was very short, and to address and seal up the envelope, before he spoke.

"I see you're using official note paper, Clinton. We're not so hard up that we can't spare a friend a sheet of paper and an envelope, you know."

"I'm writing to the Cosmopolitan Press-cutting Association," Sir Clinton explained, "and I doubt if they'd know who I was if I wrote on plain paper. My modesty, perhaps. But it's best to make sure of getting attention, and the official paper ought to do that."

"Starting an album of press cuttings about yourself?" demanded Wendover sardonically.

"Well, I think one should make things easy for one's biographer, you know," retorted the Chief Constable, with a grin. "That job's vacant, by the way. Care to apply for it, Squire? Any application from you will be carefully considered. Pity the late Huggin has passed away. After writing up the Carfax family history, he'd have been in fine form to tackle the history of my cases."

"You've still Denzil to fall back on," suggested Wendover impishly. "He'd bring the necessary understanding to his work, not to speak of imagination beyond the common."

"Bob?" said the Chief Constable in pretended doubt. "No, I don't think he'd do, somehow. In fact, I'd better take a leaf out of Griswold Carfax's book and insert in my will a clause explicitly barring my executors from employing Bob in any capacity whatever. One ought to feel certain that one won't have to turn in one's grave, and I'd be restless if I thought Bob had been let loose among my papers."

"I noticed a large bale addressed to you," said Wendover. "A few documents for this biographer, perhaps? But why trundle them about the country? Your bank would be the safest place for them."

"Nothing escapes you, Squire. But your inference is a bit out. That bale contains Atherfoldiana—that's a bit of a mouthful! In other words, Atherfold's diary and surviving correspondence."

"You evidently like your reading served up piping hot," commented Wendover disgustedly. "What do you want to wade through stuff like that for?"

"'England expects that every man will do his duty'—even Chief Constables. And no doubt it will increase my knowledge of morbid psychology."

"Undoubtedly, I imagine," declared Wendover with unconcealed repugnance. "He was a swine, that fellow."

# CHAPTER XVII
## ATHERFOLDIANA

THE AFTERNOON SUN had slipped round until it threw a bar of light across Wendover's face as he sat trying to interest himself in a book. He rose reluctantly from his chair, went over to the window, and lowered the blind of one division just sufficiently to cut off the disturbing rays. Then he returned to his seat. But instead of resuming his reading he fixed his eyes on the Chief Constable. Sir Clinton had a row of leather-bound volumes neatly stacked on the floor beside his chair, and on a table beside him were piles of old letters, fastened together in bundles of various sizes. Feeling Wendover's intent gaze, he glanced up from the volume which he was studying.

"It's lucky Miss Atherfold didn't put her nose into this production," he observed. "She'd have got the shock of her life, poor thing. It's a modern Casanova, Squire. Or rather, it reads as if Casanova had taken Pietro Aretino into partnership. You can't open it anywhere without coming on something that makes you think still worse of human nature. And, Lord knows, I've got a poor enough opinion of *that* already, without his help."

Wendover was sorely tempted. His criminological studies had given him a taste for morbid psychology, and it was plain that this Atherfold diary would throw light on that field, whatever else it did. But he had been so contemptuous in his comments on Atherfold that he shrank from the sarcasm which he was sure to draw down on himself if he showed his interest in the volumes. He found Sir Clinton examining him, with the beginning of a smile at the corners of his mouth.

"Don't sit there, Squire, looking like a cat with its eye on the cream jug. You make me nervous. I know you're burning to get your paws on this stack of self-revelation. To the pure, all things are pure, you know. Take that to comfort yourself in your fall."

Wendover shuffled uneasily in his chair.

"Any objection to my having a glance at it?" he said tentatively.

"None whatever, so long as you don't quote from it in public."

Rather shamefacedly, Wendover stretched out and picked up the first volume of the series.

"Nice clear writing on the title-page," he commented, as he opened it. "I wonder how long he kept up the copperplate."

He skimmed over some pages, pausing here and there to read a paragraph *in extenso*.

"The bookbinders must have been tickled by it when he sent it to be bound," he suggested.

"Oh, I expect he got blank sheets bound up into volumes before he wrote anything on them."

"Very likely. I see he started it on his twenty-first birthday."

"I'm working backwards through it," Sir Clinton explained. "If there's anything in it to throw light on these murders—and I've a suspicion there is, else why Huggin?—it's as likely to be recent as long ago."

"You're not thinking that Enid Carfax got mixed up with that hound Atherfold, are you?" demanded Wendover suspiciously.

"I'm not looking for anything in particular, Squire," Sir Clinton assured him. "I'm just looking, on general principles. One can't ignore the fact that Huggin got into touch with Druce Carfax for the first time *after* he'd got his claws on this diary. There may be nothing in it; but I must wade through the stuff, on chance."

Wendover laid the volume he was holding down on his knee and leaned over to pick up another one.

"This one's a newer vintage," he commented. "The writing's changed a lot; got smaller, for one thing. By Jove! He seems to have had a fine succession of lady friends: Etta . . . Alma . . .

Pauline—that must be Pauline Brent, the chorus girl who committed suicide. I remember Atherfold's name came into the evidence somehow—Peggy . . . Jeanne—French ones, too, apparently—Phyllis. . . . Needs a name index badly, this book."

"Yes, a bit of a catalogue, isn't it?" Sir Clinton answered without looking up. "It reminds me of that poem of Catulle Mendès:

> Rose, Emmeline,
> Margueridette,
> Odette,
> *Alix, Aline.* . . .

Nothing but girls' names all through. Not even a verb."

Apparently Wendover had chanced upon some incident which interested him, for he read page after page with a deepening frown on his face. Sir Clinton glanced over at him, after a while.

"What's that you've struck?" he asked.

"Oh, the Lordsmead divorce case. D'you know, Clinton, that creature Atherfold seems to have been completely a-moral and quite unable to think of anyone's good but his own. Looked at from his own point of view"—he tapped the page with his finger—"he was the only person who came out of that affair with a scrap of credit."

"The judge didn't share his opinion, so far as I remember."

Wendover closed the volume and replaced it in its proper position in the series.

"I wonder . . ." he said doubtfully as he took up the first volume again from his knee. "Is this genuine stuff, Clinton? It might be just fairy tales—what he'd *liked* to have done. Some men take a pleasure in that sort of thing: imagining stuff and putting it on paper as if it had really happened. One might almost think—"

"Oh, it's genuine enough, wherever I've checked it," Sir Clinton said shortly.

"But you can't check this kind of thing," objected Wendover. "He had at least the decency to suppress surnames when he wrote about these women, like Catulle Mendès."

"You can check it to some extent," the Chief Constable explained. "He kept piles of letters he got from women"—he pointed to the bundles of envelopes on the table beside him—"and the earlier letters in each set generally give the girl's surname in the signature. I checked one or two; because, like you, I thought it might be mere invention. But it seems sound enough. Now, if you don't mind, Squire, I'd like to get on with this job."

Wendover made a gesture of apology, took out his case, lit a cigarette, and buried himself in the first volume of the Atherfold diary. For a time the Chief Constable was allowed to read in peace, but suddenly he was interrupted by an exclamation from his host.

"What is it *now?*" he asked, rather testily.

"Just a name here. But it can't be the same."

Sir Clinton put down the volume he was reading. "What name?" he asked.

"Fenella."

"Fenella?" echoed the Chief Constable. "Oh, you're thinking of Griswold's wife? She was Fenella, wasn't she? Fenella—"

"Fenella Basnett," Wendover reminded him. "But it can't be the same girl. Not the least likely."

"What's the story?" inquired Sir Clinton. "By the way, when did this happen?"

Wendover consulted the diary.

"The date's 1902," he replied. "Here's the gist of the story, so far as the diary gives it. This girl Fenella seems to have come of quite good people. Atherfold met her, took a fancy to her, followed up the acquaintance with the worst intentions, as one might expect. There were clandestine meetings, but she fended him off; and that probably made him still keener to get what he wanted. Then came his chance. The girl's parents went off to the Continent for the summer; and as they didn't want to take her with them, she was packed off to stay with some distant cousins who had a small place in Scotland.

"That gave Atherfold a bright idea. She was young, and full of a lot of silly romantic stuff—he sneers at it in his entries, though he apparently played up to it to her. Anyhow, he produced the stale old Gretna Green romance, runaway match, and all the rest of it. It was just her style. So she went up and stayed with these cousins for a month and then left them, ostensibly to pay a visit to an old school friend. Atherfold supplied the letters from the old school friend, to make it look quite genuine.

"What she actually did, of course, was to go and live with him. But he had to quieten her with some sort of pretence of actual marriage. He wasn't taking any chances of Gretna Green, naturally. So he drew up a document in which each took the other for spouse, and they signed it in the presence of witnesses. He kept it. The witnesses weren't allowed to read the document, of course; they merely witnessed the affixing of the signatures to it.

"Well, from what you know of Atherfold, you can guess the rest. He'd got the girl, and the next thing was to get rid of her. After a couple of weeks, he let her see him as he really was; and naturally, since she was a decent girl in the main, she saw she'd made a bad mistake. Very soon she was wishing she hadn't been such a fool. Then Atherfold worked the rest of his scheme. Why not wash it all out? She could go back to her cousins again, full of invented anecdotes of her old school friend, and nobody would be a penny the wiser. And, in his usual kindly way, he told her that the 'marriage' had been only a sham and that they weren't married at all. That seems to have opened her eyes to Atherfold's character, once for all. She hadn't been very much in love with him, one suspects. And apparently that last interview cured her. She went back to her cousins with her tale. But that's the end of the story so far as the diary gives it."

Sir Clinton had followed Wendover's summary with unconcealed interest.

"That was in 1902, you say?" he asked.

"Yes, 1902; in the summer."

"And when did Fenella Basnett marry Griswold Carfax? You told me once, but I forget the date."

"In 1903 . . . Good Lord! I didn't think of that."

"And Atherfold's Fenella sounds a bit like the character sketch you gave me of Fenella Basnett, doesn't she? The kind of girl who dotes on romance and goes about looking for someone to fit into the center of it? We'd better check this up, Squire."

"Can't you let sleeping dogs lie, Clinton?" demanded Wendover, with all his distaste for raking up scandal.

"Not when they produce troublesome puppies, Squire. Besides, if there's any further evidence, it'll be here to hand." He pointed to the bundles of letters on the table. "The bother's simply nothing. Huggin gathered each set of letters together and put them into separate packets. It won't take a jiffy to find the right lot."

He rose and began to search through the neatly arranged packets as he spoke; and in a couple of minutes he returned to his chair with a little bundle of letters which he opened up.

"Yes, it would have been rather too much of a coincidence to have the ages, natures, names, and all the rest of it alike," he said as he glanced at the first document. "Here it is: 'Fenella Basnett' at the end of the first letter. That was evidently before they got on close terms, so she signed her full name."

He shuffled over the pile and examined a later epistle.

"Now it's just 'Fenella,'" he reported, "with some adoring expressions in front of it. Well, Squire, that solves one of your little problems. You know now why the Sphinx smiled."

"What do you mean?" demanded Wendover, rather at sea.

"Well, didn't you tell me once that Griswold's Fenella seemed to have some secret little jest that made her smile? I can make a guess at it. When Griswold irritated her, I've no doubt she had her own private consolation. 'You, with all your mistresses, come bullying me? Well, I had my little escapade too. We're quits, my dear fellow. Only you don't know it.' Something of that sort."

"There might be something in it," Wendover admitted. "But I hate to think of these things."

"When they happen to people in your circle, Squire. But let's get on with the job."

He put the letters together in a pile again and began to make a systematic search through them, examining each in turn as it came to hand. Wendover, puzzled by this, watched him closely. Suddenly Sir Clinton's eyes lighted up as he came upon a single sheet.

"Here it is!" he exclaimed. "I was pretty sure it would be amongst them, as a trophy. He was just that kind of creature."

He passed the sheet over to Wendover who read it:

> 3rd August, 1902.
> I, Eustace Atherfold, of 33 Lynchcroft Square, London, do hereby take Fenella Basnett, of 14, Stansway Terrace, London, as my wife; and I, Fenella Basnett, of 14, Stansway Terrace, London, do hereby take Eustace Atherfold of 33 Lynchcroft Square, London, as my husband, according to the Law of Scotland.
>
> Eustace Atherfold.
> Fenella Basnett.
>
> Jean Brand, Spinster (Witness).
> Kate Raeburn, Spinster (Witness).

"I know that Scots Law is a bit weird in some ways," Wendover declared as he handed back the paper, "but a thing like that wouldn't constitute a legal marriage."

"Oh, wouldn't it?" retorted Sir Clinton. "As it happens, I had to look into that particular aspect of Scots Law not long ago, when an unfortunate girl got let in by a scoundrel. This document you've just read, Squire, comes under the head of 'Marriages by declaration *de presenti*.' Nothing more is necessary to constitute actual marriage than a present interchange of consent, in whatever manner given, to become henceforth husband and wife. The declaration may be in writing or verbal. No particular form of words is required. And the matrimonial consent may be interchanged in the most secret and private manner. The only snag is that one of the parties must have his or her usual residence in Scotland, or must have resided in Scotland for three weeks. But if you take the story of the diary, you find that Fenella Basnett had put in that term of residence while she was staying with her cousins. That was as legal a marriage as if it had been carried out under special licence from the Archbishop of Canterbury in England."

"But it would have to be registered somewhere," objected Wendover.

"Not necessarily. If you want to register a marriage of this sort, you have to petition the Sheriff. But there's no compulsion to register it."

"But suppose it's disputed?"

"Then it can be proved by an action for Declarator in the Court of Session."

"But Atherfold himself, by his own story, didn't regard it as a marriage."

Sir Clinton smiled rather sardonically.

"I expect he knew that two English people can't rush up to Gretna Green and get married, there and then. But probably he forgot that Fenella Basnett had actually put in her twenty-one days residence. And she wouldn't know anything about the details of Scots Law, so she'd never spot the flaw in his tale. She'd take his word for it that they weren't married, and her only idea after that would be to cover her tracks in the matter."

Wendover accepted this without further demur, but a fresh problem presented itself immediately.

"I see what you're driving at. But why didn't Huggin take more care of a document like that? Why leave it amongst all these other papers, instead of keeping it in a safe place?"

"Can you think of any safer place than amongst that big pile of old letters?" retorted Sir Clinton. "An inquisitive person might unfold a single sheet of paper and take a casual glance at it. But no normal Paul Pry would have the patience to wade through all this mass of stuff in the hope of finding amusement. There's nothing so dead, to the ordinary man, as a pile of old correspondence belonging to someone else. It's as sound a dodge as the one in Poe's *Purloined Letter*."

Wendover was about to continue when a maid came into the room.

"The valet from Carfax Hall is outside, sir," she said to the Chief Constable. "He says you told him to call and see you."

"Show him in," directed Wendover.

When the valet entered, Wendover gave him a swift glance. The fellow had lost his self-assurance to some extent, it seemed. He looked rather like a schoolboy brought before the head master and not very sure of the result. The Chief Constable wasted no time in preliminaries.

"Have you put a stop to that gossip I warned you about?"

Maverton hesitated for a moment, then answered: "Oh, yes, sir, so far as I could."

"Meaning it's spread too widely for you to catch up with it?"

"Yes, sir. I've done my best," the valet replied sulkily.

"Well, it's your lookout," said Sir Clinton unsympathetically. "Don't complain if it runs you into trouble." He produced from his pocket an unmounted photograph and handed it to Maverton.

"Know who that is?"

"Yes, sir. That's Huggin, the man who was murdered."

"How do you know it's Huggin?" demanded the Chief Constable. "You never saw his body. You weren't on the coroner's jury."

Maverton evidently suspected that he was being led into a trap; but he straightened himself up and answered with a fair show of confidence:

"I saw him at the Hall, sir, months ago. He came to see Mr. Druce Carfax, I remember."

"I wonder," said Sir Clinton sceptically. "When was that?"

Maverton evidently performed some abstruse chronological calculation before he answered.

"It would be about the beginning of April, sir. I remember it because it was just about Miss Carfax's birthday and there were some people staying at the Hall. It comes to my mind that they all were playing some kind of a game in the hall of the house when Huggin dropped in. I had to take Huggin through them to show him into the library to wait for Mr. Carfax."

"I'm just going to test that memory of yours," said Sir Clinton, unpleasantly. "What people were in the hall when you say you showed Huggin in? Tell me the names of as many as you can re-member."

"Mr. Druce Carfax wasn't there. I'm sure of that, because I had to go and look for him after I left Huggin in the library. Miss Carfax was; I remember her well enough. And Mr. Julian, he was there too. And Miss Dersingham from Culmore Park, she was there. She was staying the night. And Mr. Finborough was talking to her. I remember the two of them standing by the newel post of the stair. And there was a Mr. Hawkslade. He was staying, too. I don't know where he came from. And Miss Ennerdale—"

"You seem to have it pat," said the Chief Constable. "How long did Huggin stay?"

"I can't tell you, sir. I didn't see him again. Mr. Carfax must have shown him out himself. I don't remember his ringing to have him shown out. But you could ask the maids, just in case one of them did that."

"You're making no mistake?" asked Sir Clinton incisively.

"Oh, no, sir. Huggin's a queer sort of name; it sticks in one's mind. And he wasn't the sort of man we got as a visitor at the Hall. You could see by the look of him that he wasn't quite 'it.' That made me give him a glance or two, enough to remember him by."

"Very well. Now kindly write this down on that retentive memory of yours. You're not to mention that you've been to see me to-day. Understand that clearly? If you mention a word of this conversation to anyone, it'll be very much the worse for you. Is that plain? Well, then, you can go."

# CHAPTER XVIII
## THE LAST RESERVE

"THIS IS TUESDAY," Wendover pointed out as he glanced across the breakfast table at his guest.

The faint accusatory note in his voice did not escape the Chief Constable.

"So the newspaper tells me," he replied mildly. "Useful things, newspapers. And I admire your conciseness of speech, Squire. What you mean is that Huggin was murdered on Monday, last week; Carfax and Phelp were killed on Thursday; the police have done nothing in the meanwhile; and the Chief Constable ought to be sacked."

"Well, you didn't seem to do much yourself, yesterday," grumbled Wendover. "The rate payers expect zeal, if nothing else. I speak as one of them."

"I, too, have not been idle," quoted Sir Clinton. "I did quite a lot of telephoning. Mind pushing the toast out of your reach and into mine? Thanks."

"Masterly inactivity seems your long suit at present," complained Wendover.

"*Tout vient à point à qui sait attendre,* Squire. Or, in plain English, 'Everything comes out with a click to him who knows how to bide his time.'"

"I haven't heard any click yet," said Wendover, dryly. "It happened before you came down to breakfast. The flap of your front-door letter box made it."

240

He pushed across the table an envelope, from which Wendover extracted three slips of paper. The top one had a press cutting gummed to a leaflet:

Cosmopolitan Press-Cutting Association
Extract from
THE MORNING ARGUS

London

20th Aug. 1936

WANTED BY COLLECTOR, the inset in the Crescent Theater Programme of 17th inst. announcing illness of Thelma Campion. £1 for first copy received. Other copies will be returned. Send to Closeby R. Montague, Poste Restante, G.P.O., London.

The other two cuttings were similar, except that one had been clipped from the *Courier-Press* and the other from the *News of the Globe*.

Sir Clinton waited until his host had glanced at all three; then, imitating Wendover's dryness, he suggested:

"Something to be said for biding one's time, perhaps, Squire. And now, if you have done your worst to this excellent breakfast, I propose to gratify your yearning for activity. Let me do some telephoning and then we shall become brisk and bustling. Half an hour or so, and I shall be with you once more."

The Chief Constable picked up the portable telephone as he spoke and retired with it into Wendover's library, shutting the door behind him. It was rather more than half an hour later when he emerged again.

"You've time to smoke a couple of cigarettes yet, Squire. Our appointment is not due for half an hour. You can have the car brought round, if you're on pins and needles and want some outlet for your energy. Have you got all your prepossessions about the case in good order?"

"I have my ideas in order, if that's what you mean."

"Nothing like an orderly mind, is there? No matter what's in it. Well, run along and leave the commander to plan his tactics undisturbed."

"Do you know the difference between strategy and tactics?" asked Wendover sceptically.

"Strategy is getting your troops onto the battle field; tactics is the employment of them when there. I did my strategy over the phone. Now I've got to think of my tactics. See?"

"The essence of tactics is surprise," Wendover pointed out. "It's sometimes one side that gets the surprise, sometimes the other. Are you quite sure you know which side you are?"

"Well, I've got the big battalions, anyhow," Sir Clinton declared, "and I think Marshal de la Ferté was right when he remarked to Anne of Austria that Providence was on their side."

"Napoleon said Providence was on the side of the last reserve," Wendover declared. "That's not quite the same thing. And I'd reckon Napoleon as the better authority."

"Well, we shall see. Now suppose you go and order that car."

Half an hour later, they were on their road to Carfax Hall. At the foot of the avenue, Cumberland was standing waiting for them, accompanied by a uniformed constable whom he had brought as a passenger on his motorcycle.

"Got your warrant?" asked Sir Clinton, as their car pulled up.

"Yes, sir. I called for it on the way over. Everything's in order."

"Then come along after us."

Accompanied by the motorcycle, the car sped up the avenue to Carfax Hall. The Chief Constable's ring was answered, after some delay, by a scared-looking maid. Her face perceptibly lightened as she caught a glimpse of the police uniform.

"I'm that glad you've come, sir," she broke out as she threw the door wide open. "It's been a terrible business here, this morning. Scared to death, we've been. Poor Mr. Maverton, he's half killed, sir. If you'd heard his cries, sir; they went through me like a knife. I never thought a man could scream like that. Oh, it was horrible, sir, the way he got treated."

"Is Mr. Finborough here?" demanded the Chief Constable sharply, to put an end to the lamentations.

"I don't know, sir. It was him as did it, with a hunting crop. I ran away and locked myself in my room while it was going on. I couldn't bear it, with the screaming and moaning he made. I put the bolster over my head and still I could hear it going on."

"Is Miss Carfax here?" Sir Clinton demanded, impatiently.

"She went out in her car, sir. That was before it happened. He waited till she was well gone before he took and thrashed poor Maverton."

"Where is Maverton?"

"He's in the drawing-room, sir, on the sofa. More dead than alive, sir. I'm so glad someone's come."

Sir Clinton waited for no more but brushed gently past the girl and walked into the room she indicated, followed by the others. Maverton was lying on a chesterfield and he looked, as the girl said, more dead than alive. Blood had trickled down his cheek, and his face was disfigured by a couple of cruel welts across it. He tried to lift himself into a sitting posture as the group entered the room and made a feeble, beckoning gesture to the Chief Constable.

Sir Clinton turned to the girl who had followed them to the door in morbid curiosity.

"Bring me a glass of brandy," he ordered, curtly.

Maverton beckoned again, and the Chief Constable went to his side.

"He's about done me in," Maverton whispered. "Finborough, it was. He's killed me," he whimpered as he sank back on the cushions.

The girl came back with the brandy and Sir Clinton put the glass into the valet's hand.

"Here! Drink that down," he ordered.

The neat spirit seemed to revive Maverton a little.

"Run over him," Sir Clinton directed Cumberland, as he took the glass back from the injured man.

The inspector, expert in first-aid work, made a quick examination of the valet.

"No bones broken that I can find, sir," he reported finally. "I thought the bridge of his nose might be gone, with one of these lashes over the face, but it seems all right. Did he kick you?" he asked.

"No," said Maverton, faintly. "He just thrashed me with a crop.—Oh!—I never thought it could hurt so— He's done for me."

"Not a bit of it," said Cumberland, unsympathetically. "No need to make such a song about it. You'll be all right in a week or so."

"I can't stand."

"Nobody's asking you to," said the Chief Constable, with even less sympathy than his subordinate. "Finborough found out about your gossiping habits, didn't he? Well, you've been asking for this, and now you've got it. How did it happen? Come on, you're not half so bad as you think you are."

Sir Clinton's total lack of sympathy reacted on Maverton, and the brandy helped to pull him together. He beckoned again, and the Chief Constable bent over him.

"He called me into the hall—about half an hour ago—" the valet explained, speaking in gasps. "I saw he was—going to be nasty as soon as I set eyes—on him. He said Caleb Yerbury—spiteful old blackguard—had told him—some things I'd been saying—about Miss Carfax—I told him I'd—kept quiet after you'd—warned me— and he said—'Was that—last night when you—sneaked over to see— Driffield?'—Someone had told him—about that.—Then he took a— crop from the wall—and hit me—over the face.—I thought my eye had gone.—I can't see with it.—Then he flogged me—awful it was.—Then he asked me—what I'd said—to you on Sunday—and I told him."

"Oh, you did, did you?" ejaculated Sir Clinton. "Where's he gone now?"

"I don't know.—He pitched me down—after he'd beaten me— some more—and I think he—went upstairs.—O-o-oh!—And then I crawled in here—and—"

"Go through the place," snapped Sir Clinton, turning to Cumberland. "If he's gone, find out which way he went. He can't have gone down the avenue in a car. If he had, he'd have been bound to run into either you or us on the main road."

Cumberland darted off, taking the uniformed man with him. In a couple of minutes he was back, with one of the maids.

"This girl saw him leave by the back premises, sir, just about when we came to the front door. Making for the golf links, she says."

"After him, then," ordered the Chief Constable, setting an example.

They made for the front door, emerged on the gravel sweep, and took a winding path through a little plantation. As they came out from among the trees of this, they caught a glimpse of the head and shoulders of a human figure just vanishing over a fold in the ground.

"He's making for Leisurely Lane," said the Chief Constable. "Now don't straggle. Take the pace of the slowest man and keep together. We can't afford to come up on him one at a time. He's in an ugly temper and we must make sure of him."

"The big battalions, eh?" said Wendover, slackening his pace as ordered.

"Four to one should do it," said Sir Clinton optimistically. "But he's a powerful brute and I don't want anyone to get more hurt than's necessary. I hope he isn't armed."

Running on, they took the line towards the hoarding on Leisurely Lane. The fugitive was now concealed from them by the fold in the ground, and they could make no guess at how the chase was going. Sir Clinton was the first to reach the crest of the gentle slope, a few minutes later.

Some distance away, he caught sight of the hut and the archery targets which Denzil had described to him, but the fugitive had vanished. Sir Clinton stood for a moment, scanning the landscape before him. Then something sang in the air, he heard a dull impact, and an arrow stood quivering almost at his feet, deep-set in the ground.

"Back, there!" he shouted, with a restraining gesture to the rest of the party. "Don't come over the crest."

He himself retreated a few steps, then threw himself down on the grass and began to creep forward cautiously.

A second arrow whizzed over his head and stuck in the turf with a vicious clap. Evidently the archer had drawn his bow at a venture hoping to strike one of the party on the reverse slope.

"He seems to have got us held up," Sir Clinton admitted, turning his head to address his followers. "Ingenious devil! We'll need to think this out. I've no wish to get one of these arrows through me."

Another arrow hurtled over them, but this time it was high in the air and landed somewhere out of sight amongst the dips in the ground between them and the Hall.

"That wasn't meant for us," the Chief Constable commented. "What's he after, now?"

Wendover retreated a few paces until he was well protected by the forward slope, then rose to his feet and scanned the landscape behind them.

"It's Denzil coming," he reported. "Evidently he was in sight from that hut, on the further slope."

A fourth arrow soared over their heads.

"That fellow can draw a bow," Cumberland commented wryly. "Hear the swish that arrow made?"

Wendover, keenly followed the flight of the missile, gave a gesture of relief.

"It just missed him," he said, and then added with a laugh, "It made him jump, though! But he's all right. He's discovered he isn't wanted hereabouts and taken shelter."

"I wonder he noticed that he wasn't wanted," growled Sir Clinton. "I never knew him take a hint before. What the devil brings him here now?"

"You can ask him yourself in a minute or two," Wendover declared, sinking to the ground again. "He's making good time. He must have seen us. I think he's got into dead ground now, so he's safe enough."

Very soon Denzil ran up the slope and threw himself panting on the grass beside them. When he recovered his breath, he turned to Sir Clinton.

"Well, alguazil, I dropped in to pay a duty call," he explained. "What's all this? Rural sports, I suppose. Give me a programme, will you? I may as well keep abreast of the events as they come."

"This one's called Frog-shooting. '*A was an Archer who shot at a Frog.*' You're the Frog, Bob. The Archer is one of your friends, ensconced in that hut over there. It's all very jolly and well-meant."

He lifted his head and gazed over towards the hut again.

"I don't see how we're going to get at him," he observed perplexedly, after a cautious reconnaissance. "He means business with these arrows, by the look of him. We'd stand no chance if we tried to cross this open ground."

A thought seemed to occur to him and he turned to Denzil.

"You've been inside that place, Bob. What's it like?"

"Just a big square but with windows on each side," Denzil explained. "Some racks for bows and some cases for arrows. A locker or two. That, and some camp chairs stacked in a corner, was all I remember."

"Many arrows in stock, did you notice?"

"Some dozens, anyhow, I should think."

"Windows on all sides," mused the Chief Constable. "That means he can get at us, no matter on what side we come up."

He lifted his head and, shifting his position slightly, made another inspection of the terrain.

"There's a long, shallow fold in the ground beyond him," he reported. "One might be able to get into it at the near end and crawl along under cover to within fifty or sixty yards of the hut. But even a fifty-yard rush would leave one or two of us as casualties. That's no good."

Denzil turned to Wendover.

"Sad to see the alguazil suffering the slings and arrows of outrageous fortune, isn't it?"

Sir Clinton pricked up his ears at the remark.

"Shakespeare's often helpful in adversity," he observed. "By the way, Bob, the roof of that place looks like tarred felt from here. Is it that, do you remember?"

Denzil pondered for a moment.

"It is, I think. Laths underneath, unless I'm mistaken. But the waterproofing is tarred felt."

"Ah!" ejaculated the Chief Constable, as if relieved. "Well, I think the arrows have had a fair show now. It's time the slings had a look in."

"More rural sports?" queried Denzil. "If it's a slinging competition, though, you can count me a nonstarter. I've no Balearic blood in my veins. I couldn't hit a haystack."

"Neither could I, most likely," rejoined the Chief Constable. "Still, one can but try."

He turned to Cumberland and gave him in an undertone some instructions which seemed to surprise the inspector somewhat, to judge by his expression. He took his instructions without demur, however, and set off back towards the Hall.

"Careful, when you get out of the dead ground," cautioned Sir Clinton. Then he turned to the uniformed constable. "Work your way along under cover of this ridge until you get beyond him and then cut over so as to get between him and Leisurely Lane. If he comes out on your side, don't try to get to grips with him. He'll have his bow, most likely. All I want you to do is to follow him up if he tries to bolt. Keep at least three hundred yards from him and you'll be quite safe. He'll not be able to do anything at that range. Take no risks, remember."

The constable saluted and set off on his errand. It took him some time to make the necessary detours, but finally Sir Clinton reported that he could see him, standing out of range on the top of a hillock which gave him a clear view.

They had to wait longer for the return of Cumberland, but he put in an appearance at last, carrying various small parcels.

"I took my motorcycle down to the village, sir," he reported. "It seemed the quickest way of getting the stuff. And when I was there, I got on the phone and sent out the call you pre-arranged."

He began to empty his pockets of a series of stones of various sizes; then he produced a large roll of cotton wool; and then from a parcel he extracted several bobbins of fine garden wire. Finally he took a quart bottle from his pocket and laid it with the rest.

"That's the lot, sir, I think."

Sir Clinton checked over the articles and began to stow them into his pockets.

"I hate damaging property," he said, thoughtfully. "But it would grieve me more to get an arrow in my ribs, I admit. And we can't waste time over a siege. Ugh! Paraffin oil is stinking stuff! I shan't get the smell of it off me in a hurry, worse luck."

"Going to smoke him out?" inquired Wendover, who had been examining the inspector's burden with interest.

"I'll have a dash at it, anyhow."

"I see your dodge. Get down into that fold in the ground. Work your way along it till you're as near the hut as you can get. Tie some wire round a stone and some cotton wool, leaving three feet of loose wire. Make a torch of the cotton wool with paraffin. Swing the thing round and round with the loose end of the wire and let go. If you land it on the roof, the tarred felt catches fire."

"And there we are," interrupted Sir Clinton. "I wonder you didn't suggest it yourself, as it's so obvious. Now for your parts in the affair. If our friend down there gets driven out into the open, minus his weapons, then you can come down and give a hand. If not, then you stay here and leave it to me. Don't go showing zeal by blundering into range and getting hurt. I'm taking all this trouble just to avoid that."

He left them and moved along under cover of the ridge they were on until he was out of range of the archer. Then he began to cross the stretch of grass which separated him from the beginning of the fold in the ground for which he was making. Evidently the bowman fathomed his plan, for arrow after arrow came from the hut in a vain attempt to reach him as he crossed the exposed ground. Wendover was suddenly struck by one possibility in the situation.

"Suppose the beggar makes a sally when Driffield comes near the hut. He'd be able to put an arrow through him at close quarters without the least risk," he exclaimed.

"He won't try that, if he thinks we've got firearms," Cumberland pointed out placidly.

"But we're not armed," Wendover retorted, testily.

For all answer, Cumberland tapped a bulky object in his pocket.

"Then why didn't you give it to him?" demanded Wendover.

"'Cause he never asked for it, sir. I gave him back your automatic yesterday—the one I borrowed to try these experiments with, up by Leisurely Lane. He didn't give it back to you? I thought not. You can make your mind easy, sir."

Wendover heaved a sigh of relief and turned with an easier mind to watch the Chief Constable's progress. From their higher elevation, they could see into the dip in the ground along which he was making his way, though it was invisible from the hut. The bowman had evidently detected the Chief Constable's object, for now he began to shoot higher in an attempt to drop his arrows into the little gully; and once or twice one of them landed close to Sir Clinton, who quickened his movements. Working his way along, he reached a deeper part of the channel and passed out of sight of the three watchers above. For some minutes the hail of arrows continued, but it was evident that the bowman had now no idea of Sir Clinton's position in the gully and it was only by chance that an arrow fell near him.

Then there came a pause when both sides remained apparently inactive.

"He must have got there, now," Wendover hazarded.

"Our alphabetical friend in the hut can't touch him, if he has," Denzil pointed out. "To drop an effective arrow within fifty yards you've got to shoot towards the zenith or thereabouts; and you can't do that from inside a window with any comfort. Not from those windows, anyhow, so far as I remember them. The alguazil's fairly safe now, unless he's been pinked on the way along."

"I'm going to follow him up," declared Wendover suddenly. "He may have been hit and be lying there, hurt and helpless."

The inspector, recalling his orders, put out a restraining hand. But his gesture was unnecessary. A faint report came to their ears from the direction of the hut.

"Hear that?" said Cumberland. "That's a paws-off notice. Fired in the air, I expect, just to warn Finborough that he needn't try any rush tactics."

Unconsciously, Wendover had risen to his feet in his excitement; but he dropped back to safety again as another arrow swept down from the air with a noise like an angry wasp. It struck a patch of hard soil, broke in two with the force of the impact, and the longer part of the shaft glanced up and passed over their heads.

But they hardly heeded it. Down by the hut, something rose in the air, leaving a faint trail of greasy smoke as it moved.

"Missed it that time," commented Denzil, as the flaming missile dropped to earth again before reaching the hut.

"Difficult to estimate the range," said Wendover, watching intently. "There! That's got it!"

A second flare soared up out of the little gully, rose to its culmination and began to sink towards its objective.

"That's it!" ejaculated Wendover. "It's hit the top of the roof!! Curse! It's sliding down on the far side. It'll fall off without setting the thing afire."

They waited, all on edge, for the next attempt. But there had been no need to make one. In a few seconds, they saw a heavier smoke appearing from behind the rooftree; then, by and by, flames began to lick over.

"Come on," ordered Cumberland. "We'll move along nearer now. Keep under cover, though. He's still dangerous."

They began to make their way towards the hut, which was now blazing along the roof as the tarred felt caught the flames.

"He can't stick out much longer," Wendover said, lifting his head over the crest. "It's a perfect furnace. . . . Look!"

They saw Sir Clinton's figure appear round the corner of the hut, hesitate for a moment, and then enter the doorway. At that moment, a puff of wind disturbed the stillness of the air, and a great billow of smoke swept groundwards, hiding the hut from their eyes.

"Now's our time!" cried Cumberland, starting to his feet.

He pulled out a whistle and blew a shrill call to attract the attention of the uniformed constable. Then he began to run to Sir Clinton's assistance. The others followed. As they ran, the smoke blew aside for an instant, and they saw the Chief Constable outside the hut, kneeling beside a recumbent figure. Then the veil closed round him once more.

"He's got him!" ejaculated Cumberland, making an effort to mend his pace.

In the rush across the intervening distance, Wendover fell a few yards behind the younger men. He blinked as he came into the smoke cloud, but when his eyes cleared again he was beside Sir Clinton. And then he pulled himself up in amazement. For the figure on the ground was not Finborough. It was Enid Carfax, pallid, smoke-begrimed, and unconscious.

"She's fainted," snapped Sir Clinton. "It's getting a bit hot here. Help me to shift her further away."

They carried her to clearer air, away from the burning but which was radiating like a furnace. As they did so, the uniformed constable ran up and stared in astonishment at the girl.

"You're a First Aid expert," said Sir Clinton to the inspector. "See what you can do. She must have been half choked by the smoke and when I got to her she'd fainted. The Hall's the nearest place where you'll get water. Off you go for some," he ordered, turning to the uniformed man, "and tell them to bring down a mattress or something, so that we can get her carried up to the house. She won't be fit to walk for a bit."

In less than half an hour, they got Enid Carfax up to her own room at the Hall. While the others were bringing her up on an improvised stretcher, Sir Clinton went on ahead.

"I'll ring up and get a doctor for her," he explained as he left the party. "She looks as if she needed one."

Wendover, completely confused by this last turn of events, helped with the transport of the stretcher. As he trudged slowly along, he tried to fit the jigsaw puzzle together so as to take in this last series of events. He had the ordinary British juryman's dislike for condemning a girl; and as he glanced down at the inert slim figure on the stretcher, he felt more pity than vengefulness in his mind. Surely a girl—at least a girl like that—couldn't be mixed up in a whole series of crimes. But then came the recollection of these arrows. No half measures there! She had meant mischief; no denying that! She'd been shooting to kill; or at any rate she'd meant to put her pursuers out of action at any cost. And if she'd do that, was it so unlikely that she'd done the same thing before?

And then a sudden idea came to him the motive. She was the next in succession to the estate, now, if anything happened to Julian.

There had been lies enough told in the case. Perhaps, after all, she *had* been blackmailed by Huggin, though she denied it. An uncomfortable affair, altogether, Wendover reflected ruefully. Then a fresh facet of the case flashed on him. Why had Finborough bolted that morning? But an obvious explanation occurred to him immediately. Finborough had left Maverton in a pretty bad way. Perhaps, when his rage passed, he began to fear that he'd gone the length of manslaughter and had bolted in order to avoid immediate arrest. That was just on the cards.

Still puzzled and depressed, he helped to get the stretcher upstairs and, coming down again, he encountered Sir Clinton in the hall. The Chief Constable, he knew, had no finer feelings where female criminals were concerned; and Sir Clinton's air of satisfaction jarred on him.

"I've got a doctor," the Chief Constable announced cheerfully. "Well, I suppose you feel it awkward, Squire, being a friend of the family. I won't press the matter. The main thing is that we've got the criminal under lock and key at last."

"I congratulate you," said Wendover, not too cordially.

"Time's getting on," observed the Chief Constable, glancing at his watch. "Suppose we go over to the Grange and wait for lunch? Cumberland's in charge here, and there's nothing more for me to do at the moment."

"Has she recovered consciousness yet?" asked Wendover.

"A bit confused still. Hardly fit to make any statement worth taking, even if she agrees to say anything. Cumberland will see to all that. Let's slide along to the Grange."

# CHAPTER XIX
## SOME POINTS IN THE CASE

"THERE'S STILL A LOT TO DO by way of filling in details," Sir Clinton confessed candidly. "But that's a matter of routine: checking minor points and getting corroborative evidence where we can. In its main outlines, the thing's clear enough. It was the lack of motive that made it puzzling. If Druce Carfax had only made a clean breast of things to us when we interviewed him, he'd be alive to-day and the whole affair would have been cleared up in a week."

"You think so?" said Wendover, sceptically.

"If he'd told us *exactly* what happened at the time of the Carfax family row," declared the Chief Constable, emphatically, "we could have put our finger on the criminal immediately. Because Carfax knew who killed Huggin. Of that I'm practically certain. And he got polished off himself because he knew it. At least, that was one reason for eliminating him. But he couldn't bring himself to be honest with me; and the result was what it was."

Wendover fidgeted a little in his chair. He could not keep his mind away from Enid Carfax. Horrible to think of her, guarded by callous officials waiting their chance to extract one of those "voluntary" statements which take hours to extort and yet boil down in the end to a page or two of manuscript. More horrible still, though, to think of her going coldly to that dreadful work in Leisurely Lane and Apsley Spinney. What was it Denzil said about her? "Pretty cool," "might flash up and explode to some purpose." That last trait might well have come down from her father. Druce Carfax

254

had had it also. Wendover made a determined effort to put the pictures from his mind; and to help in that he turned to Sir Clinton.

"How did you get at it?" he asked.

"Mental arithmetic: putting two and two together and sticking at the job until they made four. But sometimes it took a while to get the total right. Want a rough outline? I don't mind."

"Go ahead," said Wendover, determined to concentrate on this subject in order to exclude the other from his mind.

"Very well, then. Start with the Huggin murder. What did we find? No burning of the clothes about the wound; no pistol. Not suicide, apparently. No report heard, although some people were well within earshot. No bullet found. No sign of a ricochet from the fence. *Ergo,* it wasn't a firearm that did the trick. But you'd told me about the Carfax craze for archery. Possibly Huggin was killed by an arrow at close range and the arrow pulled out of the body as soon as he was dead. An archer could have hidden himself in the undergrowth and bushes beside the lane, at short range. Compare the Badminton book on the penetration of the long bow."

"So that was how you came to talk about Mr. A so early in the case?"

"Well, it seemed to fit, didn't it? But assuming that explanation, one or two things followed. Whoever shot Huggin could use a bow expertly. That looked like one of the Carfaxes, since they were the only local toxophilites. Further, we soon heard that Druce Carfax's 'God Send You Back to Me' bank note had got into Huggin's pocket. So that looked like Druce. And, further, the assailant must have been someone who had foreknowledge of that appointment between Huggin and Druce Carla; since he must have concealed himself and his bow in the undergrowth before Huggin appeared on the scene. But one had also to allow for the fact that the archery hut was not locked up—*teste* Bob Denzil—so anyone could get a bow and some arrows without even the asking. Still, it was an expert who put that arrow through Huggin."

"I can't pick a hole in that," admitted Wendover. "I know I couldn't have hit him so cleanly myself even at close range, especially in the twilight."

"Then came the bank notes," Sir Clinton went on. "Putting that £100 alongside Huggin's assets, it was clear that he'd had a windfall. It fairly cried 'Blackmail!' But then one got landed in the difficulty you saw at the time. If Druce Carfax killed Huggin, why did he leave that damning bundle of notes on the body? And if Druce was the murderer, how had he managed to pay over the notes to Huggin and then conceal himself amongst the bushes and shoot Huggin almost immediately? He could hardly have talked to Huggin with a bow and arrow in his hand, could he? And even so, Huggin would not have stood still to be shot down. The raising of the bow would have given him time to do something in the way of self-defence. So it looked as though Mr. A was somebody different from Druce Carfax."

"Unless someone else was being blackmailed and Druce was the accomplice who shot down Huggin from the undergrowth," Wendover suggested.

"I kept that in mind also," Sir Clinton assured him. "But at the time there was no evidence one way or the other. All I was sure about was that Huggin was a blackmailer who'd got his deserts."

"Well, what next?" inquired Wendover.

"The next thing was that I missed a clue completely," Sir Clinton acknowledged frankly. "You remember that Bob Denzil told us a tale about meeting Huggin outside Somerset House? Of course everyone knows that copies of all wills are stored at Somerset House. I ought to have followed that up. That's plain enough now. But I was led off on the wrong track and assumed that Huggin had gone to Somerset House to hunt up particulars of Atherfold. It was only much later that I tumbled to the real object of Huggin's visit. Of course he went to Somerset House to look up old Griswold Carfax's will and see how Fenella Basnett's bigamy affected the Carfax family. But one could hardly have guessed it at that stage."

"No, hardly," Wendover admitted. "It certainly never crossed my mind."

"The next thing was our little talk with Fairbank-Finborough at Rookery Park. It sounded all right on the surface. Very well done, I must say. But in retrospect it didn't look quite so well. First of all, he'd been careful to say that he was at the second show at the Crescent, which started at 9 p.m. That gave him an alibi for the time of Huggin's murder. And there was the programme lying in his room as supporting evidence. He was too clever to drag it out and fling it down on the table before us. He knew we'd get on to it for ourselves. And to clinch the naturalness of his talk, he spoke about Thelma Campion's turn and praised it up. The point was, of course, that Monday was the night of the murder and Monday's show was the first time Thelma put her new sketch on at the Crescent. So if he'd seen it and could praise it—well, it looked as if he'd been there. But, unfortunately for him, as you know, Thelma didn't appear at the second performance on Monday night. And the fact that he didn't know that was a clean knock-out for his alibi. So naturally, as soon as I learned about her illness, I began to suspect that G. Fairbank was not exactly truthful."

"I suppose I ought to have recognised him," Wendover confessed, "but he was just a hobbledehoy when I saw him at Carfax Hall in Griswold's day and he's completely changed in looks since then."

"Thinking over it later," Sir Clinton went on, "I recalled his marked objection to coming down to identify Huggin's body. Also his pretence that he didn't so much as know the name of Abbots Norton. I didn't see why he shouldn't help us to identify Huggin. It was a merely formal affair, and it was better that he should do it than his landlady, whose nerves would be no better for the experience. And then the coincidence of the initials cropped up in my mind. If it suited him to be Fairbank in town and Finborough at Abbots Norton, naturally he wouldn't want to come down here as Fairbank and at once be hailed by the natives as Finborough. That would be curious in itself; and it would give away the fact that he had a foot in both camps by being a friend of Huggin's and a relation of the Carfaxes. Assume that G.F. covered both Fairbank and Finborough, and some facts dovetailed neatly into the case.

"We learned from Mrs. Hassop that he had a car and that he kept it in some near-by shed. That meant he could take it out and put it back again at any time, without anyone being a penny the wiser. If he'd kept it in a garage, someone might have seen him take it out or bring it back, and that might be awkward. But using a shed, he was safe.

"Without straining times, it was quite possible for him to go to the first show at the Crescent, get his programme, come out immediately, get into his waiting car, and drive down here in time to be present at that interview between Huggin and Druce Carfax. Further, brought up as he was at Carfax Hall in old Griswold's time, he would know how to handle a bow like the rest of them."

"But how could Finborough know the time and place fixed for the meeting between Huggin and Carfax?" objected Wendover.

"There you have me," Sir Clinton admitted. "I don't know. Still, like the subject of the Siren's Song, it's 'not beyond conjecture.' I can give you one or two possibilities. Druce Carfax may have got the Rookery Park phone number from Huggin and may have rung up to make the appointment. It was Finborough's phone, you remember; and Finborough may have answered the call, recognised Druce's voice, and pretended to take the message for Huggin instead of calling him to the phone. Said he was out, or something of the sort. Or else Druce may have wired and, seeing the wire in its envelope, Finborough may have rung up and asked for the wire to be repeated. You can get that from Telegrams Inquiry, as you'll see if you look at the foot of a telegram form. Or else the contents of the wire may have been phoned and Finborough may have answered the phone. But that's not likely, seeing the phone was in Finborough's name and not in Huggin's. I don't profess to know exactly how it was done; but done it was, in some way."

"You might get the Post Office to look up their file of telegrams," suggested Wendover, "or their trunk-call accounts from Abbots Norton."

"That's being done—part of the routine business," Sir Clinton replied. "But even assuming all this, I was still completely in the dark as to the motive for the Huggin murder. Except that blackmail of some sort was at the root of it. And here I missed a second clue, though I don't blame myself for that, much."

"Atherfold's diary, you mean?"

"I do. But who on earth would have looked there for any light? Still, I might have been on the alert when Finborough stupidly let out that he'd played some part in getting Huggin to take on the biography. And he admitted, too, that he'd read the diary itself. What's more, he almost gave himself away then, but just pulled up in time."

"I don't remember that," Wendover acknowledged.

"Well, he said Atherfold was a client of his. 'He knew my . . .' 'mother' was the missing word, obviously, if one thinks of Atherfold's character and Judy Finborough's notoriety. But if he'd finished that sentence he'd have risked betraying his dual identity, for I'd have asked a question or two, there. So he broke off and substituted: 'We had common acquaintances.'"

"I've some hazy recollection of that, but it never struck me at the time," Wendover confessed.

"I was more interested in Huggin's cash transactions myself," Sir Clinton admitted. "You remember I pointed out to you that his payment of £65 into his bank on 5th May was curious. What I ought to have seen—but I missed it at the time—was that Huggin's contract for the Atherfold Life was not so long before that. It was dated 23rd February, 1936. But I didn't spot the connection then. It was only later that I put two and two together and began to link up these facts. It's obvious now. Huggin got his contract in February. Then he began to go through the diary and the correspondence. And while he was at this, he hit on the intrigue between Atherfold and Fenella Basnett. Then, I expect, he hunted about to see if he could find what had become of the girl eventually—just a bit of ordinary biographical research. He'd want to know if she was alive, since then he'd have to be careful of libel if he wrote up the incident. So off he went to Somerset House to consult the records. And between her marriage and the Carfax will he saw the chance of a nice bit of blackmail. By May, he was all ready; and he extracted his first £100 from Druce Carfax, paying £65 of it in cash into his bank."

"And it was then, wasn't it, that Finborough got on his track?" inquired Wendover. "Maverton told us that Finborough was at the

Hall and must have seen Huggin that night when he called on Carfax in May. That would put Finborough on the alert."

"Yes, and he probably tumbled to the diary as the thing to look into. Well, I missed that line for quite a long time, Squire. If I'd followed it up, we'd have had the motive almost at once. One can't think of everything."

"The next thing was that you interviewed Carfax," Wendover prompted.

"Yes. He was a damned bad liar, in both senses, poor chap. All we got out of him confirmed the suspicion that blackmail was going on. He couldn't give any account of how he came across Huggin. His talk about a Carfax family history was simply ludicrous. And his explanation of his cash transactions with Huggin wouldn't have convinced a six-year-old. Finally, he was in a blue funk lest we came across anything concerning him when we examined Huggin's papers. And that made me certain that someone was putting the black on him."

"And then Denzil came in with his information about village gossip. By the way what's happened to him? I forgot all about him when we came away from the Hall."

"I suppose he's hanging round with smelling salts or cordials, in the hope that Cumberland will let him have a chat with Enid Carfax. He'll be disappointed. As a sleuth, Bob was a complete washout. The only useful thing he did was to tell us about the family row up at the Hall; and we'd have got on to that sooner or later ourselves. Still, he did collect one phrase which would have thrown light on things if we'd only known a little more at that time."

"What phrase?" asked Wendover.

"Well, Finborough called Druce 'a damned cuckoo.' Like a fool, I took that as merely an ordinary bit of abuse; but it turned out to have more sting in it than I thought, then."

"There was another phrase," Wendover recalled. "Maverton gave us it. Something about neither Druce nor Finborough being able to touch each other without it all coming out."

"That was another fairly straight tip, if only we'd been able to see the point of it," Sir Clinton confessed. "All one could see in it then was that each of them had a hold on the other and yet neither of them could make a move without losing by it. I naturally assumed that one of them had a hold over the other on account of the Huggin murder. That seemed the plainest solution. But what the counter-grip was I simply couldn't make out. It's plain enough now."

"Pretty obvious," agreed Wendover. "You mean that Druce knew Finborough was mixed up in the Huggin murder. That was his trump card. But Finborough knew that Druce was illegitimate—the son of a bigamous marriage—and so had no right to the Carfax estate. So if Druce gave Finborough away, Finborough could turn on him by getting him hoofed out of the property—and, by Jove, getting Julian the push, too, so that Enid would come into it. Now I see what he meant by calling Druce a 'cuckoo.' He meant he was sitting in some other bird's nest and squeezing the rightful heir out."

"It was a shade more complicated than that, I believe," Sir Clinton said thoughtfully. "Finborough knew that Huggin was blackmailing Druce Carfax. The Atherfold diary and Huggin's visit to Carfax Hall must have put him on the track; and of course he must have known all about the 'legitimate heirs' clause in the will, since it was actually directed against him and his likes. Now, Finborough was hard up, or he'd never have been living in those rooms in Rookery Park. He pretended he could go to better quarters if he wished, but I simply didn't believe that tale. And he wasn't a gentleman with any refined sense of honesty. That tale he told us about his little flutter in shares was proof enough of that.

"Now, we know he hated Druce from childhood upwards. Is he the sort of man to sit quiet and let Huggin suck Druce dry, when all the time he had the same information as Huggin had? The facts prove that he isn't. He meant to get his paw into Druce's pocket. Now, he might have gone to work independently and blackmailed Druce on his own account. But that meant dividing the spoils. If Druce had to buy two men's silence, he could only do it by paying less to each of them than if he had a single blackmailer to square. Besides, Huggin might make some exorbitant demand and drive Druce to exposure, and where would poor Finborough be then?

"No, the obvious thing was to eliminate Huggin and then black-mail Druce for all he would part with. If we knew what actually happened at that stormy interview between Druce and Finborough, we'd have it all cut and dried. But one guess is a safe one. Druce in some way spotted Finborough's hand in the Huggin murder. Most likely he had no more than a suspicion, nothing whatever in the way of actual proof. But suspicion was quite enough, once it was voiced, to bring Finborough to his bearings. He couldn't afford to let so much as a whisper like that get afloat. So there they were, each with a clinch on the other, and neither of them able to make a move.

"Well, then, how was a deadlock like that to be loosened? Suppose Druce were out of the way, Julian was the next heir; and anyone could blackmail a creature like that in perfect safety. So Finborough decided to carry the good work one step further and eliminate Druce in his turn. That was done in Apsley Spinney. But Finborough made one slip, there."

"What was that?" queried Wendover.

"He shot the keeper with Phelp's own gun—at close quarters. Now, a keeper on the alert for poachers wouldn't part with his gun— *except to someone he knew and didn't suspect.* My reading of it is that Finborough waited for the keeper near the lodge, joined him when he came out, and walked up with him to the Spinney, ostensibly to lend a hand against the mythical poachers. When he knew that Druce was in the offing—he'd be able to learn that from Phelp, who probably had an appointment with Druce—he asked to have a look at the keeper's gun; and as soon as he got it into his hands he shot Phelp on the spot. The report would bring up Druce, who'd think the poachers were firing; and Finborough shot him down as he approached. That fits in exactly with all the facts about the spinney, and nothing else that I can think of will cover the ground."

"But what about that 'WELLWISHER' message, typed on Huggin's machine and posted that morning in the village?"

"Well, let's take the whole typewriter business together," Sir Clinton suggested. "Finborough knew he'd have to write a letter to Druce to lure him to the spinney, if he failed to bring off his black-mailing coup. This affair was planned in advance, obviously, and as much was foreseen as Finborough could manage. Clearly he could not write with a pen. His handwriting would have given him away, even if he had tried to disguise it. So a typewriter suggested itself as the alternative. But Finborough knew well enough how easy it is to identify a typewriter from its typescript; so he fought shy of using his own office typewriter, if he has one. Also, the purchase of a typewriter for that special occasion might have left a clue. But there was one machine to which he had access, after the Hassop family were all asleep: Huggin's typewriter."

"That fits, I admit," agreed Wendover. "But how could he be sure of the date to put on his letter about the spinney? For all he knew, Druce might have taken it into his head to go up to town, and then the letter would have the wrong date on it, if he had to hold it up till Druce came back to the Hall."

"Simple enough. Why assume that Finborough typed only one letter signed 'WELLWISHER'? What was to hinder him from typing half a dozen copies and dating them consecutively? Then he'd have a copy bearing the date of any day in that week which suited his purpose, if anything prevented him from acting on the Thursday."

"Yes, I see that. But why all these maneuvers with the commissionaire?"

"Because he knew how easy it is to identify a letter as having come from a particular typewriter, of course. If the 'WELLWISHER' epistle was traced to Huggin's machine, the trail would lead almost immediately afterwards to Finborough himself, who had access to the typewriter at Rookery Park. Obviously the game was to see that Huggin's machine was *spurlos versenkt*. Bury it in the Euston Left Luggage Office, with the ticket for it wandering about in a letter addressed to a nonexistent person, and no one was likely to lay hands on it for six weeks or six months. So he put it into Mrs. Hassop's head to sell the thing to that second-hand dealer— so that he might know where to find it when he wanted it. And before it went out of his reach he typed another series of letters on it addressed to the Corps of Commissionaires and no doubt dated consecutively like the 'WELLWISHER' lot."

"But he enclosed just about the right amount to cover the price of the machine and the commissionaire's charges. How did he manage to gauge the figure so neatly?"

"Look at what he did on the Thursday of the spinney affair. He'd cleared up matters with Druce on the Wednesday night. On the Thursday morning he picked out the 'WELLWISHER' letter dated that day and posted it in the village. Then he went off to London. You remember that Bob Denzil saw him saying good-bye to Enid Carfax on the links. And when he got to London, he went straight to that second-hand shop. If the typewriter had been inside, he'd have found some excuse to look at it and learn the price. But actually he was saved from that by finding the thing in the shop window with a price ticket on it. All he had to do then was to shove the requisite notes into an envelope along with the properly dated copy of the letter to the Corps of Commissionaires, and there was the thing done. But he forgot one thing in spite of all his cleverness."

"You mean he forgot that copies of letters written by Huggin on that machine could be got from Huggin's literary agent?"

"Exactly. And once they were compared with the others, the identity of the typewriter was proved beyond a doubt. And hence suspicion centered immediately on the people who had access to that typewriter before Mrs. Hassop parted with it. And, as you'll remember, Squire, I'd seen specimens of that typewriter's work when I glanced over Huggin's unfinished Life of Atherfold. It's just the usual tale. The clever fellow can't be content to be moderately clever; he overdoes it, sooner or later, and so gives us an opening."

"He certainly was clever," Wendover declared. "He took me in completely when he produced that programme inset to establish his alibi."

Sir Clinton smiled wryly.

"He very nearly diddled me with that," he confessed. "I simply couldn't see how he'd managed it, at first. That was as neat a bit of work as I've ever come across. He must have done some very quick thinking when he learned that Thelma Campion hadn't appeared at the second performance and that he'd committed himself badly in that first interview with us. Obviously the only hope was to get a copy of the inset; and the only way to do that was to advertise for it and chance that his advertisement didn't fall under our eyes. He had the luck to get it. That phrase '£1 for first copy received' was a stroke of genius. It meant that anyone who had a copy would rush to post it at once, so as to be first if possible; and so he'd get it at the very earliest moment. Very smart work. And of course the crumpling concealed any original creases that had come by folding the sheet to fit an envelope. Finborough really had a gift for details, Squire."

"And a talent for plausible explanation, too," added Wendover. "The way he talked about his weakness for folding up bus tickets was damned clever. He bamboozled me completely."

"Yes, but he'd made his blunders at our very first interview, and he couldn't wipe that out by any smartness later on. Still, he cost me a bit of hard thinking before I guessed how he managed to trot out that programme inset."

"When you'd got on to the idea, why didn't you send a man to the British Museum to hunt for the advertisements?"

"Because I prefer experts when I can get them," Sir Clinton declared. "That was all in the day's work for a press-cutting agency; and they'd have all the papers on hand, without wasting time going to the Museum Reading Room."

Again the picture of Enid Carfax, alone, under arrest, swam up in Wendover's mind.

"I see your points," he said, after a pause, "but I don't understand how that girl comes into it. You've hardly mentioned her."

"Just wait a moment. We'll get the stop-press news, if there is any," suggested Sir Clinton, going over to the telephone.

He dialed a number, asked for Cumberland, and then, after a minute or two, evidently got in touch with the inspector.

"Well, anything to report?" Wendover heard him say. "Oh, indeed? . . . Very wise, I think. . . . I suppose you gave her no tips? . . . I mean you gave nothing away about Finborough. . . . Quite right. Then presumably she's telling the truth? . . . Well, if you think so, it simplifies matters. . . . No, the Director of Public Prosecutions wouldn't look at it. . . . Oh, yes, the Prevention of Crimes

Act. But I don't think it's advisable, Inspector. It would be damnably unpopular, you know. I doubt if we'd even get a verdict. . . . Better call off your minions. But go through Finborough's luggage first, and pick up what you can. . . . Yes, congratulations! Very smart bit of work."

The Chief Constable put down the telephone and turned back to Wendover.

"She's made a statement, Squire, and it's left things in a rather queer position."

"So I gathered," Wendover observed. "But what has she said?"

"This is how it goes," explained Sir Clinton, resuming his seat. "This morning, Finborough told her he'd got into trouble. Oh, no, not a word about murder. He'd been embezzling, he confessed; and he had a 'sad case' tale all ready for her sympathetic ears, as one might expect from him. She swallowed it. I guess she knew he wasn't as straight as a die, so it would be no surprise to her. But she was very fond of him, as we know. All he wanted, he told her, was a chance to slip away quietly before the police came down on him."

"So he must have suspected that things were moving on your side? I wonder why."

"Probably the more he thought of his mistakes, the bigger they seemed, in the watches of the night. And he may have made more mistakes, for all we know. Most likely he felt it was well to go while the going was good. Perhaps the news that I'd been questioning Maverton again gave him a jar. Or he may just have lost his nerve and decided to clear out. I don't know. The point is, he told Enid Carfax this cock-and-bull yarn about embezzlement in order to enlist her help without too many questions.

"He asked her to take her car round to Piney Ridge Farm, so that he could walk over the golf links, up Leisurely Lane, and pick it up. By clearing out in her car, he hoped to make it more difficult for us, since he thought we'd be after a car with his number, if we sent out a hue and cry. I suppose he meant to get over to the Continent and lie low.

"She agreed and went off in her car to Piney Ridge Farm. He didn't hurry to follow her. I expect he wanted to give her plenty of

time to get to the rendezvous, just in case she'd been delayed on
the way by anything. Then, probably, it occurred to him to square
accounts with Maverton. There was no need to hold his hand
longer, since he was bolting in any case; and to do him justice, I
think he was genuinely bitter about the way the girl had been slan-
dered. So he took it out of Maverton's hide as we found; and I certainly feel no sorrow about that. And in the course of that fracas, out
came the facts about Maverton's interview with me. Finborough found
that I'd got on to the fact that he'd seen Huggin at the Hall on the
occasion of the first blackmailing expedition. You can guess how that
looked to Finborough. And on top of that came our arrival on his
tracks. So he bolted without more ado, via the back premises.

"Meanwhile, apparently, Enid Carfax had got tired of waiting
at Piney Ridge Farm. She took the car key and walked down to meet
Finborough. (This is the rest of her story I'm giving you now.) She
met him just as he arrived at the archery hut, and he told her the
police were after him. She gave him the ignition key, and he ran
off, after asking her to delay us as much as she could.

"Well, we've had some examples of what the Carfax strain can
do when it's put to it; and she seems to have a fair dash of it in her,
too. She knew pretty well that we weren't likely to waste time talking to her, so she couldn't count on delaying us that way. The archery hut gave her the idea, and how she held us up, you know for
yourself, Squire."

"She's a plucky girl," Wendover declared, with a frank admiration wholly unbecoming to a magistrate. "But it looks as if she'd
run herself into bad trouble over this. She's made herself an accessory after the fact, by helping Finborough to get away."

Sir Clinton noted the depressed tone in which Wendover ut-
tered the last part of his speech.

"You seem worried about her, Squire. In a murder case, acces-
sories after the fact may get penal servitude for life. Three years
penal is the minimum sentence. Dreadful, you'll think, that such a
nice girl should get landed like that. But observe the good fairy
coming up through the trap. I represent the good fairy, I may say,
so that you'll make no mistake."

"Oh, don't try to be funny," Wendover broke out. "It's too serious a thing for silly jokes."

"You won't let me tap your skull with my magic wand and produce a brain flash? Well, as you please. Now, will you tell me, Squire, what we should charge her with? You'll observe that she acted as she did under the impression she was aiding and abetting an embezzler. But we're not charging Finborough with embezzlement. And she didn't know he was a murderer. So she hadn't the guilty knowledge which constitutes an accessory. Most annoying, isn't it? All we could charge her with is obstructing the police in the performance of their duty. Prevention of Crimes Act, 1871, section 12. Penalty £20 or six months. And if we did, do you think we'd get a conviction? I have doubts about it. With a few sentimental old codgers like you on the Bench, she'd come out of it with a nominal penalty and all the airs of a heroine. And that would be a bad thing, you know. Undermine respect for the law, and that sort of thing. No, it wouldn't do any good. So we'll just pretend that she didn't obstruct the course of justice. As a matter of fact, she didn't, to any appreciable extent."

"What do you mean?" demanded Wendover.

"Well, naturally I took a few precautions, just in case he slipped through our fingers at the Hall. The whole of the police on duty in the County were on the lookout for a car bearing any of the Carfax numbers. We picked him up before he'd gone five miles. So now it's all over but the routine work of filling in every detail for the Director of Public Prosecutions. Tedious, but not so difficult now that we've fixed on the right man."

COACHWHIP PUBLICATIONS

COACHWHIPBOOKS.COM

ISBN 978-1-61646-392-2

COACHWHIP PUBLICATIONS

COACHWHIPBOOKS.COM

THE
DANGERFIELD
TALISMAN

J. J. CONNINGTON

ISBN 978-1-61646-329-8

COACHWHIP PUBLICATIONS

COACHWHIPBOOKS.COM

J. J. CONNINGTON

# JACK-IN-THE-BOX

ISBN 978-1-61646-318-X

COACHWHIP PUBLICATIONS

COACHWHIPBOOKS.COM

# A MINOR OPERATION
## J. J. CONNINGTON

ISBN 978-1-61646-337-3

COACHWHIP PUBLICATIONS

COACHWHIPBOOKS.COM

ISBN 978-1-61646-338-0

COACHWHIP PUBLICATIONS

COACHWHIPBOOKS.COM

THE
BRANDON
CASE

J. J. CONNINGTON

ISBN 978-1-61646-328-1

## COACHWHIP PUBLICATIONS
### COACHWHIPBOOKS.COM

ISBN 978-1-61646-330-4

Lightning Source UK Ltd.
Milton Keynes UK
UKHW010635120321
380227UK00001B/162